LAY ME DOWN

ALSO BY NICCI CLOKE

Someday Find Me

NICCI CLOKE

Lay Me Down

VINTAGE BOOKS
London

Published by Vintage 2015

2 4 6 8 10 9 7 5 3 1

Copyright © Nicci Cloke 2015

Vintage
Random House, 20 Vauxhall Bridge Road,
London SW1V 2SA

A Penguin Random House Company

 Penguin
Random House
UK

www.vintage-classics.info

The Random House Group Limited Reg. No. 954009

A CIP catalogue record for this book
is available from the British Library

ISBN 9780099593652

The Random House Group Limited supports the Forest
Stewardship Council® (FSC®), the leading international forest-
certification organisation. Our books carrying the FSC label are
printed on FSC®-certified paper. FSC is the only forest-certification
scheme supported by the leading environmental organisations,
including Greenpeace. Our paper procurement policy can be found
at: www.randomhouse.co.uk/environment

Printed and bound by CPI Group (UK) Ltd, Croydon, CR0 4YY

To my dad,
who put me on the plane

As harps for the winds of heaven,
My web-like cables are spun;
I offer my span for the traffic of man,
At the gate of the setting sun.

Joseph Strauss, chief engineer of the Golden Gate Bridge
Golden Gate Bridge opening ceremony, May 1937

31 December 2011

London

She holds the glass above her, watching the
bubbles drift upwards. Around her, lights flash:
pink, green, blue behind their filters, and a beat
thuds through the floor in short, insistent pulses.
Treading water in the swells of warped sound, she
grasps at words as they pass

> I said to him, I said you can go and f
> > I love this song
> > Hey, isn't that the guy
> and he said he didn't give a sh
> > I don't get it though, how can pants be out of
> > control

> > > > but they blur too
quickly back into one, the threads slipping away.
In the rush of white noise, the bubbles stream on
and on to the surface.

The red ceiling above them grows heavy with moisture; it pools in peaks and drops softly in fat flowers. She twists the stem, disturbs the flow. She is not having a good night.

'Babe!' Someone grabs her from behind; the glass tilts sideways. The wine inside slops onto her wrist, the bubbles foaming briefly, furiously, on her skin. He is her friend, but his face pushed close to hers is suddenly terrible; exaggerating words to be heard over the music until it seems his mouth is stretching in slow motion, his face collapsing.

'*My new friend*,' he says in awful, yawning syllables. '*Meet my new friend*.'

He gestures towards a blonde man standing alone at the crowded bar and then steers her towards him, his glass still pressed in one of his palms and spilling more of the sticky wine on her dress. 'Be right back,' he bellows in her ear, letting go. And then, lower, 'You're welcome.'

She looks up at the stranger and smiles, embarrassed. 'Sorry about him,' she says.

The stranger, who is not tall but is tall enough, smiles back. 'No worries. Seems like he's having a good night.'

He is older than her; this registers instantly, but she knows it is only because, though twenty-six, she still feels eighteen. His tanned skin is well preserved, but he still carries with him a certain air of age, a weathering. He smiles at her.

'You okay?'

The weathering is very attractive. He has blue eyes and an accent, slight but undeniable. Some of the vowels have been broadened and the consonants hardened into a mongrel sort of British, but it is still unmistakably other. It is also very attractive. 'Where are you from?' she asks.

'The US,' he says, and then he holds out a hand. 'Jack.'

'Elsa.' She shakes it, likes the way her hand feels small in his. 'How long have you been here?'

'Almost three years this time. My mum's British though so I grew up here.'

'Oh, okay.' She nods, a small warmth spreading through her, and finishes her drink. As she puts the glass down on the sticky bar, a girl in the crowd behind her pushes closer to the front, elbow sliding across her back, and she is forced a step or two towards him

Forget about it babe he's a right dick

where she can see the faint trace of blondish stubble along his jaw, the fine lines around his eyes.

'How about you?' he says, leaning a little closer. 'Are you having a good night?'

'I don't know,' she says, her fingers still lingering on the glass's base. The clock above the bar reads 11.30. 'It's too early to tell.'

His eyes meet hers and they seem suddenly grey, suddenly silver. She looks into them and then she looks away, hair slipping across her face. Behind them and beside them the conversations continue, the clock hands inch forward. 'This is a terrible party,' he says eventually. 'Can I buy you a drink?'

'Yes. Thank you.'

'Better make it a good one. It's bad luck if you aren't drunk at midnight.'

She presses closer to him, studying the row of bottles behind the bar. 'Very true,' she says.

As they wait, he watches her. He sees the way she shifts her weight from foot to foot; the way she drags her long dark hair over one shoulder and then the other. The curtain of it pulled back, he looks at the paleness of her skin above the silvery sheen of her dress. People pass by

Did you see what she's

I told him if he's going to be like that, at midnight he can kiss my

but still he watches. She makes small, looping movements with her hands, fingers tracing the melody, and when she glances up at him, he looks away. As he orders their drinks, she watches him lean on the bar; surveys the taut lines of his arms, the broad expanse of his back. She takes her glass from him, their fingers brushing. 'Thank you,' she says, and he nods. 'Happy New Year,' he says, and he knocks his glass against hers.

'Same to you,' she says, and she drinks. Behind her, three boys do shots, one after the other, the empty glasses slamming the bar. 'And what do you do, Jack?' She is instantly annoyed with herself for asking a question she always hates answering.

'Construction,' he says. 'I'm an ironworker.'

'Oh,' she says, taking another sip.

He smiles; a small, secret bridge between them. 'Basically I build structures for buildings and stuff. I make stuff stay up, let's say.' He realises what he has said and his smile becomes embarrassed.

'Oh,' she says again, and she is smiling back. 'Okay. Wow.'

'And you?'

Her dark eyes dart away, taking in the crowd again. 'This and that,' she says airily. 'I'm sort of in between things at the moment.'

A girl in an acid-green dress pushes past them, her face chalky. They watch her progress through the crowd, another girl, a drink in each hand, trailing in her wake. The one in the green dress doesn't make it; she doubles over, out of sight, and the people closest turn away in disgust.

'How did you end up in this place?' Elsa asks, leaning back on the bar. It is a confident gesture but her teeth tug softly at one corner of her lower lip as she does it and he finds it hard to look away.

'My housemates wanted to come,' he says, shifting his weight against the bar. 'They're Australian,' he adds, as if this explains it. 'And younger than me,' he finishes, which perhaps does.

'My friends dragged me here too,' she says, moving closer. 'I hate New Year's.'

'Me too.'

'Last year was worse,' she says. 'We went to a place where you had to queue for an hour to get to the bar, and the toilets were flooded by ten.'

'You didn't stay till midnight then?'

'Well, yeah, that's the thing – I mean, you can't even picture this place –'

In the bobbing crowd, they are an island. She talks and he listens (he's an excellent listener). He nods and laughs in all the right places. There is a dimple in his left cheek when he laughs; it catches Elsa off guard. When he talks, she watches, sipping wine and smiling. There is a roughness to his voice which travels through her in waves, drawing her closer. Time edges on, and as it does, they talk and they laugh, tentatively they touch.

And now the counting begins. People surge towards the dance floor, where the music has been silenced. A television screen behind the DJ's booth shows the Thames; Trafalgar Square; a girl in a fur-collared coat. As the seconds fade, the last, hasty pairings are made. In the centre of it all, real-life couples stretch out their arms to take photos frantically posted to Facebook: your girlfriend checked you in at, your boyfriend tagged you in a post, your friends like this a lot. Groups of girls and groups of boys link arms – THREE – and pour drinks, and the countdown – TWO – is at its climax now, the DJ's finger hovers above the button – ONE – and the room erupts; the same three words yelled, whispered, repeated as fake champagne ejaculates in plastic glasses and lips meet lips, lips meet cheek.

And back at the bar, Elsa's eyes meet Jack's, and a sense of daring overtakes her. 'Happy New Year,' she says, and then she leans up and kisses him.

EVE

2012

Eve was the first. Looking back, Elsa will think that it all began there; that while things were already pivoting on the point at which they'd fall, the descent really only began when Eve stepped onto the bridge. There were other factors, of course; other people whose parts became just as important in the unwinding. But Eve's is a thread in the tale which stands out amongst the others.

Before Eve, there was only San Francisco.

It is September when they arrive; New Year's Eve nine months and London an eleven hour flight behind them. The airport is hushed and the sun is sinking towards the runway as Elsa queues at immigration. Jack, with his British mother and American father and the dual nationality that goes some way to make up for a childhood spent over the Atlantic, is already through his channel and collecting their luggage. Elsa watches the people ahead of her shuffling forward, often glancing down to check the passport and landing card in her hand. It is her first trip to America, and the air seems satisfactorily different, the quietness of the queue appropriately reverential.

She has slept for much of the flight and is a little puffy-eyed, perhaps a shade pale, the faint freckles across the bridge of her nose made starker under the sharp white light. These freckles, once hated, are something she has recently grown fonder of. Often, when Jack's face is close to hers, his finger or his thumb will trail across a line of the faintest three, isolated from the others and beside her ear. Out on the concourse, he is thinking of them now.

The queue moves forward again, bringing her tantalisingly close to the front. She tugs the elastic from her wrist and pulls her hair back into a ponytail. Brushing down her clothes, she rolls her neck, still stiff from the flight. She imagines Jack out in the baggage hall waiting, the collar of his shirt turned up, a hand pushed carelessly through his hair as he leans against a wall. The thought, as always, sends a small and intense thrill through her, and she rolls her neck again, trying not to smile.

The woman in front of her is carrying a baby; it goggles at Elsa over its mother's shoulder, small mouth sucking at the strap of her vest top. She covers her face and plays a brief but enthusiastic round of peekaboo with it and, spurred on by a wobbly smile, she crosses her eyes and sticks out her tongue. The queue moves forward again and she glances at the stony-faced immigration officers at their desks. *No pulling crazy faces at customs*, she chides herself, and she smiles at the mother who turns to shift the baby from one hip to the other.

In sight of the desks now, she is restless, excitable. She glances down; checks her landing card again. She shifts the bag on her shoulder and looks down at the carpet, a pattern of muted blues and greys. Fidgeting her canvas trainers back and forth on it, she hums a few bars of a song that has been stuck in her head since the taxi to Heathrow. She wishes she had Jack here to chatter to – or at; she's afraid she's going to burble a stream of nonsense at the desk. The woman with the baby is directed to a channel and Elsa makes an exaggerated excited face at the child, who gurgles and buries its face in its mother's neck.

Eventually, finally, it's her turn; called forward to a tanned man with burst blood vessels in his cheeks, his beige shirt sweat-stained, who does not return her smile. She passes over her documents and he glances at them, small eyes set deep in his face.

'How long are you here for?'

'Six months.'

His eyes flick up to her, and then down to the visa inside her passport. 'Where are you staying?'

'With my boyfriend. He has a house here.' *Boyfriend*. Embarrassingly, it still makes her want to giggle.

'He a US citizen?'

'Yes.'

'Has he got a job?'

'Yes. He's an ironworker.' He continues to watch her. 'His new job is on the Golden Gate Bridge.'

A nod. Her passport is closed and handed back to her. 'Have a good stay.'

Walking into the baggage hall, she has a sudden urge to laugh. The silver loops circle slowly, loose tracks ticking as they pass through their gates, rubber flaps slapping slowly against the belts. She finds a screen and then their flight number; heads for the corresponding carousel. Within a few steps, she sees him. His hair is now, by his standards, in need of a cut, but she likes the thickness of it, the unruly way it creeps out of the neatly shorn style he favours. A few more lines around the eyes, and his eyebrows also beginning to revolt; growing coarser and more wiry, perhaps the first hint or two of grey, but, up close, the eyes themselves are still the same magnetic shade of silvery blue, the eyelashes blonde at the very tips. Standing at the far end of the hall, their bags gathered around him, he spots her and grins.

Smiling back, she heads for him with quick, eager strides. Skirting round a family and their fortress of luggage, she puts up a hand to smooth her hair in its ponytail. She slows to let a couple with two trolleys pass, and then, in a few short steps, she is beside him. 'Hey,' she says, tipping her head to receive a kiss.

'They let you in then,' he says, giving her hair a tug.

'Just about.' She stoops to pick up a holdall, clicks and extends the handle of one of the suitcases.

'Let me take that,' he says, removing the holdall from her

shoulder and slinging it over his own. The rest of the bags are already stacked on a trolley. He sets one hand on its handle, the other at the small of her back. 'Ready?'

She beams back at him. 'So ready.'

He leads her away, his hand lingering briefly on her back before joining the other on the trolley, and they walk through the airport, following the signs for the taxi rank. 'You excited?' he asks, reaching out to squeeze the back of her neck.

She nods. 'Are you?'

'Yeah. Feels weird, doesn't it?'

She slips an arm round his waist. 'Yep. In a good way, though.'

'Good weird not bad weird.'

'Exactly.'

He smiles, and she leans closer, linking an arm through his.

'Your dreams are coming true,' she says, and then they are passing through the sliding doors. Out on the pavement, they stare out across the highway and the yellowing sky, where the sun is slipping behind a dusty hill.

'Welcome to America,' he says, and he leads her over to the line of cabs idling at the kerb. The driver of the first in the queue jumps out to help them, waving Jack away and heaving bags into the boot himself, skinny arms straining. She pushes a holdall into the back seat and then climbs in after it, her handbag discarded in a footwell. She clicks her seat belt into place as the boot and the two front doors slam slam slam and then Jack says, 'Potrero Avenue, please,' and the car pulls away from the kerb. They are on their way.

She looks out at the hills; fawn slopes stubbled with pale grass, soft dust clouds catching the last of the light. She fans her ponytail across her shoulder, twisting strands of it between her fingers, and watches as a bird rises from a rocky lay-by into the sky.

'You here for vacation?' the driver asks, as the bay comes into view.

'No,' Jack says, and the sound of his voice still runs through her in waves. 'We just moved.'

'Where you from?'

'Seattle, originally. Elsa here is from London, though.'

'Oh, no way. That's cool.'

'Are you from Frisco?' It sounds funny on his lips, like something someone older, someone more securely American, would say. She smiles to herself, looks out of the window again.

'Yeah, born and bred. You been here before?'

'Not since I was a kid. Any tips?'

She looks out at the gentle, grey mass of the water, the setting sun casting the last bands of white across its shallow peaks, and wonders, as she often has, with a cool and calming sense of horror, what it would be like to drift down, looking up at the light. On land, the beginnings of the city start to rise. She squints, trying to see if the red arches of the bridge are visible in the distance. On their descent, the pilot announced that it would be on the left side of the plane; she and Jack were seated on the right. She still can't see it; only towers grow ahead, the tallest thin and needle-shaped at its peak, emitting a sickly green light against the fading grey of the sky.

She settles back in her seat, the fabric soft and sun-warmed, a faint fug of cigarette smoke and fake pine rising from it. Her neck is still a little stiff and her eyelids are growing heavy. She rests her head against the window and tunes back into the conversation in the front seat.

'... in the Mission, that's a great place. You should definitely check it out.'

'Cool, thanks.'

'Potrero's kind of far out, how come you're staying there?'

'Long story,' Jack says, though it is not. The house belonged to an aunt, who has recently died, leaving it to her brother, Jack's father. As stories go, Elsa considers it rather short, but as is often the case with families, what is written between the lines takes up many pages.

'Is it an okay area?' she asks the driver.

'Sure, not too bad,' he says, which seems to her an answer she can be satisfied with.

The road bends, the water now out of sight. There is still excitement, still a bubbling in her chest, but it is close to and covering anxiety too; fear of the new and of the uncertain, with only a six-month tourist visa to her name, a nine-month romance between them. She recalls the moment he asked her to come; a moment she keeps to hand, turns over in her mind with a furtive feverishness, a talismanic necessity. She spends much of her time remembering scenes of their relationship – up close, very close, they play out across her eyes. Memories so well worn, so often called upon, that they are handily shaped into a highlights reel; a best-of. As she cranks open her window, the breeze lifts stray strands of hair from her face and their story unfolds. Winter mornings spent under covers; summer days left lounging in parks. They turn in circles on a pebble beach; they huddle closer at a table set for two. Smile as they hold hands; avert your eyes as he slides her dress up her thighs. But always she returns to this: her at the hob, him still in his work clothes, the news of the job offer he has received related as she removes the plates from the oven. Her shoulders slump, a smile is plastered on before she turns. And then, him, tentatively: *You could come with me.*

They pull up beside a row of three neat little houses. Clad in wood, each has four small windows and a porch, and is painted a different, pastel colour. A white picket fence for each, though chipped in places and daubed with graffiti. The taxi parks outside the middle of the three; painted pale yellow, the wood lining the porch and the two dormer windows upstairs a dark red.

'It looks like a Disney house,' Elsa says, laughing, as she climbs out of the car. She hasn't noticed the graffiti. It is almost full dark now, a chill in the air, and she shivers as she watches the last of their belongings being stacked on the pavement.

'Told you it wasn't always warm here,' Jack says, rubbing her slender bare arms with his hands. 'Let's get inside.' He unlatches the small gate. 'After you,' he says, stooping to pick up several of the larger bags.

Heaving a bag under one arm and wheeling the last suitcase behind her, Elsa makes her way up the short path. Outside the front door, Jack fumbles for the keys, and she shivers again, no longer cold. He pauses, glancing back at her with a smile; a very particular secret smile which, though now familiar, still sends an electric bolt through her, and then he turns the key in the lock. As the door swings open, he leans down to kiss her.

'After you,' she says, and she follows him into the darkness.

The house has been empty for almost five months. There is a swooping as they step into it; an enveloping. She breathes in, draws it closer. The air is heavy and there is a smell of something sweet and slowly destroyed, like apples turning on an autumn lawn. Jack clicks a switch and the short hallway is illuminated by a bare bulb which swings solemnly above them. The walls are papered with a peeling layer of thick, embossed cream, and Elsa runs a hand over a flap of it. The paper is patterned with flowers; looking closer, she thinks she sees lilies. Behind it, the plaster of the wall is chipped and greying and a damp smell rises from it, the paper curling in her hand. The narrow staircase is in front of her, darkness above, and the only other thing in the space besides their bags is a small table. Elsa picks up an ornament from it. There are several more still sitting on the lacy tablecloth, china figurines painted with fading pastel colours. The one in her hand, a young girl, has a chip in its base, and the colours of her face are all but gone.

'She had a certain sort of taste,' Jack says, heaving the cases into a pile and closing the door behind him.

'That's one way of putting it,' she says, but she is smiling as she wanders into the living room. More of the paper awaits her here, along with a battered blue sofa and armchair. For the first time, she glances down at the carpet; brownish, thick, the tread scuffed in different directions. At the far end is a large window, beyond which she can see a short expanse of yard and a grey concrete wall. She opens the door beside her, sticky in its frame, and finds the kitchen. Here, thankfully, the walls are not papered; painted instead in a paleish blue which is greasy in patches, while the floor is grey lino. At one end is the sink, and above it another window, this one with crooked blinds, which also affords a view of the bleak garden. There is a small table and two mismatched chairs, and, behind her, another sticky door leads her into a tiny room where a washer and dryer stand side by side and a huge cobweb covers one corner of the ceiling. The window here looks out onto the street, its blinds thick with dust.

She steps back into the kitchen to find Jack looking at her nervously. 'What do you think?'

She looks around slowly, and then smiles. 'It's perfect,' she says.

Later, they sit on the sagging sofa, an empty pizza box on the floor beside them, a bottle of red wine half-empty. Elsa lies against the arm, her feet in Jack's lap.

'What do you want to do tomorrow?' he asks.

She grins. 'Walk around. See things. God, I love being in a new place so much.'

He squeezes her toes. 'There's the unpacking to do, of course.'

She raises an eyebrow. 'Please say you're kidding.'

He laughs. 'I'm kidding. I say we go for breakfast, take a walk around the Embarcadero, maybe go for lunch somewhere in North Beach, walk some more, and then if there's time we can come back and unpack together. Then on Tuesday, while I'm at work, you can start thinking about what you're going to do to all these walls once we strip them down.'

She closes her eyes and sighs happily. 'Now you're talking.'

'Great.' He reaches over and grasps the wine bottle, filling her glass and then his.

She opens her eyes. 'Is it weird, being here with her things?'

'Not really. I can't remember her that well. The last time I saw her, I was about seventeen I think.'

'Wow. That is a long time ago.' She draws her knees instinctively up to her chest, smiling, but he doesn't rise to the bait. 'Did you call your dad?' she asks, resettling her feet on his thigh.

'Not yet. He's working nights.'

'Will he come and visit?'

'Probably. Once we've settled in a bit.'

'It'll be nice to meet him.'

He stretches his arms, leaning his head back against the sofa and closing his eyes. 'I'm knackered.'

She places her wine glass carefully on the floor before reaching up a socked foot to stroke his face. 'You look it.'

'Right –' he grabs her ankle; she shrieks gamely – 'That's it!' He hoists her over his shoulder, slaps her playfully on her behind. 'What did we say about respecting your elders?'

He carries her up the stairs where, for now, thoughts of tomorrow – and of yesterday – are forgotten.

1981

When he is dying, these are the things he will remember. Behind his eyes, through thin lids of backlit red, there plays a life in free fall; events spooling away, voices unravelling like ribbon. Photocopied photographs find their way from family albums to display themselves neatly in quick succession, tossed up momentarily on the wave of time and then borne away again, replaced by faded footage.

He is born on 7 March 1976 as James Edward Finn but he is never James, he is always Jack. The early years are the stuff of family folklore; sun-browned pictures of a mother and father shockingly young, shockingly happy, of RVs and motels. A 'Welcome to Las Vegas' sign drifts past, lights flashing, bumped softly in the current by a Texan landscape, a New York skyline. Snatches of old records swoop by and catch on each other, skipping, fading.

There is a picture that exists that he will always remember. In years to come, he will trace the faces with a fingertip; a couple and their little boy, behind them a bridge. His father is saying something, the camera – operated by an aunt – flashing too soon, and they are laughing. His mother, belly huge and taut, holds his hand as she laughs, looking down at his small, tanned face. His father looks at her, mouth caught on a sound, a smile half-emerged. Behind them, the bridge. Swooping cables, orange smile against the sky. The sun blazes down and the camera flashes too soon.

And now a baby's cry – the birth of his sister, and here his first real memories, here the change from sepia to greyscale, to Seattle. Small, shuttered house, thin walls and curling floors. The music becomes words, voices raised but far away, sentences twisted and stretched as they travel past, echoing as they disappear. They don't belong together; they are many strands of a year-long fight. Rain, always rain, and the windows run with sheets of water. Standing by the crib, his face pressed to the flat wooden bars, he stares at the baby inside. Her small pink face, her fingers bunched into fists. Legs kicking softly, her body warm and round in a fleecy sleepsuit.

Downstairs now, he is seated at the table, unwanted food in front of him. A door slams, and it echoes back and forth between his ears, the picture trembling each time.

'What do you want from me?' his father asks from somewhere behind his left ear.

'I want to go home!' his mother yells from somewhere beside the right.

Isn't this home? his five-year-old brain asks from deep inside the one which is remembering. Light moves across the vinyl floor and he presses his face against her damp shirt. The rain keeps on falling.

And then there is a plane. His face pressed against the damp window now, he gazes out at the wing. His mother, the baby on her knee, holds a spoon out towards him.

'Take this, sweetie. It'll make you have nice dreams.'

He shakes his head, presses his lips together.

She smiles, his favourite face in all the world, and his mouth drops softly open.

'There,' she says, as the plastic meets his tongue. 'When you wake up, we'll be home. You'll see.'

His sister's fat hand is wrapped in his, and the seat belt is strapped tight around him. His eyelids droop. The ground is moving and from somewhere high above, small symbols light up with a click. The seats shake and his eyes close and the last thing he sees is the sky rushing up to catch him.

He thinks of those words as he drifts into a cloudless sleep, and later, he remembers them often.

When you wake up, we'll be home.

2012

He wakes on Tuesday and everything is still. He drinks coffee and stares out at the street, the dryer rumbling lethargically beside him, and he listens to the gentle, settled rhythm of his heart as if it is — as it feels — a stranger's. *Here we are*, he thinks, over and over, and as he rinses his cup he smiles.

Riding the bus, he watches the road outside and remembers a flight. He remembers being five, being afraid, being ignored, being fought for. He remembers a photograph of a family and a bridge. He removes a piece of paper, a printed-out email, from the inside pocket of his jacket and reads it again. The words are simple: `Meet at 9am at the office. Directions here if you need them.` but his smile keeps growing and he turns his face to the window as he puts the paper back.

Normally, the journey from their new home on Potrero to his new job on Golden Gate will be made up of two bus services: one from the house to Market Street, the next from Market out to edge of Marina, where it is a short walk to the bridge. As he rides the first, he watches the streets roll past and tries to pretend he remembers seeing them for the first time, aged four, him and his father and his pregnant mother, driving these streets in a hire car, his aunt's house behind them.

Everything was gold there, his mother said once, later, much later, in England. She was being bitter but now – looking out at the clear blue sky, the email in his pocket – he can't help but agree.

He shifts in his seat, watches the next stop approach. The bus is fairly empty, the only other passenger nearby a woman of about thirty, who sits across the aisle and openly eyes him. He glances at her and she smiles; a small, slow, lascivious thing which twists at one side of her lipsticked mouth. He returns the smile with a well-practised one of his own; tight-lipped and polite, dismissive. The sun is out over the buildings and it floods through the windows of the bus, squares of yellow light which warm the already-tanned skin of his arms. The woman across the aisle squints and reaches into her shiny handbag for a pair of sunglasses.

'Market Street,' the bus's tinny speakers announce, and he heads out onto the sidewalk.

Still early for his meeting, and in the full force of the soft September sun, he decides to skip the second bus leg and walk the rest of the way to the bridge. He sets off with a rough but confident idea of the direction he is heading, long and certain strides which take him quickly away from the commercial streets around Market.

The roads in this part of the city are on a steep incline, each block to the west another step up in gradient. As he passes through Chinatown and Nob Hill and into Pacific Heights, the streets to his right fall away, rolling downwards at a cartoonish angle. The houses are all tall, most of them three storeys, with steps leading up from the sidewalk to their front doors. Many are painted in pastel colours – pink, green, blue – and trees line the pavements outside. The sun is still climbing but it is early enough that the air has a certain morning coolness to it; the day still a promise and not yet a threat.

Often, he too revisits the moment he asked her to come. He remembers her, barefoot in the kitchen, her hair pulled back, the windows warm and fogged. The job had been a possibility for several weeks, but each time they met he'd found a new excuse not to mention it to her. And now he had received the email, had an undeniable answer, and the time for excuses was over. That evening she was bath-soft and tiny, the counter dusted with flour.

'I have some news,' he'd said, resting on the arm of a chair.

'I've been emailing an old friend,' he'd said, watching her drain water from a pan.

'He told me about a job,' he'd said, and she'd smiled.

'It's something I've wanted for ages,' he'd said, as she bent to get the plates.

'It's back in the States,' he'd said, and he'd seen her back stiffen, her toes curl against the tiles.

She turned, and she smiled; kissed him and congratulated him. But in her eyes there was a fear, and suddenly he felt it too, sharp and scrabbling. 'You could come with me,' he said and then it was gone.

He begins to whistle, hands jammed in his pockets. He has finally reached Marina, the thick muscles of his calves taut with walking, and he slows to admire the area; one of the wealthiest suburbs, the houses larger and more generously spaced. The roads here level out as they lead him towards the water, and the day's first real rays begin to reach him, heat seeping over the back of his neck. He looks up at one window, a large, bay bedroom, where a tall vase of lilies press against the glass, and there is a momentary stuttering, a falter in his stride.

'Could you help?' a woman calls from a car across the street, and Jack turns to see a husband in blue pyjama bottoms peer out from an open front door. The boot of the car slides open to reveal neat stacks of grocery bags, and the husband makes his way out of the house, barefoot against the warm tarmac. Jack keeps walking. Though he is still in the day's yellow light, he is no longer warm.

Weaving his way out of the neat blocks of houses, he finds himself on a main road; wide and flat and curving. He looks across it to the marina. The sun is just high enough now to catch the bright white hulls of the yachts, and the sky is a glorious, clear blue, the water calm. Crossing the road, he lets himself smile. At the water's edge, he pauses again, watching the waves lap slowly at the rocks. He looks to his right, where the city stretches out along the shore, Alcatraz Island sitting sullenly in the bay. He takes it all in; skirts the skyline and follows the progress of a pair of kiteboarders, his hand turning a coin over and over in his pocket. And then, with a deep breath, he turns to his left.

And there she is. The bridge, bright and orange and blazing against the sky. His heart turns over in his chest and he grins. He gazes up, hand finally stilled. And then he begins his walk towards it, the sand kicked up in fine jets by his heavy boots.

Unlike Elsa, he was relieved when, through the tinny speakers, the nasal voice of the pilot announced that the bridge could be seen on the left side of the plane as they descended. Unlike her, he did not crane his neck to try and catch a glimpse anyway. He squeezed her hand back as her fingers linked through his, but he kept his eyes on the small screen in front of him, his attention on the last scenes of the cheesy film he had – reluctantly – been watching. He has been like this throughout all of their breakneck packing; while she flicks through guidebooks and travel sites, burbling facts – 2.7 kilometres long, 746 feet tall – at random intervals and without further comment, her excitement on his behalf so infectious and endearing, he has fought to keep his mind on the straightforward and essential: paperwork, boxes, storage. Since accepting the job, he has become gradually convinced that it *cannot* be as momentous as it seems, as important. He has prepared, silently, for disappointment, and in his doing so, this moment has become more swollen, his expectations higher. And now, climbing the many steps up the hillside to it, he looks up at the two huge towers, at the cables traced on a bright blue sky, and it is every bit as momentous as he had thought it would be.

He is to be shown the ropes – *cables*, he thinks, old ironworker humour – by Bart Miller, a stocky man with a flushed red face and thinning grey hair. His voice still has the traces of a soft Southern drawl although, as he is quick to inform Jack, he has worked on Golden Gate for twenty-five years. He walks Jack round the workshop at a brisk pace, pointing things out with the bored, flat tone which says that he thinks these things are quite patently obvious, but that he is obliged to spell them out.

'There's a permanent shop crew,' he explains, 'but if the weather's bad we all pitch in down here.'

'How often's that happen?' Jack asks.

Miller wrinkles his face, his nose bulbous and soft-looking. 'Fog can get pretty bad but you get used to it. Unless it's really coming down we can get out there most days.' He moves on, gesturing at cupboards as he goes. 'Harnesses here, but we always have 'em on the trucks. These are just spares. Same goes for the helmets and stuff in *there* –' he glances back at Jack – 'and to the cones and whatnot in *there*.'

Jack is keenly aware of the other workers in the shop, who are all watching the tour from behind their benches. Miller has not bothered to introduce him. He nods at a couple as he passes, his hands back in his pockets. Remembering a line from one of Denny's emails – *great guys, they've all worked there for ever* – he wonders how long it will take for him to stop feeling like the new boy at school. A while, he suspects. Jobs on the Golden Gate crew rarely become available. He thinks of Denny, sleeping on a sunlounger in his Florida retirement community, and thinks, not for the first time, that he owes him a drink.

The tour has run in an untidy circle and they have arrived back at the workshop's door. Miller presses a hand to the back of his neck, considering Jack. He sighs.

'Okay, let's get out there.'

They walk out into the small parking lot, where rows of miniature pickup trucks are lined up. The cab of each is just big enough for two grown men, though standing beside it, Jack, not a particularly tall man, is comfortably head and shoulders above its roof. The truck bed is filled with the safety equipment he is familiar with – harnesses, clips, fluorescents. 'Climb in,' Miller says, starting the engine.

They beetle out of the parking lot and onto the stretch of road leading up to the bridge. 'You worked on bridges before?' Miller asks.

'Yeah,' Jack replies, his knees pressed against the dashboard. 'One in Washington, one in the UK.'

Miller nods, grunts in approval. 'Golden Gate's special, I guess, but that's good. You gotta place here?'

'Yep. Out on Potrero.'

'Not too far, lucky you. Most of us live out of the city, drive in. You have a car?'

'Not yet. Working on it.'

They have reached the bridge, where the rush-hour traffic floods through six lanes. Miller pulls the truck up onto the sidewalk. As they drive along it, Jack's eyes follow the cables, studying the fixtures. In his mind, he sketches out diagrams, calculates distances, constructs models. He turns them round in his head, turns the bridge inside out and back to front. He is the happiest he has been for as long as he can remember.

They pass under the first tower and, gazing up – way up – at its red underbelly, he lets out a long, low whistle.

'We'll get you up there later,' Miller says. 'Show you around. It's quite a view. Can see the whole city. The whole county, pretty much.'

Jack looks out at the city's skyline again. The climbing sun reflects off the glass of its buildings, the sky behind them still completely cloudless. To his left, beyond Miller's rugged profile, the bay widens out into the ocean; a calm, clean expanse of blue.

'Pretty nice place to work,' Jack says.

'Sure is.'

After they drive beneath the second tower, Miller begins to slow the vehicle. Up ahead, the orange cables are obscured by wire fencing, and several men in fluorescent jackets and helmets are moving large lengths of scaffolding. There are three more of the miniature pickups parked in a line here, and a small building hastily assembled from rectangles of plywood.

'So, here we are,' Miller says, hopping out. 'Today's work.'

'Scaffolding for the painters?' Jack says. Denny, clumsy and quiet, but always efficient, always thoughtful, has already laid out what Jack can expect his main duties to consist of. *Obviously an amazing place to work*, one of his emails has read, *but some of the day-to-day stuff can be a bit dry for a young guy like you.* He finished with *Worth it though*, and Jack, looking out at the bay again, can't disagree. Across the road, a completed set of scaffolding has been erected, and the length of the bridge it covers has been hidden with huge sheets of plastic. Occasionally visible are men in white paper suits, tight hoods up around their faces and ventilation masks obscuring much of what is left exposed.

'Yup,' Miller says and, clearly determined to deliver his speech, he continues. 'The bridge needs painting all the time. Keeps it from rusting, see?'

Jack does see.

'So,' Miller says, leaning over to pick up a piece of litter from the ground. 'We're here to help them. Put the scaffolding up, take it down. Rinse, repeat. In between everything else we got to do, of course.'

He turns his attention to the men moving the scaffolding ahead of them. 'Hey, fellas!' he yells. 'New kid on the block's here!'

It's later, as Miller shows him the place where he can park his car, when he finds one, and the place where he can eat his lunch

– and it is these details which really, finally convince Jack that it is true, he works here – that the question arises.

'There's one other thing,' Miller says. 'It's not a big deal, we all do it, but you don't have to, it's voluntary –' He pronounces the word strangely, elongating it. *Vol – un – tair – ee.*

Jack nods. 'Sure.'

'Well, we all sign up to be on call for jumpers. So when someone's up there, on the chord, whoever's on call gets their gear on and goes out and tries to get 'em back, see?'

He knows of course. He thinks of another line in Denny's email – `there's the jumpers thing, you know about that, right?` – and he sees Elsa, cross-legged on the sofa with her laptop balanced on the arm: *Have you read this? Did you know how many people* and then he blinks her away. He knows, he is prepared. He knows, and it's going to be okay.

'Anyway,' Miller is saying. 'Like I said, it's voluntary. Nobody's gonna make you do it if you don't want to. And there's always at least two of you out there, it's never just you on your own. There are procedures and stuff, you keep each other safe.'

'Sure.' Jack nods. 'That makes sense.'

'I'll give you the training stuff we have. Read through it and let me know what you think.'

'Sure,' Jack says again. 'Of course. Happy to help.'

And perhaps that's where it really begins; a pivot point far subtler than the one to which Elsa will eventually attribute everything which comes next. Later, alone, he watches the sun sink slowly back towards the bay, his hands on the rail. Behind him, cars continue to stream past, into and out of the city, and pedestrians skirt around him on the walkway. He has done it, he is here: he has the job he has always dreamt of.

And yet, somehow, he cannot bring himself to look down.

1986

He is ten years old and another summer has arrived, the last day of school over and the concept of another term too far off even to contemplate. He sits back in his chair, the air vent blowing softly above him. Beside him: another small window, another wing. The faint taste of nausea lingers at the back of his mouth from the long, early-morning car journey. His father sits beside him, Aimee in the seat next to the aisle. Too large for a lap on this flight; his little sister five years old and sitting grandly in her seat, her elbows parked on the armrests. His nylon backpack is wedged under the seat in front of him and he misses it already, misses having something to hold on to.

Looking up at his father again, he tries to commit the details of his face to memory. A lot can change in six months, and it does, each time.

He, for instance, has lost teeth; he has changed the way he wears his hair. The differences to his father are much smaller and yet all the more pronounced. His skin is tanned still, but the new lines around the eyes and mouth remain stubbornly white. *Dad*. He looks worn. He looks old. It is a frightening and yet fascinating thing; he finds it hard to look away.

In his backpack he has a book and tucked into it is a photo. It shows a couple and their son, behind them a bridge. At home, he keeps the photo under the top-left corner of his narrow mattress. Along with the book, he has packed two comics, a bag of sweets, an old sweatshirt in case he is cold. He has a pair of sunglasses which are too big for him but which he wears because they are orange and orange is his favourite colour. They are his mother's but she has not missed them; there are few occasions to wear sunglasses in York.

'I wish Mummy could come with us.' Aimee's voice is plaintive, cutting through the gentle hushing of the vent. As she sits up straight in her seat, her feet hang above the ground; blue shoes with yellow laces. Her accent is an easy English, a miniature version of his mother's. His own is still hybrid, stranded somewhere in the Atlantic where it will flounder for the next twenty-six years; an island which is a territory claimed by neither parent.

He glances up at his father, whose face remains impassive, impossible to read.

'You'll see her soon, hon. We're gonna have fun, I promise.'

He makes many promises, and usually they are fulfilled. But

these victories are hollow, the rewards not worth the wait. Jack shifts in his seat to view him properly. 'You don't have to work?'

His father nods. 'Yeah, I do. But not too much. There'll be plenty of time for fun stuff.'

'Where will we go?'

'You guys will sit with Mrs Campbell. Like last year, remember?'

He turns back to the window. He remembers. Mrs Campbell, the next-door neighbour, old and milky-eyed. Her house smells of vinegar and she lurks in its corners, leaving them to their own devices. The hours are long there. Aimee, though talkative, is not a suitable playmate; unable or unwilling to sustain a game long enough, ignorant of the inner workings of a spaceship or a submarine.

'Can't we come with you?' he asks. 'I like seeing your work.'

'It's not safe for kids,' his dad says, standing up to put his jumper in the overhead bin. Sitting down again, he glances at his son. 'Maybe one day,' he relents. 'If you're good for Mrs Campbell.'

The plane begins to taxi and he fiddles with the window shade, watching the tiny beads of rain start to stream, right to left, across the glass. *Maybe one day* is as good as yes, and he is triumphant. He likes the sites, likes the men who work on them. There he is always Jackie, there he is clapped on the back, his hand pumped firmly by rough, blackened fists. They give him a helmet to wear, let him watch them work. Once, during a summer three years ago, he was present for the final day of a construction, a skyscraper. The last beam was signed by each of the rough, blackened fists, and, last of all, by his own small, pale one. He wonders if that will happen again. He hopes so. He likes the idea of his carefully printed name next to his father's scrawled initials; placed high up and hidden in a thing which is, he thinks, as close to permanent as a thing can be.

The plane turns slowly, approaching its runway. The engines begin to whine, the water frantic on the glass. He glances at his father, who looks back at him.

'You ready?' he asks Jack, and Jack nods.

2012

At breakfast, she sits at the chipped table with a map unfolded in front of her, a pen hovering over the different districts. Her other hand twists and untwists her hair into her fist, while a cup of coffee sits, forgotten, beside her. Her thoughts are often an almost tangible thing, unfolding from her and filling the room like haze, making it difficult to hear his own. He leans against the counter to watch her, his own coffee mug in hand, the memory of a summer twenty-six years ago suddenly forgotten.

'Els,' he says, and he loves the way she looks when she looks up at him. 'You don't need to worry about fitting everything in. We've got ages to see it all.'

'Well, that's true,' she says, and she smiles. She leans back in her chair, dressed in a T-shirt, her bare legs pale against the seat. 'So, where should I go today?'

He takes his coffee over to the table and pulls out the chair opposite hers, trying to distract himself from the soft skin of her thighs. 'Just wander. Take a bus somewhere and wander.'

She gets up now — they are rarely still, the two of them, at least in these, the early days — and walks barefoot across the linoleum floor to his chair. Sliding into his lap, she takes the mug from him and drinks the last mouthful, her dark eyes meeting his over the rim. 'Sounds perfect,' she says, the empty cup cradled against her knee.

'Just stay away from the Tenderloin. And thanks for making me lunch.'

'You're welcome. I managed to resist putting peanut butter and jam — sorry, *jelly* — in the sandwiches.'

'I think you're taking this American thing too seriously.'

'I just want to embrace the culture!'

'Admirable. So, I think that makes it my turn to get dinner. What do you fancy, my little snickerdoodle?'

'What the hell is a snickerdoodle?'

He pinches her small, upturned nose. 'I think you need to give your American studies a little more work.'

'Hmm,' she says, scrunching her face against his hand. 'Can we have Thai?'

'But of course, mademoiselle. Your wish is my command.'

'I knew there was a reason I liked you.' She gets up, her hair slowly unwinding itself. Opening the fridge, she hands him the Tupperware box containing his lunch. 'Be good,' she says, and he kisses her.

*

After he is gone, she folds the map and slips it into her satchel. In the bedroom, she slides on jeans and glances in the mirror. She piles her hair into a dark knot and haphazardly applies mascara, smudges on a little lip balm. Today is the first day which is free, can be shaped any way she wants, and she is eager for it to begin – though, despite her initial protests, she has actually enjoyed the unpacking; enjoyed finding places for things, finding the flaws of the house: which drawer sticks, which step creaks, where the draughts are. 'You don't need to do it all,' Jack told her yesterday when he called during his lunch, but she is glad that she has. It feels secure somehow, it feels a statement.

Wrapping a scarf around her neck, she glances briefly at the jackets which are hanging in the hall. *It's California*, she thinks. *I'm not wearing a bloody coat*. She takes her keys from the side – and the feel of them in her hand is still something which makes her stomach flip, something which is tiny and ordinary but to her is further proof of them, of this thing which is now theirs. She heads out of the door without a second look at the coats, and she is in luck; outside, the sun once again hangs high in a bright blue sky and the streets are bathed in cheerful yellow light. Closing the door behind her, she turns her face up to the sun and lets out a contented sigh.

She is studiously ignoring Jack's ominous warnings of fog.

She made it out once yesterday, early in the day when it became clear that cupboards would need to be cleaned before their things could be put away inside them. A quick turn around the neighbourhood and she has the essentials mapped out in her head: convenience store four streets down, supermarket five streets up and three across, and finally, the bus stop, just two blocks up from the house. Heading for it, she glances back at the house behind its white picket fence and smiles. Her flip-flops pad against the pavement and the road is quiet, the cars few and far between.

When she thinks of London now, she sees it in smudges; shades of grey and black and beige, the faded fabric of Tube seats and the strange, pale light of the sun breaking through an overcast sky. The specifics of her life there have quietly melted back into the cityscape, years folding neatly into themselves, until now, just three days into their stay, London is simply 'a place I used to live'.

She likes it better that way.

The bus pulls up with a shuddery sigh, its doors clapping open. She steps on and they creak back into place, a single slap behind her.

'A return to Market Street, please,' she says to the driver.

'In the machine, honey,' the woman says, gesturing to a black box perched on the edge of her cab. Elsa slides the money in; two dollar bills, one at a time, and the woman presents her with her ticket. 'Have a good day, hon,' she says, pulling the bus away from the kerb.

The bus is almost empty. Elsa takes a seat near the back, watching the houses flash past. Her eyes follow them, left to right slide, and then flick back and begin the journey again and again. People they pass blink against the sun; the wood of the houses glows. After the houses there is a hospital, whose outside wall is covered with a huge, brightly coloured mural. Yellow and blue circles, a rainbow. Painted children play with a skipping rope near the centre, patches of their cheeks and clothes worn so that the red brick beneath shows through. Elsa moves her feet, restless: up onto her toes, arching; flat; down onto her heels, toes curling. Her flip-flops slap quietly against the vinyl floor. With them she ticks off things in her head: clothes unpacked; toiletries bought; linen washed.

She rides the bus all the way up Market Street, the main parade of shops and businesses which bisects the city's neat blocks at a diagonal. Here, the traffic stops and starts, the bus heaving itself forward in drunken lurches. She looks out at the people hurrying across the pavements; phones pressed to ears, shopping bags jammed over wrists.

Sometimes, she thinks of the evening they met and wonders why he stayed. In the dark, sickly space of the bar, he seemed a reluctant observer, but yet he was there, he stayed, even after his friends had dispersed and his slipping away would have been easy. She remembers leaning up to him, her mouth at his ear. *Let's get out of here.* Her hand in his, the year's earliest air whipping at her legs. A short taxi ride to her flat and then she was against the door, keys still in hand, his face close to hers. The rhythm of her feet against the floor grows faster.

At the junction with Montgomery Street, she gets off the bus. Out on the street, she unfolds the map, tracing the route with a chipped coral fingernail. The buildings here are tall, most made of glass but one, huge and grey and pillared, of stone. An escalator beside her leads down into the BART station, but she bypasses it, heading up Montgomery.

It's a little cool, not as warm as the brightness of the sun would have her believe, but she's okay in her T-shirt, the cotton scarf pulled loose and hanging down, no need to knot it. Montgomery is a long street, at first quiet and lined with banks and office buildings, then beginning to bustle as it edges around Chinatown. At the corner of one of the crossroads, an old man in a cap plays a keyboard to the cars waiting at the lights. She reaches into her bag for some change but he has no hat or cup and so she settles instead for putting a couple of coins down carefully beside his chair. Crossing the street, the opening chords of a new song drift after her until the rush of traffic snatches the rest away.

Back in England, they might now be sleeping. They are both restless sleepers; together at first but pushed back and forth, close again and then away, limbs tangling as the hours pass. She often wonders what he dreams about, wishes she could carefully lift the lids as they flicker and see what plays beneath. Not knowing – *There's nothing to know*, he would say, if she were to ask – makes her nervous. But it appeals to her too. They are both restless sleepers; the silence suits them.

She has reached the beginning of Little Italy, where the street is lined with awnings and neat little tables. It is still early; waiters in waistcoats setting out gilded menu stands, waitresses opening white tablecloths with soft, butterfly cracks. She slows her pace as the road begins to rise.

Why has she come? It seems a simple answer, when she thinks of it: because she wanted to. Others had warned against it – it's too soon, they'd say, or there's so much to leave behind. But the fear that seized her at the thought of him leaving, the thought of going back to where he was not, was appalling, the lifeline offered – *you could come with me* – too simple, too perfect to ignore. *Why would I stay?* she asked them, and the answers they could provide were flimsy and fragile: she didn't have to push hard to see them crumble.

She turns off Columbus, away from the restaurants and into North Beach, heading for the water. There are small sounds – cars accelerating uphill, strands of conversation – and the sun climbs steadily above her. She fiddles idly with the edge of the scarf as she walks, its lace edging twisted between her fingers.

'What will you do?' her mother asked, one weekend in August when she went home to break the news. It seems a simple answer, when she thinks of it – *just be* – but in reality it is more complicated. She has modest savings and her visa, though expensive, does not allow her to work. 'We hardly know the guy,' her father said, and that, in its straightforwardness, was easier to address.

'You know me,' she had said. 'You know I'm happy.' This could not be argued with. When she thinks of their last meeting; of the two of them hugging Jack – *Look after her for us* – and of the cheque pressed into her hand, she has to swallow hard. She must call, she thinks.

The issue of money, though, is not as easy to forget as she would like it to be. She has worked hard to save in the weeks leading up to their arrival, but her funds and her visa will be as fleeting as each other. After them, uncertainty looms once more. She needs a plan in place. Jack continues to dismiss her concerns – *I can take care of us* – but at this she has just laughed. Her legs are warming as she walks, her breath coming a little harder. A plan a plan a plan. There are things she can do; she just needs to find them. And there is time.

Finally the buildings become hotels, and around a corner, she catches a glimpse of the water. Just a small strip between the white buildings of the piers, but there all the same, still and blue, the green hills beyond just visible. She crosses the busy road and makes her way to the railing. The smell of the sea has been one of her favourite things for as long as she can remember, and she closes her eyes, inhaling

and it is March, it is London. Clapham Junction. Jack is pulling her onto a train to Brighton. She has nothing with her, just the clothes she is wearing, not even a toothbrush. The weekend runs in fast-forward: a worn-out guest house on the seafront, full of paintings of kittens and paisley curtains, wind whistling in the eaves and furniture creaking. Freezing cold, but what does that matter: they spin in circles on the pebbles, salt lashing at their faces, wind whipping at her dress; he lifts her against the bedroom door, her legs around his waist, her hands in his hair; they lie in the chipped enamel bath together, her hair splayed out in soapy water, sticking to his chest in strands.

Exhale, and back to September, back to the pier, sun still beating down. She grips the railing and leans back, letting it warm her face. It's easy to feel small here, under and above all this blue. Even Elsa, determined as she is not to believe in approaching bad weather, cannot help but stop to soak it in. Like everything, it is finite. But why else, she thinks, would it be beautiful?

She starts to move again; heading along the front in the direction of Pier 39. It's not one of the places Jack has mentioned that she might like; in fact, his only comment on it has been disparaging: *touristy*. But it is on the water and besides, for this week at least, and on her own, she's happy to feel like a tourist. She lets her handbag drop from her shoulder into her hand, swinging it as she walks. From somewhere behind her, somebody shouts

Don't!

and then the sound is snatched away by the radio of a passing car; a short, emphatic blare of rap that takes her the final few steps to the dark boards of Pier 39.

Jack has warned her that it is touristy and he is right – and she loves it. A two-storey promenade of shops and restaurants, wooden boardwalks and wooden storefronts, old-fashioned signs hanging outside each. Windows packed with beads and sweets, bustling restaurants where waitresses call out surnames over tannoys, plucking waiting patrons from the benches and balcony outside. She wanders idly through it all until she comes to an unobstructed view of the bay. Here, she pauses once more, resting her bare arms on the warm, splintered wood, and looks out at the desolate buildings of Alcatraz. Above her, two gulls wheel in circles and, far to the left, the bridge sits serenely over the water. She gazes at it, her heart thudding softly in her chest. It's got her too, unexpectedly. All day long tourists pause here, amazed to be amazed by something as simple as a bridge. Nobody is immune.

Sometimes, when he is concentrating or distracted, she looks at him and feels afraid. He is a solid thing – broad back and heavy boots, muscle and metal – but often she considers him ethereal, as though she might blink and he will be gone. The stillness and the largeness of the bridge are irresistible, and she pushes back from the wooden beam, studying it.

'Home,' she says softly to herself, trying the word out. The bridge smiles back at her.

She dawdles as she follows the boardwalk around, trailing her hand along the railing. At the corner, where she will turn away from the bay and back towards the road, a group of people huddle together to watch something in the water below. She finds a spot and peers down. Bobbing in the harbour are a group of wooden floats, attached to each other by chains, and lazing on them are twenty or thirty sea lions. The fetid smell of them drifts upwards; a round-faced child in front of Elsa pinches his nose and makes a face at his mother. The animals roll lethargically across the floats, occasionally snarling at each other, sometimes sliding gracelessly into the water. A sign in the centre welcomes visitors in old-fashioned lettering.

She watches, strangely fascinated by their sluggish, slug-like bodies, the surprising beauty of their round, wet eyes as they turn their faces upward. The child and his mother depart, holding hands, and she takes their place next to a freckled man who snaps photo after photo of the creatures. She finds herself surprisingly reluctant to leave. They are not attractive creatures; not dramatic or exotic or beautiful. But they are strange, and their strangeness is appealing to her. They make piggish sounds as they drag themselves across the boards, layers of fat rolling through their tumescent bodies in waves. She lets out a small snort of her own, and the red-haired cameraman glances at her.

'They're weird, aren't they?' she says weakly, the spell broken. 'I've never noticed that before.'

'I guess,' he says, but he has already turned back to his camera, aimed now at Golden Gate. It clicks rapidly, an occasional break as he checks the digital display screen. She watches his finger twitch on the shutter, the noise growing louder, more intrusive. She glances past, at the bridge, and her fingers begin to twist at the scarf again.

There are few pictures of the two of them and often she remembers this and resolves to take more. The ones they have are rarely posed; always their shapes caught unaware in someone else's frame, their faces turned towards each other. Previously, she has liked this; as if the thing they share can only be exposed in secret, captured by accident. Now, though, her hand goes to her bag, where, among the crumpled receipts and empty wrappers, it closes around her brand-new, good-luck-gift camera, bought for her by her friends back in London.

'Make sure you use it,' Jenn, who is good at gifts and practical with gadgets, had said, and Elsa dutifully removes the small silver square from its pouch and aims a few experimental clicks at the bridge. She leans over the railing and snaps a couple of shots of two particularly fat sea lions lolling against each other, their eyes looking balefully back at her. She slides the camera back into its sleeve and drops it into her bag, hitching the strap higher on her shoulder, where the fabric of her T-shirt has grown hot in the sun. She rolls the sleeves up a little, determined to tan though the skin there is stubbornly pale.

Her stomach growls, neglected. Beyond the sea lions is Fisherman's Wharf, another hub of restaurants which looks reassuringly run-down. With a final glance at the animals below, she makes her way back through the crowds and out onto the road.

The car park in front of Fisherman's Wharf is empty except for small knots of huge seagulls which scatter at her approach, only to regroup a few steps further across the asphalt. She eyes them, her pace faltering. Her mother insists that she has been afraid of birds since birth – *Even in your pram, Elsie* – but Elsa is certain that she can remember the dream which began the fear, a dream when she was perhaps eight or nine, a dream which plays now in some small, musky screen in the cinema of her head. It's a remake, the original lost to time, and like all modern takes on old films, it is exaggerated, subtleties replaced by special effects. Its potency has been diluted in the process. A strange man in a three-piece suit approaches her. They are abroad, where – Italy? Why not. The scenery emerges quickly, apologetically behind the man: a veranda, yellowish hills, Tuscan sunset. He is holding a live bird, a gull. It struggles against his hands, wings pinned tightly to its sides. Its head jerks from side to side; beady eyes, the yellow of its bill too bright. He holds it out to her, and though he does not speak, his meaning is clear to her. (Perhaps in the original, there were words. It seems likely. How else would one interpret such a gesture in such a way? But now they are erased, edited by logic and replaced with a menacing expression, an innate knowledge. She must eat it.) Her mouth is pried open by invisible fingers and the gull's eye meets hers one last time before its head disappears into the sudden cavern of her mouth. The feathers coat her tongue as the fingers force her to bite, mash, swallow. The gristle of the legs is the worst. The webbed feet bat against her chin as she chews.

She shivers, and the birds watch her as she passes, their wings bristling. Her shadow cowers at her feet, the sun high behind her. Her stomach is still growling.

Selecting a restaurant in the middle of the short strip, she steps in, blinking in the sudden dark. It's still on the early side of lunch, a little after twelve thirty, but the restaurant is busy. The man who greets her has a narrow, sallow face and an apron tied over his jeans. 'Where d'you want to sit?' he asks. 'At the bar or in a booth?'

She chooses the bar, not wanting to take up a whole booth by herself. He shows her to a red vinyl stool, and then puts a menu on the steel bar in front of her.

'That's okay,' she says. 'I know what I want. Clam chowder, please.'

He grins. 'Where you from?'

'England. London.'

'Thought so. One clam chowder coming up. Anything to drink?'

She orders a Coke, which is delivered to her in a frosted plastic pint glass full of ice. The tip of the straw is covered with paper which she slips off, rolling it into a tiny ball between her fingers.

'You're from London,' a voice says beside her. Its owner is an old man wearing a polo shirt with the collar turned up. His white hair is thinning and combed across a brown-spotted scalp. He has a pair of Ray-Bans pushed up over it.

'Yes,' she says. 'Well, from Shropshire originally. London most recently.'

'I like England. My first wife was English.'

'Oh really?'

'Yeah. From Oxford.'

'Very nice.'

He shakes his head. 'Nope. She wasn't.'

'Well, I hope she didn't put you off.'

'Nope. The third one was English too. Swansea.'

'That's actually in Wales.'

'Oh. Right. I remember now.'

She takes a sip of her drink. 'Do you live here?'

'Yup. Five years now.'

'Do you like it?'

'Oh sure. We love it. You here on vacation?'

She shakes her head. 'No. My boyfriend just got a job here.'

'Oh yeah? What's he doing?'

'He works on Golden Gate Bridge.'

He whistles. 'Wow. That's great. What a great place to work.'

The waiter arrives with her soup. Served in the traditional hollowed-out bread bowl, steam rises from it in soft curls. 'Thank you,' she says. 'This looks delicious.'

The man beside her murmurs his agreement. 'This place does the best seafood in the city. Only problem is their portions are just too big,' he says, eyeing the plate. 'Hey, Mike! Wrap this up to go for me while I use the bathroom?'

When he returns, she is halfway through the chowder, the map unfolded in front of her again.

'Fort Mason,' he says. 'Be a nice view up there today.' He collects the white polystyrene box with his food now inside. 'Hey, nice to meet you,' he says. 'I hope you enjoy your stay.'

'Everything okay for you?' the waiter, passing, asks and she nods.

'Yes,' she says. 'Everything's great.'

1990

When she is dying, these are the things she will remember. Elsa Jane Unwin, born on 5 March 1985. Early years a showreel of first cuddles, first smiles, first steps, first words; a soft static background sound, the faint clattering of an ancient projector. Her sister is born and the two of them slouch together on a squashed corduroy sofa; tubby toddler and floppy newborn. Birthday candles are blown out, hands clap as they sit under the Christmas tree. She lingers by the front gate, little school blazer and brand new shoes.

The earliest memory – the first that is real, reliable – is not long after that. They are in the car, all four of them. It is raining outside; icy almost-sleet that patters against the window in streaks. Anna dozes in her car seat, the velvet headband around her peach-soft head slipping down towards her eyes. Her father is driving whilst her mother reads a paperback, folded over and pushed against the window so that she can catch the glow of the street lights as the day begins to fade.

They have been to a party; she looks down at her legs in their white tights, shiny shoes winking back at her as she wiggles them. The dress is her favourite: stiff gold skirt, black velvet top with puffed sleeves. She puts a hand to her hair, checks that the matching gold bow is still there.

'Okay back there, Elsie?' Her dad's eyes wink at her in the rear-view mirror.

'Uh-huh.'

He fiddles with the radio, finds a station and turns it up. It is a Sunday evening and the Top 40 is coming to an end, 'Tears on my Pillow' announced as number one. Her eyes are growing tired, but she smiles, because it is one of the many songs her dad often sings in the kitchen or, like now, in the car.

'I'm going to pull in here, love,' her father says to her mother, and whether it is for petrol or for food, she can't remember. On the radio, Kylie Minogue sings of starting anew and taking things — it is people, it is a person, but, always, remembering, she will think of it as actions — back. Anna splutters and the car is filled with the sour sweet smell of vomit.

'Good timing,' her mother says cheerfully, though perhaps she has added this line herself.

In the car park she stands and watches while her mother leans into the back and mops at the baby, the seat. She secs her father at the till, paying for the petrol, and she smells the petrol, at the pumps behind them, and the vomit, spattered on Anna's outfit, now peeled off and temporarily abandoned at her mother's feet. She takes a step or two back, the evening air shuffling at her party dress.

'Hello,' says a man, and she looks up at him, dark against the sky. The shadows and his coat mean that in memory he is almost a crow.

'Hi,' she says, and for a minute they say nothing.

'That's my mum,' she says, and the crow-man looks away.

'We're always looking for each other,' he says, and the words are the clearest of them all.

'Get away from my daughter,' her father says, and though his shirt is tucked in and his shoulders are narrow, his voice is mythical across the empty forecourt in her mind.

The crow-man melts away, but, often, later, when she is dreaming or when she is remembering, she sees him. She sees him, and she remembers him, and she wonders if he has been found.

2012

He knows it won't take long. Just a few short shifts, a few jokes shared, and he'll be part of it. He's been through the process plenty of times. It doesn't make being the new guy any more fun. But it's okay. A few short shifts, and it'll all be okay.

He sits at the small Formica table and opens the Tupperware box Elsa has carefully packed for him. Where is she? He likes to wonder. He likes to picture her and her map, out in the sunshine. He bites into a sandwich as he reaches for his phone. Thinking of you, he writes, because it is true. The room is narrow and there is an orange stain on the wall beside the microwave. Paper coffee cups fill the small bin, the tendrils of a banana skin groping their way out. The tap drips into the stainless-steel sink, a slow tattoo.

Once there was a night when the roof began to leak. It started slowly, a welling, while they were still sticking to the sofa, clothes trailed down the hallway. He got up to fill a glass with wine and something, a strangeness, made him look up. The first drop fell and he studied it, an inch or two from his bare foot.

'What is it?' she asked from behind him, her arms sliding around his chest.

'The roof's leaking,' he said, and they both watched the puddle grow.

'So let it,' she said, her lips pressing against his back.

The door to the kitchen jerks open, letting in a rush of light. A man carrying a baguette in one hand and a wrench in the other walks in. They eye each other, both wrong-footed. Jack puts down his sandwich, extends his hand.

'Jack,' he says. 'I don't think we were introduced yesterday.'

'Alex. I was out sick yesterday. Good to meet you.' The hand which he extends is neat and clean; unusual for someone in their trade. Jack has spent years taking great pains to keep his own in a similar state – though, if you look close enough, there still exists the thinnest layer of black, the tiniest fragments of metal which collect along the loops and whorls of his fingers' skin like fat in a heart's artery.

'You too,' he says. 'How long have you worked here?' On closer inspection, he decides that Alex is probably several years younger than himself, perhaps only just into his thirties. He has

66

dark curly hair, with no threads of grey visible, and his face, though badly shaven, is fairly unlined.

Alex pulls out the only other chair and sits down. 'Two years. Where were you before?'

'The UK. Did a couple of long-term jobs out there.'

'Bridges?'

'One. A couple of tower blocks. And a shopping centre – a mall, sorry.'

'Cool.'

'How about you?'

'This is my first bridge. But I was an apprentice here for six months back when I was training.'

'And you like it?'

Alex looks at him, an eyebrow raised. 'You're kidding, right?'

'Right. That's what I thought.'

'So where are you from? The UK?'

'Difficult to say, to be honest. Dad's from Seattle, Mum's British, which makes me a bit of both. Been back and forth a lot with work. States for a couple of years, England for a few, rinse, repeat.'

Alex nods. 'Cool.' He spins the wrench around on the table with a finger.

'And you?'

'Cape Cod. And then New York.'

'Yep, thought I caught a hint of that. You like New York?'

'Sure, of course. But it was time to move on. And when a Golden Gate gig turns up …'

'Yeah.'

Jack takes another bite of his sandwich as Alex unwraps the baguette and picks a slice of salami out of it, dropping it into his mouth. 'You live in the city?' Jack asks.

'Yep, in the Mission. You?'

'Yeah, out on Potrero.'

'Just you?'

'No, my girlfriend too.' It still feels strange to say. *Girlfriend*. Like he is a teenager again.

'Cool. What's the rent like out there?'

'Actually we're not renting. The house was my aunt's, she died earlier this year.'

'Oh. Sorry, man.'

'Nah, it's okay. I didn't really know her.'

Alex plucks another piece of salami from his sandwich. 'You ever lived in San Fran before?'

'Nope. Worked up in Long Beach once, about a million years ago. That's it for my Californication.'

'So I guess you'll be needing someone to show you the ropes? Where to hang out, that kind of thing?'

'Absolutely.'

'Want to grab a beer after work?'

'Sure, yeah. That'd be great.'

'Cool.' Alex gets up, fishing his phone out of his pocket. 'I've gotta make a call,' he says, 'but I'll catch you back out there, okay?'

'Cool,' Jack says, and as the door to the kitchen closes, he looks at his sandwich for a moment. And then, with a smile, he nods.

He spends the afternoon sandblasting rust with a small crew of painters; undressing a section of the bridge which will then be painted anew, another fresh start. It is deeply satisfying and when he clocks out at three, he feels more relaxed than he has for a long time. He heads towards the parking lot and finds Alex at the entrance, talking to Andy, the crew member Jack was paired with on his first day.

'How's it going?' Andy asks him. 'Finding everything okay?'

'Yep, all good, thanks.'

'We're heading out for a few beers,' Alex says. 'I'm going to tell him all our dark secrets.'

'Well, someone's got to.'

'You want to come?' Jack asks.

'I'd love to but I've got to get home. My wife and daughter both have stomach flu.'

'Well, good luck with that,' Alex says. 'We're gonna go get drunk.'

'See you later, guys.' They watch him reverse out of his parking space and both lift a hand in a wave as he passes them.

'Nice guy,' Jack says.

'Yeah, he is,' Alex says. 'He's like one of those people who never says anything bad about anyone.'

'Not many of those about.'

'Nope.' Alex unlocks his car; a rust-red sedan with a sizeable dent in the door of the passenger side. 'All aboard.'

Inside, the car smells of marijuana, McDonald's and Dr Pepper and the seats have been re-covered at different times in different fabrics. 'This is my baby,' Alex says, and starts the engine.

As they drive away, the bridge looms in his wing mirror. He watches it grow smaller, caught in the smudged glass like a souvenir. 'Just another day at the office,' he says, and Alex nods.

'Just another day at the office.'

Viewed from above – a gull's-eye view – the scratched red roof of the car beetles its way through the nice neighbourhoods of Cow Hollow and Pacific Heights, and into Hayes Valley. It crests and descends the hills, bobbing like a tiny boat on a rough sea. Finally back into the flats, it crosses Haight Street and cruises into Fillmore, reaching the Mission thirty minutes later. From this gull's-eye view, the house on Potrero can also be seen, eight long blocks over. Out there, Elsa is just arriving home, her key turning in the lock as the car pulls in beside a large apartment building, pale blue with rusting fire escapes criss-crossed down its side.

'Home sweet home,' Alex says.

'Nice place,' Jack says approvingly, and he means it. 'Just you?'

Alex shakes his head. 'Me, my girlfriend, and a room-mate.'

'Cool.' He climbs out of the car, looks around. The streets here are wider than in the city, yet it feels crowded; smaller and more dense. The smell of marijuana persists, heavy and sweet, and somewhere nearby the tinny sound of dance music comes from a car radio.

'C'mon,' Alex says. 'There's a great place a couple of blocks along.'

The street is lined with buildings just like Alex's; all painted in pale colours and peeling, iron fire escapes lacing their way up and down. At the corner of the street, they give way to businesses – restaurants and bars, a liquor store, a bicycle shop. They walk past a busy Vietnamese restaurant, a cloud of scent – lemongrass and something sweet, something sticky – enclosing them briefly. 'Awesome place,' Alex says.

'How long have you lived around here?'

'Couple of years. The whole time I've been here. It's really a great area.'

'Yeah, I like the look of it,' Jack says, as they approach a bright yellow building on a corner.

'Here we are,' Alex says, gesturing at it. 'Spanish. Turns into a salsa club at night. Gets kinda crazy, people still there at three, four a.m.'

It doesn't sound particularly crazy, but he is glad. He has always been bemused by London Elsa's talk of after-parties and after-after-parties. Not that he is averse to second chances. Quite the opposite, in fact.

They enter the bar, which at this hour – just before 4 in the afternoon – is almost empty. A large, square room with wooden floorboards and exposed brick walls, it is dominated by a black stage at its far end. Paintings on the walls show flamenco dancers and close-up portraits of dark-eyed girls. A pretty barmaid stands alone behind the vast oak bar, stacking glasses on a low shelf. 'Hey, Rosie,' Alex says, and she smiles.

'Alex,' she says. 'How are you today?'

'I'm good.' Alex sits on a bar stool. 'How are you, *mamacita*?'

She smiles at him. 'Yes, good too. Who is your friend?'

'This is Jack. Jack, Rosie.'

Jack extends a hand across the bar. 'Rosa,' she says, shaking it.

'Nice to meet you.' He pulls out the chair beside Alex, who says, 'Two beers, please, Rosie baby. The usual.'

'Sure thing.' She gets them from a fridge behind her, takes the folded note from Alex's hand with small, delicate fingers. A phone rings somewhere, the sound low and insistent, and she slides the change towards them as she hurries past to answer it. There is a sureness in the way she moves; an assertion. Jack is almost entirely sure that she and Alex have slept together.

'So, the UK,' Alex says. 'What's that like?'

'Pretty good,' Jack replies. 'London's a lot like New York, actually. Less snow. More rain.'

Alex makes a gesture with his hands which suggests that these two things potentially balance each other out. 'And your mom's a Brit?'

'Yeah, she's from York. Nice city. Spent a lot of my childhood there.'

'Oh yeah?'

'Yeah, my parents divorced when I was a kid, so we moved back there. Then me and my sister'd spend each summer over in Seattle with my dad.'

'Sounds kinda rough.'

'Not really, it was nice to travel a lot. And when you're a kid you don't really know any different, do you? Once I was old enough to leave school I came over to the States for good though, qualified here and worked here a while.' As is often the case, the teetering comes without warning. Remembering is sometimes easier, sometimes harder. He takes a pull of his beer and it recedes. 'I don't know,' he says, and it is easier again, 'I guess I got bored quickly. So I went back and forth every couple of years, job here, job there. Could never really settle.'

'I'm kinda like that. Guess it goes with the territory.'

'Or the territory goes with us.'

Alex raises his bottle in Jack's direction. 'Yup. Or that.'

'So, how long'd you live in New York?'

'Five years. You been?'

Jack nods and there is a faint sense of vertigo again, a tower about to tumble. He takes two quick gulps of beer, swallowing hard. 'Sure have. What work'd you do there?''

'Skyscraper, what else? Before that just small jobs, you know how it is – putting an elevator in an apartment block, rebar stuff, that kind of thing. It's like you said, I wasn't too sure about sticking around any place too long. But she got me, New York. In the end.'

'Ever think about going back?'

Alex shakes his head, his mass of curls trembling. 'Nah. I have this theory that when you leave a place you don't go back, you know?'

'Yeah,' Jack says. 'I do.' It isn't always easy.

'Besides, this is such a great gig. Seriously.'

Jack smiles, his hand relaxing around his beer. 'So what're they like, the other guys?'

'They're great. Most of them are older – well, except the apprentices but they're not there long enough to count. Miller's a good guy, though you're not gonna see him smile no matter how long you work there. Andy's great, he'll do anything for anyone.' He drains his beer, considering. 'Chase and Tony, they're the jokers, stick with them if you're having a rough day. Who else ... Oh, watch out for Price, he's got a kind of mean streak but he's mostly harmless if you know when to avoid him. And Eddie's the nice guy, everyone likes Eddie.' He looks up at the ceiling, trying to picture the rest of the crew. 'Yeah, everyone else is pretty cool, just normal guys, you know. Long-timers.'

Jack gestures to Rosa, who has returned from the phone and is busy fixing bottles into optics, for two more beers. 'Sounds nice.' He hands his money to Rosa. 'Thank you.'

'I like him,' she says to Alex. 'He has manners. Not like you.'

'Already making me look bad,' Alex says with a shrug. 'Me and you might not be friends, new guy.'

Jack laughs. 'I'll bear that in mind.'

Rosa smiles and heads back to the bottles at the other end of the bar, twisting her hair up with a pencil as she goes. 'So,' Alex says, finishing one beer and exchanging it for the next, 'how'd you get the job? They don't advertise them in England, right?'

'No. It was a friend of mine, actually. He knew I wanted to work there and he knows some of the crew.'

'How come?'

'He used to work on the bridge too. Retired now, but he's still in touch with some of them. Miller, Andy too, I think.'

'Oh wait, you mean Denny?'

'Yeah, you know him?'

'Sure, yeah. Well, not *know him* know him. But he was around when I did my apprenticeship.'

'Oh yeah, of course'

'Good guy.'

'Yeah, he is.' Jack takes a sip of beer. 'He really is. He heard there was a job opening up, put my name forward. It's always been kind of a dream of mine.'

'Cute.'

Jack shrugs. 'I guess I am.'

'No, seriously dude, that's cool. You're lucky, too. I heard they had like three hundred applications for that spot.'

'Seriously? Wow.'

'I know, right.'

They drink in amicable silence for a few minutes, before Alex turns to look at him. 'The jumpers thing bother you?'

Something sharp kicks suddenly in Jack's chest. He has to stop himself putting a hand to it, forces himself to answer. 'Nah.

Just part of the job, isn't it? I guess I'll just get used to it. Same as any big bridge.'

Alex nods. 'Yeah,' he says, taking a swig of his drink. 'You just get used to it. It's sort of weird how that happens. Just part of the job.'

Rosa is moving up the bar towards them, cleaning it in small circular movements with a yellow cloth. 'Hey, Alex,' she says when she is closer. 'Why you never come to dance any more?'

Jack is struck suddenly and overwhelmingly by a memory of Elsa. New Year's Eve, late, 2 or 3 a.m. He is in the corner of the room, the damp wall against his back, and Elsa approaches, her fingers linking through his. *Why aren't you dancing?* she asks, lips against ear, and she pulls him with her into the throng of people, threading her arms around his neck and pressing her body to his.

'You salsa?' he asks Alex, feeling dazed.

'No,' Alex retorts. 'She's confusing me with someone else.'

'Whatever you say, fella.' Jack, regaining his footing, smiles at Rosa. 'Why don't we get Twinkletoes here a little shot of something.'

'I like him,' she says to Alex. 'He's fun. Not like you.'

Two beers and another tequila later, the bar is slowly beginning to fill with people. Small groups of young people in smart clothes clutch smartphones, drinking bottles of beer and talking loudly. A couple of older men sit on stools further down the bar, their backs to the smart groups. Another girl has joined Rosa behind the bar; her T-shirt is tied in a knot over her navel, the short expanse of exposed skin curving over the waistband of her jeans. It is still light outside, and weak sunshine floods through the low windows and onto the worn wooden floorboards.

'So,' Alex says. 'Your girlfriend, what's she called?'

'Elsa.'

'Elsa. Nice name. Sounds English, I like it. How old is she?'

'Twenty-seven.'

Alex eyes Jack admiringly. 'Nice. So, it's pretty serious, huh? For her to move here with you.'

Jack shrugs. 'That's just Els. When she wants something ...' He trails off. He takes another gulp of beer. How can just the thought of her still turn him on? 'How about you, how long have you been with your girlfriend? What's her name?'

'Claudia. Six – no, wait, seven years now.'

'Long time.'

'Yeah. She wants to get married, have kids, you know ...' Alex scrunches up his face. 'Me ...' He shrugs. 'I don't know about all that shit.'

'Yeah.' Jack drains his beer. 'Another?'

Alex slaps the bar. 'My round, man.'

Rosa comes to serve them, her hair braided loosely over one shoulder, the pencil tucked behind an ear. 'You guys staying to dance?' she asks, putting their drinks down on the bar.

Jack laughs. 'Not me.'

'Don't worry, Rosie,' Alex says. 'We're staying to drink.'

She winks at him as she walks away. 'I'll get you dancing,' she calls over one shoulder.

'Can't believe you salsa,' Jack says.

Alex smiles as he picks up his tequila. 'You'll be surprised what this city makes you do.'

1992

September light breaks slowly through the dark. He blinks, each rise and fall of his eyelids bridging a gap of twenty years – San Francisco sunrise, Yorkshire bedroom. Thirty-six, sixteen. Relenting, he closes them again. Sixteen then, and free.

Waking up that Monday, he has a sudden sense of free fall. The decision he has lived with all summer is suddenly concrete, irrevocably fact. No more school. The years yawning ahead, nothing to fill them. He swings one foot over the edge of the bed, where it kicks over an empty glass before meeting the worn carpet. He stretches, his arms wiry. His hands are still soft and clean. A yellowish tang of cigarette smoke rises from his sheets and skin.

Getting up, he shuffles through the crumpled clothes and magazines which litter the floor.

He bends to pick up a battered packet of ten cigarettes, checks inside. There is one left, a hairline crack near its base. He fiddles idly with it, kicking around in the rubble for a Rizla to patch it with. There is a fluttering in his chest and he can't quite seem to catch his breath. He presses a hand to his head, where a faint bruise still lingers at one temple. Fists meet his face often, though not as often as his meet faces.

He throws the cigarette aside, tugs on a T-shirt. As he walks downstairs, the house is silent. The air is cooling rapidly, the stairs creak suspiciously beneath his feet: this is a place which is quickly becoming somewhere that is not his. At the foot of the stairs, the threadbare carpet surrenders to entirely bare boards. They take his weight but not willingly, and his footsteps seem to shudder in the silence. He stands in the kitchen doorway and touches his head again, resting a shoulder against the frame.

The edges of this house are always lit in memory; even in early autumn they glow.

He shifts back into an upright position. The kitchen is empty, the back door open. He makes his way over, a terrible taste in his mouth. His mother is kneeling by the flower beds, a fork prongs down in the grass, a trowel in hand.

'Why aren't you at work?' he asks, lurking in the doorway.

She glances up at him, her face sun-warmed but cold. 'It's my morning off. And I might ask you the same question.'

He sniffs, running the ridge of his foot across the small step. She turns back to the soil.

'The paper's on the table. Job section's near the back. I'll make you some breakfast in a minute.'

Back inside, he stares into the fridge. He removes the juice and drinks from the carton, letting the fridge door swing shut. The paper is open on the wooden table, pages frail and fluttering in the breeze from the garden. He wanders back and forth as he gulps. The faint sound of next door's radio drifts through on the cool, gold air. The juice is pulpy in his mouth. Aimee's school timetable is stuck to the door of the fridge, and he studies it, imagining her in each class. Not clever, by any stretch of the imagination, but she is quiet and receptive and she cares. She is good. It's easy being Aimee, he feels sure of it. The fluttering feeling has not gone away.

His mother's tempers cool quickly but are ferocious while they last. He has come to enjoy igniting them, has often smiled as he turns his key in the door in the early hours of the morning, as he leaves ashtrays on windowsills or bottles in bins. But this, this long and half-hearted detachment, is difficult to adjust to. Aimee would brazen it out; talk without being answered, shrug and smile her way back into favour, but he can't bring himself to. Easy being Aimee. He recaps the juice and leaves it on the table. The paper's pages flutter; he takes a step closer.

Something is stirring beside him. The kitchen flickers, fades; his lashes twitch. He opens his eyes, Elsa's body warm against his chest.

2012

As Elsa wakes, Jack's arms slide around her, his skin hot against hers. Sun streams through the window.

'I forgot to close the curtains,' she murmurs sleepily, and he yawns beside her.

'That's okay,' he says. 'It's nice.'

'How long have you been awake?' She rolls onto her back, pushing hair out of her face.

'A while. I was just thinking.'

'Thinking about what?'

He smiles and pulls her back into him, resting his cheek against her head. 'I don't know really. Nothing much.'

'What time is it?'

He stretches out an arm to the bedside table behind him. Fumbling, he finds his watch. He squints at the face. 'Just before six.'

She pulls the duvet up over her face. 'You have to go, don't you?'

'Yep.' He burrows down beside her, kisses her forehead, her cheek, her chin. 'But you go back to sleep.' She murmurs, running a hand across his chest, but her eyes are already closing. 'I'll see you later,' he whispers. He climbs out of bed. On his way to the bathroom, he draws the curtains.

When she wakes again, several hours later, he is gone. Stretching out on the bed, she stares up at the ceiling. She lifts one leg and then the other, letting them flop down to the mattress. *Time to get up*, she thinks, but instead she rolls over, running her fingers over the empty space on Jack's side. The sheet is a faded blue, the duvet cover white; both brought with them from Jack's Clapham flat. She pulls the duvet back up and over her head, breathing in his scent. The house is silent, and under here, it's easy to imagine that nothing else exists, that beyond the bed there is only white noise. Her eyelashes brush against the fabric as she blinks; at her opposite end, her toes flex back and forth against the cotton. *What shall I do today?* she thinks, but it is an abstract question, a stranger's, because the bed is all there is.

A sound: sharp hum, death rattle. Once. Twice. She pushes the cover away from her and the room rushes back in. Dragging herself up to a sitting position, she looks around. Her phone is on the bedside table, its little light flashing expectantly.

1 new message.

She lies back down as she unlocks it, tugging a pillow up behind her so that her head is propped up.

Jack.

Up you get, lazybones. Lots to see ... xx

She smiles and locks the keypad. Putting the phone on the pillow beside her, she looks up at the ceiling again, willing herself into action. *One, two, three and up* then: she sits and stretches, wiggling her toes over the edge of the bed. The muscles in her legs are stiff from walking; she rolls her feet, clicking the joints, and then stands. She walks across the room and over the tiny landing and into the bathroom without pausing to dress. The air is cool and her skin prickles as its tiny fair hairs rise. Shutting the bathroom door, she turns the shower on full before sitting to pee. She looks down at her feet, purple toenails against grey tiles, elbows on knees, and yawns. The mirrored cabinet over the sink has begun to steam up, a cloud which passes slowly across the glass, billowing from left to right. Standing, she pulls the shower curtain across and steps into the bath – chipped grey enamel still cold as the warm water spatters it. The curtain is white plastic, yellowing and black-spotted with mould. She studies it as she lathers up her hair. Inside her head, a map of San Francisco unfolds, buildings rising up in 3D. Question marks appear over areas – shower curtains sold here? Or here? Red dotted routes spread out from the house on Potrero, some stalling and retracing their steps, others abandoned halfway. She reaches for the soap and turns to let the water fall on her face.

When he is here, the house is different. She isn't sure she

believes in ghosts, but in this tiny house, there is a strange, baited silence. *The walls are watching*, she thinks as she turns off the shower. She knows little about Christine, the aunt who lived here for forty years — was she kind? Resentful? Haunt-ish? Old, she knows that much, far older than Jack's father. She wraps a towel around herself, turbaning another on her head. The air is warmer now, tiny water molecules drifting listlessly around her, caught in the fluorescent beams of the plastic-cased light. Brushing her teeth in the steamed-up mirror, she wonders if the things that Jack isn't saying about his aunt and his father are things which might make a person who has passed hold a grudge. The extractor fan drones unevenly and she listens for words, a message from somewhere beyond, toothbrush still in her mouth. None is forthcoming. She spits.

In the bedroom, she dresses quickly, shivering. She pulls the curtains open; another bright blue day. The glass is already sun-warmed; she pauses a moment and lets the rays heat her cheeks. She needs to call her parents: this day is too blue not to be shared. She does a quick calculation: 7 p.m. in the UK. Dinnertime; she'll call them in an hour or two, when they are flicking through channels and drinking the last of their wine.

Turning back to the dresser, she runs a comb through her hair and plugs in the hairdryer. She stands with it above her head, moving it idly from side to side so that the hair flies out and back again, left to right, right to left. Bored, she leaves it half-finished and heads downstairs. *Coffee*, she thinks, an expectant bitterness blooming across her tongue. She slips her feet into canvas trainers and grabs her keys from the side and her bag from its place beside the stairs. Scarf tossed over shoulders, she opens the door and steps out into the sunshine.

There is an old lady outside.

She stands by Elsa's gate in a voluminous floral nightgown, a withered hand shielding her eyes as she stares down the street. The other hand grasps the gate, its fingers curved like talons.

'Can I help you?' Thoughts of coffee are forgotten – already she is considering the hospital further up the road, picturing a hand on an elbow, slow steps, gentle voice. Grateful nurse, kind Samaritan.

The woman turns towards her, startled. She is small, birdlike beneath the nightie. Her hair is dyed a peachy blonde, its roots white. It stands up from her broad forehead in a short, fluffy cloud. Her cheeks are pouchy but her chin is small and pointed.

'Are you okay?' Elsa tries again, beside the gate now.

The woman wears horn-rimmed glasses and, behind them, she frowns. Her fingers leave the gate. And then they are extended. 'I'm sorry,' she says, and her voice is unfeminine and forceful. She rasps as she speaks, giving the words an almost-echo, a rattle. 'I didn't see you there. I'm Pearl. Your neighbour.'

It is Elsa's turn to be startled. 'Elsa,' she says. The hand is soft and small in hers. 'Were you looking for something?'

Her neighbour looks down at herself, then at the road. 'Oh, right,' she says. 'I'm looking for my grandson.'

'I'm sorry?'

Pearl stares at her. 'My grandson. I left the door unlocked and he got out.'

'How – how old is he?'

'Five.'

'Oh my God.' Elsa opens the gate. Practicality is returning; it floods through her like silver, her limbs moving quickly and smoothly, brain ticking over. 'We should call someone.' She reaches for her bag and then remembers the phone on its pillow upstairs.

'He can't have gotten far,' Pearl says, but her voice is uncertain, and now they are both moving; heading downhill and away from the city. 'He's my great-grandson, actually,' she says, her hand still shielding her eyes. 'He and his sister are staying with me. They're normally so good.'

'Where's the little girl?' Elsa asks. 'Is she okay?'

'I locked the door,' Pearl replies, as if this answers the question.

Elsa looks around. The road is still reasonably quiet, but it's wide and will soon become busy, shuttling traffic back and forth between the city and the airport and, beyond, San Diego. A bus trundles towards them and she quickens her pace. 'How long has he been out?' she asks.

'I don't know, five, maybe ten – oh!'

They have reached the intersection with 21st Street and there, sitting on the kerb, is a small boy. He is stroking a cat – mangy thing, mouth damp – and laughing.

'Sam!' Pearl hurtles forward and grabs him by the hand.

'Hey, Gramma,' he says. Elsa's eyes lock with the cat's.

'Are you trying to give me a heart attack?' Pearl asks, tugging him to his feet. Dressed in a T-shirt and pyjama bottoms, he has a head of thick chestnut hair, and no shoes on. 'Hi,' he says to Elsa.

'Hi.'

'Do you like cats?'

The cat mews, prowling back and forth along the pavement. A section of its ear is missing.

'I like some cats,' Elsa says diplomatically.

'Let's get you inside,' Pearl says.

They walk back up the hill, the three of them in a line. 'My cat's called Snickers,' Sam says.

'That's a good name.' Elsa glances at Pearl, who is fishing in a pocket of her nightie for the keys. They have reached her gate, and she pauses, uncertain. 'Can I help with anything?'

Pearl looks up, the keys retrieved. 'Oh, we're okay,' she says. The way she says the word makes the syllables sound round and separate: *Hoe-Kay*. 'But why don't you come in? I can make you a coffee. We can introduce ourselves.'

'I'm Sam,' says Sam.

Elsa glances at her own house. 'Erm, okay. Lovely. Thank you.'

As they walk up the short path, Elsa looks down at her neighbours' feet: one set small and pale; the other, shuffling in a pair of slippers, pinched and blue. Her own seem out of place in their ordinariness.

'Here we are,' Sam says, and when Pearl unlocks the door, he bolts into the dark hallway.

'Just like his mother,' Pearl says, following him. She holds the door open for Elsa, clicking on the light with a shaky hand.

'Thank you.' Elsa pulls her shoes off; toe to heel, toe to heel. The house is identical to theirs but entirely different. Warm, yeasty air hangs in sullen clouds. From somewhere a cartoon voice is laughing. The hall, red-walled and red-carpeted, is lined with bookcases which are all filled with yellowing paperbacks, their spines cracked and lettering foiled. 'So many books,' she says, and Pearl shrugs.

'It's kind of a hobby.' She gestures for Elsa to enter the living room. 'When you get to my age, you need them.'

The living room is so full of furniture that it seems half the size of theirs. A three-seater sofa and two armchairs crowd around a glass coffee table, whilst a gas heater is guarded on either side by two end tables, both covered with framed photographs and strange ornaments. Another row of bookcases fills one wall, and a flat-screen television lurks in one corner. A cartoon rabbit dances across its screen.

'My grandson gave it to me,' Pearl says, noticing Elsa looking at it. 'I don't watch TV but a gift's a gift.'

'Uncle Harry got it,' Sam says. He has taken his place on the floor beside his sister, a toddler who has sparse curls the same rich brown as his hair, and who is studiously ignoring their presence. 'He's rich.'

'It's very nice,' Elsa says, to all of them, and then, to Pearl, 'How many grandchildren do you have?'

'Too many. I had two sons, which was enough work, and

then four grandchildren, and now six great-grandchildren. These two are the smallest.'

'It's lovely to have such a big family,' Elsa says.

Pearl laughs; a hoarse, smoky sound. 'If you say so. So, coffee? Or tea?'

'Coffee would be great, thank you.'

She disappears into the kitchen, leaving Elsa alone with the children. They stare up at the screen, their heavy heads tipped back between skinny shoulders. The cartoon rabbit is in conversation with a bear now; it is difficult to tell the politics of the situation. Elsa edges her way to the sofa and takes a seat, watching the two of them. There is a strangeness, she feels, in being left alone with more than one child. One child appears innocent, but two together seem primeval; ancient and wise. Elsa is immediately sure that there is communication occurring between the two, in a language she cannot hear or speak. The little girl's shoulder twitches once. Sam turns to look at Elsa, who smiles. He maintains his gaze for a beat and then returns his attention to the screen. One of his small hands curls and uncurls into a pudgy fist against the thick carpet.

'Here we are,' Pearl says, tottering through with two mismatched mugs. She shunts the coffee table closer to Elsa and puts one down in front of her. Sitting in one of the armchairs, her nightie puffed out around her, she eyes Elsa over the tops of her glasses.

'Well, that's one way to meet your new neighbour, right?'

'It's memorable, I'll give you that.'

'I kept meaning to drop by and say hi, but these two have been here all week.'

'I'm glad you didn't – the house is still such a mess Jack would've been mortified.' Elsa picks up her coffee and blows on it uncertainly, then replaces it.

Pearl waves this away, taking a noisy gulp from her own mug. 'How are you finding everything?'

'We love it. I love it.'

'And your husband, he's Christine's nephew?'

'That's right. We're not married though.'

Pearl frowns. 'I'm sorry, I don't know why I thought that.' She takes another sip of her coffee. 'So, I'm guessing by your accent that you're British?'

'Yes. From Shropshire and then London. Which is where I met Jack.'

'We went to England once. In the sixties. London and then down to Devon.'

'You and your husband?'

'Yep, me and Tom. He's gone now though. It's just me here.'

'And us, Gramma!' Sam pipes up, and Pearl smiles. 'And you,' she agrees.

'I'm so sorry,' Elsa says, taking a sip of her coffee. It is grainy on her tongue.

'Long time ago.' Pearl settles back in her seat. 'So, what's the story? You've emigrated?'

'No, I'm just on a tourist visa. Six months and we'll see how it goes. I'd like to apply for a professional visa after that.'

'To do what?'

Elsa takes a gulp of her drink and then another. 'I'm not sure yet. I was a PA back in England.'

'Well, now you can be anything you want, right?' She gestures around her expansively with a mottled hand. 'The land of opportunity.'

Elsa puts her cup down. 'I suppose so.'

'Good for you.' When she isn't talking, the muscles of Pearl's mouth tense and relax with a soft, wet sound. Her lips purse as she takes the final sip of coffee.

'How long have you lived here?' Elsa asks.

'In this place? Ten years almost. Before that we had a place out in Marina, big house, a lot of cleaning.'

'Have you always lived in the city?'

'Yup. I was born not far from here, actually. Looked a lot different back then.'

'Gramma,' says Sam. 'I have to go to the bathroom.'

'Okay.' Pearl heaves herself up. 'Let's go.' She glances at Elsa. 'He's afraid to go by himself'.

'Do you want me to take him?' She panics at the thought; she'd have no idea what to do.

'That's okay. We know what we're doing, don't we, Sam?'

They disappear into the hall and their steps sound overhead like heartbeats, one small and rapid, one slow and heavy. She looks at the little girl, whose shoulder twitches again, her head tipping slowly to one side.

'Are you a sleepy girl?' she asks, and the child looks up at her with slowly closing eyes. She reaches small arms up towards Elsa. Elsa hesitates and then picks her up, surprised at the weight of her. She tucks her against her chest and sits back down. The girl's arm slides slowly down her own, her small back rising in sleepy breaths.

'It's okay,' Elsa says. 'It's going to be okay.'

1994

Another rain-spattered window, but no wings, no sky. Just the endless grey of the highway. He stares out at it, at the wide lanes of the pale road, at the unfamiliar fonts which appear everywhere: licence plates, road signs, gas stations. He has been here every summer for twelve summers and yet only now does it seem a place he does not belong. He rubs at his face, still dry from ten hours' air conditioning, his mouth thick and fuzzy.

His father leans into the wheel, the radio up high and the windscreen wipers squealing back and forth. How much does he know? How many phone calls from his mother have there been, late at night or early in the morning, how many calls in the few waking hours they share? Does he know about the first police car ride home, or the second, or the third? Jack is just shy of eighteen and he has spent ten nights of his life in cells, countless more on lawns or in the backs of cars. Does he know about the girls, or about the boys who break furniture and vomit in gardens and on carpets?

His face is just as difficult to read as Jack remembers. They drive, and it rains, and he is in America. His backpack is in the boot – *trunk* – and ten times the size of the small one he stowed under the seat on his first summer return. Now it is not summer and he is not a child. Now he is his father's son.

'You eat on the plane?' his father asks, as the car bumps onto the exit ramp.

'Yeah. Sort of.'

'We can pick something up, if you want. If you're hungry.'

'Nah. I'm okay.'

'Okay.' His father fiddles with the radio, searching for the news. Voices reach out from the static and are swept away. The speakers emit sharp noises, occasionally silenced, and then burst into clear sound, a woman's calm voice reading the traffic report.

He thinks unexpectedly of Aimee, imagines her asleep in her white-framed single bed, the small TV, with its bunny-ears aerial, burbling quietly in the corner, occasional currents passing across its screen. Will she take his room? It would be fair; hers is far smaller, the window letting in little light with which to view the books she pores over. At thirteen she has become gangly and thin, her hair growing long and tangled down her back. She wears glasses but not in public. The rooms of their house are the only ones she sees well.

Will she be okay? Will they, the two of them, women together, in their yellowing semi, the walls bearing scars he has inflicted with ease? The answer is almost certainly yes. Leaving to catch his flight in the early hours of the morning, he did not wake Aimee. He does not think she will mind.

Arriving at the house, his father jerks open the boot and they both hesitate, staring at the bag inside. He reaches out a hand to hook the strap, heaving it over one shoulder.

'You got it?' his father asks belatedly, and he closes the boot.

Inside the house, the air smells faintly of oil. Dropping the bag in the hallway, he tugs his trainers off.

'You must be tired,' his father says, and he shrugs.

In the living room he drops onto the brown sofa, stretching cramped limbs and reaching for words.

His dad gets there first, selecting just one. 'Beer?'

'Please.'

Returning with the bottles, Jeff hands him one and says, 'I guess you should really eat something.'

'I will. In a while.'

His father sits down in the armchair opposite him. They take long pulls on their beers. His father lets out a slow breath which stutters and stalls halfway to being a whistle.

'Well, here we are.'

Here they are.

'You know where your room is, obviously.'

He does.

'And you know I'm not much of a cook.'

He does. Emphatically.

'We'll just see how we go.'

Jack takes a second, vicious gulp of his drink. A pressure is building in his chest. 'Thanks,' he says, and it pauses. 'I appreciate you doing this,' he says, and it begins to recede.

His father gives an uncomfortable shrug, twisting the bottle back and forth against the arm of his chair. 'S'no trouble,' he says. And, then, unexpectedly: 'You're my son.'

They sit in silence, the bottles emptying. 'I'm going to fix you something to eat,' Jeff says, rising, and Jack nods.

In the doorway, his father turns. 'I'll take you to the union on Monday. Introduce you to the boys. We'll get you started.'

And Jack nods.

1995

The sun sits high above the playground, heat coming up from the tarmac in waves. They circle through them, sweatshirts tied around waists, school shirts soft against damp skin. Her hair is coming loose from its braid, curling in strands around the edges of her face. She picks up the plastic hoop, its surface gritty. She rolls it against the ground, her shadow short at her feet.

'Whose turn is it?' she asks, and two girls are arranged, belly to belly. She lifts the hoop and slides it over them. They lean back against its edge and loop their arms around it, holding it up. 'Ready?' she asks, and they all giggle.

'Spin,' they yell, and they all take it up.

Spin   Spin   Spin   Spin   Spin

Her hands grip the hoop and others join her. They turn the hoop, slow at first and then faster.

The two girls spin with it, their hands clasped together, and then the others in the circle release them and they stagger in loops, trying to keep their balance. Their knees give way and they stumble, two other girls rushing forward to catch them.

'That was a good one,' they say.

'That was so funny,' they say.

'Elsa, it's your turn,' they say.

She reaches down to scratch a calf, the skin hot and with its first faint down. 'Okay,' she says.

'Hannah, you too,' someone says, and she is face to face with her best friend, knees touching, palms pressed damply together.

'Ready?' someone asks, and they are. They are the best at this game; so aligned that their feet land as one, each body balancing the other. They almost never fall.

'Ready,' she says, and then she looks up. In the bright light which bounces off the school's sand-coloured buildings, she sees Anna, haloed against the sky. Her little sister, who is now both big and small; shorter than her peers but rounder too, her cheeks plump behind hair cut too short. She makes her way across the playground, sticking close to the shelter of the classrooms, head tilted down. She is alone. Alone like always.

Elsa pulls herself free of the hoop. 'Anna! Over here!'

Her little sister looks up, her face suddenly lit. Anna waves back eagerly, one of her socks sliding down. 'Come on,' Elsa says, beckoning to her.

Anna takes quick, waddling steps towards her, and then she falters, her smile disappearing. She is no longer looking at

Elsa, but past her, at the herd of baby Bambis to which her sister belongs. They flick their glossy ponytails. Their fresh, freckled faces, smug and sniggering, their arms folded. Hannah, still in the hoop and with a hip cocked lazily to one side, rolls her eyes.

'Come on, Elsa. It's our turn.'

'Yeah, come on, Elsa,' they say.

'This game's not for kids,' they say.

'This game's just for us,' they say.

She looks at them, her heart thudding, and then she turns back to her sister. She remembers the things she has overheard; her mother, tearful. *The teacher says she's being bullied.* Her dad, calm and firm as always. *She'll get there.* One night, when he came to tuck her in, he sat at the edge of her bed and held her hand. *You need to look after your little sister for us,* he said. *Can you do that?*

She looks at the small, round face which looks back at her, two ugly stripes of red forming across it,

'Come on, Elsa,' Hannah says.

and then she holds out

a hand.

'Come and play,' she says.

2012

It happens on a day no different from any other. The sky is once again clear and blue, the sun just beginning to sink towards the bay. Golden Gate seems to glow; as if it has soaked up light all day and now begins to release it, a soft exhale.

The weight of its roadway is hung from two cables, which loop up from its ends and thread through the towers, giving it its two peaks. The two cables are each made of 27,572 individual strands of wire and, should you cut through them to see all these strands come together, are 36.5 inches wide. Jack, halfway through his tenth shift, is a quarter of the way up the left-hand one. A harness attaches him to silver safety wires which run all the way up the peaks and down again. It is 3 p.m., and beneath him a blue pickup truck thunders past; its bed full of brightly coloured bicycle frames, tangled together like a puzzle.

'Hang on a second,' Alex says behind him. 'I'm gonna get another clip, this one's coming loose.' They are checking rivets, of which there are 1,200,000 on the bridge, requiring almost constant inspection. It is pleasant work; methodical and satisfying. This interruption is the first in two hours.

'No worries,' Jack says, and, as he looks over his shoulder at the bay, it seems a simple truth.

'Back in a sec,' Alex says, tugging at the offending safety clip on his harness. 'Don't want to fall in now, do I?' He clumps back down the cable, humming to himself.

Jack leans back in his harness, looks up at the sky. Closing his eyes, he remembers what it is like to be five and look at the bridge in a picture, what it is like to be ten and dream of being part of a crew. *How did I know?* he wonders, and then he thinks of Elsa.

'There was something about you,' she said, once, early on, when it was probably unwise to do so. They were sitting in the park, her bare feet in his lap. She leant back on her hands, face tipped up towards the sun. Her dress was strapless and the skin above it smooth and white.

'You have no idea what you do to me,' he said, and it is still true.

Eyes open again, he pivots on the tips of his boots and looks down at the cars speeding into the city. The traffic rarely slows completely, but at this time of day it moves at a more leisurely pace, less frantic than the morning's rush. He watches the progress of a couple of cars, sunlight sparkling on the water below them.

The pedestrian walkway is on the opposite side of the road; he leans over and looks at the people walking. They are small but their details are more easily observed from here; he likes to watch. A man strolls past with his baby daughter on his shoulders, pointing at the boats passing beneath them as she slaps at his head in glee. Two teenage girls giggle, clasping at each other's arms as they whisper.

The wind whistles past him, picking up strands of his hair and pushing them back from his face. He needs a haircut, he thinks, and as he wonders where the best place to get one is, a man with a balding head and a brownish mackintosh jacket strides along the bridge, stops perhaps twenty feet from the girls, and in one swift movement, hurdles over the railing and out of sight.

Time doesn't stop; silence doesn't fall. People continue to walk and cars continue to drive. Occasional strands of conversation and song detach themselves from the flow and drift, untethered, up to him on the cable. His eyes do not leave the spot where the man in the mackintosh stood. The cable creaks and footsteps come towards him, but still he cannot look away.

'Eddie just said he has two spare tickets for the game,' Alex says from somewhere a thousand miles away. 'You wanna go?' The girls are passing the spot now; their feet touch it without pause.

'Jack?' Alex says, when he doesn't receive a response.

'He jumped,' Jack says. 'He just jumped.'

Back down on the pavement, Alex keeps a hand on his back while Andy speaks calmly into a cellphone. Eddie jogs across lanes, bouncing from foot to foot as he waits for gaps in the traffic. *Go long*, Jack thinks, and wonders if he might be sick.

'It's tough, huh?' Alex says. 'Even when you're ready for it.'

'It's not how I thought it would be,' Jack says, though these are not the words he intended to speak.

Alex pulls him a little closer, forcing him to meet his eyes. 'It gets a lot easier after this,' he says. 'I swear.'

'Okay.' He thinks he says it but he isn't sure. There is a roaring that could be traffic but which he is horribly sure is coming from his own ears.

'Okay?'

He fills his lungs with the bay's blue air, and he tells himself that this will be okay. He looks Alex in the eye and, somehow, the word makes it out. 'Okay.' When it is out, it is easier to believe.

'You wanna go to the game later?'

He turns away from the walkway, where Eddie has made it to the spot. 'Sure.'

'Cool. Eddie said he'd drive, so we can have a few beers.'

'Great.'

Alex's hand, still resting on his back, gives him a sharp slap between the shoulder blades. 'Great,' he agrees. He looks up at the cable. 'We'd better get back up there,' he says. 'Get it done before the end of the day, I bet.'

'Easily.'

They are walking now, heading for the low end of the cable where they can reattach their harnesses and begin the walk up. Alex looks sideways at him. 'We're a good team,' he says.

Jack glances up at the huge red belly of the cable which curves above them and nods. 'I guess we are.'

When he is back up above the bridge, he thinks again of Elsa. The night before their flight and she can't sleep. She sits cross-legged at the end of the bed, his T-shirt curling in folds around her thighs.

'I'm just too excited,' she says, patting insistently at the mound of his feet beneath the covers.

'I can see that,' he says, a hand shielding his eyes against the light.

She flops down on her belly beside him, chin cradled in her palm. 'Aren't you?' she asks.

He reaches out to twirl a strand of her hair around his finger. 'More than you can imagine,' he says.

'It's the beginning,' she says, and up on the cable, he nods.

Later, when the shift is over, he sits in the little kitchen area drinking a paper cup of watery coffee while he waits for Alex and Eddie. Miller comes in, the stub of a cigarette still smouldering in his hand.

'Heard we had a jumper today,' he says. 'Heard you saw it.'

Jack nods. 'Yeah. Middle-aged guy.'

'Went over without stopping?'

'Yup.'

Miller pulls out a chair and sits down. 'The guys show you what we do? Throw the flare, phone the coastguard?'

'Yeah.'

'Good.'

The coffee is cold and he turns the cup between finger and thumb on the tabletop. Miller fills a foggy glass with water from the tap. He drains it in one gulp and drops the cigarette end into the dregs.

'How often does it happen?' Jack asks.

'Twenty-five a year, maybe. One every couple of weeks anyway. But a lot are like today, straight over and we don't even see 'em.'

'And the others?'

'We keep an eye out. Some people are easier to spot than others. I give you the book thing yet?'

'Yeah.'

'You read it?'

'Bits.' He drinks his coffee even though it is cold.

'Good. Cos I'm gonna need to put you on the list next week if that's all right with you. To be on call, I mean.'

'Okay, sure.'

Miller stands by the door, fishing his cigarettes from his back pocket. 'It's all in the book. All procedure. Two of you out there, you say the right things, you get them thinking, and then you pull them back over. Keeps you safe and hopefully them too. After that, it's out of our hands and the officials take over.' He thumbs a cigarette out of the packet.

Jack pushes his chair back and stands up, crushing the empty cup in his fist. 'All sounds pretty straightforward,' he says.

Miller pauses to strike a match. He brings it to his face, and the cigarette crackles. 'Kinda has to be,' he says, tossing the spent match aside, and then Jack follows him out into the dying light.

1996

S oft focus for the montage; the building of a
building man. His apprenticeship is with a
local firm, one where his father is well known.
There are classrooms – and he has never liked
classrooms – but there are also hard hats and
harnesses, there are late-night conversations in the
kitchen about rebar and blistered hands. There are
days spent scaling scaffolding, hours hidden behind
a welding mask. In the bars after work, the men
still clap him on the back and still call him 'Jackie'
or 'kid'. His father continues to attempt to cook
and they still drink beer on the battered couch. He
calls him 'son' more frequently in those days, and
each time it seems more like the truth.

The arguments begin as they did back in England
with his mother: tiny bubbles of irritation drifting

gradually to a simmer; weeks later a raging boil. Doors are slammed, insults hurled, bottles countless. It is always his fault; he can't help it. He is twenty years old, a trainee in ironworking and an expert in baiting. He is drawn to the spark, mesmerised by the flames. Each night he staggers down the path, a stale alcohol cloud hanging over him like smog. Girls press into him as he guides them towards the house. There are many and some come more than once, but looking back they are faceless, nameless; blurring into each other, an amorphous collection of flesh and limbs, of white morning light and cigarette-stained sheets. They are always loud, he recalls that much. He always picks the loud ones.

One Friday night, his father hammers on the door at 3 a.m. The blows sound through the house, the walls finally ready to crumble. The argument is conducted with Jeff pacing the hall and Jack in the doorway, a sheet wrapped around his waist, a faceless girl spreadeagled on the bed behind him.

'This is my house, you'll show me some respect here,' his father says. There is a vein pulsing at his temple.

'Fine,' he says, and lights a cigarette.

'Fine?'

'Yeah. I'll move out.'

The door is slammed, the sheet dropped, the suspended moment collected and continued.

Then he is here, on an October morning, the key unfamiliar in his hand. A tiny apartment on the west side of Seattle, where the walls are paper thin but they belong, in the loosest possible sense and through a rental agreement, to him. His father is behind him, carrying a box of food and pretending not to notice the stink of urine in the hallway, the sound of crying from a floor above. There is a moment's hesitation when Jack knows he could turn, say something to take it all back, and just for that moment he is tempted. And then he unlocks the door and steps inside.

The street light sends bars of orange through the crooked blinds and across the plasterboard walls. There is a stain on one of them; a blackish smudge which spreads like smoke as it rises. His father puts the box down on the kitchen counter. The backpack stuffed with his things leans against the wall.

'Well.'

Well.

'This is it, I guess. You gonna be okay?'

He nods but he can't quite bring himself to look up. 'Sure.'

'You can call any time. Come over for dinner, whatever, you know.'

'Thanks.'

They almost don't, but at the last second, they do: an awkward, stiff sort of hug which neither leans into. And then he is shutting the door, his father's footsteps fading down the hall.

There is a tap at the door an hour later, and then she is there, the light behind her flickering. Her midriff bare, jeans frayed around the feet. Thin blonde hair falls round her pointed face, the shoestring straps of her vest slide down her shoulders.

Ginny. Voice softly Southern, body firm. The bar she waitresses at is just a few blocks away, and many shifts end here: shoulder to shoulder on the small bed, beers in hand, legs entwined. Mornings begin waking with her hair spread across the pillow, bare breasts pressed against him. But now, on this first night, they are still almost strangers. And yet she is here, wine in hand, midriff bare, straps sliding down her shoulders.

2012

Sometimes, in those first weeks of October, Elsa waits to wake; too certain that life is not this simple. She rises each morning while Jack showers, folding one of his shirts around her, enjoying the smell of his skin as it lingers on hers. In the kitchen, she prepares lunches for him, and when he tells her she doesn't need to, she laughs.

'I want to,' she says, and sometimes he looks at her strangely.

When he has left for the day, she showers. She studies her face in the mirror, traces the marks his lips have left on the pale skin of her neck, her breasts. Under the water she thinks of his body against hers, and as she dresses, she looks at his things – at the neat stack of clothes, at the turned-out contents of his pockets on the windowsill – and smiles. Back down in the kitchen, she studies her map and then steps out into the cooling days. She walks to the water, to the hills, to the parks. She walks through residential areas and through tourist traps, around the echoing halls of museums and galleries and through the hustling streets of Chinatown and the Castro.

When she has exhausted all of the areas she can walk to, or when walking is too exhausting, she starts catching buses. On a day when the latter is true, she leaves the house, pausing to wipe a scuff mark from the door with the edge of her sleeve, and goes to the bus stop to await the bus to Market Street, where she will catch the 73 to Haight Street, her current favourite destination. There is no evidence of it in her family history, but she is still pretty sure she's at least part hippy.

This morning, while he was dressing, she slipped into the room behind him and watched his bare back as he pulled up his jeans.

'You have no flaws,' she said, and he turned in surprise.

'What do you mean?'

She prowled slowly around him, her fingertips tracing his skin. 'No scars. No moles. No flaws.'

'I have scars,' he said, and he turned over his arm. At the crease of the elbow, running up behind the bicep; a thick white track.

'What happened?' she asked.

'Someone dropped a beam from twenty feet up.' He pressed two of her fingers to his arm, ran them along the length. 'A step closer and I would've lost my arm. Two and it would've killed me.'

She thinks of it now, that flaw. She had been sure that she had seen every inch of his skin, but she has never seen the scar. The memory of it beneath her fingers makes her body quicken and she shifts on the spot, looking down at her trainers.

The weather is still warm and clear, but she has noticed over the previous days the temperature dropping more sharply, the sun not reaching quite as high in the sky. The wind is picking up, and she unties the cardigan she has wrapped around the straps of her handbag and slips it on. She has looped her hair into a knot which is loosely pinned at the nape of her neck, strands already slipping out around her face. Her weeks of walking in the autumn sun have given her a tan — just a little; a faint flush of colour across the bridge of her nose and along her cheeks. It hides the freckles and sometimes when she looks at herself in the mirror, she tries to place what is missing.

The bus arrives and she boards, tapping the reader with her travel card. She sits near the front, where a long row of seats faces inwards on either side of the aisle. As always, the bus is fairly empty this far up the line and early in the day, and, for now, she has an unobstructed view of the road passing by through the windows opposite her.

She has not seen the children at Pearl's house since their first meeting. Alone in the house, she keeps an ear out, but rarely hears the sound of the flat-screen television brought by Uncle Harry who is rich. She has seen Pearl a few times, when one of them is on the way in, the other halfway out.

'You must come over for dinner,' she called last time, and her neighbour smiled.

'Any time,' she said. 'I got no plans.'

I must do that, she thinks now. She will choose a day when Jack finishes early, make something he likes. She runs through recipes in her head, resting it against the glass. In the empty bus, the sound of the engine is hypnotic. She lets it lull her, her hands lying loosely in her lap.

The quietness lasts for five, perhaps ten minutes, until the bus pulls up outside the hospital. Its mural looks less bright today, the sun too lazy to pick out its colours. The doors creak open, one faster than the other, the engine cutting out with a soft sigh. A woman climbs on, leaning heavily on a single crutch. Though the bus is empty, Elsa is sitting close to the door and the woman staggers into the seat beside her, an arm bumping onto Elsa's lap and then away again. The hand is heavily bandaged, the cast fresh and white for the most part, but chewed and browning around its top edge. She carries with her the smell of disinfectant and plaster; a *hospital* smell.

As the bus moves off again, the woman mutters to herself once and then falls silent. The driver whistles a few bars of a tune and then abandons it. The engine continues to drone, sighing with each stop.

She has considered the hospital as a possible place to work; has got as far as Googling their volunteer schemes. It is still a possibility – each time she passes it on the bus, she thinks of it again – but further exploration has brought further possibilities, further opportunities for volunteers in the city. The other options, more practical as a plan, are slowly forming. Discussing it on the phone with her father two days ago, she listed them: something like what I used to do, something like what I want to do. Respectively, these mean administration jobs and illustration jobs, and though the latter seem less likely, they are something she can work towards without working. In her bag now is a sketchpad, and each day more of its pages are filled. She can't remember the last time she drew so much. She can't remember the last time she drew something that wasn't Jack. *Things are different here*, she thinks, and from behind her hair she looks at the woman with the crutch and tries to commit her – the way her skin is greyish, as if it's turning stale; the way her hair is cropped unevenly, as though it was done in a hurry or to cut something out – to memory.

Two or three stops later, a distance of only a few blocks – and one of the only things she is happy to complain about in San Francisco is the unnecessary regularity of bus stops – the doors open again and admit a tall, youngish (she still isn't sure what is and isn't young any more) man in bright yellow high-top trainers. There is a handsomeness to his face but it is sharp, not easy to absorb. He reminds her of a fox. A fox in high-tops. Despite the many seats available, he chooses to stand halfway down the bus. He does not hold onto either of the handrails. She glances up at him and then away again. She is from London; she knows when to avoid meeting a stranger's eye.

At the next stop, two schoolgirls board; one talking rapidly on a mobile phone while the other clutches her arm and listens in. They sit close to Elsa and occasionally look cautiously at the fox. Elsa looks straight ahead, which seems safer. They are passing through denser streets now, and the dark-bricked buildings which line them mean that frequently she is greeted with a half-formed phantom of her own face. The girls begin texting on their respective phones, while the fox moves to stare out of the exit doors. She glances at his reflection in the glass and sees that it is changing back and forth like theatre masks: a pointy, gleeful smile; a drooping frown. Smile. Frown.

Other people board: an elderly couple with two plastic laundry bags full of shopping; a girl about her own age with a perfect, goldish afro and silver trainers; a middle-aged man in jeans and a stone-washed denim jacket. Each time, they move towards the back of the bus, and, each time, the young foxish man with the high-tops moves out of their way so politely that Elsa is sure she must have imagined the theatre faces.

They are perhaps ten minutes – allowing for the many stops – away from Market, when the bus doors open again, and a man staggers on. He lurches towards Elsa, dressed in a grey zip-up hoody and beige cords. His face is purple with broken veins, the flesh behind them sagging freely. As he sits down in the seat beside her, she is hit with a draught of a scent unlike anything she has smelt before. Trying to explain it to Jack later, she will try comparing it to many things: rotting leaves on a forest floor; TCP; old, dirty socks, but nothing will be able to convey the magnitude of it, the chord of disgust it strikes in her. It is a smell that years later she will be suddenly, briefly haunted by, before it disappears into the recesses of memory again, waiting patiently to strike. Where it comes from, why it revolts her so much, she will never know. For now, she is simply overwhelmed by the putridness of it, the chemical taste it leaves in her mouth. She draws her scarf up closer around her mouth, and as she does, she notices that in one hand, tucked into the damp sleeve of his hoody, he clutches a small glass phial, burnt black in places.

He is silent for a minute – a brief, teetering moment of safety – but as the bus slows at a junction, he begins patting himself down; systematically checking his pockets and swearing to himself. He repeats this process every couple of minutes, each time locating a tiny parcel wrapped in cling film tucked inside his other sleeve, each time relieved and relaxed, before beginning the cycle again. She tries to edge away from him in her seat, but the woman with the crutch, who has up until now been still and silent, leans towards her instead.

'Him,' she says, or perhaps it is *Hymn*. 'Him,' she says again, more assertively. She is looking at her plastered hand.

Elsa looks up at the road and is relieved to find that they are only a couple of stops away from hers.

But now the bus is stuck in traffic; Market filled with stationary cars, red lights like stars. Pedestrians pass on either side of the jam, occasionally threading between vehicles like the first water in a pebbled stream.

The fox in the high-tops begins to pace up and down the aisle. 'C'mon, man,' he yells at the driver. 'I got places to be!'

'Him,' the woman with the crutch says, in agreement. 'Places we've been.'

The man beside Elsa cries out and continues checking his pockets. She leans forward and looks at her stop in the distance. So close and yet so far.

'Hey, dude,' the fox – who is beginning to seem more like a wolf, or no, worse: a hyena – says, stepping past her. 'I need to be somewhere! Let us out of here.'

'Yeah!' the woman with the crutch says, abandoning her appraisal of her hand. 'Let us go.'

The driver, a Korean man in his sixties, shakes his head. 'No. You have to wait for the island.'

Market Street, a wide road with a busy bus route, has brick islands built at its stops. The man beside Elsa stiffens, crack pipe still clutched in his hand.

'Yeah!' he says, eyes turning blearily from Elsa to the driver to the boy in the aisle. 'Let us out!'

He leans forward and a fresh wave of the strange smell hits her. She shrinks back in her seat.

'Let us out, let us out,' the two men chant, the woman with the crutch joining in in a whisper.

Let us out let us out let us out

She is frozen in place, seized by a compulsion to join in the chant. The bus's interior seems to stretch away from her, the words echoing, her heart beating a solemn, lurching soundtrack to the lyrics. Let us out let us out let us out.

And then they reach the island and the bus stops. The doors

open and she hurls herself through them and onto the pavement, gasping for breath.

That night, they lie together. They lie without talking, curled together on the sofa, and then they lie, face to face, in their bed. In the dark, Elsa traces the lines of his features. His hand runs up and down over her hip.

'What is it like?' she asks, and he knows she is thinking about the man in the mackintosh.

'I don't know. Strange. It doesn't seem real.'

'Do you think it hurts?'

He hesitates. 'Yes.'

She presses closer and kisses him. 'Do you think you'll just get used to it?'

His hand moves down and around the curve of her back, over her thigh and up again. 'I don't know.' His mouth is close to hers and the words warm her face.

Her hand slides slowly down his chest. 'I hope you don't.'

1998

Newly qualified, he is lucky to find a job almost immediately. It is rebar work, his least favourite — the reinforcement of concrete with bars of steel, where the men are known as rodbusters and his days are spent tying the bars together with wire, fixing them in moulds so that the concrete can be poured over them in a soft sluice of grey. His evenings are often spent with Ginny; months of consecutive nights in the single bed, her thin legs looped around him. But he grows bored and returns to the faceless, fleeting girls. He forgets or doesn't ask for their names; in the early mornings he tells them to leave as he pulls on his boots. Cara — her name he remembers. He remembers her long body against the pole, the light in the club purple. He takes her home four, five times. Her skin is soft, her laugh harsh, infectious, adult. Afterwards, he returns to Ginny, and the cycle begins again. He always returns to Ginny.

The end of the rebar contract approaches, and he stops answering Ginny's calls, starts drinking at places on the other side of the city. At work, looking down at the moulds, he feels afraid. It is a shapeless fear, one which cannot be deterred by visits to the union, assurances of another job. At night, it crawls through the paper-thin walls, and when Ginny knocks on the door, he holds his breath and waits for her to leave.

On the last day of the job, he dresses slowly. There is no sun but no clouds; just a thin grey sky which stretches onwards out of sight. Collecting his tools at the end of the shift, he looks around the deserted site, fine white dust caught in swarms in the weak light.

'Jack,' someone says, and he jumps.

Bayes, the foreman, stands in the doorway, hard hat under his arm. He is a tall man with a thick, pale moustache, and he has never called him 'Jackie'. 'I got some work coming up down in Florida,' he says. 'If you're interested.'

And so begins a new phase: eighteen months of sunshine and cheap motels, short contracts and superficial camaraderie. Florida, Texas, Tennessee. And then back to rainscapes, to Michigan, Illinois. From bed to bed and bar to bar. The memories are bright and chipped, cheap souvenirs.

Eventually, a month after he turns twenty-two, he arrives back in Seattle. Back on his father's doorstep. The short-term contracts are over; the process of swinging from one to the next ending abruptly, the ride jerking to a stop. And where to go then? It is easiest to return where there is a place to stay and a union he belongs to. A phone call, a cheap flight later, and he's back on that doorstep, bag in hand.

'You have fun?' his father asks, when they are in their places on the sofa and the chair. They eye each other as they speak. Jeff seems to be silvering; the tips of his hair and the surface of his skin ashy.

'Yeah, it was cool.'

'You got something else lined up?'

The test is almost over; he has almost passed. He nods. 'Going to the union tomorrow, they said they could hook me up.'

His father settles back in his seat. 'Good.' He jerks his bottle towards the ceiling. 'Your bed's all made up.'

That night he turns up at the bar where Ginny works, a fancy hotel place where she wears a shirt and skirt. He misses her sliding straps, her exposed back. Leaning against the bar, he watches her wait tables, the way her hair falls forward and her smile is shy. He watches others watch her.

'Can I get you anything else?'

There is something in the barman's voice which he does not like. He shakes his head, squares his shoulders. 'No, I'm good.'

The barman moves away, leaves him alone, but now he notices, as if for the first time, his own clothes, the staining and the calluses on his hands. He grips his drink more fiercely, leans further into the bar. The clock hands tick round, big silver face on mirrored wall. A mumbling tide of conversation pushes insistently forward from the booths at his back, glasses clinking, muted music rising like steam.

Finally Ginny is released, her apron untied and bunched in her hand as she walks, her hair pulled over one shoulder. She is tentative towards him at first, and then her arms are around his neck, her lips pressed against his jaw. He pulls back, he studies her face. Wide blue eyes and faintly scarred cheek. Slender lips palest pink, a hairline gap between her front teeth. He pulls her closer.

'You came back,' she says.

'I missed you,' he says, and though it isn't the truth, it doesn't feel like a lie.

2012

It is 11 October when it shifts; when the unravelling really begins. It is an afternoon much like the ones which have gone before it, but Elsa, at the house on Potrero, finds herself suddenly at a window, looking out at the empty street. Jack has just finished work and, about to climb into the car, he turns and looks at the bay. A lone kitesurfer bobs across the steel water, the sinking sun sending pink ridges over the waves. Everywhere is quiet.

'What are you waiting for?' Alex says, from inside the car, and Jack starts. He looks at Alex, and then back at the water.

'Sorry,' he says, and he climbs into the passenger seat.

He closes the door behind him, shuts his eyes. *Did I forget something?* he thinks, but there is nothing. He fumbles with his seat belt, glancing back at the bridge. Alex has turned on the ignition and is fiddling with the old radio, trying to find a station, a half-eaten Three Musketeers bar clamped between his teeth. These details are recorded with perfect clarity; the sound of the radio's static mixed with the crackling of the wrapper as Alex twists his head to locate his own seat belt. The same tobacco-sweet smell of the car, the half-smoked joint in its dusty ashtray. The way his phone vibrates against his leg; short, significant pulses. Insistent. He answers it, and as he does, he notices that Alex's phone is also ringing.

And then they are moving, then he is out of the car on shaking legs, then he is catching the harness Alex throws to him from the back seat. The asphalt pounds at his feet as he runs, throwing him forward, the pinkish sky closing in and the cars speeding by, lights trailing across his vision.

Time is unhinged – it is faster, it is slower – until he sees her. Then the world lurches back into crystal-clear real time, and every tiny fragment of the scene assaults him in perfect technicolour.

She is standing almost exactly halfway along the steel beam which runs below the bridge's pedestrian walkway. *The chord*. It is a word he uses almost daily and yet now it seems other-worldly and strange. It is difficult to make out her features as he runs; she hunches forward, the shadow of the walkway casting her in shades of grey. Two members of the Highway Patrol are already on the scene, their uniforms muted and beige against the candy colours of the late-afternoon sky. One, short and fat, keeping the few pedestrians at a distance, ushering them backwards with stubby arms. The other, a taller, more muscular man with a thick wedge of straw-coloured hair, stands at the railing. He has a loudhailer in one hand but does not use it; leaning over, he is close enough to the girl's bowed head to be heard. Jack cannot make out what he is saying to her, but when the girl turns to respond, he has no trouble understanding the words.

'Don't come any closer,' she says, and the patrolman holds his hands up in a gesture of surrender and takes a step to his right, away from her. Jack and Alex are only ten feet away now and they stop running, begin their careful approach. Assured that the patrolman is no longer behind her, the girl straightens up and they see her clearly.

She is small and thin, her face narrow in profile. Her chin juts slightly upwards; defiant. Blonde hair falls in neat sheets around her face. The city is far ahead of her and she looks towards it, never looking down. As Jack secures his harness, he thinks that she cannot be older than twenty. He notices that the canvas sneakers on her feet are new. They are the same shade of blue as Elsa's.

The railing which runs along the walkway is four feet high. A little irresponsible, some might – and do – say. Jack has heard a rumour – one of Eddie's little stories, always told as he is departing, like a tip left at the end of a meal – that Golden Gate's chief engineer was very short and demanded a rail low enough to see over. A little vain, but handy now – Jack hops over with ease. He climbs down onto the chord, careful to place his feet squarely. On the other side of the girl, Alex is doing the same.

The beam creaks, and the girl whips round to face Jack. She has large green eyes and thin lips. Her skin is pale and pockmarked. 'Stay back,' she says. 'Stay back or I'll do it.'

Her voice is calm, and Alex matches it. 'Okay,' he says. 'We're staying back. What's your name?'

But for a moment, wild and frantic, Jack knows. *Ginny.* Sweat pools at the base of his neck and across his back.

She is still staring at him and he is sure she will say it. He knows she will say it.

She spits a single syllable at him instead. 'Eve.'

'Hi, Eve,' Alex says. 'My name's Alex, and this is Jack.'

'I don't care what your names are,' she says, turning her gaze back towards the city. 'I don't want to talk to you.'

'That's okay,' Alex says, 'I'll do the talking.'

It is taking a lot of effort for Jack to keep his body still, to stop himself from lunging forward to grab her. He looks and looks, calculating. Not close enough; he wouldn't get there in time.

'What are you doing here, Eve?' Alex says, and Jack moves his left foot an inch closer. Her eyes fly to it immediately and he freezes.

'This is a bad idea, Eve,' he says.

'It's the only way.' Her voice is still calm but her chest rises rapidly; short, fluttery breaths like birds.

Jack tries to catch Alex's attention. Alex tries to catch his. He jabs his finger in Jack's direction and then at his own chest, and Jack understands the message. *You be me. I'll be you.* It would once have been appealing but now, when words seem to have abandoned him, it seems impossible. He tries to gesture to Alex but his hands have become numb.

'Stop that,' Eve says, without looking at either of them. Jack notices that still she does not look down. He knows that the water is 245 feet below them, and that it is, at its deepest, 350 feet to the ocean floor. He knows, though he does not want to know, that it will take a person falling four seconds to reach the surface, and that meeting it will be like hitting solid concrete. He looks at her, at her thin arms and small face. She is not wearing a jacket.

'You must be cold,' he says.

She has closed her eyes. 'I'm always cold.'

'You should wear a coat.'

'I like to be cold.'

Her hands are braced behind her, gripping the bars of the railings. He notices the faint tracks of scars on the smooth skin between her wrist and elbow. Pink ridges. A delicate gold bracelet hangs there. 'Nice bracelet,' he says. 'Present?'

'From my mom,' she says, with a sneer.

'You should give it to me,' he says. 'If you're gonna jump, it might be nice for her to have it back.'

She sucks her bottom lip between her teeth, her fingers tightening on the bars. 'Stop it,' she says. 'Please stop it.'

'I can stop it,' he says, pushing his left foot a fraction closer. 'All you have to do is stay very still and let us come to you.' The beam creaks as Alex takes a step towards her.

'Stop it!' Her eyes fly open. 'Stop talking. Don't come closer or I'll jump.'

'Eve.' Panic is beginning to bat against his chest. His feet feel numb, concrete in his boots. 'Talk to me. Tell me why you're here.' He knows that if he keeps speaking, Alex will try again to get closer. He wants to yell out a warning, tell him to stop.

She looks at him, eyes clear. 'This is where it ends,' she says.

'Eve.' If he keeps saying her name, it will be okay. If he keeps his eyes locked on hers, she won't be able to let go. 'Okay,' he says, voice casual. 'Well, if you're going to do this, why don't you tell me your mom's phone number? So I can call and let her know.'

Her eyes turn wide and watery. 'I have to do this,' she says.

In his mind, Jack tries to turn the page of the advice leaflet Miller has given him. *Ask about a family member*, he thinks. *Then what?* 'You don't have to do anything. We can help you. There are people who can help you.'

'Nobody can help me,' she says, and the beam creaks again, Alex shifting his weight to his toes now, poised, ready. Her legs tense and her fingers leave the bars, but her eyes are locked on Jack's.

'Eve,' he says, and it is difficult to squeeze the words out, his lungs like steel. 'Don't do this. Take my hand. Let me lift you back over. This isn't what you want.'

She turns back to the view, her head tilted higher again. 'You don't know what I want.'

'So tell me.'

It isn't what she says. It isn't the sudden sound of Alex making a grab for her. Jack knows it is too late even before she speaks. 'I want it to be over,' she says, but before she does, she looks down.

And then she jumps.

MATTHEW

1999

It is late on the last day of the year; the last day of the century. Y2K and the day is all about bugs and domes, parties in the streets and arguments at home. And home is where he is — if home is a thing that exists. It springs up around him like a cardboard set; flat pack walls winched into place as he watches, the York skyline wheeled across the living-room window. Sugary snow from a giant salt shaker above settling on cartoon streets. Home — here — again. Back in his childhood bed, sometimes sober, staring up at the ceiling.

He had planned to continue his ironworking here, but that plan has faltered and stalled somewhere across the Atlantic. Back in America, Ginny still waits tables and his father still drinks, buildings and bridges still groan into being. Seattle carries on without him; he lifts out without a trace. Here, he is reinvented. He is twenty-three, he is a barman. He is twenty-three, it is New Year's Eve and it is his night off.

He goes to the bar where he works anyway, him and Tom. Tom is a year younger and just graduated from the university. While the other student staff have left, heading back to their homes to get jobs and wear suits, Tom has decided to stay a while longer. They are a good team, him and Tom. A good team, on their night off, heading to the bar because the drinks always taste better on the right side of the small space they pace every other night.

He found it harder to leave Seattle than he expected. Before he decided, it seemed easy. He was struggling to find work, tired of Ginny's increasingly tearful phone calls. The former is easier to accept as his own fault: a falling-out with some of the guys from the union, too many beers one night and a joke taken too far, its punchline a fist. The second he is less willing to take responsibility for. Their relationship, based on bottles of wine shared in a single bed, on midnight hours and the closeness of the dark, was enough for him. But not for her, and in trying to get closer she only pushed him away.

It seemed easy then. But boarding the flight, he felt fearful. *When does it end?* he found himself thinking, and he had to force himself to remain in his seat.

The fear is now thankfully gone. He likes his job, likes York, likes that he has friends like Tom who are his age and care little for permanence or structure. They approach the bar, new shirts and no jackets, damp wind battering them from every side.

Inside there are the usual familiar faces, most of them friends, but tonight they are stuffed in with strangers; underage kids in the corners, trying to blend in with the brickwork, middle-aged women with novelty hairbands and glasses, the scene studded with cheap, glittery 2's and 0's, Y's and K's fluttering like insects. They push through the crowd. Two members of staff are serving: the manager, Lou, who he often shares a cigarette break or an after-work half with, the other the new girl, chubby and scarlet-haired, pink strapless top slipping as she darts back and forth with plastic glasses thrust forward, liquid slopping out across the metal bar.

He is drunk already, several pubs down. The clock reads 11.05, and everyone is hyper, everyone is ready. Shots – tequila? It seems likely. Here they use tiny sachets of salt from the kitchen; the white packets lining the floor like the scraps of snow which linger outside. They head for a window beside the dance floor, where others wait. There are hugs and kisses, glasses clinked, cigarettes lit. A blur of faces, yelled conversations over the thudding music, dancing – dancing! He never dances – and one of the girls' hands on his arm, his on the small of her back.

The scene tumbles sideways. A shove: a body barrelling out of the crowd and into him, sending him stumbling into the group. He straightens up, shirt wet with beer and something sticky – lemonade? A group of lads are laughing, their friend retrieved from the floor, a hand or two waved in apology, but there is already a buzzing in his ears, a heat spreading through him.

Someone is yelling his name. Tom? The girl? It doesn't matter. He launches himself across the room at the group, fist meeting cheekbone, the crowd surging back like a tide. Time slows but then snaps taut; hands begin shoving him back, hard, but he's ready this time, he can't be shoved, and his fist is thrown without hesitation, and then it is the bottle, the green glass flashing in the disco lights, shattering as it meets someone's skull; then he is flying, boot to his ribs, skidding through the crowd, floor rising up to him, and he is back up, returning, another bottle in his hand; and then there is a wall of black, two sets of meaty fists dragging him across the floor and through the door and onto the pavement, head cracking the frame as he passes, air knocked out of him, and he is lying on the road and something is sticky on his shirt.

2012

November arrives, and with it the fog. It creeps into the bay each morning in slow, sly steps, taking more territory each time she turns. It seeps through streets and the tops of buildings are obscured, the towers of Golden Gate hidden like secrets. By mid-morning, the winter sun begins to break through and the fog retreats, sidling out across the water into a sullen smudge which stretches from Alcatraz to the bridge and then fades away.

Stuck in with a cold, she pads around the house in thick socks, balled-up tissues spilling out of her sleeves. She boils the kettle but forgets to make tea. In the tiny laundry room she stands, two fingers prying open a gap in the blinds, and watches Sam and his sister playing in Pearl's front yard.

Somewhere in the house, her phone is ringing. She pulls the shirt she's wearing – one of Jack's heaviest; thick, rough cotton – tighter around her and wanders through the small rooms until she finds it, wedged under a cushion on the sofa. The ringing stops when she reaches it and there is a short moment of silence, the phone weighed in the palm of her hand, before it begins again. It's Jack.

'Hey, lover,' she says, voice soft and throat raw.

'How are you feeling?' It is cold where he is; the wind whistles down the line to her.

'Just a bit dozy. I'm fine. How are you?'

'I'm good. I wish I was at home in the warm with you.'

'Me too.'

'What do you want for dinner? I'll pick stuff up.'

'No, hon, honestly –' She wanders back to the laundry room. Hitching herself onto the washing machine, she peeps through the blinds again. 'I'll go out. The fresh air will do me good.'

'You sure?' There is someone talking close by; their words flow faintly past on the breeze.

'Yeah. What do you fancy?'

'Now there's a question.'

She laughs. 'Some nurse you are.'

Someone is talking to him now; a man's gruff voice, his words difficult to make out. 'I've gotta go, babe,' Jack says. 'I'll call you when I'm on my way home, okay?'

'Okay. Love you.'

'Love you too.'

'Bye.'

And he is gone. She spins the phone around on the surface of the washing machine beside her, swinging her legs against its door. Then, determined, she hops off and heads upstairs, where she dresses in her own clothes and brushes her hair. She tugs on a jacket and slips her feet into boots. Downstairs, she pauses to blow her nose and glances at her face in the mirror. Then she leaves, locking the door behind her.

Sam glances up at her as she approaches their gate. 'Hi,' he says.

'Hi. I live next door, do you remember me?'

He nods.

'Is your grandma here?'

'Yeah. She's reading.'

'What are you guys doing?'

'Drawing.'

She leans over to look. Stubby pastel-coloured chalks litter the path between them and there are the faint ghosts of shapes on the grey paving slabs.

'That's good. I love drawing.'

Sam hesitates, eyeing her. Then he holds out the yellow chalk he is holding. 'You wanna play?'

Elsa shakes her head. 'I'm just going to say hi to your grandma. Don't go anywhere though, okay?'

'Okay.' He returns his attention to his picture. She opens the gate, taking care to close it behind her even though he could easily reach the latch and open it himself. The little girl glances up at her, a pink chalk grasped in her fist, and Elsa stoops to run a hand over her soft hair. *So small*, she thinks. *Are they always this small?* 'See you in a sec, guys,' she says, stepping carefully around them.

The front door is ajar but she knocks anyway, the sound sharp in the soft darkness of the house. She waits and then knocks again, a little harder. She glances back at the children, who are both staring at her.

'You can go in,' Sam says.

She hesitates, looking back at the open door. 'I should probably just –' she says, but then she pushes it gently open. 'Pearl?' she calls and, without meaning to, she is inside. In the dark mouth of the hallway, it is warm and close. She unzips her jacket and takes another step in. 'Pearl?'

Sam is humming, a short series of three notes which he repeats over and over. Elsa, mouth dry, takes another step, hand outstretched, towards the living room door –

It opens with a jerk, light flooding into the hallway. Pearl, blinking into the dimness, her hair in uneven tufts, a paperback clutched in one hand.

'Hi,' Elsa says. 'Sorry to disturb you. Sam said . . .' She trails off.

'I was sleeping,' her neighbour says, pushing her glasses back up her face. 'Reading,' she says, lifting the book and waggling it in Elsa's direction. 'Two pages and I'm asleep. Never used to happen.' She turns and shuffles back into the living room. 'Come sit down,' she barks over one shoulder.

Elsa follows her in. The heat of the room is stifling and toys litter the floor. She steps over a Lego set and shuffles the pieces to one side with the edge of her boot.

'Yup, you don't want to stand on one of those,' Pearl says, glancing back. 'Like stepping on a jellyfish.' She sits down in her chair with a wheezy cough, balancing the book on her knee.

Elsa perches at the edge of the sofa. 'I didn't want to bother you. It's just that I'm going to the *store* –' the American word feels strange on her tongue – 'and I wondered if I could pick anything up for you?' Pearl is rummaging in the cushions around her; triumphantly, she pulls out a bookmark. 'I noticed you had the children here,' Elsa continues, 'so I thought it might be hard for you to get out.'

Pearl closes the book and rests it carefully on the arm. She considers Elsa through thick, lopsided lenses. 'That's real nice of you,' she says. 'You're a nice girl.'

'It's no trouble at all. Do you need anything?'

'We could use some more diapers. And some milk. I'd go myself but it's hard to get the two of them ready.'

'Of course it is,' Elsa says, relieved. 'And I'm going anyway. What kind of *diapers* –' she feels a fraud – 'do you need?'

'I'll write it down,' Pearl says, and she gets up. In maroon trousers and a white, pearl-buttoned blouse, she looks even smaller than in her nightdress. 'You know, I really appreciate this,' she says, locating a pen and paper in a sideboard. 'I wasn't expecting to have them today.'

'It must be hard work,' Elsa says. 'They're so little.'

'It's okay,' Pearl says, shrugging. 'They're good kids. I've changed plenty of diapers.'

'How often do they stay here?'

'Sometimes twice a week, sometimes a whole week. Sometimes not for a month. Their mother works shifts so I just take them when she needs me to.'

'Your granddaughter?'

'Yup. My Carrie. The only one of them still here. So I guess I should make the most of them.' Pearl tears off the sheet of notepaper and takes it, with slow, shuffling steps, to Elsa. 'They're no trouble.'

'Well, I think that's pretty amazing,' Elsa says, rising.

'Let me find my purse.'

'No, really, that's okay. We can—'

'Here it is.' Pearl unzips a small fabric purse, taking out a carefully folded $10 bill. 'I really appreciate this,' she says, pressing it into Elsa's hand. Up close, the sound of her breathing is soft and rasping, like something burrowing into damp earth. 'A nice girl,' she says again.

'Are the children okay outside?' Elsa asks. 'Do you want me to bring them in?'

Pearl shrugs, taking stiff steps towards the door to the kitchen. 'They'll come in soon enough. It's time to fix their lunch.'

When she leaves, Sam is on the step, half-carrying, half-dragging his sister with him. 'Do you want some help?' Elsa asks him.

'That's okay. She can walk but she's just lazy.'

'Oh. Okay.' She watches him heave his sister into the hallway, where he places her carefully down. The baby laughs and crawls off in the direction of the living room.

'Bye,' Sam says, and then he follows.

'Bye,' she says, and she closes the door.

Out on the street, the cold hits her again and she folds her arms across her chest, head down against the wind. The fog lifts early here though, and the sun is out at least. She walks uphill, thinking of the children sitting out on the street. She has a sudden urge to call her mother. At the thought, her phone vibrates in her bag and she jumps. She pauses to fish it out with numb fingers, heart still skipping, but it's just a text message.

Wrap up warm little one xx

Jack. She smiles, shaking her head, but as she starts walking again she buttons her coat back up and ties her scarf. She remembers his voice on the phone, the wind whistling behind him. Out on the bridge like the edge of the world.

She didn't realise it was true until she said it out loud. It seems strange but neither can remember who said it first; just that it was said. There was wine, that much is clear. Wine and food at a pan-Asian place in Bloomsbury, sitting on the narrow deck above the pavement, sharing cigarettes. There was more wine at a basement bar on a corner nearby, and then there was a taxi, jokes shared with the driver, and a stop at the twenty-four-hour place near her house to pick up another bottle. There was the sofa, and glasses, and long conversations about parents and places and things, and then the rest becomes a blur. There was the bed, and there was his skin against hers, her hair fanned out across the pillow. And there were the words, whispered in a soft storm of others, breathed back and forth between them. *I love you.*

Crossing the road, she looks around. Potrero Hill, the neighbourhood which Potrero Avenue borders, is usually quiet, but 18th Street, which she is crossing, has a busy strip of cafés and diners. Two months in, she has visited most of them in a carefully conducted survey, and is proud to have definitively awarded such labels as Best-Place-to-Get-Coffee and Best-Place-for-Sunday-Brunch and Best-Place-for-Hangover-Food.

The first time he said it sober, they were waiting for the bus. It was about to rain, the sky swelling, and they were hungover. The bus stop was busy and they were forced closer together, people surging towards the approaching 345. She caught his eye and fanned her face.

'Urgh,' she said. 'Grey sweat.'

'Grey what?'

'Grey sweat. You know, like when you're either going to be sick or faint and you go all sweaty and grey?'

'Yeah ...'

'It's called a grey sweat.'

'By who?'

She thought about this. 'By me.'

He laughed, and then caught her in the crook of his arm, pressing his lips to the top of her head. 'I love you,' he said.

Two blocks down, on 16th Street, is the Safeway centre.

Elsa collects a cart, dumping her handbag in as she pushes it through the automatic doors. She rummages inside the bag for Pearl's list, which she holds in her hand, half-crushed against the handle. The handwriting is not old-fashioned or feminine, as she has expected, but made up of tight, small scrawls, an occasional loop dipping at random on the page. She glances over it, then up at the signs which hang suspended over the aisles.

Making her way through the shop, she collects items, dawdling through the fruit and veg section. She has no list of her own and faintly formed ideas of dinner drift fruitlessly around her. She fishes in her sleeve for a tissue as she considers a display of squash. Selecting one, she weighs it in her hand, lost in thought.

'Oh!' Beside her, a bag slides to the floor, spilling its contents onto the speckled vinyl. Its owner, a young woman about her own age, crouches to collect it, swearing quietly to herself. She has a baby on one hip; it watches, passive, as she begins to scoop things towards her.

Elsa bends down to help, collecting a set of keys from the dusty space beneath the shelves. 'Here.'

'Thanks.' The woman looks up, pushing hair out of her face. She has dry, flaking skin, and her hair is bleached but growing out, telltale streaks of dark beginning to break through. There is a patch of something sticky in it, congealing. The baby considers Elsa, a tiny finger resting between its gums.

They stand. 'Thanks,' the woman mutters again, and then she is gone, hitching the bag onto her shoulder and shifting the baby higher on her hip. Elsa looks down and sees that the squash is still in her hand. She places it in the trolley and moves on, consulting the list again.

She worries sometimes. It catches her off guard; when she is showering or scraping food from plates. The house is small and its walls often don't seem solid. Sometimes she wishes for something that would cement them; sometimes she looks to him and waits for the right words or a look, something that will remind her why she came.

She looks at the rows of nappies now – *diapers* – and tries to imagine what it would be like to be shopping for them with him, what it would be like to send him out to the supermarket while she did the bathing, fixed tiny lunches.

Stupid, she thinks, finding the kind Pearl has listed. *Stop.*

Instead, she moves to the end of the aisle and takes her phone from her bag. Opening Jack's message again, she presses Reply.

On the road to recovery, she writes. But still in need of a good nurse xx

She is just paying the cashier when his reply comes through.

I can make you feel better, he says, and as usual, he is right.

That night, they eat soup. Elsa is fresh-faced and warm from the bath, damp hair drying in waves. Steam rises as they eat; the kitchen window is wet and cloudy. Below it, in the sink, are pans and a blender crusted with orange clots of soup.

'This is really good,' Jack says, reaching over to pull off another chunk of bread.

'I called my mum for the recipe.' Elsa puts down her spoon.

'How is she?'

'Good. She said Anna's doing well at work.'

'That's good. Did your dad get that roof sorted?'

'Yeah. Apparently the guy's been there all week fixing it.'

'No rain?'

'No. She said it's been overcast though.'

'Well, that's reassuring.'

'Mmm.' Elsa lifts up her feet, hugging her knees to her chest. She gazes out of the window, idly moving the spoon back and forth against the rim of her bowl. 'I wonder what she does.'

'Who? Anna?'

'What? Sorry. I was thinking about next door again. I wonder what the mother does as a job.'

'My money's on hooker.'

She rolls her eyes and smiles. 'Be serious. It's just strange, isn't it? Leaving the children with an old woman. And they're there *all* the time.'

Jack pushes a piece of the bread around the edge of his bowl and tosses it into his mouth. 'Why do I get the feeling you're about to get way too involved?'

'Well, if I can help ...'

'You're too nice, you know.'

'Well, that's lucky, isn't it? We balance each other out.'

He throws a chunk of bread at her. 'Come on then, Good Samaritan. Let's watch some TV and have a cuddle and you can give me that cold for safekeeping.'

'Yes, sir,' she says, laughing. 'I like it when you say "cuddle".' She rises, taking the dishes to the sink. 'It sounds funny.'

'I know you do.' He slides his arms around her and turns on the tap. He starts to wash the dirty pan, keeping her trapped against his chest. 'That's why I do it.'

She runs her hands over his arms. The skin is warm, the hairs still sun-blonde. 'That's very generous of you.'

'I'm a generous kind of guy.'

The buckle of his belt presses against the small of her back. She leans her head against his shoulder and closes her eyes. *I can make you feel better*, he says, and as usual, he is right.

2000

'Come on, hurry up!'

She jogs to catch up with Hannah, school bag slapping against her thigh.

'Jesus, Elsa, what are you doing?'

'It's these shoes.' She gestures down to her new school boots, which are maroon leather and against the rules. Their pointed toes stick out from underneath the carefully selected turn-ups of her trousers. The trousers are low on the hips while the shirt rises up, the strap of her bag rubbing against the sparse flesh there. Her school jumper is stuffed inside the bag.

'Worth it though, aren't they?' Hannah looks down, considering them. 'Wish I'd got them now.'

'Come on,' Elsa says, glancing back over her shoulder. 'Someone's going to see us.'

'Er, yeah,' her friend says, rolling her eyes, the lashes emphatic and clogged. 'That's what I keep *saying*.'

'Go on then!'

Hannah pushes back the hedge to reveal the wire fence behind it. 'It's somewhere here,' she says, and she starts kicking at it with her own boots: pointed too, but black leather, gold studs around the ankle. 'Here!' she says, pushing at a flap of fence, and it peels back and lets them through. A strand of her pale red ponytail catches in the loose wire; it flutters in Elsa's face as she passes.

Elsa pauses to check the hedge has fallen back behind them; tucks her own hair behind her ears. She hurries to catch up with Hannah, who has clambered out of the clearing and onto the pathway which runs behind the school.

'We're free!' she yells, and Elsa laughs.

'Shhhh. Deakin's classroom is *right there*.'

'He won't care! He hates us!'

'He hates you,' Elsa points out. 'And that's only because you keep asking him if he likes what you're wearing.'

'Ha.' Hannah links her arm through Elsa's. 'He does though. He loves it.'

'Let's get going. We've only got an hour.'

They walk along the path, which in an hour's time will be filled with pupils walking home from school. Sunlight filters through the leaves, polka-dotting the uneven paving.

'Got any fags?' Hannah asks.

'No. We smoked them this morning, remember?'

'Arse.'

'They'll serve you in Fazal's. They always do.'

The path leads into a quiet residential area and their footsteps seem suddenly shockingly loud. The houses are all neat and silent, the occasional flickering television screen visible through a window.

'I feel like we need to whisper,' Hannah says, in a not-very-quiet stage whisper.

'We probably do.' Elsa looks around. 'You know what they're like round here, they'd probably call the school.'

'Look at those girls,' Hannah hisses in a mock-shocked voice. 'Look at their slag shoes and their see-through shirts. Someone call the vicar!'

'Stop it!' Elsa says, but she is laughing.

At the end of the road is Fazal's, where they buy cigarettes – ten Sovereign – and sweets – jelly babies and ice-cream flavoured Chewits – from the moon-eyed proprietor who tells Hannah, as he always does, that she is a bad girl. 'Very bad girl,' he says mournfully, counting the stack of 10p and 20p pieces they have given him.

They follow the road along the river bank and into the tiny town centre. A small parade of shops lines the pavement; two takeaways, an optician's, a bike shop, and a tanning salon which is painted bright blue and has the residents up in arms.

'Oooh!' Hannah grasps Elsa's arm, glancing behind her. 'FSF alert.'

'Fuck. Which one?'

'Wait and see ...' Hannah says, giggling, which means that it is the fittest of all the fit sixth formers. They both swiftly rearrange themselves, tossing hair and ensuring there is an uninhibited view of their swinging hips.

'In three ... two ... one ...' Hannah says, and the black Ford Escort glides past, its seats filled with FSFs, windows rolled down to let cigarettes hang out.

When it has disappeared round the corner, they relax. 'Did they look?' Elsa asks.

'They so looked.'

'They did, didn't they?'

'Er, yeah!'

They cross the road and make their way over the small bridge, cutting through the grounds of the only bed and breakfast and hopping the fence into the meadow. The sky is cloudy but there is sun and it is warm and the grass smells sweet and impossibly green. They wade through it towards the water, and then follow the bank along until they find a relatively flat spot to sit down.

'Perfect,' Hannah says, flopping onto her front.

Elsa takes her jumper out of her bag and spreads it out. 'Have we got a lighter?' she asks, sitting down on it.

'Course, babe!' Hannah plucks it from her bag and tosses the Chewits towards Elsa. 'Suck on one of those, bitch.'

They lie on their bellies side by side and blow smoke towards the river, half-chewed sweets pressed into their molars.

'What you going to wear at the weekend?' Hannah asks, clicking her jaw in an attempt to blow rings.

'I don't know. Maybe my new skirt.'

'White one?'

'Yeah.'

'Nice. You can wear my blue top if you want.'

'Cool.' Elsa blows on the cherry of her cigarette, watching it burn brighter. 'Thanks.' The smoke tastes thick in her throat.

Hannah nudges her with her shoulder. 'Do you think you'll get off with him again?'

Elsa blushes, tokes on her cigarette again. 'I don't know.'

'Was he in the car?'

'I didn't see. Did you?'

'I think he was.'

Her stomach turns in a series of quick loops. She pulls on the last inch of cigarette.

'I'm done with Duncan,' Hannah says.

'Really?'

'Yeah. He's too … you know.'

'Yeah.'

Hannah stubs her cigarette out in the grass and turns onto her back. 'Imagine,' she says. 'In ten years, we'll be twenty-five. We'll have jobs and boyfriends.'

'Husbands,' Elsa corrects.

'You reckon?'

'At twenty-five? Yeah.'

'That's weird, isn't it?'

Elsa chips her cigarette carefully out and lies down beside her. 'Yeah,' she says, looking up at the sky.

'Do you think we'll still be friends?'

'Of course.'

'You'll probably have kids and I'll be their favourite. I'll be cool Auntie Hannah.'

'Obviously.'

'And my husband will be famous and rich and we'll have a huge house and loads of sex.'

'Lovely.'

Hannah sighs, tossing a jelly baby into her mouth. 'It seems a long way off, doesn't it?'

'Yes,' Elsa says, and it does.

2012

It happens slowly at first; almost too slowly to notice. The *thing* that has been kept safe finds a chink; a way to creep out, and suddenly, each time there is a silence, each time he looks at the spot on the bridge where Eve jumped, he is aware that it is unravelling, that it is overwhelming. He blinks it back, swallows it down, but there is a panic which is growing and which can't be stopped, and being with Elsa, touching her and feeling her against him, no longer quells it like it used to.

'Good morning, San Francisco!' warbles the radio in the corner, and Jack, still groggy, glares at it. Behind the small, chipped desk, Nathan, the salesman he has just spent thirty minutes with, is scrabbling through a pencil-holder to find a pen that works. He wears a pale grey suit of a shiny sort of fabric which looks as though it might be sticky. His shoulder-length hair is coated in a kind of wax and the place where it touches his shoulders is almost definitely sticky.

'You got a job to get to?'

'Yeah.' Jack shifts position, glancing at the phone he has half-fished from his pocket.

'Won't be long now. Pete's just looking for the registration. What kind of work you in?'

'Ironworker. Out on the bridge.'

'Golden Gate?'

'Yeah.'

'Well, that must be pretty great.'

Jack pushes the phone back into his pocket. 'Yep, it's not so bad.'

There is a loud crash from behind the door marked 'Office' in the corner of the small grey showroom, and then someone yells, 'Fuck!'

'Won't be a second,' Nathan says, clicking a pen and scribbling on a pad of paper. 'Ah ha,' he says, looking down at the mark.

The office door opens and Pete, sweating, emerges, brandishing a piece of paper. 'Got it.'

'Great,' Jack says. 'Thanks.'

Nathan slides this and a wedge of other paperwork into an envelope, and hands it and a set of keys to Jack. 'She's all yours.'

The front seat is still warm from the test drive, and Jack sits for a moment, looking out over the forecourt as the sun begins to break its way through the fog. The fabric of the seats is grey and smells of cheap soap, and the grey leather of the steering wheel is rough in patches. He runs his hands over it and across the dashboard, where the faint traces of a long-gone sticker have turned black and gummy. He turns the key in the ignition, puts the car into reverse.

Out on Van Ness, he winds the window down. The day is cold and blue, the fog already retreating back out to sea, and he turns the radio on, skimming through stations. Finding one which has sudden clarity in the sea of static he turns up the volume, drumming his fingers against the wheel. There are few cars around, the city still waking. He winds the window down further, lets the wind run hard fingers through his hair.

He finds it difficult to think of living in London now. When he does, it suddenly becomes just a little less easy to breathe. He can't imagine himself in its busy streets; can't picture himself waiting on a crowded Tube platform or pressed up against others in the aisle of a bus. He can't imagine any existence other than this; driving through wide streets towards a bright blue bay, the bridge cresting the horizon. This is where he should be; this is where he has always been. He tells himself this often, pushes the unravelling away.

He has had plenty of practice at this kind of reinvention.

Parking the car, he looks back at the city and then up at Golden Gate. The lot is not too far from the photo spot where families pose, the bridge perfectly in frame behind them. He should bring Elsa here, really. They have done a little exploring together; walks around the Mission, a Sunday in Golden Gate Park here, a Saturday hiking along the coast there. He'd like to talk Miller into letting him take her up to the top of one of the towers, but his not-so-new-guy status still feels a little unsteady and so for now his head is staying firmly down.

He remembers who said it first. He remembers looking down at her, his body above hers. Her cheeks flushed with wine, her hand on his face. He leant down to kiss her and heard the words escape. He pressed his lips against hers to push them back, but finding the words still on the air, he was surprised how easy it was to say them back. In the March morning light, she looked up at him as he dressed, still curled in their sheets. 'Last night,' she said. 'We said it, didn't we?' When he nodded, she bit her lip. 'Did I say it first?' she asked, and he hesitated.

'I don't remember,' he said, and he climbed back beside her.

They say it often now and there is no fear. Before, it was a rule, it was one of the things that would keep him safe. But that was before, and now there is Elsa. Saying those words back to Elsa has become the thing that will keep him safe; it has become essential, a religion.

Besides, there are plenty of other rules which he takes care not to break.

He collects his tool belt and hard hat from the back seat and heads towards the office. There are only a few of the miniature pickup trucks left parked in their row beside the small building, and as he approaches them, the door to the office opens and Andy strides out, carrying a bolt bag and a road cone.

'Hey,' Jack says.

'Hey. How you doing?'

'Good, thanks. You?'

'Not too bad. Want a ride?' He puts the cone in the bed of one of the trucks and climbs into the driver's side.

'Thanks,' Jack says, climbing in beside him.

'Real quiet out there today,' Andy says, reversing the truck out of its space. 'Miller, Eddie and Chase are all out sick.'

'Flu?'

'Yup.'

'It's going around. Elsa had it.'

'Oh, she did?'

'Yeah, she's fine now though. And so far I haven't caught it.'

They pull onto the sidewalk on the left-hand side of the bridge, which isn't open to pedestrians and which offers an unrestricted view of the ocean. Jack glances up at the cable as they pass beneath the spot where he stood and watched the man in the mackintosh jump, and then looks out to sea.

'Gorgeous day,' he says.

'Yup. Not much fog this morning.'

'No.'

'Won't stay like that for ever,' Andy says, and Jack does not reply.

There are plenty of bars in the Mission, and some that are closer to the bridge, but somehow, over the weeks, their drinking place of choice has become a dive bar in North Beach, which is halfway across the city. Cool and dark and full of Beat Generation memorabilia, it is a rectangular room which is often empty. At the far end, just before the toilets, is an ancient piano, often played by a small old man who wears a fedora and rarely turns round. Jack is not sure he has ever seen his face. Sometimes he sings, his reedy voice wavering in a thin stream into the room. When he is not there, there is no music; just the steady dripping of the bathroom's taps.

They are on their third beer of the evening, and Alex has just come back from the bar with two chasers of whiskey.

'You see that girl over there?' he asks as he sets them down.

Jack glances over to the bar. 'Yeah.'

'She's giving me "the look".'

Jack takes a swig of his beer. 'Yeah. Sure.'

'Seriously.' Alex sits down. 'When I was over there, she couldn't take her eyes off me.'

'Too bad you've got a girlfriend then, isn't it?'

'Yeah.' Alex looks glumly into his whiskey. 'I guess it is.'

'Claudia's a lucky girl.'

'Ha ha,' Alex says, gulping half of the drink. 'Hey,' he says, brightening. 'Did you hear what Andy said today? About a TV crew coming to film us in the summer?'

'Yeah.'

'That's awesome, right? We're gonna be famous. Well, me, probably. I look pretty good on camera. I'll probably get a lot of offers.'

Jack laughs. 'Right.'

'That's what we need though, something to shake things up. You hear Price complaining about someone drinking his Coke earlier?'

'Yeah. He wasn't happy.'

Alex tips the last drops of whiskey into his mouth. 'That's the most exciting thing that's happened at work all week. Seriously. Come on.'

Jack raises an eyebrow. 'I think I prefer it that way.'

'Shit, yeah. I don't mean … You see those girls last week with the flowers?'

Jack did. Two girls, wrapped up against the cold, looking out at the city with the wind driving their hair across their faces. The flowers float past him now, one by one, solitary stems descending to the surface of the water. They did not cry, but when it was done, they held each other for a while.

'They were there for her, right? The blonde girl.' Alex picks up his bottle and stares into it.

'Eve.'

'Yeah, that's it.'

Jack pushes his chair back. 'Same again?'

'Sure.'

The woman behind the bar has a face predisposed to look irritated and a tattoo of a shooting star behind one ear. 'Two more, please,' he says. 'Two more chasers, too.'

Her sour expression softens when he speaks. 'Where you from?' she asks.

'Seattle,' he says, because this is easiest. 'But I've travelled a bit.'

She nods, satisfied, and pours the whiskeys. She sets them in front of him and opens the beers in quick succession on the bar. 'Eighteen dollars, please.' He hands her a $20 bill and takes the whiskeys to the table. Returning for the beers, he leaves the two dollars on the bar, and she smiles at him; a stiff tightening of her mouth. 'Have a good night,' she says, which strikes him as odd because he is not leaving.

The bar is busier than he has ever seen it; hardly any of the few tables free. The man at the piano plays on to the wall, oblivious to the crowd behind him. His hands dance from side to side, his small voice struggling through the low, humming tide of conversations. Jack sits down and nods in his direction.

'He's on one tonight.'

'On one?'

'On a mission. Like, really going for it.'

'Oh. Yeah. Think it's his fan club.' Alex points the neck of his bottle in the direction of the table closest to the piano; a large round one with six or seven mismatched chairs. Sitting around it are a youngish group, three boys and four girls, drinking pale ale from cloudy glasses. A plastic pitcher sits in the centre of the table.

'Backpackers,' Alex says. 'French. That one is, anyway –' He swivels his bottle to a dark-haired girl sitting with her back to them. 'Heard her talking at the bar. Or German, maybe.'

Jack laughs. 'Languages aren't your strong point then.'

'I get by just fine.' He takes a pull on his drink and glances at the table again. The group are singing along to 'Hotel California'. The dark-haired girl takes picture after picture, making her way around the table, ushering her friends into poses, before beginning the journey again. One of the boys holds his glass up in a toast, and they all join in, ale slopping onto the scratched wood below. 'Guess they're having a good time,' Alex says. 'Speaking of which — you like it here, right? Not planning on escaping back to London?'

'I like it. It has its good parts.'

'You're talking about me, right?'

'No. I am not.'

'What about Elsa? She settling in okay? Happy?'

'Yeah, she's always happy.'

'When you gonna let me meet her, anyway?' Alex takes another gulp of whiskey, wiggling his eyebrows suggestively over the edge of the glass.

'Never, if you plan on making that face at her.'

'I'll be good, I promise.'

'We'll see.'

Alex becomes suddenly serious, chewing on his lip. 'You tell her about the girl — Eve?'

Jack glances at his drink. 'Yeah, of course.'

'She was your first, right?'

'Yep.'

'I'm sorry, man. That's rough.'

Jack shrugs.

'You must think I'm an asshole, not remembering her name.'

'Of course not.'

Alex begins twisting his glass round on the table. 'It's just easier that way. It's like – I don't know …'

'Distance,' Jack says, and then he gulps his whiskey in one.

'Yeah.' Alex shrugs. 'Distance.'

There is a dancing here; they are both aware of it. They circle the table, eyes on each other, closer and closer to the brink. *Stop*, Jack wants to say. *What a lovely place*, he wants to sing. He wants to put his hands over his ears, squeeze his eyes shut, because there is a *thing* they are getting close to, too close, and if they aren't careful it will all crumble into the bay in a groaning mass of orange steel. Golden Gate must be protected, he must check each of the rivets that holds it together and he must fight the things which tarnish, the things which invade. That is his job.

'Elsa's going to be pissed off,' he says, though the 'off' is quieter because he is becoming unsure if he uses it or not. 'I forgot to tell her I wasn't coming home.'

'Ahh.' Alex leans back in his chair. 'She's not so perfect after all. Thank fuck for that.'

Jack smirks. 'You haven't seen her when she's pissed off.'

'Oh yeah?' Alex's eyebrows rejoin the conversation.

Jack takes a swig of his beer. 'Hot.'

'In that case, you should probably stay for another, right?'

When he finally teeters up the hill to the house, the road is deserted. His breath, alcohol warm, fogs on the thin air. The key is tricky in the lock; he rests his forehead against the door as he turns it.

The house is dark, and it is her. Her smell is everywhere; the fibres of the carpet against his socked feet and the sound of the clock which ticks on the small table are her. He takes his jacket off and tries to hang it on the banister. It slides to the floor and he leaves it there, climbing the stairs in the darkness. He treads carefully, feeling with his feet. Somehow, he can sense her up there; he knows she is awake. At the top, at the door, he pauses.

'Hi,' he says, leaning against the frame.

She lies on her side in the bed, her back to him. A lamp beside her illuminates the yellowing pages of a paperback. She does not reply.

He moves clumsily across the room, shedding his shirt and socks as he goes. He clambers onto the bed behind her, slips an arm around her. He buries his face in her hair. She turns the page.

'I'm sorry I'm so late,' he whispers. 'I missed you.'

Her breathing is the only sound. He slides down her back and presses his ear to her, listens to her living. He begins to drift towards sleep; the turning of another page brings him back.

'Hey,' he says, propping himself up. He puts a hand on her hip and tilts her onto her back. She keeps her head turned to the side, her lips pressed together. She is wearing her glasses; dark frames against her lamplit skin. 'What you reading?' he asks.

An eyebrow lifts; she quickly checks it.

'Talk to me,' he says, moving up the bed to her. 'I'm sorry I'm late. I love you.'

The eyebrow arches again.

'I love you,' he says, kissing her shoulder. 'I love you.' He kisses her neck. 'I love you.' He kisses her cheek. He sits up and takes her glasses off, folds them carefully. Reaching over her, he places them on the bedside table. He takes the book from between her fingers; she does not resist.

He positions himself above her, a hand either side of her shoulders. She keeps her gaze on the wall, but her lips are pressed tighter together now, a smile escaping. 'Look at me,' he says. 'I love you.'

'No, you don't,' she says, crossing her arms across her chest.

'No, I don't?' He lets his weight fall on her, burying his face in her hair and nipping at her ear. She cannot resist; she laughs. She pretends to push him off but her leg creeps up and over his back, holds him to her.

'You're a bastard,' she whispers, taking his earlobe between her teeth.

'I know.'

'You're a fucking bastard.'

'I love you.'

'You don't deserve me.'

'I know.'

She bites him harder; his cheek now. 'You're a twat.'

'I missed you.'

She pulls at his belt. He twists at her hair, wrapping it around his wrist and tugging her head to one side, pressing his lips to her neck. 'Fuck you,' she hisses, and then she kisses him.

2002

The months after the millennium are bruised and sharp. His mother collects him from the police station. Two days later, she hands him the phone and stands in the doorway while Lou, still bright on a bad line, tells him she's sorry but she'll have to let him go. It is a new century and he has no job. Aimee, now eighteen, does not speak to him if she can help it. The two of them, women together, tuck themselves in the small sitting room, watching hospital dramas and cookery shows on the ancient television, and leave him to roam the kitchen, pad back up the stairs.

He speaks more often to his father, who is more communicative on another continent. His calls are full of carefully weighted words, sentences which are built on sturdy foundations but which have no concrete ending: 'You need to think now' and 'You're at an age when'. 'It's time now' and, most often, 'This is a chance'.

Finally, one February afternoon when the frost is still not thawing, the weekly phone call offers something more substantial. His father has a friend and the friend has a vacancy. He can give Jack the friend's phone number, but the rest is up to him. The number begins with a Newcastle area code.

He makes the call standing in the hallway, the phone's cord stretching out from around the fridge, umbilical and essential. He makes assurances he isn't sure even he can believe in, uses terms he hasn't used for three years now, stands up straight as he speaks. He laughs in the right places and quips where he can, and when he hangs up, it is after saying, 'Thank you, that's great. I'll see you then.'

Two years and six months later, it is a Friday night in August 2002, and he is in his car. The shopping centre is halfway built and it is the first thing he has seen come up from nothing in such a way. He calls his father on Sundays and his mother on Thursdays, and if Aimee answers the phone she chatters at him until their mother pushes her out of the way.

He checks the dashboard's clock: 19.02. The sunlight is still bright and gold, the air warm. He indicates and turns into a side street.

Jamie is standing on the kerb, shock of blonde hair bleached white by the summer. He has on star-shaped sunglasses and a purple vest top, and as Jack pulls up beside him, he wrenches open the passenger door.

'Wassup!' he says, grinning in at him. 'Ready to P.A.R.T.Y?'

'What the fuck are you wearing?' Jack asks.

'Fuck off.' He bends down to pick two six-packs up from the pavement and climbs in.

'I've got a crate back there,' Jack says, pointing to the back seat, as he does a neat three-point turn and speeds out onto the main road. Jamie leans into the back, purple vest riding up over his skinny frame, and pulls two cans from the box. He opens one and hands it to Jack, who takes a swig and places it between his thighs to change gear.

'Your brother already there?' he asks.

'Aye. Katie's had him setting up since this morning.'

'You sure she's okay with us going?'

Jamie laughs. 'You mean *you*.' He glances at Jack. 'You're not *nervous*, are you?'

'Course not.'

'Don't worry, Finland. It's all forgotten.'

Jack isn't so sure. He has always got on well with Katie; with Michael, too. Since he turned up in their local two years ago, alone in the corner with half a pint, the three of them have adopted him. He likes Katie, small and loud and curvy, and Jamie is probably right, but the echoes of their argument keep ticking over

I don't care if you fuck them, just stop fucking them over you cunt

in his mind and he hopes with some intensity that

172

Jodie, the friend who was one friend too many, will not be there tonight.

'Here.' Jamie hands him a lit cigarette. 'Trust me, Katie's fine. I've shagged *all* her mates and she still loves me.'

'I'm not worried.'

'I shagged two of them at once before.'

'So you keep saying.'

'One of them was Jodie.'

'Yeah, cheers for that.'

'My pleasure.' Jamie crunches his can and throws it out of the open window. He collects another one. 'This is going to be the best night ever, bruv.'

'You still can't get away with "bruv", by the way. Just so you know.'

'I'm gonna keep trying, if it's all right with you, like.'

Jack flicks his cigarette butt onto the road. 'It's down here, isn't it?'

'Aye. Third house on the right.'

The direction is unnecessary; as soon as they pull into the cul-de-sac, they can hear the music, see the people already sitting on the front lawn and the pavement, the house overflown. Jack finds a space to park and turns off the engine.

'You should give me your keys,' Jamie says, looking over the tips of his stars.

'Eh?'

'You know, to stop you drink-driving.'

'Jamie, who's more likely to drink-drive – me or you?'

Jamie pushes his sunglasses back up his nose. 'Good point. Let's go.'

They make their way up the path, past people in bikini tops and shorts and summer dresses, girls drinking pink wine from bottles and boys drinking Coronas and kicking a football back and forth. Instead of heading for the front door, Jamie ducks left and down the passage beside the house. Everywhere seems to pulse dully with music. Jack opens another beer.

The passage leads out into the tiny garden, where Katie and Michael are sitting around a white plastic table with eight or nine friends, while others sit in clots along the low wall.

'All right, boys,' Michael says, standing up to shake their hands. He is taller than Jamie, broader too, and his blonde hair is cut close to his skull. When his hand closes around Jack's it presses a small plastic package into his palm.

Jamie has leant down to kiss Katie on the cheek. She looks at Jack over his shoulder. 'All right, chick?' she asks him with a wink, and he feels instantly lighter.

'All right, Kate,' he says, and he sits down on the wall.

'Great party, K-Dog,' Jamie says, but he is already turning away from her, headed eagerly for Jack. He raises his eyebrows in a silent question and Jack nods and presses one of the pills into his hand. 'Great party,' Jamie says again, and they both put their hands to their mouths.

*

Later, much later, he realises he is sitting on a sofa in a living room he assumes is Katie's. His skin feels white hot and his eyes are slow to catch up, dragging behind as he turns to look around the room. Furniture loops and spins, the low light of lamps bouncing back and forth.

'You haven't done this before, have you?' a voice asks beside him and he turns, smiling. She is slim and pretty and wearing a red top which is cut very low. 'Do you like it?' she asks, taking the cigarette from between his fingers and putting it to her lips, which are also red. His eyes try to roll but he keeps them in place, keeps them looking at her lips.

'Yeah,' he says.

'Have some of this.' She holds out a bottle of whiskey and he puts it to his mouth and drinks. It burns his throat but the pain is far away and the heat is irresistible.

'Everything feels amazing, doesn't it?' the girl says. She leans closer. '*Everything.*'

His mouth is dry and his smile sticks to his teeth. He drinks more of the whiskey and takes the cigarette back from her.

'Try this,' she says, and she puts her hand in his hair, runs her fingers down over his scalp and across his neck. This time, his eyes roll, and he lets them, bringing the bottle to his mouth again. 'Good?' she asks, and he moans. Her fingers tighten on him, they tip him towards her, and her lips press on his. He moans again, pulls her onto him, his hands running down her back. Hers slide over his chest, leaving a trail of fire as they go.

And then she is gone, pushed aside, and Jamie's face looms instead but the words are hard to process and instead his own slow thoughts fill the space

Have I got lipstick on my face?

and he stares blankly up at his friend, who is grabbing him by the shirt and pulling him outside and onto the front lawn. Everything is swimming, people bobbing brightly past, but Jamie is shouting and he tries to catch hold of the stream

She's my ex I told you she was my ex what are you playing at why do you have to fuck everything that moves

to make sense of it, tries to apologise but his mouth is too thick to form words apart from simple, short ones: *sorry, I didn't, it was*. On and on, Jamie goes, his face red beneath his white hair, and he can feel it before it happens, feel the fist working itself up, but when it comes towards him he cannot duck.

The terrible, unstoppable rise of the anger begins immediately and he tries to hold it down, tries to keep the warm shield around him. 'I'm sorry,' he says, but the fist hits his face again and now he can't stop it, it pulses maddeningly through him and the face of his friend is there and he hates it and –

No. It's Jamie, he must not hit Jamie. He takes a shaky step backwards, the two of them staring at each other. Jamie is still shouting

Fucking pussy you're a fucking pussy look at you you're a dick you're just

but it is difficult to hear over the pounding in his ears, the grinding in his jaw. With legs that feel like lead, he turns away, his steps staggering at first but soon finding the rhythm of a walk. He realises that he still has the bottle in his hand and he brings it to his mouth, hoping to wash away the buzzing sound that presses down on him. Somewhere Jamie is still shouting and with numb fingers he finds his keys. He gets into his car and stares down the road, away from the house. He brings the bottle up again, his eyes still rolling, his breath coming in shallow through his nose. His fist is still clenched; it throbs and he bangs it on the wheel, trying to loosen it.

And then he's starting the engine, reversing down the cul-de-sac, whiskey to mouth, hand clenched around steering wheel. He drives blindly and everything is fast, everything is going too fast, the radio up loud, whiskey again again again, fingers burning, throat burning, foot on accelerator, *fuck's sake how has this happened again*. He blinks hard, over and over, trying to make his eyes catch up, black – road – black – road. The whiskey is almost empty; he tips it up, head tilted back, but his hand is shaking and the bottle tumbles down *whoops* bounces off his knee *shit* and under his seat. He needs it he puts a hand down chin against the wheel fingers grasping glass hand closing around neck –

Back up to the wheel wrong side of the road silver car coming round the corner girl screaming.

Black.

2012

It is 6 November, and across the country, exit poll data begins to flood in. Social media outlets and news broadcasts urge voters to stay in line, assuring them that if they are in line they will be allowed to vote. In San Francisco, where polling stations will remain open for another three hours, people queue in garages, in schools, in restaurants, in a temple. Many locations are crowded; voters crouch on the floor to complete their ballots. They are given stickers as they leave. Some complain that, contrary to rumours, there are no doughnuts. In bars across the city, those who have already voted, or who will not, watch televisions, check smartphones. In some they will be offered election-night specials, discounts when proof of voting is presented. But the streets are otherwise subdued, the hours carrying on as normal.

Elsa is in Chinatown. It is not a place she usually walks; too busy, the hills too steep. She prefers being out by the water, or in the wide streets of the Mission and the Castro. But variety is the spice of life, and she needs chillies to make dinner. She crosses the forecourt of a rust-red temple, following a narrow street out onto a busy section of one of the steepest hills. She pauses beside a bakery, trying to get her bearings. Dressed in a skirt with thick woollen tights, boots and a military-style jacket she found at a thrift store in the Mission, she feels young; bundled up like a little girl. People flow around her, hurrying as the sky begins to darken into a grey twilight. She glances into the bakery's window. A tiny place, it is packed with customers, all pushing towards the single, smeared display case. The door is open and a muddle of their voices makes its way out on the yeast-warm air. One, young and male, is louder than the rest; its owner a tall, white American with long wavy hair tied in a ponytail. His jeans are low on his hips, the bright blue waistband of his underwear visible beneath his checked shirt, and he is speaking in quick, confident Mandarin while the other customers stare at him. Watching him, she is fascinated. His hands move back and forth across the glass, indicating items which are immediately bagged and placed in front of him. The woman serving him laughs, coos a couple of words at him, and he smiles.

A couple push past Elsa, knocking her off balance and away from the yellow light of the bakery. They walk on without turning back, huddling together against the wind. Shaken, she zips up her coat a little further and carries on up the hill.

This morning, when he was leaving, Jack asked her if she had thought of visiting her family at Christmas. 'If you want to go home for a week, I'll pay for your flight,' he said. 'It can be your present.'

She'd pressed the lid of his lunchbox down, taking time to check the corners. 'That's really sweet,' she said, 'but you don't have to do that.'

'I don't mind,' he'd said. 'I know it's kind of a big thing for you guys.'

'No, really, Jack. The flights are so expensive this time of year.'

'That's okay.' He'd reached out a hand to stroke her hair. 'I still have stuff saved from selling the Chicago house. I know you want to see your family.'

'I'll think about it,' she'd said, leaning her cheek into his palm. 'But really I'd be happy just being here with you.'

'You're cute,' he said, bending to kiss her. 'I'll see you tonight.'

The Chicago house. He does not mention it often, and she knows that it is because he lived there with a woman. Beyond that, she doesn't ask questions; this is how they work. This is how they have always worked, though it has never been explicitly stated, never expressed by either. Somehow, they both just know. She had the answers she wanted, asked them on the first night and again on the first morning. Are you married? No. Do you have children? No. And that was enough; that was all she needed.

But now, turning onto a quieter street in Chinatown, she

isn't sure if that is still true. Now, alone in the cold, the phrase keeps resurfacing. *The Chicago house.* He has been a homeowner. Somehow, the easy way he refers to it makes it stranger to conceive of. It cannot be the first time he has said it that way, but it is the first time she has noticed. She racks her brain for the things he has said about it before but comes up empty-handed. She has spent too long kicking away from any mention of the past; now the fragments have been borne out of her reach.

Tourist shops litter these streets, filled with ridiculous and inauthentic souvenirs: parasols, fans, lucky cats with their weighted paws waving in long, leaden rows. T-shirts touch windows, sleeves and sides rumpled against the glass. Fake orange Alcatraz uniforms, others white with ironed-on images of landmarks: Lombard Street, Coit Tower, Golden Gate. She stops, surprised at the sudden silence. It hasn't taken many steps, and this felt the right direction, but this is not the street she expected. She hesitates, shivering, and then turns away, downhill, her boots tapping against the pavement.

At the bottom of the slope, she finds what she is looking for. A street filled with supermarkets, flickering white light flooding the damp grey pavement. Chicken carcasses line doorways, tanks of lobsters bubble against walls. Trays of familiar and unfamiliar vegetables spill out onto the streets; their trays lined with green felt. She chooses a store at random and stops. In the white electric light, she shivers again, and draws her coat tighter around her.

She will admit that it is not just the phrase (and remembering it now — *the Chicago house* — sends a fresh, unpleasant feeling through her) that has unsettled her. She is almost afraid to think it, afraid to be *that* girl, but she can't help it. Try as she might to silence it — and she is trying very hard, with an almost heroic effort — there is still a small voice, tiny even, inside which asks, *Doesn't he want to spend Christmas with me?*

Pathetic. She picks up an onion, shaking her head at herself. It is an extremely generous offer and she is grateful. She puts the onion down, moves on. It is an extremely generous offer and she doesn't want to take him up on it.

'I'm just looking, thanks,' she says to the man who approaches her as she examines an aubergine.

He frowns, tilts his head to one side. 'No, thanks,' she says, trying to be clearer, and he nods and turns away. She finds a box of chillies and picks out a few. Taking them to the till, she pays, smiling at the man as she offers a crumpled note. 'Thank you,' she says as she leaves, and he shakes his head as if she has asked a question.

She passes back through the souvenir streets, past the rows of cats, who watch, paws taking slow swipes. The streets step up more steeply in this direction, each block winched up a little higher. With each increase, there is less sound, less life. Shutters have been pulled, curtains drawn, the last of the daylight sinks away. The cold air feels rough in her lungs and yet she has a sudden urge to run.

At the top of one block, and out of breath, she stops and turns to look back. Behind her, the street sweeps down towards the water and, just visible between buildings, the Bay Bridge, grey in the growing gloom. Down at the waterside, there is a pier she likes to visit when her walks last until after dark. It is simple wood with old-fashioned street lamps and a single bench, and against the velvet black of the sky and the water, it and the Bay Bridge behind it glow bright gold. She sits there often, looking out at the bridge, and she has sometimes thought that the secret beauty of this view is far more special than any of Golden Gate. It makes her feel somewhat a traitor.

She turns right and makes her way towards North Beach, more familiar territory, the bag of chillies clutched in her hand.

There was a time when they came close. Arriving at the house in Clapham, she felt it before she walked through the door; a closing-in. It was April then, the weather warming, and she had on a new dress, fitted in the waist with a full, knee-length skirt. *A lady's dress*, Anna would have called it. Two of his housemates were out; the other, Charlie, answered the door.

'He's in the kitchen, mate,' he said. 'Been slaving away in there all day.'

The house smelt of cooking, but in the kitchen he was only sitting at the table, his back to her. He was still, very still, as if he was watching the wall. She put a hand to the frame, wanted to run. Instead, she took a step inside the room, kept her voice bright.

'Hey,' she said, putting a bottle of wine down on the side. 'Charlie let me in. How's it going, Heston?'

He turned to her and his eyes were wide and red but he

managed to rise, managed to hug her, to pour her a glass of wine. He talked her through the menu, through his day, through the recent argument between Charlie and another of their housemates, but all the time he was elsewhere, his eyes bloodshot and frantic. Eventually he fell silent, watched her sip. He watched her and she tried to look away, tried to find a way to take them safely past, but it was no use. She has never been able to avoid his eyes. She looked into them then and put down her glass.

'Are you okay?' she asked, and he breathed in; a slow, soft pulling, his eyes closing, and she felt the world tilt.

And then the lights went out, a sudden, swift fall. The gentle humming of the oven gone, just the sounds of their fluttering breath.

'Guys?' Charlie, in the hallway. 'I think I blew the fuse.'

She could have asked him, afterwards, when the light was back and the dinner was ready. He no longer wanted her to but he wouldn't have resisted, she could tell. Instead she watched him serve and when he sat down, when he looked at her and paused, she simply smiled.

'This looks great,' she said.

It seemed important then. *Keep moving forward.* It seemed the right thing for them.

I'm going in circles, she thinks now, as she walks down the hill with her legs bowing out gracelessly in an effort to keep her upright.

Closer to the supermarkets again, a street sweeper makes his way slowly across the road, his broom dragging vegetable detritus and sodden paper with it and sending a rotten, plasticky smell back to Elsa. She smiles at him and he turns away. As she passes a silent shop, she looks through the dusty, yellowed glass of the window. Tanks line it; through the brownish filter of the window and the stagnant water, she sees fish crushed together, their flat eyes pressed outwards, their bodies barely moving. She presses a hand to the glass, watching them. The wind whistles down the street behind her; a strand of her hair breaks free and twists across her face, and suddenly she finds herself thinking of the crow-man. *We are always looking for each other.* She shivers, glances at her watch. *Time to go home.*

It's too far to walk but she has spent her last dollar on the chillies, and so she heads towards Little Italy, in search of funds and her bus stop. She finds a cashpoint – *ATM*, she thinks, *it's called an ATM* – at the junction of Montgomery and Columbus. Joining the queue for the two machines, she tucks the paper bag of chillies into one of the big pockets on the front of her jacket. The jacket is made of stiff, coarse fabric in military green, and cost her $10. It is her favourite thing, the best she has ever bought. She tucks her chin into its funnel neck, ears pink with the cold.

The couple in front of her have identical tattoos on the napes of their necks. She leans closer to see it: a date – 06/21/11 – with a tiny heart beneath the last 1. She wonders what happened on this particular date; studies their backs for clues. They hold hands but don't look at each other. His foot taps in time with a silent beat. A woman ahead of them takes her money from the machine and moves away, and they take a single step forward, left foot and then right, eyes still fixed in front.

Beside them is a wheely bin, its lid propped almost half-open by the rubbish bulging out of it. As Elsa looks at it, her card already in her hand, an elderly Chinese couple approach and open the lid all the way. They rummage through the contents without speaking, selecting several items and then moving away, shoulder to shoulder. Nobody but her notices.

'Nobody understands me,' she tells Jack later, undressing in the bedroom. 'I thought Americans loved a British accent.'

He laughs. 'You thought you'd be treated like the third Middleton sister, didn't you?'

She swats at him with her tights. 'No.'

'Yeah, you did.'

'Fuck off.'

He sits down on the bed to remove his socks. 'Who doesn't understand you, baby?'

'Bus drivers. People in shops. Pearl, half the time.'

'Poor Elsa.'

She kneels on her side of the bed, fluffing her pillow. 'What are we doing this weekend?'

'I don't know.' He climbs into bed and offers an arm up to her. 'What do you want to do?' She slides beneath the duvet and tucks herself into his side, her head on his chest.

'I don't mind.'

'How about ...' He tugs at a strand of her hair, twisting it around a finger. 'Lunch on Haight, Saturday?'

'Sounds good. Or we could take a boat over to Sausalito. Pearl was saying how beautiful it is out there.'

'Maybe. I think I'd just like to take it easy though. I'm so tired this week.'

She flicks at a hair on his chest. 'Okay.'

'Let's see how we feel.'

'What about Friday? Are you going out with Alex?'

'Probably. It's Andy's birthday so it'll be a few of us.'

'Sounds fun.'

They lie in the limited light, watching headlights travel across the closed blind.

'I'm glad he won,' she says, listening to the thud of his heart.

'Me too.'

'People online are calling it "Hope 2.0".'

'Cute.' He picks up another strand of her hair and lets it fall.

'I thought it was rather beautiful.'

He considers this. 'When you say it, it is,' he says finally.

She turns to look back at him, propping her chin on his chest. 'Can I ask you a question?'

'Of course.'

'The Chicago house. Who did you live there with?'

Perhaps it's the light, but she's sure she sees a muscle twitch in his jaw. 'My ex. For a while.'

'Oh.'

He picks up another piece of her hair, holds it carefully but does not drop it. 'Does that upset you?'

'No.'

'Good.' He looks at her for a moment, his head tilted to one side against the headboard. 'You've never asked that before.'

'I know.'

'You okay?'

She swallows. *Ask him.* But she can't. She is too afraid. It crawls through her and she clings to him. 'I talked to my sister earlier,' she says, running a hand across his chest.

'Oh yeah? How is she?'

'Okay. I don't know. I'm worried about her.'

'Why?'

'She didn't sound herself. She kept forgetting what she was saying, or suddenly changing the subject. Then she'd go quiet, like she was falling asleep.'

He looks back at her, waiting.

'I think she was drunk,' she says, resting her cheek against his skin.

At this he laughs. The sound is deeper where she lies; it travels through her jaw. 'I'm not joking,' she says, lifting her head, and then, when he lets out another snort, she says it again. She sits up and studies him, stung.

'I'm sorry, honey,' he says, a hand held out to bring her back. 'I just don't see why that's a problem.'

'My sister doesn't get drunk,' she says, lying down on her own side of the bed. 'And she definitely doesn't get drunk at ten a.m.'

He turns onto his side and smiles at her. 'Come on, don't overreact. She's not a baby any more.'

'I know that. She has a husband and a house.'

He takes her hand in his. 'You're too protective, Elsa. You worry too much. They're all okay. You're inventing problems.'

She sighs. 'That's not what I'm doing.'

'No?' He slides an arm across her stomach, drawing her close. 'She's probably working too hard. You said she got promoted, right?'

'Yeah.'

'Well then.'

She slips down, resting her head against his shoulder. 'Always here to talk me down, aren't you?'

He is silent.

'Sorry,' she says, turning to press her lips against his skin. 'I didn't mean ...'

'I know.' He kisses the top of her head but it is a small thing, not affectionate, a full stop. 'What are your plans for tomorrow?'

She closes her eyes. 'I don't know yet. A museum maybe.'

'Sounds good.' He reaches over her to turn off the lamp. 'Sweet dreams, babe.'

'You too.'

They settle into the darkness. A siren echoes as he begins to sleep, a single sound in the orange night.

2002

Few opportunities offer themselves in those initial hours. His right to remain silent. His right to a phone call. The phone call that will spark a chain of phone calls, their words the only break in the silence of the following days. His, from the police station, to his mother in York. And then hers, frantic and frequent, to the hospital in Newcastle; constant requests for news on the girl's condition: we can't tell you we still can't tell you she's stable that's all I can say critical but stable she's recovering she's been discharged.

He receives a court date, and it becomes a throbbing, unseen thing which takes almost all of the air in the house and fills every sentence. His mother seems to wither in front of him, smaller and smaller, until he comes to think of her as a fairy-tale person, a thimble hat, a matchbox bed.

Smaller and smaller until, one day, another phone call. She looks at him, bewildered, as she hangs up.

'She won't give evidence,' she says.

'What?' His voice sounds far away. 'Why?'

'The poor girl won't give evidence,' she says, and she looks at him and suddenly it is him who is small. 'The lawyer thinks you'll get away with a ban and a fine,' she says, with an edge, and as she walks away he realises that this edge is disgust.

The relief should make him fly but instead he sinks. He thinks often of the girl and tries to picture a face so scarred that it can't be shown in a courtroom; tries to imagine a person so scared that she can't leave the house. The not-knowing is the thing, but there is no way *to* know; he is allowed no information and he is too afraid to ask. The imagining and the not knowing fill him up, and suddenly it is him who isn't leaving the house.

His lawyer — a sharp-faced, short man whose services are paid for by Jack's mother after another series of phone calls between his parents — is right. A three-year ban, a fine. All he can think is that it's nothing. It's not enough. He hates the lawyer as he shakes his hand: hates him for doing his job. But he's relieved to be leaving, relieved to be free, and for this he hates himself most of all.

The last phone call in the chain is his, to his sister. Aimee sounds New York brash, a room-mate yelling something in the background, but still, as she's speaking, he's picturing the little girl with her feet dangling over the edge of a too-big plane seat.

'You need to get away,' she says. 'You need to come back.' It takes him a second to realise that these two actions are the same.

'Okay,' he says. 'I'll come back.'

'There's something else,' she says. 'It's Dad.'

He picks at a loose flake of wood on the door frame and his voice comes out small. 'Is he okay?'

'He's in trouble, Jack. I can't get him to tell me how bad, but he's doing stuff he shouldn't be. Money stuff.'

The flake lets go; it crumbles in his fingers. 'It's okay,' he says. 'I'll come back.' But his words sound hollow, even to himself.

He arrives late in the afternoon of a Monday in September, and on a tip from an old friend, it's Chicago where he lands. The immigration official smiles. 'Welcome home, sir.'

Jack looks at him, and then down at his passport. 'Thank you,' he says, but he doesn't smile.

Checking into a hotel, he draws the blinds against the daylight. The room is several shades of beige and the blind has a large, tear-shaped stain in its upper-left corner. He stares up at it for a moment, bag still in hand. He blinks but his eyes are dry and sore. Turning off the light, he climbs under the starchy sheets without undressing and sleeps. When he wakes in the middle of the night, he sits in the grainy armchair and peers out at the street. Rain has fallen and everything is silvery and slick. As the sun begins to rise, he lets the blind fall again. The television is switched on and the tinny voices of infomercials pass over him as he sleeps.

He wakes at three, rises and showers. Under the flow of water, he closes his eyes and is frightened by the blankness he finds there. He dresses slowly, his muscles stiff.

Outside on the street the rain is gone. He catches the bus to Commercial Street, where Local 63, the Chicago branch of the union, hides in a cream building on an industrial estate. The bus pulls away, leaving him standing there. A child on the back seat watches as, through the greasy glass, he grows smaller and smaller.

Golden Gate Bridge, Elsa reads, idly skimming another travel site as she tries to think of exciting anecdotes to tell her sister, to assure her in her cheeriest email voice that everything is still okay, everything is still golden, is travelled by around 112,000 cars each day. The number seems huge; she shakes her head. *How many places can one bridge lead?* she thinks, and she wonders if she should add this to the email.

At 5 p.m. on this Monday night, two people in San Francisco speed towards the same destination. One, a man in a tattered suit, walks towards the orange hulk of the bridge. The other sleeps on a sofa in a tiny house on Potrero Avenue whilst his girlfriend types an email at the kitchen table. The second man is dreaming. He sees a motel room, he hears his sister's voice. The other, the first man, looks out as the last lights flicker on in the city, and then he hoists himself onto the barrier and slides a leg over.

In the kitchen, Elsa pauses, a tiny white arrow hovering over the icon marked Send. She glances up. Beside the sofa, a phone begins to vibrate, its screen flashing blue in the dim room.

Jack's sister sounds disapproving. 'This is not a great time,' she says, and then Jack wakes with a jerk. He blinks, eyes adjusting, as he answers the phone. His replies drift into the kitchen as sounds instead of words and Elsa turns away from her laptop.

'I have to go,' he says, stumbling against the kitchen door frame as he tugs on his boots. She watches him, pale-faced and not knowing what to say. *Good luck*, she almost tries, but that seems too cheerful, too thoughtless. *I'm sorry* she dismisses instantly as too defeatist. She presses her lips together in the ghost of a kiss and then he is gone.

On the way to Heathrow, she caught him looking at the tickets. It was still only almost-morning, the first streaks of grey appearing slowly in the sky like cracks. The taxi driver spoke in low murmurs on his phone, swapping hands to change gear. She had worn a scarf bought specially for the plane (she is always cold on planes); blue and red Navajo print, it unfolds into a shawl which almost covers her. Tucked under it in the back seat, she dozed against the window. The excitement of the previous night had been dulled by the early start (she has never been a morning person) but occasionally it resurfaced through her like a spark, and she would start awake, stomach circling. Each time, she would glance at him; sometimes sleeping, sometimes watching the road, but once, just as the first sign for Heathrow's exit appeared, looking down at the tickets in his hand.

She remembers his face now, the small smile playing at the corners of his mouth, and hugs her knees to her chest. She reads the words on the screen, her own, and she hates their shallowness, the exclamation marks which appear too often amongst them. Moving the cursor back and forth, she considers deleting them. Instead, she finally hits Send and then clicks the laptop's lid carefully shut.

In the car, Jack hunches over the wheel as he speeds across the city. The dream lingers and he is afraid. He thinks of his family, he thinks of his father; he thinks of the first time he saw his haggard father after arriving back in Chicago, the thundering free fall of fear as he saw something of himself in the wreckage of that face, and the back of his neck breaks out in a cold sweat. He focuses on breathing; drawing in air as deep as he can, blowing it out through pursed lips until there is none left. He drives past the Safeway, follows a bus up Divisadero Street. In the back window, a little girl looks out at him. Her mother is talking on her phone. At the end of October, Price and Chase arrived on a call-out to see a man throw his toddler son from the barrier before following him over. *I can't do that*, Jack thinks now. *I can't see that.* He pulls onto the highway, changing lanes erratically, and then the bridge is in front of him.

'A bridge is what you want,' his father said to him once. 'A bridge is where you really see it.'

He was fourteen, the first summer when Mrs Campbell did not have to feature in their plans. Old enough to sit alone and look after Aimee, but more often than not, hanging around the site while his sister was left to read her books in the low light of Mrs Campbell's porch. 'Where you see what?' he asked, then, his voice tight and unruly, skin rupturing.

'What we can do,' his father had said, swinging a wrench around one finger.

He swings into the parking lot and his usual space and finds Miller waiting for him on the kerb, a harness in hand. 'Let's go,' he says.

They don't have to travel far. They round the observation deck beneath the first tower, and see the two tired-looking Highway Patrol officers. This time there is one man – possibly one of the two from the last time, but his back is turned and Jack can't tell – and a woman, short and slight with red hair tied in a stubby ponytail at the nape of her neck.

'He's responsive but jumpy,' the female officer says to Jack as he passes. She presses a hand to her mouth. 'Oops. Wrong word.' She has a small scar bisecting her lower lip. He stares at her and she smiles. 'Good luck.'

The man standing on the chord is in his late thirties, perhaps early forties, Jack guesses, squinting against the sinking sun as the last blaze of it bounces off the bonnets of the cars speeding past. The sky above them is turning a dark and bright blue, and Jack glances up at it as he climbs over the railing. *Easy does it*, he tells himself. *All going to be okay.*

'Get back,' the man shouts, before Jack's feet have even touched the beam. 'Stay away from me!'

He is crying; jagged, hitching sobs which shake his body. His suit is shabby and does not fit him properly; the sleeves too long and the legs shapeless. The cuffs of the trousers are dusty – sandy, Jack thinks, looking closer – and his face is unshaven. His hair is thinning and unstyled, tufts of it drifting up from his head in the calmest of evening breezes. He stares frantically from Jack to Miller, still sobbing with an open mouth which makes wheezing, hollow sounds as he struggles to breathe.

Jack glances at Miller, who indicates with a casual motion of one hand that Jack should begin talking. Jack does not know why people keep assigning him this role.

'Okay,' he says to the man. 'I'm not moving. Tell me what you're doing here.' This is not, he realises, a question with many potential answers.

'I have to do it,' the man says.

'You don't have to do anything,' Jack says. 'What's your name?'

The man turns to look at him. Snot runs onto his top lip. A gull lets out a single cry overhead. 'Matthew,' he says.

'Okay, Matthew. Why don't you let us help you back over? There are people who can help you.'

Help, help, help.

'It's too late.'

'It's never too late,' Jack says, and hates himself.

'What do you know?' Matthew reaches a shaking hand

behind him, feeling for the steel bars. A flash of gold catches the twilight. *That's something*, Jack thinks, with something like relief, something like horror. He grabs at it, wonders if it will keep them afloat.

'You married?'

Eyes slide sideways to look at him. 'Yeah.' Matthew takes a stuttering breath.

'What's she like?'

Somewhere in the city, Elsa presses Play on a TV show she has taped. She watches Britney Spears deliver her verdict on Arin Ray's rendition of 'American Boy'. Simon Cowell smiles. She tries not to cry.

'She's great,' Matthew says, and he hiccups. 'She doesn't deserve this.'

'That's probably true,' Jack says. His harness feels damp in his hand. 'I don't think anyone deserves this.'

'She deserves better than me.'

That's true, Jack says, clenching his hands into fists. 'This isn't the answer,' he says.

'What is?'

I wish I knew, Jack thinks, and he has to fight a horrible urge to laugh. 'Go home to your wife,' he says instead, his voice quiet. 'Nothing is worth this.' He looks at the man's watery eyes, the bubble of snot which swells and shrinks with each breath. He holds his gaze, willing himself not to glance at Miller, who creeps closer, unexpectedly agile. 'Nothing is worth this,' he says again, quieter still, but somehow the words are harder to get out.

'I don't know what to do any more.' Matthew's voice is just a whisper. It drifts down to the waves and sinks beneath the blackness. Seals circle it; a lost and lonely shoe bumps it on its way down.

'Me neither,' Jack says, and the two men look at each other.

It takes for ever; it takes a second. Matthew reaches out his hand to Jack and starts to cry again. 'I don't want to die,' he says, and as he does, both Jack and Miller swoop in. They grab his arms and they heave him up between them. He pivots for a second on the edge of the railing, suspended, and the two Highway Patrol officers are suddenly there to help pull him over. His body is surprisingly slight; it feels unexpectedly other. When his weight is transferred and they are left alone on the chord, Jack feels significantly lighter.

As he climbs back over, his legs wobble and give way. He sits on the kerb and watches the policemen who have just arrived restrain Matthew. The blue lights of the silent sirens flicker back and forth across the faces of the small crowd. He wants to go back to his car and drive away. He wants to watch Simon Cowell smile.

Miller is already leaving, a phone pressed to his ear. He stoops as he walks, digging his chin towards his chest. His silhouette bobs into the darkness. Jack pushes himself up from the pavement and stands watching as the Highway Patrol officers try to lead people away. Matthew is still crying, the hooping sounds carrying across the water where they fade like smoke over Alcatraz. A policeman cuffs his wrists behind his back and pretends not to notice the crying. As he and his partner lead Matthew towards the car, he nods at Jack. But Jack looks at Matthew, who looks back. There should be relief but instead he is searching; he is trying to see if in these tears there is a regret, a decision to come back. *We always come back*, he thinks, and he doesn't know why. He doesn't know why the two of them have become a we. He looks at Matthew, and Matthew looks back.

'Remember,' Jack says, but the words run out before the sentence. As Matthew is folded into the car's back seat, he catches another glimpse of the wedding ring.

2003

They arrive at Goldsmiths an hour behind schedule; her father's car neatly stacked with her boxed belongings. She and Anna squash into the back amongst her bin-bagged duvet and her brand-new books, and Anna looks out of the window often, bottom lip wobbling. Her parents are bright and chatty though occasionally she catches a dangerous thickness in her mother's voice.

'You okay back there, girls?' her dad asks, for perhaps the tenth or eleventh time, and she remembers car journeys from long ago, babies in car seats and shiny new shoes.

'Almost there, I think,' her mother says, looking round to smile at her, and her heart jumps a little.

She still can't quite believe this is happening. A year ago, getting ready to apply, she remembers lining up options; practical, mature, plan-type options: Law. Management. Finance. She remembers her dad passing her at the kitchen table, running a finger over one of the course titles. She remembers the way he looked at her face, then pulled out a chair.

'What you thinking, then?' he asked, and she tried on the ideas of the courses for size, wondering if she could make them fit. She remembers him listening, remembers him asking 'What do you actually *want* to do, though?' and she remembers the way he listened again, remembers the way he batted away the worries she had worried they would have; worries which had by imaginary osmosis become her worries too – art isn't really a career, what can I do with it, am I good enough – and the way he simply smiled and pushed away the prospectuses. 'You must do what you want,' he told her, and she remembers the last part best. *We believe in you.*

Tucked safely among the taped-up boxes and bin bags of clothing, it is the thing she is bringing with her which is most important of all.

The halls of residence are a pale brick, neat rows of square windows up each side like spider's eyes. She stares out of the car window as they park, her application statement echoing in her head. *Art is my.* A short expanse of grass, a beige feathery bush stirring in the breeze. *A career in illustration is.* An undergraduate volunteer in a yellow vest motions them forward. *I am a.* The same girl beams up at her a minute or two later as she hands her a set of keys, shows her how to use the fob to enter the building. *I will be.* Anna is sniffing beside her.

In the stairwell now, breathing in their scent of plastic and new things. She feels carsick and tired, each step an effort. She thinks of Hannah, halfway to Manchester, their other friends on routes which stretch out from home like fireworks. None are in London. She can't quite remember, now, why *she* is in London.

At the top of the stairs, they find the door to her floor wedged open with a small box marked 'Books and shit'. Doors in the corridor gape open too, more boxes and empty bin bags lolling across the denim-blue carpet. The sounds of a television are already coming from someone's room; a song on the radio

That was Jet with 'Are You Gonna

in another. They pass the kitchen, where someone else's mother is carefully stacking plates and pans into one of the narrow cupboards.

To her room, the fourth on the left, the door unlocked. She pushes it open, her mother close behind her. It sticks in its frame at first, needs a shove, and when it opens it lets out a yelp which echoes down the corridor.

She stands in the centre of the room, looking around. It is small and square, the tang of paint still hanging in the air, but it is light and in the distance there is the faintest view of the city. She has a headache. The single bed, its mattress wrapped in plastic, crackles as Anna sits down heavily on it. The bin bag of clothes she's been carrying is left to sag at her feet.

'Plenty of space for you to come and stay,' Elsa tells her, and Anna manages a smile.

'Enough space in here for all of us to stay,' her mum says in a too-cheerful voice, and Elsa manages a smile for her too.

She walks over to the window, runs a finger along its frame; freshly painted in thick, uneven white paint. From it, she can look out over the car park, where a steady trickle of families and belongings work their way into the building like ants. Her father stands in the doorway behind her, shifting the boxes into a neat line with his toe.

'Best get the rest of it in,' he says. 'Then maybe we can all go for dinner.'

'Yes,' Anna says, brightening a little as she traipses out after him. 'I think I saw a Mexican place down the road. I love Mexican!'

She stays behind and arranges her things as the three of them ferry the last boxes from the car. The sounds of the flat go on, but she hears them less as she watches her hands place and replace things, touching them with fingertips, bunching them in fists. She peels back the bed's plastic and spreads on a sheet, a mushroom cloud of fabric softener family scent filling the room.

'We'll do all this, love.' Her mother is balanced on the small desk, stacking books onto the shelves above. 'You go and introduce yourself.'

Back out in the hallway, her heart begins thumping. She goes to the door beside hers and hesitates. No voices come from inside but there is certainly sound; the rustling of bags and the occasional cardboard scratching of boxes on the floor.

She knocks, hating the faltering sound, preparing her introduction in her head. A boy at the other end of the corridor yells 'Mum!' in no particular direction.

The door opens and a pretty blonde girl grins at her. 'Hi.' Dressed in shorts and a hoody, she is holding a wad of BluTack in one hand and a glass of wine in the other.

'Hi. I'm your neighbour, I'm Elsa.'

'Oh good, you're a girl. Come in! Have a glass of wine. I'm Jenn, by the way.'

The door swings shut; it is as easy as that. Her parents knock an hour later, halfway through a conversation about gap years (neither has had one) and boyfriends (both have just disposed of one). She leaves her glass of wine amongst the stacks of books and clothes on Jenn's desk and goes out to them. Her room has been transformed; everything in a place, everything in order. Her posters are tacked at perfect angles; framed photos are lined up on the windowsill.

'Well, this is it.'

'Have fun. Enjoy yourself. Call us tomorrow and let us know how you're getting on.'

'Thank you so much for doing this.'

'Don't drink too much.'

'Love you.'

'Text me.'

'Don't forget to tape that thing at seven.'

'Be safe.'

'Love you.'

'Love you.'

They nod, they hug. She holds Anna that little bit longer, that little bit tighter.

And then another door swings shut, and they are gone.

That evening, they round up the others and go across the concrete car park to the halls' bar. Jenn orders a bottle of wine for the girls while the boys drink foamy pints from plastic glasses. Refilling her glass, Elsa looks around at them, trying to keep their names, homes and courses straight. Beside her there is Lily, a flower with a floral dress, and then Max, chain-smoking and leaning back in his chair. Barney sits next to Jenn, smart in a shirt and asking too many questions, cracking too many jokes. Lastly, there is Emily, the girl who will leave the next day without telling anyone why, but who sits with them tonight chatting away, laughing at Barney's jokes. There are still other rooms in their corridor to be filled, but for now, it's just them.

She refills Lily's glass and then Jenn's. Emily shakes her head and presses a hand over hers. All around the room, she can hear the same questions being asked:

Where are you from?

What are you studying?

Do you smoke?

Her own answers are already well worn and shaped to her, like old shoes.

Shropshire.

Art.

Only when I drink.

Their group is now past these introductory stages; moving on to music, film, opinions. The first fragile in-jokes and catchphrases are already forming, there is talk of having roasts on Sundays and film nights on Fridays. She settles back in her seat, brings her glass to her mouth to hide her grin. Is it how she has hoped? She can't even remember, now, what she had wanted. This supersedes it instantly; eclipses it totally. It is all possibility, all potential; it is intoxicating.

Jenn, hand halfway across the table to accept a cigarette from Max, catches her eye. 'What are you smiling about?'

It is a moment of euphoric, unguarded honesty.

I'm just really happy.

2012

The back yard was perhaps once smooth but now its surface is broken apart, its wall slowly crumbling with its barbed-wire crown. Weeds push their way through and she has watched them grow and it is now enough. Today – a Sunday – is the day. Weeds cannot be allowed to grow. She does not want the cracks to take hold.

Jack pushes at a mossy corner with the toe of his boot, hands in his pockets. 'Going to rain,' he says.

She grasps an offending stub of green and pulls it out, fist full of grainy soil. She studies it upended; fine filigree of silvery roots against a storm-grey sky. 'I liked last night,' she says. 'I still ache though.'

'I liked it too,' he says, crouching to study a large hollow in the concrete of the wall.

'I've never done that before.'

'You're a natural.'

She glances up and the temperature drops. 'You have, I suppose.'

He straightens, moves his attention to a wide crack in one corner of the yard. 'It doesn't matter, does it?'

She tosses the weed aside. 'Of course not.'

He laughs. 'I love it when you're jealous.'

'Yes, I've noticed.'

'You do this thing with your mouth. It's very attractive.'

'I'm glad you find tormenting me so appealing.'

He passes behind her, heading for his toolbox. His fingers graze the nape of her neck. 'If I remember correctly, you enjoy being tormented very much.'

She stirs, pushes the hair away from her face. 'Your memory rarely serves you correctly.'

He retreats, chisel in hand. Back in his corner, he begins chipping away. She watches the muscles in his back as he works. The blonde of his hair seems silver in the grey of the day; the summer's heat it has held retreating.

'Tell me something,' she says. 'Can you remember all of them?'

'Elsa,' he says. 'It's not my fault I've had a lot of sex.'

She is silent, still on her knees in the centre of the yard. She looks down at her hands, at the dirt under her nails.

'Most of them,' he says with a shrug. 'None of them were like you.'

She uncurls, catlike, and smiles. 'You would say that.'

'Probably. It's true though.'

'It's freezing out here,' she says, pulling the sleeves of his jumper further over her hands. Her chin dips into the neck of her coat.

'Think how nice it'll be in summer.'

'Me sunbathing, you barbecuing ...'

He runs a hand over the wall. 'Sexist.'

'You know your place.'

'Thankfully you're always here to put me in it.'

She laughs, pulling up another clump of weed. 'I take my job very seriously.'

'And you do it well.'

Something sharp is on the air; a scent like smoke, a thing which hangs between them. They shiver; they bristle. In the house next door, a child begins to cry. The first fat raindrops begin to fall.

'Let's go inside,' he says. As they cross the short space, he puts an arm around her.

In the house there is little light and the kitchen has a sticky, stale smell. Last night's plates are stacked and crusting beside the sink. He pushes in the plug and runs the water, wordlessly sliding the dishes under the surge of bubbles.

'Sorry,' she says, shedding her jacket. 'I was too busy with ...' She trails off.

He turns to look at her, surprised. 'It's fine.'

She takes a tea towel and stands beside him. The plate feels fragile in her fingers. 'This week's my housework week,' she says. 'I promise. What a terrible wife I am.'

There is a bang from somewhere far off. He starts, and something painful shifts position in his chest.

'Don't be silly,' he says. She loves the way the word sounds in his voice; one long line of sound. 'You're not the housekeeper.'

'I know, but that's the deal, isn't it – you go out to work and I take care of you. That's only fair.'

'Elsa.' He puts another plate down on the draining board. Its suds run back to the sink, some left stranded on the steel. 'That's not the deal. I didn't bring you here to take care of me. I brought you here to have fun.'

They are kind words but suddenly she feels close to tears. 'The Chicago house,' she says. 'The woman who lived there with you. Did she take good care of you?'

He looks at her and then down at his hands. 'Yes,' he says. 'She did. For a while.'

She reaches out to take the plate, dries it with hot hands. He is still watching her. They are silent, and she keeps her eyes on the plate. 'So, do you like seeing me jealous now?' she asks.

'No.' He takes the plate from her, puts it back down on the side. He moves up close to her, draws her into his shadow. 'No, I don't. I'm sorry.' His voice is low; its weight pulls his mouth down towards hers. 'I don't live in Chicago any more,' he says, and her eyes close.

'You live here,' she says, and his lips graze hers.

'And so do you.' He runs a hand up her back, taking a tide

of the jumper with it. He slides it over her skin, tugs it over her head. It pools softly on the ground, one arm extended. They are sinking slowly, her eyes still closed. He unbuttons her shirt as he presses her against the cabinets, his forehead against hers.

'You can ask, if you want,' he whispers, but before she can speak, he kisses her.

Fingers skim skin, light slides slowly across the ceiling. The tap drip drip drips. The child is crying again. A bus passes the house; aboard it a woman breaks up with her boyfriend by text and another watches the street lights stutter into life. At the top of Market, two homeless men are arguing about a lost shoe. A third watches from his place on City Hall's steps.

Out on the bridge, two teenagers climb the struts of the North Tower; a six-pack in a plastic bag slung over the first's arm, two neatly rolled joints tucked behind the ears of the other. Fog obscures the top; they climb above the clouds. In the parking lot, Bart Miller climbs into his car and drives away. He is planning to call his daughter tonight. His daughter, in Massachusetts, is bathing her two small children and wondering if her father will call.

And somewhere, in some other time, there is a girl who has just started university, and a young man who is attending a birthday party.

2003

It is a birthday party for Franklin's wife, Nicole. Franklin, a friend from sunny states and short-term gigs those long and short years ago, is the one who made him go to Chicago, and he is the person who has made him stay. He is the person who has got him his job: a roller-coaster construction at the Six Flags theme park, and he is the person who checks up on him without checking; who knows enough about England and the accident that he knows not to ask. By now, six months into the Six Flags job, Jack is safely established in the crew. There are plenty of weekends spent playing golf or watching games with Franklin and Denny, another member of the team he has become close to. He has left the studio he moved into on landing and now has an apartment with rooms; at twenty-seven, he has his first double bed.

He has only met Nicole once or twice. Nonetheless, when Jack arrives at the party there are huge smiles and hugs, thanks for coming let me take your coat I can't believe Frank organised this all for me. Happy birthday, he says in return, handing her the flowers he has bought at a 7-Eleven down the street.

He makes his way through to the kitchen, where Denny is drinking beer and bottles of wine and spirits are lined up on the counter. It is October outside and dark already; people's words condense against the window. He works his way over to Denny and they make small talk, sports talk. Franklin comes and goes, bringing with him stray guests; whiskery men with leathery handshakes, plump women with smudged lipstick. Jack is the youngest there by quite a margin; he drinks continuously but cannot get drunk.

An hour in and Denny's attention is held by a small woman with large hips and a dark tan, her hand on his arm and her head bobbing as she talks. Someone is playing a Stevie Wonder album in the living room. Jack leans back on the counter and watches people mill about, conversations stall and restart, drinks spill. His own, the seventh or eighth of the evening, remains firmly in hand. He looks at Denny, at his neat moustache, and runs a finger across his own lip, wondering if he could pull one off himself. The head-bobbing woman laughs and it is a large sound, its note thunderous.

And then there is a hand on his arm, Nicole beside him.

'You two should meet,' she says, and then she slips away.

The particulars of the girl she has left behind register with him slowly and methodically (perhaps he is drunk after all). She has hair which is gold and not blonde and shines sharply in the light. She has green eyes. She is smiling. 'I'm Beth.' She is holding out a hand to him. 'Beth Coogan.'

She is wearing a red dress. It is a neat dress; old-fashioned, simple and straight and red. A little too large for her, the neckline baggy and exposing the bones of her chest. Her arms are bare and the skin of them is smooth and sun-soaked.

'Jack,' he says, and her hand is small and strong in his. 'Nice to meet you.'

'How do you know Nicole?'

'I don't, not really. I work with her husband.'

'Oh, on the roller coaster?'

'Yeah.' He sips his drink, shifts his weight uncertainly. 'How about you?'

'Well, actually, I work with Nicole. We're both assistants at the same company.'

'Are you from Chicago?'

'No, Wisconsin. I'm a country girl.' She studies him, birdlike. 'Are you British?'

He lets out an awkward half-laugh and regrets it. 'Sort of.'

Another smile is playing on her lips; her soft, watercolour lips. 'I've never met someone who was sort-of British before.' She looks behind him at the rows of bottles. 'I'm pretty thirsty,' she says.

He reaches for a cup behind him, her hip pressed to his. The red dress rises and falls over her ribs. He pours wine, he watches her breathe. He speaks, and he watches her laugh.

Even now, he watches her laugh.

2012

It begins to rain as she leaves the house, the drops exploding fatly on the pale path. She knocks on the door and edges closer to it, seeking shelter. She weighs the paperback in her hand and looks down at a spiral of ink at the corner of the back cover. The chilled breeze snakes tendrils of hair across her face as she runs a finger over the mark. A deep scar, the work of a cheap biro; someone testing to see if it still had ink. She flips the book back over and looks at the peeling foil of the title. The girl beneath it stares mournfully back at her, a lurid sun setting behind her slender left shoulder.

She shifts her attention to the book in the other hand; stiff and new and unread. *Everything You Need*. It still has a small yellow sticker on its back cover; the name of her favourite Mission thrift store's name faintly printed at the top and '$1.50' stamped underneath. She tucks the sunset girl under her armpit and hurriedly peels it off as the door opens.

'Hello?' Pearl has a way of answering the door as if it is a telephone. Her glasses are steamed up at the bottoms of their lenses, and her hair sticks up on the left-hand side, a candyfloss wave across her head.

Elsa holds up the sunset girl. 'I brought your book back.' She holds up hers. 'And I thought you might like to borrow this.'

'Oh.' Pearl considers the two covers for a moment, her head bobbing. 'Great. Come in.'

Inside the house, breathing in its warm, bread-sweet air, she follows Pearl, who leads her, unusually, to the kitchen. She feels a small burst of triumph, as if she has conquered a new level of a computer game called Being Friends with Pearl. The kitchen is like a distorted version of their own: smaller fridge, larger table, curtains where they have blinds. She puts the books down on the table's plastic tablecloth.

'Do you want some coffee? I was just about to have a cup.'

'Thanks, that'd be great.'

She watches as Pearl pours the coffee, her hands trembling. It is an effort to resist offering help, but she is learning. The rules in Pearl's house are simple and clear.

'So, what did you think of the book?' Pearl places two mugs of coffee on the table and pulls out a chair. She lowers herself into it, gnarled hands flat against the tabletop.

Elsa turns it round on the table and pretends to study it,

avoiding the sunset girl's eyes. 'I thought it was ... very romantic.'

Pearl smirks. 'You didn't take me for a romantic, did you?'

'I have to confess, I was surprised.'

'The old broad next door likes a love story.'

'You're full of surprises.'

Pearl takes a gulp of her drink. 'So are you, probably.'

'Probably.' She takes a sip of her own coffee, pushing its silt across her tongue. 'How's the knee?'

'Much better.' Her neighbour considers her. 'How are you?'

'Fine. Good.' She is surprised at the brittle way the words feel leaving her mouth.

Her neighbour nods. She looks at Elsa over the wings of her glasses, picks up a book from the edge of the table and slides it towards Elsa. 'Here. It's the sequel. I just finished it.'

'You're a fast reader.'

'I gotta get my kicks somewhere.'

Elsa laughs. 'Don't we all.'

There is a noise from somewhere in the house; a tiny sparkling shatter. 'Oh damn,' Pearl says, putting down her cup with a start. 'I almost forgot they were here, they were so quiet.'

'Oh, you have the children?'

The phone begins to ring. 'Damn.' Pearl rises, steadying herself against the counter as she goes, gold rings clinking against the granite. 'Could you –'

'Sure.' Elsa puts down her coffee. And then, to herself: 'No problem.'

The door to the living room is open and the cause of the sound is instantly identifiable: a light bulb fallen from its fixture; its fragments strewn across the floor. She stoops to try to gather them, places the pieces she can collect carefully on a shelf of the nearest bookcase.

'You guys okay?' she asks. Both children are kneeling in front of the glass coffee table, undisturbed by the broken light. Sprawled in awkward positions in a circle around them, as if felled by a disastrous phenomenon whose centre is these two small people, are about twenty plastic figurines. She steps closer and sees farmyard animals, a Barbie face down beside the armchair, a Buzz Lightyear doing unthinkable things to a hapless goat a foot or so from the table.

Sam, who is pushing a cow across the surface of the table with a determined squeal, glances over his shoulder. 'Hi,' he says.

'Hi,' she says. 'Your grandma has to take a call so I thought I'd come and see what you two were up to. That's okay, isn't it?'

Sam considers this. 'I guess it's okay if you know some games,' he says.

'How about hide-and-seek?'

Sam shakes his head. His hair flies out and from side to side.

'No,' Elsa says, relieved. She taps her chin with a finger as she thinks. '"What's the time, Mr Wolf"?'

The boy studies her, eyes narrowed. 'No,' he says eventually, turning back to the cow.

His sister sits with her back to them, a toy chicken in one hand and a tractor in the other. Holding them close to her face, she moves them back and forth, a silent dialogue whose outcome is uncertain.

'I'm not shy,' Sam says suddenly, turning back to Elsa.

'No,' she agrees. 'I can see that.'

'Skye's not shy either,' he says, glancing at his sister, who has removed the chicken from a clearly heated situation and is now pushing the tractor back and forth across the carpet. 'She just can't really talk yet.' He considers this. 'Or she might be shy but we don't know yet.' At the sound of her name, the baby looks up.

Skye. 'I suppose that's true. How old is Skye now?'

'One. She came out of my mommy's tummy.'

At this, Skye laughs and crawls a few steps towards them.

Sam points towards Elsa's hand. 'What's that?'

'It's a book I'm borrowing from your grandma.'

'Oh. Gramma *really* likes books.' He elongates the 'l's of really, rocking cheerfully from side to side.

'I do too.' She places the book primly on her knee. 'Do you?'

'Yeah. But my mommy has to read to me.' He pauses. 'Unless the book is really short.'

'Well, soon you'll be able to read anything you want whenever you want. That'll be good, won't it?'

Sam nods, pleased. He is edging closer, a small finger tracing the letters on the cover. 'What's this one about?'

'I haven't read it yet but I think it's probably a love story.'

This nod is small, solemn. 'Gramma likes love stories.'

'Most women do,' Elsa says, lowering her voice.

'Do you?'

She has to think about her answer. 'Yes,' she says eventually. 'Some.'

'I like stories with trains,' Sam says, leaning on the arm and looking up at her. 'Or animals.'

Skye glances up from her seat at Elsa's feet and waves the cow figurine around in agreement.

'I love trains,' Elsa agrees. 'And some animals are actually better than people.'

Sam gazes up at her, chewing his lower lip with tiny white milk teeth. The kitchen door opens with a squeal.

'You should come back some time,' he says. 'I'll bring you my best book — it has a lion in it.'

'And a train?'

He shakes his head. 'The lion's really big.'

'Well, they're the best kind.'

'Yeah.' Sam considers her for a moment and then spins on his heel, plucking the cow from Skye's hand. He resumes its journey against the coffee table, head bent so that his hair almost brushes the glass. Skye heaves herself up by the fabric of the chair, round eyes on Elsa.

In the pocket of her skirt, Elsa's phone vibrates. She slides it out and reads the message.

Late home tonight. Love you.

*

On the sofa that evening, pyjama bottoms tucked into a fat pair of fluffy socks and the television sending blue light flickering across the dark ceiling, she mouths phrases to herself.

'I've loved you all my life,' she says. 'It's always been you.'

She watches a Hollywood couple embrace on the small screen and then she changes the channel.

'I've loved you all my life,' she whispers to a newsreader. 'I knew from the moment I saw you.'

She pulls her phone across the sofa cushions and stares at it. 'We met in a bar,' she says, 'and we just knew.' She unlocks and then locks the keypad. 'We met on New Year's Eve,' she says, 'and we just knew.' She pushes the phone aside again and changes the channel.

'He's the one,' she tells Simon Cowell. Simon Cowell glances at Britney Spears. 'He makes everything make sense.' She pours another glass of wine. Simon Cowell raises an eyebrow. 'Oh, what do you know,' she says, and she closes her eyes.

2004

Returning to London after Christmas, she practically runs up the steps from the Tube. There is a chunk of her mum's Christmas cake in foil in her handbag and the train journey has been spent exchanging texts with Hannah, but the first sight of her street brings with it relief. She drags her suitcase along the crooked pavement, coat hanging open and handbag sliding down her arm. Conversations they will all have are already forming in her head; her tongue feels heavy with sentences she can't wait to eject. She fumbles her key into the lock, listening for sounds of life as she enters the cold hallway.

She dumps her suitcase in her room and then heads for the only light in the hallway, leaking from under Max's door. She knocks, glancing back along the empty corridor.

'Yeah?'

She opens the door, letting out the light. Max is in his chair while Lily sits on the bed, still in her coat. They both beam at her.

'All right, mate?' Max says.

'I just got back too,' Lily says, patting the end of the bed. 'Come sit down.'

They recap half-heartedly, finding home-town connections too tedious to explain. Instead, they plan. There is much planning to do and they do it eagerly, taking feverish drags on the spliff Max passes between them. Jenn and Barney's return the next day secures things, solidifies them.

Lectures are few and far between that year but her calendar is always filled, activities marked out in different colours; neat strips of green, pink and yellow threading through the weeks. Netball Club, Yoga Society, Drama Club. Bar crawl, speed dating, quiz night. Every white space is filled with drinks at the hall bar, or the union, or the pub around the corner from their building. Lectures and tutorials are spent with Jenn, a fellow art student. Dinnertimes often with Max, hunched over his wok or his George Foreman grill, T-shirt and jeans and his glasses if he is hungover, his hair sticking out in tufts. Her own first tentative attempts at cooking are a surprising success, an unexpected hobby.

Anna visits one weekend near the end of January. Her hair is newly highlighted, her figure slim in a woollen dress. They take her out and Elsa watches her drink shots, watches her dance, arms up in the air, hips swaying. She watches the way Max and Barney watch her too and a wave of relief sweeps over her. She pulls her sister close, holds her phone out to Lily.

'Can you take a photo of us?' she asks, shouting to be heard over the music. 'I need a new photo of me and my baby sister.'

That night, they top-and-tail in her tiny bed, her sister's soft feet beside her. They whisper to each other after they have turned out the light, heads propped up on pillows.

'Where did you meet him?' she asks. 'What's he like?'

'At college.' Anna giggles. 'I don't know! He's nice.'

'Fit?'

'Obviously!'

'What do Mum and Dad think?'

'They like him.'

'Of course they do. Trust you to bring home Mr Perfect.' She squeezes her sister's toes. 'Anna and Mark, sitting in a tree …'

Anna kicks out, laughing. 'Stop it!'

'I suppose it's better than the year you had an imaginary boyfriend.'

'Oh right, like you never had actual, out-loud conversations with your poster of J from 5ive.'

'It wasn't J, it was Scott!'

They are both laughing now. They lie back in the darkness and listen to each other breathe. Slowly, sleep grows closer.

'Your friends are nice,' Anna murmurs.

'They liked you.'

'It was really fun tonight.'

'Mmm.' Elsa's eyes are closing.

'Everything's different now,' Anna says, her voice barely a whisper, and Elsa is asleep before she can reply.

They eat breakfast the next day in a little café down the road, where the tablecloths are checked plastic and clipped to the tabletop with small metal brackets. Only Barney joins them, the others still sleeping off their hangovers.

'Are you arty like your sister?' He spears a sausage on his fork as he speaks, studying Anna as he bites a chunk from it.

She shakes her head, pushing beans onto her fork. 'No. I'll probably do business studies. Or history.'

Barney finishes the sausage, nodding. 'You should talk to Max. He does history.'

'And you're politics, right?'

Pleased she has remembered, he spends the rest of breakfast telling her about his course. Elsa scrolls idly through her phone, picture after picture of the night before. These are the moments, she thinks, but the thought is unfinished. She sips cold tea and smiles.

Afterwards, she walks Anna to the station, their arms linked. There is brilliant and rare January sunshine, their breath cloudy on the crisp air. The streets are quiet, the station sleepy. She holds her sister's hand as they look up at the departures board.

'Will you be okay?' she asks. 'Do you know where you're going?'

Anna rolls her eyes. '*Yes*. I'll be fine.'

'Thanks for coming.'

Her sister's fingers squeeze hers. 'Call me soon, okay?'

'I will. You too. I want to hear all about this Mark.'

Their heads rest against each other's. 'One day,' Anna says, as an old man totters past, 'when we're really old, we'll look back at this and remember it.'

'You think so?'

'Yeah. We'll say "That's where it all started." And then we'll say, "Look at us now, can you believe it ..." and our children and their children will stop listening because they'll have heard it all before.'

Elsa is silent, smelling the vanilla shampoo smell of her little sister. 'Well, that'll be nice,' she says after a while. 'I'll like that.'

2012

On another wind-chilled Thursday, Jack pulls his car up alongside Alex's building. Elsa looks out through the foggy window at the peeling blue paint and the rusted fire escape.

'I like it,' she says, and Jack smiles at her.

She glances down at the bowl – thick-cut glass, engraved with fat pears and curling leaves and borrowed from Pearl – of salad on her lap. 'Are you sure this is all they wanted us to bring?'

'Yep.' He twirls his keys around a finger. 'Not nervous, are you?'

She gives him a withering look but her hands tighten on the bowl. 'Don't be ridiculous.'

The salad tilts drunkenly towards the kerb as she climbs out of the car and she rights it, hair blowing against her glossed lips. He laughs as he comes around the car to her. 'You all right there?'

She glances back at the car. 'Will it be okay left here?'

'What do you mean?'

'Well, obviously you're going to drink and we'll have to come and collect it tomorrow. Will it be safe?'

He shrugs. 'We'll see how it goes.'

'What does that mean?'

'I might drive home.'

She presses her lips together. 'Okay.'

He leads her to the building's entrance, a hand at the small of her back. A dark-haired guy in a beanie hat is holding the door open, leaning against it to let his girlfriend, who is carrying a huge, cooked turkey in a disposable tray, past. His own arms are full of Tupperware containers of food. He smiles at them as he lets them through. 'Happy Thanksgiving.'

They climb the stairs to the top floor. The carpet is a worn greenish-grey, fraying along the wall. She runs her hand across a dent in the plaster, pausing at the foot of the next flight of stairs to pluck another stray hair from her lower lip. Music plays from one of the apartments, the lyrics in Spanish. 'One more flight,' he says.

At the top of the stairs, he turns left and pushes through a door into a short stretch of corridor with three front doors. He knocks on one, pulling his phone from his jeans pocket to check the screen. Here there is a strong smell of cooking meat and something sweeter. She shifts the bowl of salad from one hip to the other, then straightens her dress. It is a cream dress with a collar and short sleeves, and though Jack does not know this, it was bought for her by a boyfriend four or five years ago.

Alex opens the door, curls haphazard, and grins at Elsa. 'Well, we meet at last.'

'We do.' She steps forward to kiss him on the cheek. 'Thanks so much for inviting us.'

'Thanks for coming. It's great to see you.' He ushers her in, then turns to Jack. 'But who invited you?'

Jack clips him around the side of the head. 'Respect your elders. How many times do I have to tell you?'

Alex looks at Elsa, jerking a thumb in Jack's direction. 'He this rude to you?'

'All the time.'

'Then let's get you a drink.' He leads her along the short hallway, which bends sharply to the right and takes them past two closed doors and the bathroom – from which recent shower steam still billows softly out – before ending abruptly in a small living area. It has wide windows which look out across the city, and two sagging, overstuffed sofas which have been pushed up against them to make space for the makeshift dining table which has been assembled from three smaller ones in the centre of the room. A woman rises from the arm of the nearest sofa, smiling.

'Stephanie, this is Elsa and Jack,' Alex says.

'Hi,' she says, stepping forward. She is strikingly beautiful; creamy coffee skin and masses of blue-black hair falling in waves across her delicate shoulders. A tiny turned-up nose and plum-

plump mouth, wide eyes framed with glossy naked lashes.

'Nice to meet you,' Elsa says. The two women have met halfway across the small room. Somehow the salad bowl has found its way in front of Elsa's body.

'It's so good to meet you. You're from London, right?'

'Yes, that's right.'

'I really love London. And you're Jack?'

And she is past, arm extended. 'And this is Claudia,' Alex says, arm around another woman who has just emerged from the kitchen. 'Claudia, this is Elsa.'

'It's great to meet you,' Claudia says. She is tall and willowy, with smooth dark skin and shoulder-length hair which fluffs softly out at the ends. 'We've both probably been a lot lonelier since these two met.'

Elsa laughs. 'We should find our own place to drink.'

'Maybe we should. Here, let me take that for you.' She takes Pearl's bowl and puts it on the table, wedging it between a tray of sliced, pale pink ham, a huge bowl of mashed potato, a tureen of a blackish soup. 'This all looks amazing,' Elsa says. 'Are you sure we couldn't bring anything else?'

'And you lived in Clapham?' Stephanie is asking Jack. *Clapham*. 'What's that like? I don't think we went there.'

'What can I get everyone to drink?' Alex says, pushing a plastic dustbin into the room. Ice and beer bob listlessly in the water inside.

'Can I have a glass of wine?' Elsa asks, as Jack fishes out a beer and says, 'Full of Australians.'

'So what do you think of San Francisco?' Stephanie asks Elsa, who is fiddling with her collar.

'I like it.' She shifts her weight from one heel to the other. 'It's a really lovely city.'

There is a knock at the door and Alex heads out to answer it. 'I hope that's my brother,' Claudia says. 'They're bringing an amazing pie.'

'It's your brother,' Alex says, returning with the guests. 'And they brought a lot of food.'

'Jasper,' Claudia says, pausing to kiss him on both cheeks, 'this is Jack and Elsa, and you know Stephanie. Jack, Elsa, this is my brother, Jasper, and Laura, his wife.'

The resemblance between Jasper and Claudia is striking, and he is equally soft-spoken. He grips Elsa's hand with his cool one, thin gold bands on the index and ring fingers. 'Nice to meet you,' he says, and she thinks how strange a custom it is to say such a thing. So far, meeting her is without adjective; the first blank space on the first blank page. She smiles.

'Nice to meet you, too.'

His wife fiddles with a strand of pale blonde hair as she talks quietly to Claudia, gesturing occasionally towards a joint of beef which has been balanced near the edge of the table.

'Did you have an apartment in London? Or a house?' Stephanie asks.

'Do you want more wine, Elsa?' Alex is already pouring some into her glass. She stares at the red imprint of her lower lip on the glass. When she takes a sip, she positions her mouth carefully over it.

A key turns, the click echoing in the hallway. A rustle of bags, a dropped bottle rolls. 'Fuck,' someone says, and then, 'Honey, I'm home!'

'Where'd he go?' Alex asks Claudia, who shakes her head.

'Hey.' The owner of the voice appears around the corner, the rogue bottle in one hand and two six-packs under the other arm. 'Oh, everyone's here.'

'We thought you were in your room,' Alex says, and then points vaguely in the direction of the others. 'Kevin Pepper, meet Jack Finn and his beautiful woman friend, Elsa. And you know Jasper and Laura, obviously.'

'Hey there.' Kevin Pepper salutes them as he pushes the bag of beer in Alex's direction. He opens the lone one with his teeth as he fumbles in his pocket, eventually pulling out a battered pack of cigarettes. Young and unshaven, he has wild, mousy hair which stands back from his head but is unable to escape the hand which he runs through it every minute or two. The hand in question is encased in a fingerless glove; its pair is peeled off with his teeth before he lights his cigarette. They watch him smoke; the single coil of grey circling up and around his head.

'Is this your first Thanksgiving?' Claudia asks Elsa.

'Yes,' Elsa replies, running a thumb around the edge of the lipstick mark, which has begun to smear. 'I didn't really know what to expect.'

'Well, they're different everywhere, everyone has their own traditions.'

'Sure,' Kevin Pepper agrees, flicking ash towards the bin of beer. 'My family's was getting loaded and then fighting in the street.'

'He loves to tell that one,' Alex tells Elsa. 'Pepper loves pretending he's from the ghetto.'

'I don't need to pretend, my friend,' Pepper replies, draining his beer. 'Now, English Elsa, I should tell you that the Thanksgiving motto in this house is "Go hard or go home".'

'I know that one,' Elsa says. 'Don't worry about me.'

'Fill the lady's glass,' Pepper says, and there is another knock at the door.

'That'll be Chase,' Alex says.

'Full house!' In Alex's absence, Pepper takes it upon himself to fill Elsa's glass. He spins away, going to the bin to collect two beers which he presses into Jack and Jasper's hands. 'Maybe we need more beer.' He flicks the stub of his cigarette into the beer's water.

'I loved Camden,' Stephanie says. 'Camden Lock, right?'

'Here's Chasey boy,' Alex says, 'and he's brought us actual food he actually cooked.'

'You're kidding,' Jack says.

'I am not.'

'Chase, this is Elsa,' Jack says, putting an arm around her. 'You've heard all about her, she's heard next to nothing about you.'

'Probably a good thing,' Chase says. 'Nice to meet you, Elsa.'

'And you.' She shakes his hand, which is warm and lined and rough. He has short, stubby fingers and a thin face which is beginning to gain jowls. Silver hair has started to creep out around his temples but the rest of his hair is a coarse dark, its specific shade difficult to determine. He smells of petrol. She likes the smell of petrol.

Claudia is retreating into the kitchen, tiny backward steps that are almost invisible. *What's the time, Mr Wolf?* Elsa thinks, and she wonders what Sam is doing for Thanksgiving. Making it to the door, Claudia beckons to Laura and disappears.

'So, Elsa, what do you do?' Jasper taps lightly at the edge of the table with his fingertips. The gold bands flash the beat in the electric strip light.

'Well … I used to be a personal assistant, back in London, but I can't actually work here at the moment, I just have a tourist visa. I'm hoping to get a professional one after this one expires, but I'm not sure if I'll go back to being a PA, maybe – I don't know what else I'd do – it was just a job, really, at the time. When I finished uni I got a bit lost, I somehow ended up in it, and then it was three years later and, well –' Relieved, she runs out of steam, and clamps her lip firmly over the lipstick line, pulling the wine through her teeth.

'Elsa's actually an illustrator,' Jack says, accepting another beer from Pepper. 'She's a very talented artist.'

'That's not at all true,' she says, looking down. A stray strand of scarlet cotton has detached itself from her scarf and is caught in her hair. She watches it drift down to her shoe. 'I mean, I'd love to be some day, but I'm not quite there yet.'

'I used to say that,' Stephanie says, 'but then I realised that you become an artist as soon as you say you're one.'

'What sort of art do you do?' Jack asks.

'I used to paint a lot, and then I went through a charcoal phase. Right now I'm mostly writing poetry.'

'Everyone's an artist in San Francisco,' Pepper says, and lights another cigarette.

'I don't know much about poetry,' Chase says, crunching his beer can in one hand.

'Well, we're all pretty shocked at that revelation,' Jack says, patting him on the back and smiling at Stephanie.

'Here we go,' Laura says, and she and Claudia walk through the room with the turkey balanced between them.

'Wow,' Jack says, and the others echo the word back and forth in a series of soft volleys.

With the turkey safely installed in its place at the centre of the table, they sit. Claudia perches at one end – 'So I can be close to the kitchen' – while Alex slouches beside her on a beanbag, gesturing for Jasper to take the seat at the other end, the head of the table. Stephanie, Laura and Chase are the first to the table and file neatly along its far side, the windows to their backs. Elsa takes her place between Jack and Pepper.

'So everyone just help themselves,' Claudia says, sweeping her hair across one shoulder and immediately fluffing it back out again.

'It all looks great,' Chase says, and they stare. Alex reaches behind him to the bin full of beer and passes one to Claudia.

'Well, I'll start,' Jack says, and reaches out to take a congealed slab of macaroni and cheese.

'This beef looks fantastic,' Elsa tells Laura.

'Ho, wait,' Pepper, who is shovelling spaghetti onto his plate, says. 'We need to tell everyone what we're thankful for.' He laughs, flicking a chunk of chorizo into his mouth.

'Do people actually do that?' Jack asks.

'Sure,' Chase says, 'some people.'

'I'll start,' Alex says. 'I'm thankful for all this food and all this beer.'

Claudia rolls her eyes. 'I'm thankful for having this great place where we can bring us all together, and to finally meet Jack and Elsa, who I was starting to think were Alex's imaginary friends.'

'I'm thankful for such great neighbours,' Stephanie says, raising her bottle towards their hosts.

'I'm thankful for my husband,' Laura says, and Pepper groans.

'I think that's so sweet,' Stephanie says. 'Hey, can somebody pass me those mashed potatoes?'

'I'm thankful that Alex found a girlfriend who can cook and who puts up with him,' Chase says, winking at Claudia.

Jasper runs his fingers across his knife and fork, still in place beside his plate. 'I'm thankful for my wife.'

'Well, I'll second the thanks for the beer,' Pepper says. 'And

I suppose I ought to thank someone for giving me room-mates who aren't total assholes.'

Elsa takes the dish of ham Jack passes to her. 'I'm thankful to be in this city,' she says, slipping a slice onto her plate. 'And for our hosts.'

'It's all pretty much been said for me,' Jack says, 'but I'll add thankful for this place to the mix, and actually, I think it's only you who's a native, Chase —' He glances at Stephanie, who nods. 'Yeah. So maybe we should have a toast to our hosts, Alex and Claudia, and to our host, San Francisco.'

'To San Francisco,' Alex agrees, and glass meets glass.

Elsa nudges Jack. 'I said that.'

'No, you didn't. You said you were thankful to be here.'

'The spaghetti's really good,' Pepper says, topping Elsa's glass up.

Chase shrugs. 'It's the only thing my wife knew how to cook.'

'Chase is divorced,' Jack tells Elsa.

'And not bitter at alllllll,' Alex adds.

Chase laughs along with them. Pepper reaches for more turkey. The sound of the spoon in the stuffing is intimate and wet.

'Jasper and Laura only got married a couple of weeks ago,' Claudia says to Elsa.

'Oh really? Congratulations.'

Laura blushes. 'Thank you.'

'Where did you get married?'

'In Hawaii,' Jasper says. 'It was a dream of Laura's from when she was small.'

'My grandparents took us on holiday there when I was seven,' she explains, studying her plate. 'My mom was very sick and it was their gift to her, I guess. It sounds strange but even though it was a sad time, Hawaii reminds me of being happy. It reminds me of hope.'

'That's beautiful,' Stephanie says, and nods at Alex who is silently offering her a beer.

'It is,' Elsa says. 'Did you get married on the beach?'

'Yes. I know that's kind of tacky.'

'It's not.' Elsa puts down her fork. 'It's not at all.'

'It was just a small ceremony,' Jasper says. 'Just a few guests. Claudia of course, and our parents, and an aunt who came all the way from Belgium. Then Laura's father and her grandparents, two of her cousins and her best friend from childhood.'

'It sounds wonderful,' Elsa says.

'And you get a built-in honeymoon,' Jack says. 'That's pretty smart.'

'Oh, I forgot,' Laura turns to Claudia. 'Did you take a look at Michelle's photos yet?'

'I did.' Claudia lowers her voice. 'Did you see the one —'

'Jack, could you pass me the stuffing?' Stephanie asks.

Elsa turns to Pepper. 'So, what do you do?'

He laughs and lights a cigarette. 'Good question.'

She picks up her fork again and waits. 'I'm from LA,' he says after a long toke. 'And I came here to write.' He laughs again at himself and taps ash onto the edge of his plate. 'But now I'm working at a bar.'

'What do you write?'

'I've got two halves of a novel sitting on a laptop but they don't match. Two beginnings and no ends.' He rolls the cigarette against the plate, sharpening it. 'Now I want to write a screenplay.'

'What about?'

He blows a series of rings, his jaw clicking with each. 'Being at the end of your twenties and fucked up and in the city.' He snorts. 'You know, *On the Road* for the Facebook generation.'

'I hated *On the Road*.'

He raises an eyebrow. 'You serious?'

'Yeah. It's just self-indulgent, self-important shit.' She drinks some more of her wine.

Stephanie is listening by now. 'No way, really?'

Elsa pushes at a piece of ham on her plate. 'Yeah ... I don't know, I don't think it's shocking any more. It's just about a couple of guys who just want to get fucked all the time instead of growing up and facing the real world.' She takes another slug of wine. 'I don't know, it's not my thing.' She drains her glass, cheeks warm. 'I didn't like *Catcher in the Rye*, either,' she finishes, as if this in some way explains her deficiency, putting her glass back down.

Pepper stubs out his cigarette at the edge of a mossy patch of stuffing. 'Well, it's always good to get constructive feedback.'

'Oh, no – I didn't mean ... Your script will be amazing, I'm sure – because it will be modern and relevant, and I don't feel that Kerouac is any more, you know ...'

Stephanie reaches out to take some more mashed potato. 'I totally understand what you're saying but I think he's so relevant, I think those human feelings of isolation and loss are even more relevant in the modern world.'

Jack opens another beer and says, 'Sure, yeah.' Elsa looks sideways at him.

'I haven't read it,' Alex chimes in, 'but me and Claud went to see the movie and I agree with Elsa, it was kind of boring. I fell asleep for some of it.'

'The girl from *Twilight* was in it,' Claudia says.

'And the girl from *Spider-Man*,' Alex adds, forking up more macaroni into his mouth.

Pepper laughs. 'Critical analysis at its finest.' He tops up Elsa's glass and pours one for himself.

'I can't even remember the last time I went to a movie,' Chase says. 'I don't even watch TV any more.'

'Well, that's a lie,' Jack says, grinning. 'I heard you and Andy talking about *X Factor* at work last week.'

Chase shrugs. 'Well, *sometimes* I watch TV, I check the news, you know.'

'You watch *X Factor* religiously,' Alex says. 'You love Demi Lovato.'

'Who the hell is Demi Lovato?' Jack says.

'She used to be a Disney actress and now she's a singer,' Elsa explains. 'She's really good.' She turns to Chase. 'Who's your favourite?'

'Tate, I guess.'

'Mine's Paige. I think she's brilliant.'

Jack shifts in his chair. 'You think you know someone and then you find out they watch *X Factor*.' Everyone laughs. Elsa drinks more wine.

'Well, I don't even have a TV yet,' Stephanie says. 'I have to come visit these guys when I want to watch something.'

'When did you move in?' Jack asks.

'A couple months ago.'

'And where were you before?'

'In San Diego, with my husband. But we're getting divorced so I wanted to be somewhere new. This is like my little bacholerette pad.' She laughs; a sparkling, sharp sound like breaking glass.

'I'm sorry to hear that,' Laura says, and Stephanie shrugs.

'It's really okay. We just aren't right for each other any more, but there's no regrets, I'm glad we got married. I don't think divorce is such a big deal these days.'

'That's because you've never had to pay for one,' Chase says.

'Not bitter at alllllllll.' Alex leans back in his chair as they laugh.

'Seriously, though.' Stephanie fixes Laura with her wide eyes. 'We're still friends. We had a great time together.'

'Would you ever get married again?' Jack asks.

She considers this, a small hand toying with the ends of her hair. 'Probably not.'

He nods, helps himself to more turkey.

'All this talk of weddings is making me nervous,' Alex says, opening another beer. Claudia slaps him lightly on the arm.

'How long have you been together?' Elsa asks.

'Seven years.' Claudia smiles. 'Seven long years.'

'How did you meet?'

'I was building a lift in Claudia's building,' Alex says.

'In New York,' Claudia says.

'And we got to talking. Claud found me irresistible, obviously.'

'Obviously.'

'And you moved to San Francisco when?' Elsa asks.

'Two years ago, when Alex got his job on the bridge.'

'And I followed two months later,' Jasper adds. 'I missed my little sister too much.'

'And then you met me,' Laura says.

'And then I met you.'

'Actually, *I* met you first,' Claudia says. 'And the rest, as they say, is history.'

'The rest is Hawaii,' Alex says, stacking empty plates. 'Now I hope you all saved some room, because this is where the real action starts.'

'Don't get too excited,' Pepper says, getting up and heading for the kitchen. 'Because I was in charge of pies and I can't be held responsible for the quality.'

'If we have any complaints, we'll write to the 7-Eleven down the street,' Alex says, taking Elsa's plate and following him.

'That would be best,' Pepper agrees.

The desserts are served and another bottle of wine is opened and positioned between Pepper and Elsa. The paper tablecloth is soaked with sullen rings and empty beer bottles stand sentry among the foil dishes of food. The Spanish-sounding music has grown louder, and Alex rises to put on some of his own.

'Hey,' he says, returning to the table and forking cheesecake into his mouth before continuing. 'Did you guys see that article in the *Chronicle* yesterday about the guy who tried to jump off the bridge five years ago and now he's a millionaire?'

Nobody did.

'I wish I'd been the one to pull him off,' Alex says, reaching for another bottle. 'Think about the reward he'd give you.'

'Could've been me,' Chase says. 'Or Miller. Any of us pretty much. You two are the only ones who've been around less than five years.'

'Do people ever come back and thank you?' Jasper asks.

'A few. Some send letters or try and call, but not many.'

'Some of them must try again,' Pepper says.

'Probably.' Chase reaches out to take another piece of pie.

'Miller — he's the foreman — he's pulled the same girl off three times before,' Alex says.

Chase nods. 'Yeah. I remember her.' He taps his head with a stubby finger. 'Real problems. They hospitalised her a couple times, I don't know what happened in the end.'

Elsa reaches out to pour more wine and spills a little on Pepper's plate. He mops it up with his cookie and carries on eating. 'They made a film about it once,' he says. 'About the jumpers.'

Chase opens another beer with the edge of Pepper's lighter. 'Who'd want to watch that?'

'I agree,' Laura says. 'It's so morbid.'

'I think it's sort of beautiful,' Stephanie says, and Elsa laughs.

The phone rings and Alex gets up to answer it.

'It's just the way it is,' Chase shrugs. 'It's a thing that happens.'

'So, Elsa,' Pepper says, lighting a cigarette. 'What do you think of Thanksgiving so far?'

She sips her wine. 'It's lovely, but it's not as good as Christmas.'

'Hold up, the best part is yet to come.'

'Better than my turkey?' Claudia asks.

'Okay, the second best.'

'Oh,' Elsa says. 'Well, in that case, I'll reserve judgement for now.'

'Hedging your bets, huh?' Pepper says, blowing out a plume of smoke. 'Smart girl.'

After the dishes have been cleared, the group file one by one onto the fire escape. It's dark outside; a pure and velvet dark, a last band of light fading slowly into the city. Their breath fogs in soft cotton strands but Elsa's cheeks are still red-wine warm. In the centre of the iron-slatted ledge is a ladder.

'Thisaway,' Pepper says, climbing one-handed. In the other he is holding a bottle of vodka which is thick with ice and a cloudy yellow inside. The rungs of the ladder feel strange beneath Elsa's hands; hot and rough though they are smooth and metal. Behind her, Alex clutches a stack of paper cups between his teeth, a red beak which points up as he climbs. She reaches the top and Pepper helps haul her up, her bare knee catching on the pale grey gravel that covers the flat surface of the roof. 'Welcome to my kingdom,' he says, and she turns in a slow circle, looking out over the city; over the crooked, sprawling streets of the Mission and the Castro, of the neat lines of the Financial District in the distance. The wind tugs at her, pushing her dress against her thighs and pulling her hair away from her face and out into a storm behind her. The moon is low and bright.

'What do you think?' Pepper asks her.

'It's amazing,' she says. He lights a joint and passes it to her, and she sits down cross-legged and abruptly.

'I'm going downstairs to get a sweater,' Stephanie says. Jack shucks his off and hands it to her. The moon twitches.

Alex passes the frosty vodka bottle to Elsa. 'It's pineapple,' he says. 'It's Pepper's speciality.'

'How long is it till midnight?' Laura asks.

Jack checks his phone. 'Three hours.'

'What happens at midnight?' Elsa asks.

'It's Black Friday,' Pepper says, sitting down beside her. 'Everyone goes out shopping in the middle of the night. Big sales, total chaos, that kind of thing.'

'That is the most American thing I've ever heard,' she says, laughing. 'Let's be thankful for what we have and then go out and buy loads of new stuff!' She laughs again, a shrill sound that shivers in the moonlight. Somewhere in the street below, an alarm is sounding. She takes the vodka back from Pepper and he passes her the joint with it.

Jack takes it from her before it reaches her mouth and tokes on it himself, his body turned away from them. He takes several steps away from the group, away from the city's skyline, and looks out at the dark masses of the Twin Peaks. Out on their shrouded slopes, three teenagers lie beside their tent, looking up at the moon. A coyote stalks through the trees at one summit, eyes alien gold in the smooth dark. A nameless man lies forgotten in the leaves, hidden from the light. Jack's feet are close to the edge of the roof, and he closes his eyes and lets himself drift.

2004

Beth's stuff is still in boxes though they've been living together six months. In other ways, though, they are organised; moving through the stages of their relationship in simple steps. From first date to first night together to the first time he tells her he loves her, in easy (some might say hasty) jumps. On this Sunday, another first, they are taking a walk in the tiny Wisconsin town she grew up in, the first lunch with the parents still digesting. It is a cool day in April and Beth is pleased with how things have gone. It is the first time he has had to perform in such a way but her parents are quiet and polite and there have been no uncomfortable silences – even a couple of jokes cracked – and so, all in all, he feels he can count it as a success.

He lets her lead him through the quiet streets of her home town. The buildings are pale brick, some pillared, the street lights and the balconies iron and old-fashioned. Most of the stores are closed and there are few other people around. He leans closer to her.

'I like seeing you here, country girl.'

She looks up at him, mouth twitching. Grabbing his hand, she drags him down a narrow alley. The specifics of the moment are clear even though the memory is worn and hazy. The freckled skin of her hand as she runs it along the cool bricks, laughing. The thin spiral of blonde hair blown back towards him as she glances over her shoulder at him. The way their footsteps sound in the small space, clattering upwards like birds disturbed. He clings tighter to her fingertips and smiles.

They pass out into a deserted lane and she is ahead of him now, moving in and out of shadows, heading towards the sunlight which streams through the stone arch at its end. Her fingers slip from his and he wants to call out to her. But the words won't come, and then they are through the arch and in a sloping garden, the green of its grass so bright he squints against it. A small play park fills one corner; swings at its far end and a roundabout spinning slowly in the breeze. In the centre of the garden is a round fishpond, fenced in with black iron railings. An empty bench faces it, another with its back to them.

'Come on.' Beth turns to look at him, eyes bright, hair defiant in the wind. She is taking off her shoes and he copies her, the damp grass pushing between his toes. The two children who are playing on the swings stare at them, open-mouthed. There is a strong gust of wind and the iron frame of the swing set creaks; a warning sound, a lurching.

Beth opens the latch on the pond's pretty gate and lets it swing open. It moves too slowly; hypnotised. She steps slowly onto the ledge which runs around the water's edge and walks along it, one foot placed carefully in front of the other.

'What are you doing?' he says, but he's already following her, his toes bent right over the cold stone as he tries to keep his balance. He looks down into the green water, clouds of silt passing though it in slow shoals, and his hand tightens on the railing.

Halfway around, she stops and sits slowly down, her feet disappearing into the water. He laughs, one short sound, and then in a rush of daring, does the same. The shock of the water makes him gasp, but her face is peaceful, serene.

'This is my favourite place,' she says.

They sit; the iron fence at their backs, their calves and feet submerged in the cold water. A fish brushes against his leg, darts away again. He threads his fingers through hers; she tips her head against his shoulder. They sit there for a long time, the sun setting behind them. The children are long gone, the fish lurk somewhere unseen. The hairs on his arms and the back of his neck stand up and he looks down at her.

'Marry me,' he says.

2004

A netball team night out, wearing their bibs and short skirts. Hers is denim, frayed hem soft on her thighs. Pointed shoes and painted nails, her hair carefully ironed straight. They go from bar to bar, they drink purple shots and drinks mixed with flat lemonade. Acid lime taste, vodka-hot breath. They sing as they walk, they share cigarettes. She sees a fleeting glimpse of herself in a window; fingers linked with another girl's, name now forgotten.

He is standing outside, on the phone. There is a voice down the line who is instantly forgotten, left hanging for ever as he watches them pass. She walks by, her skirt riding up. She lets go of the girl's hand, pauses to say something to another. Her eyes meet his and he winks. That wink, momentary, is eternal. It will always exist in its exact and perfect state, a Polaroid never touched by the flood of time which slowly sweeps away the details of the rest. She turns back to look at him, surveys his face. Narrow features and wide eyes. Light brown hair swept across his forehead, long around his ears. He smiles. She walks a few steps backwards, watching him watching. The girls tug her away, they laugh.

Later, she waits to buy a round. The wall behind the bar is mirrored and her face is one of a swarm, all clamouring for a reflection. She shifts up onto her elbows, kicks a shoe idly against the faux-marble front. Her eyes keep returning to her reflected face and there is something there she likes, something that is strange. And then he appears beside her.

He leans close to speak to her, lets his lips graze her ear. 'I'm Kieran.'

Soon, they are dancing, his body pressed against her back, his hands on her hips. His mouth against the curve of her neck.

'Let's go.' Him or her? She can't remember.

The taxi ride is frantic and breathless, bare legs on leather seat, one of her shoes discarded in the footwell. The driver turns the radio up, winds down his window. Arriving at the address, a crumpled tenner is pushed through the Perspex, Kieran already out on the pavement without collecting his change. She grabs her shoe, hops out after him.

His house is dark, the hallway cluttered. She trips over a football and he catches her, pulling her to him, pressing her against the wall. His hands are in her hair, his hips sharp against hers. Frayed hem soft on her thighs.

*

There is coffee by the bed when she wakes. She stares up at the ceiling, piecing things together again, and then she rises sharply, making the room spin. She clamps a hand to her head as she staggers around the room, collecting her clothes. There is a fluttery feeling in her chest. She needs to get out. She needs to get back to her flat.

She finds her bag and sits down on the edge of the bed. Sweat cools on her chest; she takes a shaky sip of the coffee and wishes it was water. Pawing through the small bag – something sticky there, on the front, and a smear of ash on the fabric beside it – the fluttering rises again, its wings beating faster. But everything is there; her phone, her driving licence, a scrunched-up five-pound note. And a small piece of yellow paper, folded carefully. She takes it out, brow creased. Unfolding it, she notices her hands trembling. It is a small Post-it with slanted, looping handwriting.

His number. 'Call me!' A kiss.

2012

The restaurant is busy, the music too loud. Thanksgiving is over but as he looks around the crowded room, Jack feels as though the edge of the roof is still close, the swoop still only a step or two away. He shifts onto his toes and off again, his shoes stiff and unfamiliar.

'It looks nice,' Elsa says, giving his hand a brief squeeze. 'It's really lively.' But Jack is glad when the maître d' leads them up a set of steps and to a table on the quieter balcony. *Getting old*, he thinks. The maître d' pulls out Elsa's chair for her and he waits, watching her legs as they fold into place, as the chair is pushed in behind her. He settles himself in his seat as the man leaves and Elsa smoothes back her hair; smiling. It is a nice restaurant and she is pleased and he is pleased. While she looks around, he looks at her. It is one of the days when she has crept up on him; he is drunk on the dark mass of her hair waterfalling over her white shoulders, electric with the slimness of the straps which hold her green silk dress against her body. She is looking at him with the same, soft smile with which she has viewed him across countless dinner tables, and he feels almost delirious with the familiar intimacy of it. He used to enjoy this intoxication; tonight he feels afraid of it.

'It's so nice to be out,' she says.

'Yeah.' He reaches for the drinks menu, a small shiver in the very tips of his fingers. 'You look gorgeous.'

She grins, reaching for her own menu. 'You brush up rather well yourself.'

A waiter arrives, a small but round man with wet, brown eyes. 'Can I get you anything to drink?'

'I'll take a beer,' Jack says. 'Which would you recommend?'

Elsa orders a cocktail, the tiny white half-moon of her nail running along the description as she speaks. The small but round waiter watches it in a daze.

'Do you need a couple more minutes on the food?' He retreats, the shiny fabric of his waistcoat catching in the low light.

An older couple are seated at the table opposite. The woman, grey hair twisted up behind her head, has a cream scarf over her sweater and one of her hands plays idly with it as she sips a cloudy glass of white wine. Her companion is wearing cream trousers and canvas deck shoes even though it is misty and raining outside. Jack watches them sit and thinks of his father.

Our father, he thinks. *Who art*. And then he stops. 'What are you going to have?' he asks Elsa, whose brow is furrowed with concentration.

'I don't know.' She sighs. 'Either the sea bream or the risotto. Or the chicken. Are you going to have the steak?'

'No, not tonight. I feel like a change.' *What does a change feel like?*

'Perhaps I will then.'

A waiter is showing the older couple another bottle of wine. The husband nods, the bottle is uncorked. An inch is poured into his glass and the wife and the waiter watch, heads inclined, as he sips. 'It's weird, isn't it?' Jack says, and Elsa glances up. 'All this,' he says, gesturing around, and then he looks back down at his menu.

'You're strange tonight,' she says.

'I guess I am,' he says.

Their waiter is returning with their drinks. Jack watches him making his way across the room with the two glasses on a tray and wonders if they will fall. To Elsa, he says, 'I'm really happy we're here.'

She looks up, surprised. 'Me too,' she says and she reaches out to touch his hand.

'Here we go,' the waiter says, setting the drinks down in front of them. 'Are you ready to order?'

'I think so,' Elsa says. 'I'll have the seafood salad to start, and then the chicken.'

'Sure,' the man jots it down. There is a bead of sweat in the soft, fleshy hollow between his nose and the curve of his cheek. As Jack watches, it seems to swell.

'I'll have the scallops,' he says. 'And the pork fillet.'

'Great,' the waiter says. The bead has still not fallen. 'Can I get you guys anything else?'

'I think we're okay,' Elsa says, closing her menu and handing it to him. 'Thank you.'

When he is gone, she says, 'I wish I'd had the steak now.'

'I'll cook you steak tomorrow,' Jack says. *A lot's at steak.*

'You are good,' she says, picking up her drink. It is pale pink and sugary; it leaves white flecks on the surface of the glass as she tips it towards her.

'How is it?' he asks.

'It's great,' she says, taking another appreciative sip. He returns to his own drink, which is also good; a wheat beer, almost floral in taste. *Our father*, he thinks. *Who art.* And then he shakes his head.

'I've been thinking,' she says, putting down her cocktail and leaning forward in her seat, 'about the living room. What do you think about grey? Grey and blue. Not dark, obviously, that would be depressing. Soft shades. If we had some white furniture – a table, well, two tables, really, at the ends of the sofa, and perhaps a chair, wicker maybe – it would look so pretty. It would make the room look much bigger.' She stops. 'Why are you smiling? I'm being serious.'

'I know you are, honey,' he says, still smiling. 'You just look so beautiful when you're excited.'

She raises an eyebrow and takes another, larger sip of her drink. 'Well, it makes me feel like a child,' she says. She stares over the balcony, where a band are setting up on a small stage in the middle of the busy dining room.

He scrambles in a momentary free fall, and takes a sip of his beer, trying to regain his footing. 'I'm sorry,' he says eventually. 'That wasn't what I meant at all. Blue and grey sound great. Maybe tomorrow we can go and look at samples.'

She looks back and smiles; a smaller, tighter smile than before but one just large enough to find a foothold in. 'I'd like that,' she says.

'I love you, you know,' he says.

'I know.' She covers his hand with hers. *Take my hand.*

'You've finished your drink.'

'So have you.'

'Close your eyes.'

She does, never questioning, and he reaches out a hand to remove the small speck of something caught in the corner of her eye. The tip of his smallest finger presses against her lashes and then the lid, soft, the slight curve of the orb beneath it. *No resistance.* 'There,' he says, wiping it away on the tablecloth.

'I wonder if these are ours,' she says.

They aren't; the plates are delivered to the older couple instead. They are just far enough away that conversation doesn't carry; he watches them speak as they start to eat, trying to make out the words which are washed away by the band. 'A little cold,' he thinks the woman says. 'Very good,' the husband. He stops trying to decipher and starts inventing. 'I want to fuck the waiter,' the wife says. 'Me first, Eve,' replies the man.

'This must be ours,' Elsa says.

'Would you like to order some wine, sir?' asks the waiter. The bead of sweat is gone.

'You choose,' he tells Elsa. She has very good taste.

As they eat, her foot finds his calf under the table. He reaches a hand down and grabs it, following the taut muscle of her leg upwards. She is wearing tights – *stockings*, he hopes – and the flimsy fabric of them clings to his fingers as they move. 'How's your food?' he asks, releasing her.

'Very good. And yours?'

'Nice.'

He takes a sip of the wine, coarse and metallic on his tongue. 'Hey,' he says, leaning forward, fork in mid-air. 'You remember that time we went to that tapas place?'

'In Angel?'

'Yeah. And it was raining like hell and we just sat in there for five hours, eating.'

'And getting absolutely hammered on sangria,' she adds.

He looks at her, not smiling. 'That was really amazing.'

She looks back at him. 'I just remember the hangover,' she says.

One hour and two courses later, they sit among the ruins of the meal, the last dregs of wine shared between their glasses. The couple at the table opposite have been replaced by another.

Jack, watching them, has decided that they are either friends – not particularly good friends – or on a first date. The band on the stage below have also been exchanged for a lone pianist, the mood in the room calmer, people moving more slowly.

'Do you want dessert?' Jack asks, and she shakes her head.

'Another cocktail, maybe.'

She speaks a little too quickly, her eyes a little too wide, and he knows she shouldn't have another. He feels nervous but he isn't sure why. He checks his watch. 'I guess we could have another.'

'There's something, isn't there?' she says suddenly, messily, and his heart lurches.

'What do you mean?'

'There's something you aren't saying, but I *know* it, I can see it in your face every day.'

He tries to smile. 'Els, I don't know what you mean. Maybe we should—'

'The Chicago house,' she says, changing tack, and each word is a separate shot to his chest. 'Who did you live there with? What's her name?'

There is a roaring in his ears and he forces himself to swallow. 'Beth.'

'Did you love her?'

He puts a hand to the balcony's rail to steady himself; stares down at the people below. 'Why are you doing this to yourself?'

Tears have sprung to her eyes, and she lacks either the will or the control to hold them back. Drunk, he watches her cry with a kind of quiet fascination. He takes a sip of his wine and waits. Embarrassed, she tries to compose herself, smearing the tears away with the flat of her hand. He reaches across the table. 'Don't,' she says, pulling away. And then, 'People are looking.'

They aren't, actually, but he understands why she feels that way. He feels watched too, all the time, more and more each day. He gulps down the rest of his wine and stands up awkwardly.

'I'll get you a drink.'

She nods but doesn't meet his eyes. She stares over the balcony instead, breath hitching in her chest. The pianist plays on. Jack turns away, tripping over the leg of his chair as he goes.

While the drinks are poured, he stares down at his fists as they press into the bar, focuses on pulling air in and out of his lungs. *Going to be okay*, the part of him which is hardy and designed for preservation chirps. *All going to be okay.* He pays the bill and nods once, twice to himself. 'Okay,' he says, aloud, and then he returns to the table.

'Can we start again?' he asks, putting her drink down in front of her. She looks sullenly up at him.

'What am I to you?'

He pulls out his chair and sits back down. *Take my hand*, he thinks, without warning. She stares at him and her face seems suddenly unfamiliar to him. 'This isn't like you,' he says.

She snorts. 'Maybe you just don't know me.'

He looks sadly back at her. 'You think so?'

'I don't know what to think. When we came here, I thought this — *we* — were a fresh start.'

'If you want a fresh start then why are we having this conversation?' he asks, and his voice is harsher than he meant it to be.

'Because it's not about us, is it? Sometimes I feel like you don't mind if I'm here or not. Golden Gate's the main attraction, I'm just the fucking B side.'

'I'm not sure I know what that means.'

'I'm just a bit of fun. I'm not, you know, "The Real Thing".' She makes wobbly inverted commas in the air as she speaks. 'But you are to *me*.' She is dangerously close to crying again. 'I'm starting to feel like we're not on the same page.'

'Or listening to the same track.'

It's a precarious moment; through someone else's eyes, he watches them teeter there. And then she laughs, takes a shaky sip of her drink. 'Yeah. Or that.'

'Let's go home,' he says. 'I want to hold you.'

Later, he comes up behind her whilst she is cleaning her teeth. He wraps his arms around her shoulders and rests his rough cheek against hers, studying their faces in the mirror.

'You know,' he says softly. 'The B side is always more interesting than the single.'

2005

The things he remembers of the wedding day, he remembers clearly.

He remembers the night before, him and Franklin alone in the house. Some platitudes exchanged — *Best call it a night; See you on the other side* — and he gathers the few empty cans, the empty pizza box. Out in the garden, there is something in the centre of the patio; small, black, star-like. The stones of the patio are damp under his bare feet, the bag sagging in his hand. He reaches the object, leans closer as he squints in the half-light.

A bird, pure black except for its beak and feet which stand out like scars against its tiny mass. It has fallen onto its back, its wings spread out and crumpled, feet curled up to its chest. He picks it up with the thin membrane of the bin bag, and the weightlessness of it, the fragility of its frame in his hand, repulses and fascinates him. The night is still warm, but when he shuts the bin's lid on the small body, he shivers.

He remembers the morning, though he does not remember rising. In shorts, he jogs down to the mailbox. Just one thing inside; another of the cheap white slips of paper, a visiting order from the prison. His father wants him to come, but his father lives in another life. The previous two letters have been thrown away without pause, but this one he folds and puts in his pocket. He does not understand the reasons his father has for stealing other people's money, but, for the first time, he feels he might be prepared to listen. He heads back to the house, feeling warmed. Inside, Franklin is in the kitchen making breakfast.

He remembers the car. He is in the car and his heart is beating fast. The cornfields flash past, the city disappears behind them. The sun beats down on everything and burns it bright and white. He loosens his tie.

He remembers the church. They are pulling up outside the church and his mother and Aimee are already waiting. He climbs out to greet them; hugs them tightly, one under each arm. Both seem smaller, both feel fragile to the touch. There are tears in his mother's eyes as she looks up at him and he looks down at her and nods; a small, simple movement which feels overdue and essential.

He is at the altar, sweat beading at his temples. It's too hot for April, too small in the church. People fan themselves with sheets of primrose-yellow paper, the orders of service. A baby begins to cry in one of the pews near the back. And then there is her. Then there is the gigantic, heart-stopping moment of her, and the church is silent and the church is breathless. Beth appears, her blonde hair loose and tumbling down her shoulders.

He is outside the church, they are all outside the church, camera flash smile just the bride and groom now please. His mother stands in the shelter of a tree with Beth's mother beside her. They are greying but the white light erases all and the tree sheds tiny yellow petals on the grass around them. Aimee smokes a cigarette at the edge of the crowd, talking on her cell. Her mouth moves quickly, her head is bowed. He puts an arm around Beth's waist, brings her body close to him, tiny and precious and porcelain.

He remembers the dinner, though he does not remember the food. They are in a marquee in the grounds of the golf club, the spring air still sultry, white linen white candles white flowers. Franklin is speaking into the microphone, round face red, tie pulled open and lolling down his front. Denny is at his table and his girlfriend's head bobs as she laughs. He glances at Beth and she is smiling and all the people at the tables are smiling and he, most of all, is smiling.

He is dancing, the day's first nerves returning. Round and round they go, his heart racing. Eyes everywhere, eyes all on them. But he looks down at Beth and everything is still, everything is gone. White train against vinyl dance floor and them.

He remembers the room, he remembers the room best. They are in their hotel room, they are lying on a huge bed. They are flat on their backs beside each other, and they are laughing.

2012

She sits one afternoon and draws the children as they watch a DVD. She sketches the shapes of their heads, the smallness of their bodies. She tests strokes in one corner, trying to imitate the soft shininess of their hair. She fills another page with noses, and then three single eyes, each looking in a different direction. She blows the pencil's dust away, dampens a finger to smudge at lines.

'What are you doing?' Sam asks her. He has forgotten the TV and is edging closer.

'I'm drawing you,' she says, and turns the page to consult the noses which have gone before. Satisfied, she returns to shading a floating pair of tiny lips.

'Why?'

'Because your grandma asked me to.'

'Why?'

'Because she thinks it would be nice.'

'Why?'

'I think she'd like to give it to your mum as a present. But that part's a secret.' She glances up at him. 'You can keep a secret, right?'

He nods. 'Can I see?'

'Of course.'

He comes up beside her and looks down at the page. She flicks back through the pages and shows him the skeletal versions of him and his sister, then the sheets of features to be transplanted on. He laughs at all the noses. 'That's funny.'

'It is, isn't it?'

'Which one is mine?'

'I'm not sure yet. Which one do you think?'

He leans forward to look closer, arms resting on her knee. 'I think this one,' he says, pointing at one near the top of the page.

'Oh really? I was thinking more this.' She points to an eye, and he contracts in a peal of laughter.

'That's not a nose, that's an eye!' He looks up at her. 'You're funny.'

She nods. 'I know.'

Skye wobbles closer and gazes up at both of them. 'Eye,' she says, and it is Elsa's turn to laugh.

Afterwards, she sticks her head into the kitchen. Pearl is sitting at the table with her back to the door.

'I'm off,' she says. 'I'll try some things at home and bring them to show you next week.'

Her neighbour is dressed in her nightdress again today, her book unopened beside her. Elsa takes a step into the room.

'Pearl?'

The sound of her neighbour's breathing is shallow and wet. She steps closer. 'Pearl?'

Pearl looks up, eyes blinking slowly behind the thick lenses of her glasses. 'Sorry,' she says, her voice rough. 'I forgot you were here.'

'Are you okay?'

'Yup. A little tired.'

Elsa pulls out a chair. 'Are you sure?'

'Yup. The kids okay?'

'They're fine. Sam's teaching Skye to say his name.'

'He's a good kid. He reminds me of my boys.'

'They're both lovely children.'

Pearl studies her. Her mouth moves unevenly, lips rolling against each other. 'I know you think Carrie's a bad mother,' she says. 'But she's not.'

Elsa shakes her head. 'I don't think that.'

'She reminds me of you, you know. You're a lot like her.'

'Well, I'd love to meet her.'

'Always got a smile, my Carrie. Never lets you know what she's thinking.'

Elsa nods. She is considering this likeness; she does not know how she feels about its fit. 'She's lucky to have you,' she says.

'Are you happy?' Pearl asks, leaning forward in her chair. Her glasses are sliding down her nose. 'You can tell me.'

Elsa looks at the book on the table in front of her. *Everything You Need*. 'I'm not sure any more,' she says.

'Don't take any shit.' Pearl reels back in her chair. 'You're smarter than that.' Her mouth makes small smacking sounds as she talks.

Elsa puts her sketchpad on the table. 'Do you want me to stay for a while? I can make the kids something to eat.'

'What time is it?'

'Just before six.'

'I need to take my pills.'

'Okay.' She rises from the table. 'Let me get them for you. Where are they?'

'The drawer over there. The second one.'

She finds the small orange cylinder, reads the prescription label. Shaking two into her hand, she finds a glass and fills it with water. 'Here,' she says, putting them down in front of Pearl. 'I'll stay,' she says.

'No, no need. Carrie's friend comes to pick them up at six-thirty.'

'Pearl.' Elsa puts a hand out to touch her shoulder; surprised at the frailness of the bone. 'Is it serious?'

Pearl shrugs. 'I'm going. But we all are, right?'

'I suppose we are.'

Her neighbour glances up at her and smiles; a dry, difficult thing that is nevertheless affectionate. 'Just like my Carrie.

Don't think bad of her. There are all kinds of mothers. I ought to know.'

Elsa squeezes her shoulder, just a little, and feels like crying. 'Can I get you anything?'

'I'm good. You should go.'

Out in the hallway, Sam is looking at the bookcases. 'You okay?' she asks him. 'Where's Skye?'

'She's sleeping. I put her blanket on her.'

'She's very lucky to have a big brother like you.'

'Do you have one?'

'Me? No. I have a little sister though, like you do.'

'Do you look after her like I look after Skye?'

'That's right. They're hard work sometimes, aren't they?'

'Yeah!'

'Don't worry. They get easier as they get older.'

Sam looks up at her, his head on one side. 'I wish you were my big sister,' he says.

'Do you?' Her eyes water unexpectedly. 'Well, we can pretend, if you like. I'd love a little brother.'

'You can look after me.'

'Yep.'

'And I can look after you.'

'That sounds like a fair deal.'

Sam smiles at her. 'I brought my book to show you.'

'The lion one?'

'Yeah.'

She takes his hand. 'Well, why didn't you say?'

'It's ridiculous, them being in that house all the time,' Jack says. 'She's an old lady. They should be with the parents.'

'Parent,' Elsa says. 'She's a single mother. And she has to work.'

'There's got to be someone better than their great-grandmother.'

She opens the oven, looks in at the lasagne inside. The steam hits the thin chain of her necklace, turning it hot against her skin. 'Not everyone has the perfect situation,' she says, shutting it and shrugging. 'Some people have to make things work.'

'You don't have to tell me that,' he says. 'I spent my childhood flying across the Atlantic, remember?'

She touches his arm as she passes. 'And you turned out just fine.'

'Debatable.'

'I was being polite.' She watches his back as he sifts through the junkmail on the side. 'When am I going to meet your family, anyway?' she asks, trying to keep her voice light. 'When will your dad come and visit? Or your sister? She's in New York, right?'

He shrugs, doesn't look up, but she thinks she sees the muscles of his back tighten. 'Soon, I guess. Flights are expensive.'

She nods, even though he is not looking at her. 'Of course. Yeah.'

He goes to the fridge and offers her a beer. 'I'm going to have a bath,' she says. 'Save me one.'

She climbs the stairs and shuts the bathroom door behind her. Leaning her forehead against it, she closes her eyes and pulls the breath through her nose, blowing it softly out against the white-painted wood. From below, she hears the TV being switched on, the faint sound of a newsreader's voice. She forces herself to cross the tiny bathroom and turn on the tap. Tired, she sits on the edge and watches the bath fill. There is a crack in one side of the grey enamel and she watches the water sidle towards it, thinking of the tide and the moon and the way a nose looks alone on the page. Adding the cold, she stands and undresses, letting the many layers which now make up her California uniform drop to the floor.

In a different room, on a different level of the house, Jack slides lower in his seat, feet up on the arm, as Elsa slides below the water above him. She has misjudged; the bathwater is too cool. She sinks lower in it, letting the water soak slowly up her hair as it drifts around her shoulders. The channel is changed; a sports commentator's more urgent tones pushing up through the floorboards. She traces a number on the side of the bath with her nail, over and over, a number which becomes a date which is a date she finds herself writing often, but always like this, always without making a mark. She imagines writing it in places people will see. A status update? An email signature? A tattoo – wrist or rib? People will have to ask. People will wonder. What does it mark, they will ask. What is it for? A death, she will say. The simple truth. A death.

Is that how I think of it?

She frowns, unsure of the correct answer. She tries the idea on for size. *No*, she thinks decisively, though the truth is, if she thinks on it for too long then the answer will become fluid, the concept ballooning out and away from her. *It marks an event. A catastrophe.* She sinks lower still in the bathwater.

When she thinks of the men she has loved in her life, and the certainty with which she loved them, she is always surprised at herself, always bewildered. There have been several versions of Elsa, but the newest is no longer sure, as the others were, that she is the final and true Elsa. How can she trust herself when herself is a thing which changes often and without warning? She thinks of herself pressed against the hallway wall of a student house. She thinks of herself pressed against the door of a bed-and-breakfast bedroom. She traces the date again.

When the water is cold, she climbs out and dries herself carefully. She leaves the clothes in their sad sprawl and walks softly down the stairs. At the doorway, she pauses, watching the rise and fall of his chest.

'I'm here,' she says, but what she means is *I'm me.*

He straightens, turns to see her. He holds out his arm and she moves across the room to him, folds herself onto his lap. 'You're here,' he says, and he smiles.

2005

It's a month before her twentieth birthday, and Kieran is busy, his friends also elsewhere and the house empty for the night. The house where she likes to live now, though her things remain somewhere in stasis between her halls bedroom and his bedroom floor. She wanders through the rooms, watching the time tick by. *Get a grip*, she tells herself, and on impulse, she picks up her bag and heads out.

Returning to halls, her footsteps sound hollow on the pavement. Her key is stiff in the lock, her abandoned canvases sticky against a wall in the hallway.

'You're back.' Jenn appears in the corridor, a slim silhouette against the flickering light. 'Coming out?'

'Yeah.' She nods after the word, underlining it. 'Let me just get changed.'

Her fingers fumble with buttons, her face pale in the glass. When she leaves her room, they are waiting by the front door for her, Jenn and Barney lost in conversation. Outside, in the dark street and orange street light, she tries to keep hold of the words, tries to place names. Jenn offers her a plastic bottle filled with vodka and flat Coke and she takes large gulps, shivering.

When they turn the corner, the bus is just pulling up at the stop and they run towards it, catch it just in time. They tumble down the aisle and into the back seat. Lily falls into the seat beside her and smiles. 'It's so great you're here.'

'How are things, Lil?'

'Oh, you know.' Lily looks out through the window, blonde curls falling out of their bun. 'Hey, did I tell you about that guy I met?'

It's easy to let Lily's words wash over, filling in the spaces between them as effortlessly and efficiently as water. When they arrive at the union she is afraid to get up, afraid to be back on uncertain land.

She checks her mobile as they enter the club. Screen blank, thumb twitching. *Should I text?* But no. She is not *that* lost yet. She slides the phone back into her pocket, takes her drink from Max. His hair still needs cutting and she wants to reach out and ruffle it. 'It's changed in here,' she says instead, looking around as she sips.

Questions, casual but insistent, are aimed at her. Where has she been, how are things? Jenn talks about a lecture she has missed, asks if she wants to borrow the notes. She nods, smiles, sips. The bottle is cold, its label soggy. She peels at it with damp fingertips.

Jenn's body is angled towards Max. *They're sleeping together.* The realisation is soft and far off. Lily's arm presses against hers as she crushes a cigarette in the foil ashtray, the material of her sleeve static against her skin.

They are talking about a programme now, a comedy. A new series of a show she liked before. They quote lines from it, they laugh. Faces turn to her expectantly.

'I haven't seen it,' she says.

There is a thump as the band begin setting up onstage. Someone behind the bar yells out for more ice. Max lifts his pint and gazes at the tabletop. 'You've changed, Elsa. You've changed.' Lily laughs nervously but the others are silent, the others agree.

Later, she dances, floor tacky under silky shoe. There is another bottle in her hand and Barney is beside her. Barney is speaking, though the words seem distorted and distant to her. 'Things are okay, though, yeah?' His jaw is tight, the teeth moving back and forth behind the flaccid white skin of it. His pupils are wide and black.

She nods, glances at her phone.

'That's great.' His hand ruffles her hair. 'That's really great.'

She leaves the club early, slips out without saying goodbye. This was once Lily's trick but never hers. She sends a guilty text to Lily and not Jenn because she knows that this way it will go unnoticed until the end of the night when the union's lights stutter back into life. The muscles of her face feel tense; she puts a hand to her jaw, trying to rub them loose. Each step of the journey is essential, an achievement. Out of the club. At the bus stop. Pay the driver. On the bus. The road outside groans past, the light behind her too bright, too yellow. *I should go back*, she thinks, but she leans closer to the glass.

Arriving at her stop, she clambers out, silky shoes blackened, soles gritty. Leaving the main road for their silent street, everything cast in strange night light. The neighbour's cat sits on the wall, tail flicking from side to side. Her key echoes in the lock.

The house hums with faraway voices. Paulo's bike is in the hallway, Justin's guitar case beside it. She trails her fingers across them, along the spindles of the banister as she passes the stairs, thunk. Thunk. Thunk. She opens the kitchen door and the room is empty, though the voices are closer. Through the kitchen then, both hands out now, fingers trailing over table, counter. Round the corner and into the living room, where short, fat lamps glow and dark figures crouch. Smoke curls up to the ceiling, sweet and acrid. The joint is held out to her, but she shakes her head, asks her wordless question.

'He's upstairs.' Paulo points, his hand flopping back down beside him with the effort.

Up the stairs she goes, lifting her bag from her shoulder, sliding her jacket off. The hallway is dark, just two thin stripes of light across its carpet. Someone is in the bath; she hears the soft sluice of the water as they sink lower. She heads for the bedroom door, silky shoes discarded on brown carpet, handle smooth and cool in her palm.

The bedroom is lit by the sharp white light of the desk lamp which points towards her, inquisitive. The room behind it falls into pools of blue, darkness creeping from the corners. His shape is vague on the edge of the bed, his back to her, phone pressed against ear. She crawls onto the mattress, pressing star-shaped hands against his spine. His arm reaches back, palm finding her belly, sending a white-hot shock through her. He glances back at her, grins. The conversation goes on.

She sits against the wall, bare toes splayed against white sheets, watching him. Her phone buzzes in her bag and she reaches for it, teeth grinding. But his hand closes around her wrist, his call ended.

'Come here,' he says, pressing her down into the mattress. 'You went out without me,' he says. 'You bad girl.' He bites her lip.

'I'm back now,' she says, pulling him closer.

2005

They are driving home – *he* is driving, and it feels different and the same and frightening – one evening after visiting Beth's family. The Chicago house is only an hour and forty minutes' drive from her parents' home, and weekends are often spent here. Despite his inexperience, he is surprisingly good with her parents. It has so far won him access to her father's golf club and a place of honour in her mother's kitchen. On this particular visit, he has also been subjected to the scrutiny of her two sisters, and, it seems, passed. In the car, pulling away from the house, Beth turns to him.

'That was nice,' she says. 'Wasn't it?'

'It was.'

'Dad says you're getting better.'

'He's just being kind.'

'You're his new favourite.'

He turns to grin at her. 'Jealous?'

She kicks her shoes off, rubbing her toes. 'Nope. I'm glad he's finally got the son he always wanted.'

'What cake did your mum give us this time?'

'Carrot.'

'My favourite.'

'Of course.'

'Lucky me.'

She settles back in her seat. 'I love you,' she says, leaning her head back against the headrest and closing her eyes.

Ninety minutes into the journey, and almost home, there are flashing lights up ahead. Even though they are innocent and yellow, they evoke a special kind of childish fear in him and he thinks of his father, thinks of heavy closing doors and electronic locks. Drawing closer, he sees a car parked on the hard shoulder, its hazard lights blinking feverishly. Though the road is otherwise deserted, he clicks on his indicator.

'Don't.' Her hand, a pale splay in the moonlight, clutches his arm.

'What?' He slows and turns the wheel anyway, not waiting for the answer.

'I have a bad feeling about this.' She turns away, folds her arms.

He pulls the car in beside the other and turns off the engine, leaving his headlights on. 'Come on,' he says, removing his seat belt. 'Let's see if we can help.'

'I don't want to,' she says, but he is already closing his door behind him. Reluctantly, she follows him, pulling her thin cardigan closer around her.

Approaching the driver's side, he sees that the car is empty. He tries the door: locked.

'They must've broken down,' he says. 'They've probably gone for help. We should drive around, see if we can pick them up and give them a ride.'

He is standing beside the back seat now, his face pressed to the window, his hands cupped around his eyes. Inside is a baby's car seat, and beside it, a woman's coat, folded neatly. Expensive; the fabric thick and with a sheen. Down in the footwell is an empty plastic water bottle and a floppy rag doll, one arm twisted beneath its body.

Moving back to the driver's door he peers in again. The armrest between the seats is open; inside it another bottle of water, this one half-full, and a glasses case. On the dashboard is a book of maps, open at a page of the area.

'I don't like this,' Beth says, but he ignores her, moving round to the passenger side. He finds nothing, straightens up.

'I hope they're okay,' he says, looking around him at the dark road. Moving back towards her, he pauses, trapped in one headlight while she shifts uneasily in the other. He bends down and picks up a keyring. A single ring, no keys attached. He lets it drop back to the dusty road. He is shivering.

'Let's get back in the car.'

They drive slowly, but they see no one. The next morning on his way to work, he passes the car again. On his way home, it remains.

For three days he passes it. And then it is gone.

2012

'I didn't know that about Miller,' Jack says, when he is joined at the edge of the roof by Chase. The Thanksgiving moon is full and yellow and low. 'About that girl. Same girl, three times?'

'Yeah,' Chase says, staring down at the roofs below them. 'That was rough.'

'Wonder what happened to her,' Jack says, turning his face up to the moon.

Chase looks at him and then looks away again. 'Fourth time lucky,' he says, and Jack takes a small – almost (but not quite) imperceptible – step away from the edge.

'Seriously?'

'Yeah. Year or so later. Miller wasn't on call. Eddie was. Real shitty day for Eddie.'

Though the story has settled, hard and small and

immovable, somewhere in him, Jack and Eddie are yet to go on a call-out together, and perhaps that's why, when Eddie approaches on a normal day at the end of November, Jack feels no vertigo.

'Letter here for you, Jackie,' Eddie says, tossing an envelope towards him. 'See you tomorrow, fella.'

'See ya,' Jack says, but he is already looking down at the small white envelope, on which his name is indeed printed, along with the address of the Golden Gate Bridge Authority. The handwriting is childish; rounded and generously spaced. He turns the envelope over and opens it. Inside is a single sheet of paper, thin and folded into quarters. He unfolds it, turning it round so that he can read it, and he notices detachedly that his hands have begun to shake. The same childish handwriting fills two lines in the centre of the page.

Then the devil left him, and behold, angels were ministering to him.

At the bottom of the page a phone number is scrawled. Jack studies it for a long time, and then he folds the piece of paper back up and slides the envelope into his pocket.

He is about to leave when Alex comes bounding in, grinning. 'What. A. Day,' he says, swinging open the dented door of his locker and pulling out a carton of juice. He takes a long pull on it, then another, and belches. 'Let's go get drunk.'

'Sure,' Jack says, shrugging.

'Eddie tell you about this morning?'

Jack shakes his head.

'Five a.m. call-out, some chick on the chord. We got her back, it was like –' He clicks his fingers. *Just like that.*

'Congratulations,' Jack says, trying to ignore the hammering in his chest at the mention of the chord.

'So, let's go.'

'Usual?'

'Nah, I'm sick of it there. Let's go to the Spanish place.'

Jack pulls on his jacket. 'Sounds good.'

As he follows Alex's car down Divisadero, he glances occasionally at the shard of his face which is caught in the rear-view mirror. The hair – even Elsa would admit now – really does need cutting, and the eye which stares back at him is wide and frightened, the lines at its corners deeper than ever. He reaches up a hand and tilts the mirror away.

The car. It is a long time since he has thought of that. He remembers the frightened way Beth looked at him and the hairs on the back of his neck stand up. *Who did it belong to?* he wonders. *Where did they go?* He presses his foot a little harder on the accelerator, inches his bumper a little closer to Alex's.

He finds himself thinking again of the night in the tapas place in Angel, of how they finally braved the rain. Drunk on sangria and desperate for each other, they stood at the door and looked out at it hammering down, the street deserted. He remembers the way she looked up at him, remembers the way she took his hand. 'Ready?' she asked him, and they ran.

Outside Alex's building, he parks and glances up at the apartment. On the fire escape, a girl is sitting on the steps between first and second floors, smoking. She is the only other person around, and for the first time since he has visited this street, there is no music coming from any of the houses. The letter in Jack's pocket crackles as he climbs out of his car and despite the empty street, he is sure that someone is watching him.

'I wonder if Claud's home yet,' Alex says, glancing up at his window. 'Probably not.'

'How's she feeling?'

'Much better. She went back to work yesterday. Think I'm catching it though.' He gives a small, testing sort of cough.

'Drama queen.'

'Fuck off.'

Outside the Vietnamese restaurant, a couple are arguing.

'Why didn't you say?' she says. Her T-shirt reads *Yes, it's really me.*

'I tried,' he says. 'I'm sorry.'

'No, you're not,' she tells him.

'No, I'm not,' he tells her, and then he goes back inside.

A plane passes overhead and Jack glances up at its white underbelly. He remembers a pilot's voice

> Those of you on the left side of the plane will be able to
> see Golden Gate Bridge just coming up now

and his stomach turns in several quick loops. He whistles the beginnings of a tune he has forgotten and lets the notes drift away unfinished as they walk.

'Milder out today,' he says to Alex, and then they are through the bar's doors. Rosa is cleaning a table just inside the room, caught in a square of late sunlight. She looks up and grins.

'It's you two,' she says.

'It's us,' Alex says, holding out a hand and twirling her through the yellow light and into the gloom.

'How are you?'

'We're good. How are you, *chica*?'

'I'm fine. Happy to see you, of course.'

'Of course.'

She crosses the floor and smiles at him from behind the bar. 'What can I get you guys?'

'Beer,' Alex says, pulling out a stool. 'And plenty of it.'

She takes the bottles from the fridge and opens them, slotting them between the fingers on one hand. 'Happy Friday,' she says, sliding a small square napkin in front of each of them with the other.

'Happy Friday,' Alex says, holding out a $10 bill. Someone calls for Rosa from the dark space behind the stage.

'One second,' she says and hurries to the voice, tugging her hair back into a knot as she goes.

Alex takes his first sip and lets out a low whistle. 'What. A. Day.'

'Yeah,' Jack says, taking a pull on his bottle. 'A girl, you said?' The words feel heavy on his tongue.

'Right. Mid-twenties, Goth-ish – you know, total *Girl with the Dragon Tattoo* vibe.'

'We've talked about me and popular culture references.'

'Jeez, get yourself to a theatre now and again. A Goth, basically. Well, Goth-lite. Long leather coat, all that.'

'Okay, I'm with you.'

'Obviously, with the drive and all, she was out there for about twenty minutes before we got there. Cops were there first but they wouldn't go near her. As usual.'

'So what did you say to her?'

'Oh, you know, the usual crap. Asked for her mom's phone number, that sort of thing. Then when I got her attention I asked her what was wrong. Said I'd been through shit too, and maybe I could help.' He glances at Jack. 'I always say that. It really works.'

Jack nods.

'And you know what? When she thought about it, she couldn't tell me what was wrong. She just kept saying, "I'm so sad, I'm so sad," over and over in a whisper.'

I'm so sad I'm so sad I'm so sad I'm so sad

'Poor kid.'

'Right. So while I was talking to her, Eddie just hops back over the railing, gets hold of the back of her coat, like here –' he gets a handful of his own collar and stretches it out for Jack to see – 'and just pulls her up like a little puppy or something.'

'All in a day's work,' Jack says, and hates himself.

'We're kind of like superheroes, when you think about it.'

It's not the first time Alex has said this, but it is the first time

Jack has laughed. The sound feels wrong in his throat; unwieldy and sticky. *I'm so sad*, he thinks. *And then the devil left him.*

'What are you doing at the weekend?' Alex asks, gulping at his beer.

'We're supposed to be decorating. I don't know if we will. I could sleep for a year.'

'Yeah. It's been a long week.'

'Yeah. It has.'

'How's Elsa doing?'

Jack thinks of her face in the restaurant. *I thought this — we — were a fresh start.* 'She's good.'

'She going back to England for Christmas?'

'I don't think so. I offered to pay for her ticket, but she wasn't too happy about it. She's pretty independent like that.'

Alex laughs. 'Uh, no.'

Jack glances sideways at him. 'What?'

'She wants to spend it with you, dumb-ass. Sounds to me like you don't have the perfect independent woman after all.'

Jack takes another, harder swig of his beer. 'I don't think it's that.'

'Whatever you say.' Alex rests his chin on his hand. He twirls his empty bottle against the bar.

'Another?' Jack says, but Alex is staring dreamily into space. *And behold*, Jack thinks, but instead he says, 'Anyone home?'

Alex grins, stirs himself. 'I think I'm gonna ask her to marry me.'

'Dragon tattoo?'

'Oh, ha ha. Claudia.'

Jack swallows his last mouthful of beer slowly. 'Yeah?'

'Yeah. I think it's time.'

'That's quite the turnaround.'

'Well, things like today, they make you think, right? Life's too fucking short, and too many people fucking waste it. I love her and she loves me. It's time to do this.'

Jack puts the bottle down, his palms sweating. 'Did someone give you a personality transplant out on the chord today?' he says, his voice sounding shrill in his ears. 'Are you the real Alex?'

'What can I say? My time has come. I've seen the light.'

And behold. 'Well,' Jack says, gesturing to Rosa, who has returned from the dark space, for another round. 'Congratulations.'

2006

Graduation day dawns and the sun climbs steadily in the sky. They walk through empty streets, hand in hand, feet aching.

'We're going to look terrible in the pictures,' she says.

'What time are your parents getting here?' Kieran drops her hand and tangles his fingers in her hair, tugging her head towards him.

'The ceremony's at eleven, I think they're getting here for ten. Yours?'

He shrugs. 'Who knows.'

She recognises the tone, knows where the barrier is. 'Can you believe this is actually happening?' she asks, a careful sidestep.

'What?'

'Us graduating.'

'Me? No. You?' He drags her into a headlock.

'Yes.' He ruffles her hair. 'You've always been annoyingly good at passing things without actually doing the work.'

She pulls free and skips ahead. 'Some of us have a natural talent,' she calls back. 'Don't hate the player, hate the game.'

He lunges after her, catching her and swinging her around. 'You think you've got game, do you?' The wheeling sounds of their laughter fill the silent street and rise up like birds.

They arrive home – no longer the smoky, greasy house in Aldgate, no more Justin and Paulo to share space with, but their own tiny flat, still crammed with unpacked boxes. She stands at the door and surveys it: the bed in one corner, the sofa in the other. A metre of counter, with two electric hobs, one small, one large, and a microwave. There are dishes in the sink and a pizza box on the bed. Her best black dress hangs against the window, outlined in hazy summer light.

Kieran kisses her. 'I'm going to jump in the shower.'

Alone, she kneels on the bed and listens to the sound of the water running in the next room. She sinks down into the mattress, the sheets caught up around her. Today is a day which is important and far away. Today is a day which began hours ago and is yet to arrive.

After the ceremony, she stands on the pavement outside the hall, posing for photos and sweating under her make-up. The gown feels static against her skin, the hood with its pink lining dragging it untidily down at the back. She blinks against the sun, willing the nausea back. Anna grins beside her father as he fiddles with his camera. She glances at her mother, sheltering in the shade, Kieran beside her. He talks earnestly, his hands flipping back and forth, and she watches her mother laugh, watches her mother smile. She feels relieved and smug and unsurprised. Happy and content and horrendously hungover.

'Let us take you both for lunch,' her father says, finally zipping up the camera's case.

They take them to a pub on the corner, already crammed with overheating graduates in their swathes of crow-black, proud parents looking on. They find a table in the corner, Elsa installed at the head, and her father jostles his way back to the bar, taking Kieran with him. She grips the edge of the table, looking around for the toilets. *Grey sweat*, she thinks, closing her eyes.

'Are you okay, Elsa?' Mark asks, and she opens her eyes and looks at him, Anna pressed to his side. He is kind and quiet and she scolds herself for thinking he'd be anything else. She watches the easy way they exist with each other and then she thinks of Kieran's fingers against her skin, her teeth sinking into his lip, and she thinks that it is a shame that Anna has something easy and quiet when there is so much more to feel.

'I'm fine,' she says, and she smiles at her sister. 'What are you guys going to eat?'

Three sips into her large glass of wine, she has a sudden, misleading wave of energy and orders enthusiastically: fish and chips, a side salad, onion rings to share with Anna. It vanishes instantly when the plates appear in front of her and she leans back in her seat, trying not to breathe through her nose. She picks up a chip and chews on it gingerly, her foot finding Kieran's under the table.

'Someone had a big night last night,' her dad says, and she nods and closes her eyes. The conversation goes on around her, food coming off plates in quick, neat forkfuls whilst her own dish is pushed back and forth on the wooden table. Anna leans closer to Mark, takes a mouthful of his lasagne. Kieran is talking earnestly with her father; tennis, she thinks, trying to keep hold of stray words long enough to make sense of them. She looks at the clean brown sweep of his hair across a faintly red-rimmed eye, the bare shaven skin of his sharp jaw.

'We're really proud of you,' her mother says, reaching over to take a chip from her untouched plate.

'It feels very strange,' she says, closing her eyes again.

A waiter comes to clear the table, and her father raises his glass. 'To Elsie,' he says, and the others echo him. Kieran is a beat behind, a smile playing at the corners of his mouth. 'To Elsie,' he says, his hand creeping up her thigh.

'So, guys,' her father says, pouring himself another glass. 'You did it. What's the big plan now?'

She lists the places she would like to apply to and wonders if she is speaking loudly enough for them to hear. She listens as Kieran names the agencies he'd like to work for. She watches Mark watching Anna.

'Well, that all sounds great.' Her father signals for the bill.

Outside on the pavement, he presses a cheque into her hand: 'For rent and whatnot.' When he hugs her, she holds on tightly, her cheek hot against his shoulder. 'Thank you for coming,' she says, and then she kisses each of them and watches them climb into a taxi and drive away.

She falls asleep on the bus home, her head lolling against Kieran as he plays on his phone. She jerks awake unprompted as they approach their stop, head spinning.

In the flat, she lies face down on the bed, Kieran playing idly with a strand of her hair. It is darker then, and redder too, dyed with cheap tints. She drifts between sleep and waking dreams; scenes from the previous night, the ceremony and the lunch muddled with imagined images and strange soundbites, her limbs twitching. Kieran's voice is far off and close by, coming to her in small, difficult-to-decipher segments.

'You looked great up there,' he says.

She rolls on her side to look up at him, smiling slowly. He slides down beside her.

'You look better now.'

They kiss, their lips hot and dry, air warm. His chest bare, her dress hitched up, strap twisted. Her legs ache, her hands do not belong to her. There is sleep somewhere, his arm beneath her. She wakes in the darkness and presses down on him, his body slow and then rising to meet her. They sit without seeing, her arms around his neck, his hair against her face. The grey light of morning fills the room as they move against each other.

The hours are always backwards in those days.

2006

'You never listen to me.'

'You spend all of your time on the house.'

'I can't talk to you about the things I care about.' She slams a door.

'Are you calling me stupid?' he asks, later, when the words have really sunk in.

'You never make me feel beautiful,' she ends, and he laughs, because it seems too impossible to be true.

The laugh is a mistake.

2012

It is December. People continue to jump. Elsa continues to walk. She visits galleries and museums, shopping malls and beaches. She wears more and more layers, and her fingers have taken on an almost permanent state of near-numbness. When Sam and Skye visit their grandma, she sketches them. Jack works late and comes home drunk and she is angry; she ignores him. The silences are taut and all-consuming for her, but he slips off to sleep with ease and in the mornings when she wakes he is gone. Sometimes, when she watches the clock and realises he is not coming back, she is afraid to admit that what she feels is relief.

One night, lying awake alone, she drinks wine in the dark and remembers what it is like to run through the rain and what it is like to walk in the dawn. She reaches for her laptop and tries to speak to friends in England, but the connection is slow and she can't find the words. 'What have you been up to?' they ask, and she feels like crying. She scrolls down the newsfeed, past friends who have had bad days at work, friends who have enjoyed a film, friends whose children grin toothlessly at cameras. There is a birth announcement, an engagement. There are several sets of tagged wedding photos. Mouth dry, she clicks on her own profile instead. She flicks through an album of photos first uploaded in the weeks after they arrived, when the skies were still an endless blue. There is Jack, usually in profile; caught unaware. A few of her face, tanned and grinning, on the occasions he has taken the camera from her and pushed her into shot. Hardly any of the two of them: one taken in North Beach on their first full day, a Japanese tourist behind the camera. They pose in front of a shop window, his arm around her, her head leant in to him. It is tagged with her name only: to the internet, Jack does not exist. The thought frustrates her, a now familiar pang striking sharp inside her, and she flicks through the album to find another of the two of them. This one, taken a week later in Golden Gate Park, is closer up, the camera held in his outstretched hand. Their cheeks are flushed with walking, the sky bright behind them. Her cursor hovers over the photo's options: 'Make this my profile picture'. She looks at the two of them again, looks at her own smile and the easy light in his eyes. Then she slides the cursor up and crosses the photo away.

The rest of the album is all landscapes, most of the water. She flicks through them, the yellow stretch of sand at Crissy Field, looking up at Golden Gate; the white buildings of the piers. She pauses at one with Alcatraz in the foreground, water foaming at the rocks. She glances down at the abandoned conversation, the unanswered question: What have you been up to? Opening another window, she searches for tour operators. She selects a slot, proceeds to checkout. She enters her credit card details and drinks more wine, finally falling asleep with a forearm pressed to the keys.

The next day is grey and wet, a fine sheen of constant but almost invisible rain falling, but the ferry is full and so she sits without shelter on its deck, her hair curling damply against her cheeks. The bay is filled with fog, a wall of white which hides the bridge from view. Droplets of rain cling to her eyelashes and she stares at it, trying to make out its shape. At the very top, the towers emerge, two heads above the tide.

The morning after he told her about the job on Golden Gate, she woke early. She rolled onto her side and looked at him. When he sleeps, his brow is often furrowed, but that morning his face was calm and still and as she watched, his eyes opened slowly and he looked at her.

'Did you mean it?' she asked.

'Of course.'

'People will say it's too soon. They'll say we haven't known each other long enough.'

He rolled her towards him, folded her in. 'Els,' he said, his face in her hair. 'We're not like other people.'

They are approaching the island now, a looming mass in the sea of white. Several large buildings, yellow and grey, stand on its banks, the watch tower reaching up through the fog. Some plants grow, hardy and sparse, and dark trees skulk across one slope. As they draw closer, a sign emerges at the edge of the bank: 'WARNING. Persons procuring or concealing the escape of prisoners are subject to prosecution and imprisonment.' Through the rain, she reads it wrong: sees the word as 'persecution'. She watches two gulls huddle together under a thorny bush, yellow eyes following the boat's progress. At the top of the chalky hill, a ruined building opens its glassless windows to the white sky, a toothless smile. A woman on the bench in front of Elsa's leans over the boat's railing to take photographs, a blue plastic rainhat covering her blonde braid. 'Do you think they have wifi?' she asks, turning back to the man beside her.

Kieran once told her that there are more people alive today than have ever lived. Sometimes, thinking of this number makes her hopeful. More often it makes her dizzy. She remembers his face as he said it, backlit by blue screen as he looked round from his laptop, sprawled on the sagging mattress in their stuffy studio. *Get this*, he'd said. *There are more people alive right now than have ever died. Ever.* She turns away from him, looks back out at the island. *You only ever did care about the big picture*, she thinks.

The boat docks in a series of shuddering movements, and the people on the benches around her begin to head for the gangway, shoes squeaking against the wet deck. She follows them, the woman in the blue rainhat in front of her. The queue bottlenecks where a set of steps lead below deck, the people pushing their way up dry and coffee-breathed. Elsa is underneath a ledge and water runs down her neck.

Sometimes she walks out to the bridge. As she climbs the quiet hills beside it, the fog is damp and heavy in her lungs. The trees sweat with it; a constant, slow dripping like solitary notes of a song. She goes there but she never tells him. She goes, and she gets close, but she has never put a foot onto the bridge itself. Somehow, she is afraid to.

Finally across the gangway and onto the jetty, she moves through the assembled crowd. Someone with a clipboard is explaining something but Elsa is too far away to hear. She watches the others listening, their faces smooth and blank. When they begin to walk, she walks too, following the road which winds up the hill. The rain, which has begun in earnest now, drowns out words and the wind whistles through her wet hair. She burrows deeper into her jacket.

'Where's he gone?' someone says, and she walks faster.

At the top of the hill is the main prison; a long, orangeish building with iron bars across its windows and rusty stains weeping down its brickwork. Stepping into the sudden wave of sound in the visitor's entrance hall, she joins the queue, which bends back on itself, snakelike, and passes guests through rows of institutional showers. Along one side, behind white painted bars, is the station where arriving inmates would collect their prison clothes and bedding, have their faces shaven and their hair cut. She runs a hand along the bars, looking in at the neat rows of folded trousers and shirts.

As a little girl, she was never afraid of the dark. She never had a nightlight, never slept with the door ajar. She has never been afraid of small spaces, either – has always been the one to wiggle under beds to retrieve things, to climb into crawl spaces. Now, thinking of the fish crammed in the tanks in Chinatown, thinking of the dark rooms in the house on Potrero, she is not so sure. She turns away from the bars, jams her hands into her pockets.

Reaching the front of the queue, she is called forward by a dark-haired girl with expanders in her earlobes, two open-mouthed o's, who asks 'English?'

'Yes,' she says, and is given a headset.

'Through those doors,' the girl says, pointing. 'Enjoy.'

The double doors lead directly into the cells. Three storeys high, their bars a pale green, they stretch out in front of her. She places the foam headphones over her ears and clicks the Play button with cold, stiff fingers. A stern male voice welcomes her to the tour, instructing her to study some picture boards to her left. Dutifully, she does so, craning her neck to see through the crowd. One by one, the voices of the ex-prisoners and correctional officers pictured join the recording.

She walks slowly through the concrete space, letting them direct her from cell to cell. The tour's sound effects are silly and over-acted, but around her everyone shuffles through its stops, silent as they listen to their headphones. It is creepy and makes her think of old zombie movies. She finds herself looking over her shoulder often.

The voices direct her attention to the rough hole hacked into the wall of the cell once inhabited by Frank Morris, famous escapee. *Two years*, she thinks. *Two years chipping away. How did they bear it?* She imagines the three of them, successfully out of the building and at the island's edge, makeshift raft at the ready. *Where did they go?* she thinks, and then, *Where do they go?* She is touched, just briefly, feather soft and fleeting, by the mysteries below the surface of the bay. Then her attention is caught by the dummy head, formed from soap, toilet paper and hair, which Morris put in his place in the narrow bed to avoid detection, and she thinks reflexively of her sketchpad at home, of the half-sketched faces which fill its pages. It feels good to draw again. She likes that she has a project. *Art is who I am*, she wrote on an application many years ago, and although she does not like to be defined, she thinks this is probably almost true. The feeling of taking a white page and shaping it into something new is a feeling she has forgotten, and remembering it is even better than the original discovery. *Why did I ever stop?* she wonders, but the path which leads to the answer is not one she wants to turn down.

A man who sounds kinder than the others talks her out through a narrow steel door and down crumbling steps which lead to a rectangular expanse of cracked concrete; the old exercise yard. Weeds poke through gaps and she thinks of the house on Potrero; of a fistful of soil in her hand, a thing pulled up at the roots. The wire mesh which tops the perimeter wall is broken and bent in many places, hanging down where it is torn, and across the water, just a mile away, the skyline of the city unfolds, lights beginning to come on in the gloom. One old inmate tells her that on some still nights, its sounds could carry easily across the water, distorted but recognisable, like voices heard through bathwater, music played through a phone. 'New Year was the night we always heard,' he says, and she lets out a small, irritated breath. Another explains how it felt to stand here on clear days and look out at the city's skyline. 'There's everything I want in my life and it's there – a mile and a quarter away. But I can't get there,' he says and she closes her eyes.

Back inside, the voices lead her through the offices of the prison, where some of the old radio equipment and antique typewriters are still in their places. She presses her hand against the glass and watches the imprints of her fingers crawl slowly inwards and then disappear.

'Wow,' a woman says behind her, and Elsa jumps and moves away. 'Imagine,' the woman says, but the rest of the thought is lost as the sound of a siren echoes through Elsa's earphones. An ex-guard recounts an escape attempt and she stares at the ruins of the staff's quarters, battered by wind and damaged by storms, its open windows showing only the relentless grey of the bay.

In the old dining hall, she walks to the window and stares out across the water again. Higher now, and with the fog beginning to lift, she can see the faint outline of the Bay Bridge and the dark edge of the Marin County shoreline beyond. The tour is ending; they have reached the part of the prison's tale when the gates are closed for ever and its last residents are released. Time to leave, and yet, as the final voice explains, a day which is full of uncertainty for some inmates. *What's the point in being free when you haven't got anywhere else to go?* she thinks, and he agrees. As she turns to leave, his voice echoes through her headphones. 'I was scared to death,' he says.

On the ferry back to the mainland, she pushes her way below deck, her clothes damp. She orders a coffee from the small bar and takes a seat on a crowded bench. The paper cup is too hot and she pulls her sleeve down over her hand to hold it. Removing the lid, she brings the cup close to her face, breathes in its steam. All around her, people huddle, faces bent over camera screens. They click through the day's shots, occasionally showing them to their friends. With a sudden and hollow ache, she wishes for someone to talk to.

From the bridge, Elsa's boat is just a dot on the water, hidden almost entirely from view. Jack lugs short lengths of scaffolding from a storeroom to one of the miniature pickups. In his pocket burns another letter, and in the letter is another, solitary sentence.

For wide is the gate and broad is the path which leads to destruction, and many enter through it

This time, the phone number is accompanied by a single kiss.

Back on dry land, where the rain has slowed to a faint and delicate drizzle, Elsa crosses the street and heads for the Embarcadero centre. A short stretch of delis and dessert stalls stands under fluorescent lights, defiant to the gloom outside. She makes for a juice bar near the centre where she often goes. Fruit is something she neither likes nor dislikes, and she can rarely stir herself to buy or eat it for pleasure. A smoothie or two a week suits her better; she thinks of it like putting petrol in a car. She looks up at the menu and orders an Apple Kiwi Twist, an option which fulfils both of the criteria she considers essential: it doesn't have an embarrassing name or contain banana.

'Do you want to add a booster?' the teenage boy behind the counter asks.

'Do you have vodka?'

He stares at her, panicked. 'Ginseng, B-12 or bee pollen.'

'Bee pollen?'

'Yeah.'

'I'm okay, thanks.'

She watches him push the fruit into the funnel of the blender, the flesh exploding. When he slides the plastic glass towards her, the drink inside is not green as she has expected but a greyish sort of yellow, black flecks of kiwi seeds pressed against its surface like fish eyes.

'Three ninety-five,' he says, passing her a straw, and she hands him four dollar bills and turns away. Outside the stall, she pauses at one of the tiny tables, biting the paper from the straw. She slots it through the hole in the plastic lid and drags the first gulp up, the apple gritty on the sides of her mouth.

'Hey.'

She wheels around, straw still in situ. 'Hey!' she says, releasing it.

Pepper is dressed in a tweedy, oversized jumper, his shirt collar turned up around his neck. His hair, wet with rain, is slicked back, and droplets are sent shivering from it every time his gloved hand pushes its way through the strands. 'Elsa, right?' he says.

'Right.'

'How you doing?'

'Good, thanks. And you?'

'Weather's shit, huh?'

'It's not great, no. I've just been to Alcatraz.'

'Oh yeah? How was it?'

'It was pretty amazing, actually. Have you not been?'

'Nope. Not my kind of thing.'

'Oh, okay.' She takes another sip of her drink, watching the teenage server pushing strawberries into the blender in a gory stream.

'Hey,' Pepper says after a minute. 'What are you up to tonight?'

She shrugs. 'I'm not sure.'

'There's a thing – you should come. It'll be cool, you'll like it.'

'Okay.'

'Great.' Pepper is groping around in the pockets of his jeans. 'There's an awesome band playing. You should definitely come.'

He locates a piece of folded card, thrusting it towards Elsa. She unfolds it and looks down at the hot-pink type. A bar out in Oakland, a Battle of the Bands event. 'Thanks,' Elsa says. 'Looks like fun.'

'It will be,' Pepper says. 'You'll like it.'

She smiles and takes another slurp of her drink. 'Well, I should go,' he says, pushing more water from his hair. 'Catch you later, okay? Eight o'clock.'

Elsa nods politely. She won't go. She knows she won't go.

She takes the BART under the water and into Oakland. Stepping off the escalator and onto the street, she glances around, checking the map on her phone. Her paper map, now dog-eared and doodled on, is at home, no longer required. Starting to walk towards the bar, she feels a sudden nostalgia for it, a wave of sadness. She locks her phone and puts it away.

Things are different here; the streets wider and empty, buildings low. As she walks down the empty road, there is a sense of menace, of old-westerns suspense. There are gas stations on both sides of the road, their forecourts dusty and deserted. A run-down burger joint has a single customer waiting at its service window. She crosses the road, passing an empty restaurant, a shuttered store. Up ahead, a small group of people stand smoking.

'Hey, sweetheart,' someone says, and she pushes past them and into the bar.

The place is dark, lit by red light bulbs in torn paper shades. It takes a moment for her eyes to adjust and she stands in the doorway, the carpet sticky under her shoes. The bar fills one wall, corrugated steel against the black of the floor and the walls. There is a single barman, tall, fat and bald, his head egg-shaped. Behind him, limited edition Barbie dolls line the wall in their boxes. A Russian princess, a mermaid, an air hostess. Their pinched faces stare out from behind the smeared plastic of their boxes, eyes fixed ahead. There is a certain shame to them, as though they are embarrassed by their exhibition, vulnerable on the wall. *Just look straight ahead*, Elsa thinks. *Don't look down.* She snorts at herself and looks away.

A single sheet of A4 paper has been taped to the wall, advertising cans of beer at $2. She orders one and makes her way through to the next room, where a lone guitarist plays on a small stage. She sits in one of the booths around the side of the room – orange plastic, patched up all over with black or silver gaffer tape. Sipping her beer, she looks around. Peeling stickers fill most surfaces – neon colours, torn slogans. She runs her hand across one on the table in front of her, an acid-house smiley face and the words 'TAKE YOUR TIME'. Up on the stage, a rubber chicken has been left atop one of the speakers, and the guitarist sings a song about a girl's blonde hair. He is good-looking; hair shorn short and bright green eyes in a chiselled face. Wearing a lumberjack shirt and jeans, he sits on the stool with his battered guitar, eyes fixed on a point on the floor. Behind him, a man in a Stetson fiddles with a speaker.

The room is otherwise empty except for a girl sitting in the booth across from Elsa's. Wearing a red beret and thick black glasses, a pink ski jacket, checked skirt and thick woollen tights with ballerina flats, she watches the singer with a feverish expression, mouthing the words to the song. There is no sign of Pepper.

Elsa drains her beer and makes her way to the bathroom.

The ladies' room is tiny; barely a cupboard. Two cubicles have been crammed in, but there isn't enough space to open their doors fully. She manoeuvres her way in, her bag getting trapped halfway. Inside, the cubicle is covered with graffiti. She reads it as she sits. 'I miss my sister' someone has plaintively printed, right next to a declaration that 'It's only gay if the balls touch'. 'I love Dylan' someone has written, but beneath that, in another, neater hand, someone has replied that 'Dylan doesn't hang out here any more', signing off, definitively, as 'Dylan's new girlfriend'. As she stands and flushes, the words at her eye level simply state 'I don't want to be here.' She pushes her way back out of the cubicle, listening to the owner introducing the next act. Beside the sink is a bottle of dishwashing liquid instead of soap. She squeezes some into her palm and watches the water drain away.

Shots of tequila are also $2. This, clearly, is the more economical option. She sits at the bar as they are delivered to her, alone in a patch of raw red light. More customers arrive but they lurk at the edges of the room, a swelling of the shadows. A band begin and finish their set to a spattering of applause behind her. The next act, a female singer with a red tube top and a keyboard, gets off to a better start; several whistles and one or two catcalls. Elsa ignores it all. She orders a beer. She sucks salt from the ridge where her thumb expands into the fleshy part of her hand. She stares up at the rows of Barbie dolls and laughs.

When the next band are announced, the atmosphere changes. People begin to move towards the stage, appearing from the dark en masse, leaking out of walls. They are suddenly interested, suddenly engaged. She orders another beer and slides off her stool. A little unsteady on her feet, she makes her way after the small crowd. She's wearing heels and is out of practice, legs stiff as she walks. She leans against a post at the edge of the small dance floor, watching it fill.

The band, now clambering on stage and arranging themselves behind their instruments, are all in their late thirties, and all have a neatly pressed, suburban sort of look. Four men, all in jeans and T-shirts, all with tidy haircuts and clean-shaven faces, their instruments pristine, their boots brand new. Looking at them, she pictures them behind desks and with children, driving estate cars and buying food at farmer's markets. The people who watch from the dance floor – the women in their halter tops, the men in their stonewashed jeans and sweat-stained shirts – don't seem to have noticed. She presses her back to the post and drinks more beer.

The first song begins and she is surprised to find that they are good; a classic rock-and-roll sound with a darker twist, a keening, metallic edge that intrigues her. The air smells of tequila and sweat and plastic. *Shut your legs, Barbie*, Elsa thinks, and laughs.

The bass guitarist, in particular, and for no particular reason, is the one she finds most interesting. Like the others, he is tall and neat in a pale blue T-shirt and dark jeans. He has short dark hair and thin-rimmed glasses, and underneath his T-shirt a slightly flabby stomach protrudes. There is a thin silver band on his right index finger, the only thing which marks him out. Throughout the set, she watches him, trying to imagine his life. Where does he live? What does he do during the day, where is he sitting while he isn't on a dive-bar stage? She narrows her eyes, trying to answer her own questions. The neatness of him, the cleanness, is irritating. She wants to pick up the flaccid rubber chicken from its speaker roost and shove it in his mouth; to take his index finger and place it in *her* mouth, slide the silver ring off with her teeth.

The set begins to gain momentum, more and more of the audience dancing. She returns to the bar, where the barman is texting, Ice Princess Barbie watching over him. He sees her approach but waits until she is actually at the bar to put away his phone.

'Can I have a tequila, please?'

He pours it without speaking and she watches him, cheeks warm. 'Do you like them?' she asks, jerking her head back towards the stage.

'The band?'

She shrugs.

He slides the tequila towards her. 'Yeah. They're good.'

She drinks the shot, pushes the plastic glass back towards him. 'I'll have another, please.'

He pours it and puts it down in front of her, taking his phone out again. She sips half and then the other half, wincing. She wonders how many she would have to drink before he asked if she has had enough.

The fourth song is coming to an end, and with it, the set. The lead singer thanks the crowd in between lines, the repeated chorus spaced out to fit 'Thanks so much, you guys' and 'Have a great night' and 'We hope we'll see you again soon'. The crowd cheer, calling out for one more song, but the manager is climbing onto the stage, announcing the final act, who are welcomed with a volley of boos. Elsa orders another tequila and, on a sudden whim, a packet of cigarettes.

'Thirteen dollars,' the bartender tells her and she hands him a twenty. Drinking the tequila as she moves, she staggers outside. She leans against the bar's window as she opens the cigarettes.

'Hey, baby,' a passing man in a leather jacket says. She ignores him. 'Bitch,' he says, over his shoulder, as she thumbs a cigarette out of the packet and puts it in her mouth.

'You have a spare one of those?'

She looks up and sees the guitarist blinking back at her. Up close and behind his glasses, his eyes are a pale brown, almost gold. She shrugs. 'You have a light?'

He nods; she extends the packet. As he reaches out to take one, the silver band on his finger catches the glow of the solitary street light.

'I'm Michael,' he says, but she doesn't care.

2006

He knocks on the bathroom door and waits. The thermostat on the central heating is broken, and the house is hot and hazy. Sweat beads on his back and his T-shirt clings to his skin. He glances at his watch again as he tries the handle. Locked. 'Beth?'

He can hear her running the taps, hear the bubbles foaming as she washes her hands. He knocks again and this time, after a pause, she opens it. Dressed in loose trousers and one of his T-shirts, she looks small and fluid, ready to evaporate. They face each other.

'It's negative,' she says.

'I'm going to miss my flight,' he says.

It is a four-hour flight and a ten-minute taxi ride. He has decided not to check into his motel first, carrying his overnight bag with him; the quicker he does it, the quicker it is done. He pays the driver who offers a small smile and a shrug – it is what it is you do what you can – and then is gone. As the taxi pulls away, he looks up at the building: tall and white, two central towers with two slimmer wings extending outwards. The slopes of grass are landscaped, the hedges well kept and uniform. It looks like a hospital, it looks like a hotel. He looks up at it and wishes he hadn't come.

Inside, he is shuffled through two sets of metal detectors. The second takes offence at him, screeching each time he is forced to walk through it.

'Step this way, sir,' one of the guards tells him. He pats him down roughly, and Jack imagines cartoon escape plans: a file baked into a cake, a smuggled-in spoon for digging. Satisfied, the guard stands, gesturing for him to continue.

The walls look wet to the touch, grey paint slimy. There is a strong smell of disinfectant and his shoes squeak as he walks, the sound subdued.

At the end of the corridor is another door, another guard. And beyond them, a square room, the walls pale green, filled with three rows of small, chipped tables and orange plastic chairs. He takes a seat at one and looks around at the other people in the room. At the table beside his, two women; one blonde, one redhead, both smoking. It hangs in yellow clouds around them, a fog into which they both retreat. In one corner, a teenage boy scratches at a table with his thumbnail. Finally, at a table directly behind Jack's, a man of around his own age is sitting with a little girl about five years old on his lap. She plays idly with a cord on his jacket while he stares straight ahead. In each corner is a guard; arms folded, eyes averted. The minutes tick by in silence. He thinks of Beth, back in Chicago, her face in the open bathroom door. He wishes he hadn't come.

Finally the door opposite is unlocked and the men come shuffling in. He scans their faces as they file into the room. His father's is the last, and as their eyes meet, Jack's heart stops in his chest. He takes a shuddery breath and it starts again, the world recalibrating, but the shock still remains, white hot and pulsing. His father looks old. His father *is* old, has been made old here, like a far harsher sentence served. The lines on his face carve deeply into the flesh, the cross-hatched skin sagging. His hair is grey and thin and there are freckles on his scalp.

He pushes back his chair, meaning to stand, but, unsure if this is appropriate, hovering halfway.

His father sits down and there is no embrace. 'I didn't think you'd come.'

'I'm sorry. Things have been busy, with the wedding and the house –' He falters. 'How are you?'

His question is ignored. 'How was the wedding?'

'It was good. Fantastic. Really great.' These words do not belong to him, yet here they are, flowing smoothly out.

'Your mother have a good time?'

'Sure, yeah. She had fun.'

'How's she doing?'

'She's well. Aimee too.'

His father looks down at his hands, picks at a hair on his left forearm. The silence which is growing is softer than the shock; it is filled with rainy Seattle days and brown-sofa sitting. Jack is eighteen and English; he is thirty and American.

'What were you thinking, Dad?' he asks, and his father's hand stops.

'It was a hard time,' he says, after a moment. 'I was in a corner.'

Embezzlement. It is a word that has always sounded comical to him, but now there is no humour. He looks at his father. 'I'm sorry.'

'So.' His father lifts his thumb and finger to his face to study the hair, now removed. 'How do you like married life?'

He hesitates without meaning to and is instantly flooded with guilt. 'It's great.' His voice is determined. 'Beth's great.'

His father leans back in his chair, folding his arms across his chest. He is smiling now. 'Sure. They all start out that way.'

'Dad.' It is a warning but also a plea.

Jeff holds up his hands. 'It's not easy, that's all I'm saying. It's not easy like you expect.'

'So, what's the secret?' He tries to keep his tone light. Remembering his eighteen-year-old self arriving in Seattle, he is suddenly eager to bridge the gap between them, to be the son who sleeps in a single bed and complains about the cooking.

'Don't get married.' His father lights a cigarette with shaking hands. Jack turns away. The teenage boy is reaching across the table to show a small, chubby man a photograph. The little girl is sitting on an inmate's lap, gazing up at him while he talks to the man who brought her, his hand stroking her small face. *It's negative*, he thinks, and though he hates himself for it, he is relieved.

'You'll be okay,' his dad says, flicking ash onto the tabletop. 'You've always been a stubborn asshole, just like me. You'll keep trying.'

Jack sneers. 'And that's enough, is it? Trying?'

His father shrugs. 'That's all you can do.'

2012

As Christmas approaches, the *thing* that has
been unravelling has been safely recaptured,
the shutters redrawn, and Jack begins to feel less
afraid. *You'll keep trying*, his father once told him,
and he does. He does so in earnest. Washing his
face in the mornings, he studies the lines that are
beginning to deepen and does not feel the teetering
panic he once did. Watching Elsa at her laptop, he
sees the smoothness of her skin and the darkness
of her hair and they are simple things which please
him. She is more often out now than when they
first arrived – out for drinks with people she has
met at a night he can't remember, whose names she
says with wary ease, as if trying to trip a memory
from him. Alone in the house for perhaps the first
time, he sits on her side of the bed and looks at the
things which belong to her – the bracelet and

the paperback romance on the bedside table, the hairbrush beside the mirror. Sometimes when she sleeps, he holds her hand. In the mornings when he leaves, she is rarely awake, and often he lies beside her a little longer, right up close where the warmth of her reaches him.

On 20 December, he is leaving work later than usual. He has stayed behind to help the team in the shop, collecting overtime which he is gradually piling up into a savings account. He likes to think of it as 'the escape fund', even though he has no specific plans to escape, no definitive idea of what or who he would be escaping. The simple fact that it exists has always been enough. Like blocks of a building, the amount in the account goes steadily up, more and more secure as it grows.

He has just reached the entrance to the staff parking lot, the sky rapidly darkening, when he sees a shadow beside a tangled patch of undergrowth. He takes slow steps closer, sees it morph into a man. Haloed against the orange sky, he stands with his hands in his pockets, watching Jack approach. His face cast half in shadow, he appears featureless but for a smile which grows the closer Jack gets. *And then the devil left him*, Jack thinks, pushing his own hands deeper into the pockets of his coat.

A little closer now, and the rest of the face begins to reveal itself. The man looks well, his face rounder and his clothes cleaner than the last time Jack saw him, his hair cut into a sharper style. It is strange, Jack realises, to think he looks out of place here, on concrete instead of a chord, but there it is, that is the truth.

'Hi, Jack,' he says nervously. 'I'm sorry to just show up like this.'

Absurdly, Jack shakes his head. 'Don't worry,' he says. 'How've you been?'

'I've been okay.' Matthew shifts his weight from one foot to the other, his hands still in his pockets. 'I sent you a letter.'

And behold. 'You sent me the letters?'

'Yeah. I found out your name from one of the guys you work with.'

'Why didn't you sign them?'

'I didn't?'

'No.'

'I guess I didn't.'

'No.'

'I thought you might call.'

Jack studies his feet. He wonders what Alex would do, or Miller. He doesn't think there is a guideline for this.

'I've been thinking about you a lot,' Matthew says, looking up at the sky. The first stars are shining.

'You've had a difficult time,' Jack says.

'I've been thinking you were sent to me that day.'

'It wasn't your time,' Jack says, though the words feel heavy in his throat, difficult to heave out. 'You need to remember that.'

'Someone saved me,' Matthew says, and because this is factually inarguable, Jack nods.

'Yes.'

'I'm going to try and be better,' Matthew says, looking over

Jack's shoulder at the bridge. The wind is picking up and the fog draws closer, moisture seeping through their clothes.

'That's all you can do,' Jack says, and his voice is soft and lost in the mist.

Arriving home, his face stinging with the cold, he breathes in the air of the house, clinging to it, because it is her. 'Els?' he calls out, kicking off his shoes.

'In here.' She is kneeling on the living-room floor, a line of colour charts spread out in front of her. On one wall are several neat rectangles of paint; shades of blue and grey in blocks. 'What do you think?' she asks, getting up. 'What's in the bags?'

'Dinner,' he says, putting them down on the sofa. He strides across the room and tugs her to him, pressing his mouth hard against hers. A small sound escapes her, an exhalation of breath hot on his skin, and her teeth sink gently into his lip. He draws back, hands sliding up her arms, across her collarbone, up and around her neck, into her hair.

She stares back at him. Her hair is tied up in a knot on the top of her head, and there is a streak of powder-blue paint on one cheek. She smells faintly of cigarettes, strongly of vanilla. 'What's got into you?' she asks, and smiles.

He lets his arm slide around the familiar curve of her waist, drawing her in to him. *I'm going to try and be better*, he thinks, and he shivers. He sees Matthew looking out at the bridge. *I've been thinking you were sent to me that day*, he said, but why, somehow, does it feel the other way round? He pulls Elsa closer and he cannot get warm. She rests a head against his shoulder, the sweet, smoky smell of her hair drifting up to him. They turn in slow circles around the small room.

'I missed you,' she says, and he nods.

2006

Instead of trying to find ways to argue with
her, he begins to turn even the most mundane
conversations meaningful.

'I'm tired.'

'Well, you've had a hard time lately.'

                              'Can you take out the trash?'

                              'Sure. You need to rest.'

'This weather is so depressing.'

'We'll get through it, you know.'

Each time, Beth smiles and softly presses
her lips together, each of his efforts as efficiently
dismissed as the rest. She makes her visits to the
doctor alone, the appointment cards hidden from
him. She speaks on the phone to her friends but
falls silent whenever he enters a room.

At a birthday party for Franklin's third son,
Jack loses sight of her. The party is almost over;

the children seated around the table, eating cake. The cake is yellow, previously rectangular, and now disintegrating at the centre of the table. The birthday boy, strapped into his highchair, has fallen asleep, his pudgy hand still splayed in the remains of his slice. Jack moves through the room, past its candied carnage, looking for his wife.

He finds her in the garden. She is on her knees in front of one of the flower beds in the corner, her hair twisted into a loose knot which is beginning to uncurl at the nape of her neck. As he gets closer, he sees that she is digging a hole.

'What are you doing?' There is a single tulip clutched in her hand, its stem torn. She holds it up.

'One of the kids pulled it out.'

'It won't grow,' he says. 'It doesn't work like that.'

She ignores him.

He stands and watches her, her small hands moving quickly in short strokes. The soil is dry, the sun warm at his back. She holds the stem of the flower in the centre of the hole, shuffling the dirt back in around it neatly with her other palm. When the hole is filled, she presses down around the edges and stops, considering, before kneeling back.

'There,' she says.

Beth stands and wipes her hands on her jeans, leaving green and brown ingrained in the soft blue. They both look at the flower.

'There,' she says again. 'That's better.'

BELLA

2013

I t is 6 January, and as Elsa stretches and turns over in bed, she notices the lowness of the sun in the sky and realises that it is almost evening. The sheets are twisted around her, and she flexes her toes against the taut material, preparing herself for the inevitable moment when she will have to move. She stares up at the ceiling, watching a foggy thread of cobweb flutter listlessly in a draught.

Christmas has passed with little to cling to. On the day itself, she cooked her first Christmas dinner; a reasonable success, on the whole, she thinks, though the potatoes here do not perform in the way she expects them to, her roasts always coming out soft and smooth where they should be fluffy and crisp. After dinner, they exchanged presents – as she remembers this, she twists the silver bracelet around her wrist, sliding a finger back and forth between it and her skin.

The last days of the year were quiet on Potrero Avenue; even Pearl away, visiting her grandson, rich Uncle Harry, in Los Angeles. Elsa and Jack, now unused to spending several days in the same space, approached them tentatively. There were walks. There were meals. There were afternoons spent face to face, breathless, on the floor. But often there was silence. In some ways, she preferred the silence. There was a politeness to their words, a boundary. The silence felt like a period of recharging, of recovery. On New Year's Eve, she felt hopeful again. One year since they met. She dressed in his favourite dress, took time over her hair. In the taxi ride over to Alex's place, she turned to look at him beside her on the back seat and they both smiled. Out on the fire escape, his hand in hers, she turned her head towards the light and looked up at the open sky, the low, white moon and the stars.

Back inside the party, with five minutes until the countdown, she stood beside Claudia and watched the men laugh. Claudia is engaged and there is something different about her, and about Alex; a softness and a secret. At three minutes to midnight, Elsa's eyes met Pepper's across the room and he raised his glass. Then Jack was beside her, leading her over to the window, where Chase and Price were arguing about baseball. She remembers the coolness of his hand through the silk of her dress. Somewhere in the room, Stephanie was singing. Her new boyfriend, Lorenz, gazed down at her. Her ex-husband had come to the party with them but had gone on to see another friend elsewhere in the city.

At two minutes to midnight, Elsa moved towards Jack and whispered, 'This time last year.' His hand travelled up her spine, his eyes locked on hers. He drew her closer, their faces almost touching. 'I remember,' he said, his lips grazing hers.

She should get up, she thinks now. Jack will be home from work soon, and she has recorded a film for them to watch, has plans to order a takeaway later. She shivers at the thought of leaving the bed. She has been wearing the same jumper almost every day; a faded and baggy cable-knit she found in a thrift store for $4. A man's XXL, it comes down past her thighs. Most days she folds her hands inside the sleeves and tucks her knees up inside as she sits at the table sketching or reading. The silk dress from New Year's Eve is tucked in a ball at the foot of her bed, waiting to be washed.

At just after one minute to midnight, the music was switched off and Alex hoisted himself onto a chair, one hand reaching up to the foam ceiling tiles for support. 'You know how this goes, kids,' he said. 'I'll start you off: TEN ...' Elsa's bare arm pressed against Jack's as they counted, fingers still linked, and as she yelled FOUR she glanced up at him and he looked back at her and neither of them counted any more. At the turn of the year, they were already kissing. Around them the others cheered and hugged. *Should auld acquaintance be forgot*, they sang, *And never brought to mind?* Through the thin material of the dress, she felt the heat of his body against hers. They left the party soon after.

She really should get up, she thinks, as she hears footsteps on the stairs. She sits, drawing the sheets around her, goosebumps rising across her naked chest and down her arms. The door opens, and Michael the bass guitarist pops his head round, still shirtless, his thinning hair messy. 'I made you some coffee,' he says. 'It's really cold out.'

'I have to leave,' she says, reaching out to take the mug.

Is there guilt? Yes, almost certainly. Elsa is not a person without guilt; she is in fact a person rather prone to guilt, a guilty addiction to guilt. Walking down Market Street in the late afternoon, she steps over sleeping bodies and feels guilty for her clothes and her house, for the food in the bags she is carrying. Thinking of the people on the bridge – the blonde girl called Eve, the man in the mackintosh, the others who Jack no longer describes – she feels guilty. Now, standing in the laundry room in the house on Potrero, puffing warm air into her pink hands, she feels guilty. It is a giddy feeling, vertiginous and hot. She chews at a thumbnail and imagines what it would be like to tell him. She pictures words hurled across the new, blue living room, glass shattering, tears falling. Doors slam, one by one. She winces as she blows on her hands again, the fingers still furled and frozen.

Why has she done it? Anger, she would like to say, because there is less blame in that. There has been a fight, their first, really – the first as she defines the word anyway. Over something small; him just in from work, the smell of him metallic and cold. Her at the table, an unfinished sketch of Pearl and Skye in front of her.

'Hey,' he had said.

'Did you get my text?'

'Yeah, sorry.' He sat in the chair opposite her, removing his boots. 'I don't know, Els. I'm not really up for a trip at the moment.'

'It's just a weekend away. It's only a couple of hours' drive.'

'I know. I'm just really tired.'

She put down the pencil. 'Well, why didn't you just say that instead of not replying?'

He'd slammed his fist against the table. 'Do you ever just stop?'

Her chair had made a shrieking sound as she pushed it back, timely and satisfying. 'Fuck off then,' she said over her shoulder, and she'd found herself outside the house, her coat in her hand.

Perhaps she *could* blame anger, if she had done it then, but anger took her only as far as the nearest off-licence, where she bought a bottle of wine and twenty cigarettes before returning home. He was watching TV when she let herself in, his back to her. She passed behind him and sat back at the table, a tumbler and the wine in front of her. After three drinks, the news droning through from the other room, she felt brave enough to light a cigarette, to blow the smoke through the open door. But he said nothing. Ten minutes later, the television clicked off. The light was turned out and she heard his footsteps overhead. It was later, much later, when she reached for the phone, when she wrote the text. And it was this morning, when there was still silence in the house, when she replied to a question with a 'Yes.'

Is there guilt? Yes, and with it a kind of freedom, for it is a feeling. She pulls apart the blinds and sees his car pull up outside, one hand still close to her mouth. She watches him climb out of the car, her fingers against the glass. She starts to cry.

When he enters the kitchen, she is at the sink, washing her coffee mug. 'Hey,' she says, turning to smile at him.

'Hey.'

'How was your day?'

'The usual.' He is at the fridge, a carton of orange juice in one hand. He takes a single swig and replaces it. His hair, though cut just before Christmas, seems wilder than ever. His skin is sallow looking, the cheeks hollow. She has to turn away, afraid.

'Do you want tea?'

'Thanks, yeah, that'd be good.'

She clicks on the kettle, heart pounding. Reaching up to the cupboard, she looks for the last of the tea bags they brought with them from England, collects the mugs. The simplicity of the actions soothes her, and she lets out a long, slow breath. The kettle begins to rattle as the water starts to boil, its plastic display clouding. 'You go and sit down,' she says. 'I'll bring it to you.'

He is looking absently around the kitchen, as if something is missing. 'Do we have any aspirin?' he asks, pinching his nose.

'In the odd cupboard.' She steps past him, to where things without a place live, and locates the small tube between a measuring jug and a ball of string. She taps two into his hand and runs him a glass of water. She watches him toss them into his mouth, the tendons in his hand flexing like cables. Jack's hands fill many pages of her sketchbooks.

'I'm going to sit down,' he says, and she nods.

When the kettle clicks off, she fills the mugs. She takes her time with the tea, the back of the spoon pressed slowly against the bag, the operatic curls of amber moving slowly through the cup. She squeezes lemon in hers, adds the last splash of milk to his. Taking them through to the living room, she looks around at the walls and realises she has got it wrong. It is a shade too dark.

'I'm sorry about last night,' he says, taking his cup from her.

'So am I,' she says, the tears rising. She sits down on the arm of his chair, blinking them away.

'I'm just so tired,' he says, and she nods.

'I wish you'd talk to me,' she says. She reaches out a tentative hand to touch his hair, which still holds the cold from hours in the fog.

His eyes, suddenly bright, flick to hers. 'About what?'

'Whatever it is that's bothering you.' Her fingers freeze against his skin as she says it, a sudden fear of falling sharp and crystalline inside her.

He leans his head back against the sofa and closes his eyes. It is there; the ledge. He runs his toe along the edge and thinks how easy it would be to step from it. 'There's this guy,' he says, his voice small. 'We pulled him off the chord a couple of weeks ago, me and Miller, and now he won't stop sending me letters.'

'What kind of letters?'

He sighs. 'Quotes. Weird shit. I Googled them, they're Bible stuff.'

She raises her eyebrows. 'Hmm.'

'I called the cops that took him in that night and they said he was just a normal guy — no record, no previous attempts. Married with two kids. Just a normal guy.'

'He doesn't sound very normal.'

He looks down at his tea. 'The quotes — it's like they're trying to tell me something.'

'Like what?'

His voice is growing smaller. 'They're about guilt, I think. About doing wrong.' He closes his eyes again, rests his head against her hand.

Is there guilt? His skin feels icy against hers and she is afraid. 'You should tell someone,' she says.

He opens his eyes and looks up at her. They are baleful and bloodshot and the vertigo is back. 'How does he know?' he whispers, and the words pass through her in single, sharp shots.

'How does he know what?'

He drinks his tea in several uneven gulps, and puts the mug down on the floor beside him. 'Nothing,' he says. 'I don't know what I'm saying.'

'What do the letters say?' she asks, and suddenly it feels essential that she knows.

He glances up at her. 'Els,' he says, putting an arm under her legs and shifting her onto his lap. 'I don't feel much like talking any more.'

2006

In March, they travel to England. They spend a week with his mother, who tends to Beth with a feverish, awe-struck care which occasionally extends to him; endless cups of tea, meals cooked to order, a refusal to let either of them in the kitchen. When they leave, she is wet-eyed and forlorn, pushing Tupperware boxes into their hands.

'Call me when you get there,' she says to Beth, and, to him, 'Take care.'

They travel out to the coast, to a flattened stretch of rocky hill. The owner meets them outside the cottage, which is pale blue with wooden shutters on the windows, yellowing net curtains behind their glass.

'Mr and Mrs Finn?' he asks, and when they nod he hands them the key. 'Enjoy your stay.'

'Where's the nearest shop?' Jack asks, and the man laughs.

'Head that way,' he says, pointing down the bumpy track. 'And keep going.'

They let themselves in and as Beth looks around, she lets out a small sigh. 'This isn't how I thought it would be,' she says, and he nods.

The cottage is small, its rooms easy to populate. They circle through them, leaving traces; a pair of shoes here, a coat hanging there. The bedroom is in the attic, its ceiling steeply sloped. During their stay he will hit his head countless times whilst Beth passes underneath untouched. He will stop himself spitting out curses each time his skull meets the beam, because the rooms here are reverential and the silence is a comfort.

In the kitchen there is no fridge and no oven; just two small hobs to cook on. Here he will prepare simple meals: bread, cheese, salad. The salad he will keep in a box outside the back door, where there is a small, sandy garden with yellow and green plants and a rotary washing line sticking crookedly out of the ground, occasionally creaking in the breeze. A tortoiseshell cat often lurks here. It has no collar or tag, appears at random. Sometimes this cat will leap onto the narrow windowsills and stare in at them. When he goes outside it flees, but when Beth is there it comes closer, it circles. By the end of the week it will come to her when she calls it, her pale lips making small, encouraging kissing sounds as it prowls closer. She walks along the shore with it in her wake, its tail flicking from side to side, a warning.

In front of the fire is a rug, worn and red. Every evening Beth lies there on her back, staring up at the ceiling. He makes the dinner and when it is done, he collects the plates and washes them in the small, cracked sink. He takes his time, making sure the kitchen is clean; trying to remember the way things must be done. When there is nothing else, he returns to the tiny sitting room and sits on the battered sofa, watching her. There is no television and their books lie untouched.

During the days they walk. The wind howls and the surf explodes against the rocks in short, hushing bursts. They add few sounds of their own. Sometimes they stand still and watch the waves. He puts his arm around her and rests his head against hers and sometimes he hears a sound escape; a murmur, a moan. At night they lie together under the eaves, the darkness complete. He lays his fingers over hers on the thin mattress and they are cold and small, fragile like china.

On their last night, he takes her out onto the beach and makes a fire on the sand. Beth sits across from him, long skirt wrapped around her legs and the light from the flames flickering on her skin. He pushes at the driftwood with a stick, sending sparks circling upwards. She is talkative tonight; they smile at each other, they speak of home. As the hours pass, the sand grows cold and damp begins to seep through their clothes. Beth traces shapes in the grains with a finger. The sea is heavy and grey and far away. From somewhere behind them, they hear the faint rumble of thunder.

'It's beautiful here,' she says, and she starts to cry.

'It is,' he says.

They both look out to sea and both are still. The tide crawls towards them and the moon climbs higher in the sky. It begins to rain, the drops small as they fall, the marks they make on impact wide on the water. 'Let's go inside,' he says, but still they sit.

2007

Summer arrives, unexpected and unwanted.
It has been a year since graduation. A year
of applications, a year of rejections. A year is
seeming suddenly like a long thing and short; time
something she desperately wants to retrieve and yet
she wishes that the days that pass are ones she could
fast-forward. She stares down at the pan, bacon
pale and oozing, and up at the yellowing wall.
'How do you want your eggs?' she asks, trying to
keep her voice bright.

Kieran glances up from the bed, where he
is slouched against the wall with his laptop
balanced on his thighs. 'For fuck's sake, Elsa,
open a window. You're making everything stink of
frying.'

'Sorry.' She crosses the room, tugs open the
sash window. Hands pressed against the sill, she

draws in a lungful of the warm outside air. The laptop makes an irritable sound and he gets up, searching for the power cord. 'So, scrambled?' she asks, coming back inside. 'Or fried?'

'Whatever.'

She crouches by the ancient fridge, pushing aside the few items of food on its greasy shelves; an open packet of thin and flaccid value ham, a cling-film-wrapped chunk of orange cheese. Finding the eggs, she stands again. She opens the solitary cupboard, searching for a bowl.

'I can't be bothered to wait,' he says from the bed, turning languidly onto his front. 'Just do me a sandwich.'

'Are you sure?'

He doesn't answer. She turns back to the pan.

Things always do stink, he's right. Every day at her desk, she searches through databases and smells the cold fat smell of her clothes. Why does it matter? She shouldn't care what her colleagues think of her. It's just a stopgap job, just a way to pay the rent. It isn't part of the plan, isn't to be recorded. When she is dying, those dull desk days are not the things she will remember.

She finds the bread, discarding the top, mouldering slices. Finishing the bacon, she takes the pan from the heat. The hobs are patched with reddish stains, the same burnt orange as a bridge an ocean and half a decade away. She carries the sandwich over to him, her feet sticking to the bare floor. She sits down beside him, holds the plate out. The laptop lid is quickly shut, the sandwich taken from her.

'Sorry it took so long,' she says.

His teeth bite through the soft white bread, his eyes on the floor. His textbooks are in an unsteady pile, an almost-helix, though the beginning of his Masters is still a month or so away. He is still a student while she is a stopgap. The flat is funded by her dull desk days and his parents' reluctant handouts.

He raised his hand to her once. It was just once and she tries not to think of it. It was before the Masters masterplan, and he'd received his twentieth or thirtieth rejection that morning, a small agency in Soho which he'd spoken disparagingly of even as he typed the application. She shouldn't have let him go out that night, she knows that now; should have insisted they stay in. Paulo's birthday, the only person they speak to with any regularity, and so she had said nothing, had curled her hair, put on a pair of skinny jeans borrowed from Anna on her last visit home. 'I can't believe you don't have a pair,' she remembers Anna saying, her own sad smile in response. 'Behind the times,' she must have replied, or something like that. *Out of the loop.*

She remembers watching him drink; the tumblers of whisky gripped, one after another, in his thin fingers. She remembers trying to get him home. *Let's go. Let's go to bed.* And she remembers him shaking her off. *No way. It's Paulo's birthday.* She remembers saying please, she remembers trying to be firm. And she remembers the flash of rage across his face, the hand coming up towards her. His breath hot on her face.

Someone stepped in, someone came between them. They haven't spoken of it since, but it happened. He raised his hand to her. It was just once, and she thinks of it often. She is thinking of it now, as she sits on the bed beside him and watches him eat.

He looks up, smiling at her as he swallows. 'Back to work tomorrow.'

She nods at him. Her cheap white work shirt hangs over the window where she once had a black dress waiting. The sun casts a foggy imprint of it on the floorboards.

'I miss you when you're not here.' He returns his attention to the sandwich.

A silent sigh goes through her, a little lift. She rises. 'I'm going to wash that pan up,' she says. The limited air which drifts through the window brings with it strands of conversation from the pavement below, a bassline from a passing car.

'One day,' he says, tossing his plate aside, 'things won't be like this.'

She turns to face him, halfway across the room. 'I know.'

'Some day,' he says, looking around, 'we won't be here.'

'I know.'

He stares at her. 'I promise.'

'You promise?'

He smiles, and she takes a step towards him. 'I promise,' he says, and his voice is low. 'Now pass me that joint.'

2013

He is a haunted man. Every day he feels the eyes following him: as he leaves the house, as he works, as he drinks with Alex or drives home alone. As the end of January draws nearer, he begins to see the figure; always in the distance, always still. The letters continue to arrive. He reads them, he remembers them. He does not call. He is afraid.

His life begins to seem to him like a series of films, each on repeat. When he arrives at the bridge he becomes one character; entering his front door, another. Elsa he sees in black and white, the way she moves through the rooms of their home balletic and silent. As she sleeps he runs locks of her dark hair through his fingers, the scene turned grey in the early morning light, her limbs pale against the sheets.

One Saturday, he wakes at 4 a.m. and can't get back to sleep. He lies awake, looking at her; asleep on her side, a hand on the pillow beside him. She sleeps with one foot drawn up, the sole pressed against her other shin, and he traces the curve of her knee beneath the sheets. She stirs, turning onto her back.

There was a night like this in Brighton, the first time he took her away. It was windy outside, the floorboards in the room above creaking, and he couldn't settle. Elsa slept close to him that night, her head against his chest. Lying awake, he looked down at her and could only see Beth. He had got good at pretending that Beth was simply a thing dragged up from the depths of his imagination; that if he let go, she would sink back below the surface, the water smooth and undisturbed. But March, by the sea – how could he forget, how could he have brought her there? – and Beth would not be silenced. That night he woke Elsa, pushed inside her without speaking, her lips hot against his neck. Tonight, he lets her sleep.

The hot water clicks on downstairs, the timer set early from his week's shifts, and the pipes in the wall beside him begin to rumble, kicking out occasionally with soft thuds. Elsa turns again with a soft sigh, her back to him. He listens to her breathing slow and become heavier as she drifts deeper into sleep, her dark hair streaming across the pillow.

Since Alex's engagement, he often finds himself alone in their old haunt, watching the old man play the piano. The sour-faced woman behind the bar is fonder of him when he is on his own; often she makes casual, non-committal remarks, things which conversations cannot be formed from, but are friendly in their own sort of way: 'Warmer out today' or 'Quiet tonight'. He responds in kind: 'Sure is' or 'Hope so', sometimes beginning his own: 'Starting to rain'; 'Trouble down the street'. Otherwise, he is left alone. He sits and sometimes he takes out the letters and looks at them. He thinks of the most recent now, traces the words through Elsa's hair. *Come to me, all you who are weary and burdened, and I will give you rest.* Below it, for the first time, Matthew has added his own words. *I recognise your burden. Live your life righteously, Jack, and you will find rest.* But Jack is afraid that it is too late for that.

At 5 a.m., he gets up, dressing in the dark. Walking downstairs, he is careful to tread lightly on the steps he knows will creak. He finds his keys on the side and pulls on a jacket and shoes.

Out on the street, he heads left at the end of the block, where the road slopes down towards the Mission. *What am I doing?* he thinks, not for the first time, but his steps do not slow. The rhythm of his feet against the pavement is all that exists; the insistent beat of them keeps thoughts tamped down, maintains the silence even as they disturb it. The air is cold and dank and it presses against him, wet in his mouth. He tucks his chin into his chest and keeps walking.

At some point – he isn't sure when – he becomes aware of the footsteps that fall in time with his own. The figure behind him is faceless, all in black; a shadow. He turns back to the road, considers breaking into a jog. But he isn't sure if there is anywhere left to run. At the corner of the street, he stops. He turns on his heel, hands wedged in his pockets, and watches the figure approach.

'Good morning, Jack,' Matthew says, lowering his hood.

'What are you doing here?'

'You're out early.'

'I couldn't sleep.'

'Me neither.'

Jack sighs. 'How did you find out where I live?'

'You told me.'

'No. I didn't.'

'I think you did.'

Too tired to argue, Jack stares back up the hill. Somewhere in the shadows is his house, and somewhere inside it, Elsa rolls onto her back, pulls the covers over her face. 'I don't understand what you want,' he says.

'I want to be better,' Matthew says. 'So do you, I think. That's why we found each other.'

Jack kicks at the pavement. 'How's that working out for you?'

The smaller man considers this, his forehead puckering. 'All you can do is try. That's what you said, right? All you can do is try.'

Jack lets out a short laugh, turns away. He gazes up at the slowly lightening sky. 'I guess it is.'

Matthew glances up at the sky too. 'I can help you, you know. Just like you helped me.'

Jack looks sideways at him. 'I don't know what it is you think you know about me—

'I know, Jack. Honestly.'

'You've got it wrong. Whatever it is you're talking about.'

Matthew smiles amicably. 'I *know*, Jack. I know *you*. I can see it on your face. We're the same, you and me. The way we live is wrong. And I'm supposed to help you get back on the righteous path.'

He should be afraid but instead he finds himself smiling. 'I don't think you can. But I'm glad you're feeling better. Keep on trying. Or whatever.'

'Your girlfriend's pretty. What's her name?'

'Elsa.'

'My wife is called Sarah.'

Jack takes his first few steps down the hill. 'Good to see you, Matthew. Take care.'

'My sons are Connor and Jake.'

The first blur of the sun's light is just visible on the horizon. It bleeds between buildings, white into soft grey and up into the still-dark blue. Jack crosses the street and carries on.

'His name was Pete but he died,' Matthew says.

A car slides slowly past, its driver cast in shadow, a black paper outline on a classroom wall. Jack is almost at the next cross-street now.

'I don't go to those places any more, Jack,' Matthew calls.

'Good for you,' Jack whispers, and he keeps walking.

2007

He arrives home from work early one day and finds the front door ajar. He pushes it open with one hand, runs his fingers over the latch. Closing the door and checking the lock, he is struck by a sudden fear. He swallows it down, calls out.

'Beth?'

The hallway is too warm, the air heavy with fumes. He runs a hand along the banister and finds it covered with a sheen, a strange chemical sort of protective layer. He walks through rooms, and each is the same; each is too suddenly, post-apocalyptically still. In the living room, the vacuum stands halfway across the carpet, turned off but still plugged in, its flex curling across the floor. On the dining-room table, a duster and open aerosol can of polish are marooned on the glassy wood.

'Beth?' The fumes are thick in his chest. He walks to the window and opens it wide. Looking out at the patio, he thinks, without knowing why, of the dead bird on its back.

There is a sound coming from the kitchen; a scratching, insistent and fast. He pushes open the swinging door, heart pounding.

Beth is on her hands and knees, her back to him. The scratching sound continues, shorter strokes coming quicker. He takes a step or two closer and sees that she is scrubbing the floor. Closer, he can hear that she is humming; a taut, high melody which he does not recognise. The sound is persistent and violent, the notes vibrating on her lips. He draws back sharply.

'Stop, please,' he says from the doorway, and then, more softly, 'we need to talk.'

She looks up in surprise, pushing her hair away from her face. He notices suddenly how clean it is, sees that she is wearing make-up. When was the last time she wore make-up? He can't remember. Her hair is often unwashed for weeks while the house is continually, eternally cleaned.

It is suddenly difficult to speak. The words stick like lumps in the flesh of his throat.

'You can't carry on like this.' He drops to a whisper, tries to sneak them out that way. 'You need to talk to someone.' The last word is soft and small, it crawls out with little resistance: 'Please.'

'Everything's okay.' She stands up, takes a step towards him. She is wearing her red dress. It has always been too big for her but now seems to belong to someone else, shapeless against her small frame, straps sagging against her sharp bones. 'It's all okay,' she says.

'It's not okay, Beth,' he says, and, shaking, he reaches out to close the gap between them. He takes hold of her carefully, a gentle hand on each shoulder. 'You're not well,' he says. 'But we'll find someone who can help you.'

She takes a step closer to him, eyes wide as she looks up into his. 'We're going to have a baby,' she says, and he looks back at her.

'What?' he asks, a buzzing in his ears.

'I'm pregnant.' She reaches up to take one of his hands from her shoulder, holds it in her own. 'You see? Everything's okay. It's all okay now.'

He stares into her eyes, lets her hold his hand. Then he moves her slowly, carefully, against his chest. He rests his chin on top of her head, and he closes his eyes.

2013

In the week that follows, Elsa receives three text messages from Michael the bass guitarist. The first, on Sunday afternoon, is casual. Hey, how's your weekend? An hour or two later, the second arrives: I forgot to say – we're playing in the city on thursday, wanna come? Beside the question mark is a winking face. She deletes both messages while Jack is cooking dinner, her appetite entirely evaporated. She goes to the kitchen door and watches him dish up.

'You okay?' he asks, glancing up, and she nods. He turns back to the stove and she studies the muscles in his arms beneath his short-sleeved T-shirt, her stomach twisting. He has on soft, flannel pyjama bottoms, held loosely on his hips by a drawstring waistband, and she goes up behind him, running her hands under his T-shirt, her face pressed to his back.

'Watch out,' he says, moving her away gently. He takes plates down from the cupboard. 'Hungry?' he asks, and she nods, swallowing hard.

On Monday, at 3 p.m. when she is watching an episode of *X Factor* recorded from the previous Thursday, a third is delivered: Playing hard to get? The winking face is there again. She looks at it for a while, this small emoticon. It seems oddly hopeful, gazing back at her, and this makes her feel sad. She types a reply: ☹ and stares at it there on the screen, her finger hovering over Send. In the end, she deletes the face and goes out for a walk. That evening, Jack stays out with Alex, and Elsa watches a film and drinks wine. The film has Hugh Grant in it and makes her feel sadder. The wine is cheap and from the convenience store three blocks down. It makes her feel drunk. She tries to stay awake to see Jack come home but falls asleep in her place on the sofa, head resting on the arm and feet tucked up under her. When he wakes her to go to bed, she is irritable and disorientated, shoves him away. In the night he curls her against him but in the morning when she wakes he has already left. She stares in the mirror. Yesterday's make-up is smudged under her eyes and her lips are stained with wine. She showers with her eyes closed, a tight pain at her temples.

Finally, at 11 a.m. on Tuesday while she is drying her hair, a fourth and final text message announces itself.

What's up? Give me a call, I want to see you x

The kiss is what breaks her. Though sharp in shape, it is strangely vulnerable, alone on the screen. Feeling squeamish, she types replies and deletes them

Sorry but

Haven't been totally honest

You're lovely but

difficult time for me

Me and my boyfriend

She gives up, throwing the phone at the bed. It bounces off
and hits the carpet with a listless thud. Somewhere outside the
city, he is at his desk, and she wants to cry. *Want toy, get toy*, she
thinks. *Break toy.* And then she does cry, just a little, standing up
with a hand pressed over her face. She cries for him, but mostly
for her, mostly for the sheer sense of failure which hangs ahead
of her, a looming ledge. *I'm so sad*, she thinks, and then she goes
to the bathroom and splashes cold water on her cheeks.

Leaning over the sink, she glances up at her reflection. *For
fuck's sake*, she thinks, straightening. She squeezes toothpaste
onto her toothbrush and pushes it angrily into her mouth,
cleaning her teeth with quick, violent strokes. 'That's enough
now,' she says out loud. She cups water and splashes it into her
mouth. Standing, she dries her mouth on her sleeve and gives
the mirror a final nod. *That's enough.*

She goes downstairs and begins to tidy, punching the sofa's
cushions into shape. She picks up the wine glass and empty bottle
from beside the arm and takes them through to the kitchen.
There is a stack of plates beside the sink and she turns the tap on
full, fumbling for the plug. She is just about to plunge the first

plate into the suds when the doorbell rings. She hasn't heard their doorbell before, and she freezes guiltily, as if caught in the middle of some action for which she ought to be ashamed. 'Oh,' she says, aloud, when she registers where the sound has come from. She is talking out loud to herself more and more these days, though she hasn't noticed. Putting the plate back down on the side, she turns off the tap.

Out in the hallway, she runs a hand through her half-dried hair, straightens out her jumper. She has lied about where she lives but there is still a part of her expecting to see Michael outside. Her heart races and her hand fumbles with the bolt.

'Oh,' she says, again. 'Hi.'

It is the first time she has seen Pearl wear a coat; it makes her seem even smaller. Her hair looks brushed and neat, though it is thinner than ever, a bright candy peach against the browning skin. 'I need to ask you a favour.'

'Sure. Do you want to come in?'

'Can't.' The vowel sound of the word has a honk-like quality in Pearl's mouth. Her voice is hoarse and harsh, harder to make out than usual. 'I have to go to the hospital.'

'Are you okay?'

'It's just a check-up. But Carrie just showed up with the kids. Somebody called in sick so they gave her an extra shift.'

Elsa reaches behind her, shoving her feet in her shoes. 'I'll sit with them,' she says, grabbing her keys. 'You go.'

'Are you sure?'

'Of course.' She locks the door and follows Pearl back up the path. At the gate, she turns to her. 'Pearl, are you sure you're okay going there on your own? Don't you want someone to come with you?'

'Nope. I'll be fine.'

'Okay.' Elsa unlatches Pearl's gate.

'I'll be back soon.' Her flat, orthopaedic shoes thump heavily against the pavement. 'And Elsa? Thanks.'

The door is ajar, left on the latch. Elsa closes it carefully behind her. 'You guys okay?' She pokes her head in the living room: empty. There is a faint scrabbling sound coming from the kitchen, a thin yellow bar of light cast out from underneath the door. She puts a hand on the handle, suddenly afraid. The door opens with a low creak. Sam, sitting at the table, glances up.

'Hey, Elsa.'

She lets out her breath. 'Hey, Sam.'

Skye is sprawled on the floor, scribbling on a piece of paper with a fat blue crayon. It makes a scratching sound against the lino. She looks up and laughs, her hair sticking up on one side.

'Has Gramma gone?' Sam asks, returning to his own picture. His colouring is slower and he presses harder, the felt-tip pen squeaking against the paper.

'Yeah. She won't be long.'

'That's okay.'

Elsa steps over Skye and takes a seat opposite Sam. He has drawn a face; a girl's, she thinks, taking in the lips and the hair, and is now colouring it in with intense concentration. 'That's nice,' she says.

'It's you.'

'Is it?'

'Yeah. Cos you're drawing us.'

'Well, I'm flattered.' She leans over and gives Skye a gentle wiggle. 'And what are you drawing, miss?'

'She doesn't really draw,' Sam says, pushing a pink crayon off the edge of the table to his sister. It falls without turning, bounces against the paper. *Splash*, Elsa thinks, and is sickened. 'She just does *that*,' Sam says, gesturing at the scribbles.

'A lot of grown-ups would think *that* was art,' Elsa says.

Sam wrinkles his face. '*I* don't.'

'Me neither.'

'Where's your picture?'

'It's at home,' Elsa says, truthfully. 'It's almost done,' she adds, not so truthfully.

'Do you think my mommy will like it?'

'I hope so.'

Skye pushes herself into a sitting position, her picture either forgotten or completed. There is a bookcase in the corner of the room and she heaves herself up and totters over to it. Clinging onto the wood, she runs a tiny finger across the spines, murmuring cheerfully to herself.

'Elsa?' Sam says, reaching for a red felt-tip pen, with which he begins to shade her lips.

'Yes, Sam?'

'Why do you do it?'

Her hands tighten on the edge of the table. The bottom lip is finished; the top begun. 'Why do I do what?'

He glances up at her, wide-eyed. She is almost certain she sees her own reflection there, small and white and trapped in the centre of the two dark spheres. Pinioned. Exposed. It has been several moments and she has forgotten to breathe.

Then, with a crash which seems, in the scheme of things, strangely quiet to Elsa, Skye stumbles, tugging the shelf, which collapses readily. She sits down hard on her bottom and the books fall after her, thudding, one by one in quick succession, onto her small, dark head. Loose sheets of paper flutter down around her. The final one, a large, hardback cookery book, catches her with its corner just above the faint pencil smudge of her eyebrow. As it slides sideways into her lap and then rolls over onto the ground, she turns to look at Elsa, dumbfounded. There is a cut where the book has hit her. It seems to draw breath before it begins to bleed.

'Skye —' Elsa is instantly across the room. And then, with a sound far louder than the crash, a key turns in the front door. Elsa's eyes meet Skye's, and for one, teetering second, she wills her not to cry. She transmits the words with every ounce of brainpower available, heart stalled in her chest. Skye's brow creases, the message apparently unclear on reception, and then she shuts her eyes and lets out a piercing wail.

Hitching the child onto her hip, Elsa whirls wildly around for something to stem the bleeding. The front door opens and shuts, and, finding nothing, she presses the sleeve of her jumper against it, bumping the baby up and down in an attempt at comfort. Behind her, Sam begins to cry too, an unsure and stuttering series of sobs.

A woman who is not Pearl appears in the doorway. 'What the hell are you doing?'

Elsa stares back, words temporarily abandoning her. The woman is about her own age, perhaps a little younger. She has dark, shoulder-length hair with several blonde streaks bleached through it, and is wearing no make-up; her skin yellowing and her lips dark, blueish. 'You're Carrie?' Elsa asks hesitantly, still bouncing Skye back and forth, but the baby's crying drowns out the words.

Carrie strides across the small room and snatches the child away. 'What have you done to my baby?' Drawing back, she sees the blood, and the need to know becomes more insistent. '*What* have you done to my baby?'

'Nothing – she – she pulled over some books, it's just a graze ...'

Skye, who has apparently also reached this conclusion, falls into a sudden silence, her head pressed against her mother's neck. Her small body continues to rise and fall in rapid shudders and she snuffles occasionally, a fist finding its way up to her mouth.

Carrie takes a step back, staring at Elsa. She is wearing a padded black jacket and black biker boots. The sole of the left one has come away from the shoe, and it gapes at Elsa in outrage. 'Who the hell are you?' Carrie asks. 'Where's my grandma?'

'She's ... out,' Elsa says uncertainly. 'She had to pop out.

I live next door.' She reaches out for the chair behind her, steadying herself. 'She said you were at work,' she adds, her voice small.

'Sam, for the love of God, stop crying,' Carrie says, and then, to Elsa, 'I think you better leave.'

Elsa glances at Sam. 'I— '

'Get out!'

And so she does. She hurries into the hall, stumbling against the door as she pulls on her shoes. As she steps out onto the path, Sam finally stops crying. She closes the door as quietly as she can and, crossing the tiny yard, climbs over the wall between it and hers. She pushes her key into the lock with a trembling hand.

Inside, she closes the door and leans her back against it. She spreads her feet on the mat and looks down at them, her fingers tapping out a staccato pattern on the door. She sucks air in and forces it out. 'Don't cry,' she says, her voice firm. After a few more minutes of tapping, she feels in safer territory. She straightens up and heads for the stairs, still concentrating on her breathing. *In. And out. In. And out. In.*

Her phone is where she left it, face up on the bed, flashing plaintively. *Michael*, she thinks, reaching for it. But the message is from Jack.

Going for beers for Chase's birthday. Back late xx

She tosses the phone back onto the bed and then follows it, crawling sideways on the mattress and drawing her knees up to her chest. The house is so quiet that she can hear the faint strains of television now coming from Pearl's. *I'm a bad person,* she thinks. *These things* — but the thought trails off, the things too unwieldy to compress into words. The guilt is overwhelming. She wanted it to be him, she realises, even if just for a split second. She wanted it to be him, because she feels small and he thinks her special. *Playing with people*, someone says to her from far away and long ago. *Break toy*. She flops onto her back and stares up at the ceiling. *Where did we go?*

Dust circles in the thin streams of weak sunlight which filter through the clouds, and the scent of the sheets drifts around her: fabric softener; her perfume; the woody, faintly metallic smell of Jack's skin. The old mattress seems to hold their shapes as she lies across them and she traces them with the palm of her hand; here the small of his back, here her tilted hip.

They lay in bed for thirty-two hours, once. It was not planned, not even discussed at first; they just woke one morning and stayed there, talking. Lunchtime came and went, and when she heard his stomach growling she went to the kitchen and brought back supplies; the conversation continuing as they sat up among the pillows and tore chunks from the bread, cut corners from the cheese with a butter knife.

'Let's stay here all day,' he said suddenly, sliding her T-shirt over her head.

As the sun moved across the room, objects became beached around them; the lunch plates on the floor, the few clothes they had slept in at the edges of the mattress. As the room grew darker, a pizza box and a wine bottle, two glasses stained red. The TV carried in from the living room, perched on the end of the small desk. Her laptop, open at the foot of the bed, played music and when they finally fell asleep, the blue light of it glowed across his skin.

I want to do that now, she thinks, and her whole body aches for him, for that day.

Instead, she gets up. On Jack's side of the bed are a discarded pair of jeans and a T-shirt, and she stoops to pick them up. She walks to the bathroom and rummages through the laundry basket until she finds a pair of her own jeans. She throws them over her arm and selects several pairs of balled-up underwear before replacing the lid. Taking Jack's still-damp towel from its hanging place on the edge of the bath, she makes her way downstairs. A scarf hangs from the banister, slipping slowly towards the ground, and she snatches this up too, adding it to the pile.

In the tiny laundry room, she dumps the clothes on the tiled floor and kneels down beside them. She opens the washing-machine door, throwing in the underwear, the scarf, the towel. The jeans she is more careful with. She washed Kieran's trousers without checking the pockets once. There was a funny sound throughout the cycle, and when she took the clothes out to hang them on the rickety old airer, she found his phone in the bottom of the drum. They had the same model and she swapped it with her own, but the lesson was learnt. She checks the pockets methodically, pulling out the lining of each. Her's are empty, but in the last pocket of Jack's, her fingers touch a folded piece of paper. She pulls it out, tossing the jeans aside, and holds it carefully in her hands.

She shouldn't do it. She knows it is a step she won't be able to take back. She looks down, breath held. And then she unfolds it.

We are alike, the letter reads.

Banish serpents disguised as lovers, it says.

"'For wide is the gate and broad is the path which leads to destruction, and many enter through it,'" she reads aloud.

At the bottom are two words.

TELL HER.

2007

He is dreaming of his father. His father will soon be released, and his first steps as a free man are through his son's sleep, where together they walk down a Seattle street. 'How did we get here?' Jack asks him, and his father stops walking and turns to him.

'Wake up,' he says, and Jack opens his eyes with a start.

Beth is sitting upright in bed, looking down at him. Her eyes are soft and black, her hair and skin pale gold in the darkness.

He lifts himself onto one elbow. 'Everything okay?'

She leans down and kisses him. Her kisses are gentle at first, and then hard, insistent. Her hands run over his face, his shoulders, his chest, back up to his hair. They search as they touch, the fingers assessing. She climbs onto him and he moves his fingertips over her, her body hot and smooth. He runs a hand over the almost imperceptible curve of her belly, draws in his breath.

And then she is scrambling off the bed, away from him. She cowers in a corner, eyes flashing.

'Who is she?'

He is still slow with sleep, only halfway out of bed. He presses a hand to his eyes, removes it. But Beth is still there, still glaring. He approaches her slowly, his hands held out in peace. In panic.

'I don't understand.' He stops a foot away from her, wary.

'She's everywhere.' Her eyes flit across the room. 'I can feel her.'

'Beth, calm down. Slow down.'

'You taste different.' The words are sharp, they emerge from her mouth with their tips pointed at him.

'Let's get back to bed.' He holds out a hand to her.

'You taste of her.'

'There's only you.'

She stares at him.

'Beth, I promise. There's nobody else. Come here. Come back to bed.'

Finally, she approaches him, lets him mesh her hand into his. He leads her back to bed, her face soft again in confusion. 'Here,' he says, holding back the sheets for her. As she crawls in, she tucks a hand protectively across her belly. He pushes the hair back from her face, pulls the sheet up over her shoulders.

Climbing in beside her, he moulds his body to hers, holds her tight against his chest. 'Let's get some sleep,' he says, reaching back to turn off the light.

'Only us,' Beth whispers into the darkness.

2013

Somewhere over the Atlantic, near the end of his second film, and halfway through a dubious beef stroganoff, Jack dislodged an old crown which has been squatting near the back of his mouth for seventeen years. The tooth it replaced was cracked in half by a particularly dirty punch in a fight in the street in Seattle, and the crown, expensive and painful to put in place, has had a lot to put up with over the years. Frequently serving, along with the other teeth at the back of his mouth, as a bottle opener in his Newcastle days, it has also had to take the strain of a long period of addiction to hard candies; Curiously Strong mints and cinnamon balls, each carefully cracked in its centre. In more recent years, when his sleep is irregular and often troubled, it has been roughly introduced to its upstairs neighbours, ground back and forth against them. Finally, with one crooked chew, it has let go. He felt the crack, up there in the air, but by avoiding further mastication on that side of his mouth for these four, almost five months, he has managed also to avoid dealing with the removal. In a moment of weakness, a split-second of forgetting, on a Sunday night at the end of January, he has let a stray mouthful of apple cross the wrong side of his mouth, let the jaw reflexively mash down on it, and here it is: the tooth detached.

Which is how he comes to be driving to work at just after noon on a Monday, a dentist's bill in the inside pocket of his jacket, one side of his face beginning to buzz back to life. His lip feels thick and out of place; he frequently checks his reflection in the rear-view mirror, afraid of drooling.

His phone vibrates from its place in the well beside the car's ancient cigarette lighter. Pulling up at a red light, he glances down at it. Unknown number. A new development, this; three, four, five times a day. He never answers. He is afraid to answer. He is also afraid it might stop. He watches the phone edge its way across the plastic surface, turning in tiny increments. *What if*, he thinks, and his hand reaches out to answer the call. He catches himself just as his fingers reach the screen. 'Nobody has that number,' he whispers to himself, but nothing seems so certain any more. The light turns green and he pulls away. The phone falls silent.

This morning, for the first time in a long time, he was beside Elsa when she woke. He remembers her sleepy limbs entwined with his, a fistful of her hair, the constant throbbing in his jaw.

He remembers her hot, dry kiss in the taut dip at the base of his neck, between the bones of his chest. *Clavicles*. As a child, he thought of them as his wishbone.

He still wonders if he should tell her about the letters, tell her exactly what they say. Their presence in the house fills him with fear, turns his insides to water. And yet he is afraid to throw them away. They have taken on a significance, a life of their own. Perhaps if he tells her what they say, she will be able to explain, be able to laugh them away. But how can she? Her dismissal, he realises, would mean nothing. She doesn't know.

Matthew knows.

Stop it. He turns on the radio, tries to drown the thought out. *It's crazy. It's insane.* He flicks through stations, heart racing. He hears the engine begin to whine and realises his foot is pressing down on the pedal, the needle creeping slowly up. He takes it off, blows out a slow breath. He turns off the radio.

At the next red light, he leans his head against the window. He pushes at the still-numb part of his lip with a finger, pinching the rubbery flesh. He watches a woman push a buggy down the street, head bent against the cold. Her back is to him and the few strands of hair which escape her hat are a pale blonde, almost white in the winter light. He lets go of his lip and it smacks back into place, the first fingers of feeling spreading slowly through it.

He still watches Elsa sleep. He suspects she watches him too, on Sunday afternoons or weeknight evenings when his eyelids are too heavy to hold up. They often exist in these different states, different spheres. The closeness is in the passing, the pausing to view the other, suspended and still. And then their places are exchanged, or he is gone and she remains, in their little house out on Potrero. He pushes the car forward, the first view of the bridge ahead of him now, orange peaks against bright, sheer blue. The sky like this is a shriek to him; a single sound of piercing volume, the last jagged filigrees of ice still melting at the corners of his windscreen. He follows the road around the coast, the bay at his right. The traffic slows ahead and he crawls past a diner where a family of five stare back at him, glassy-eyed through the picture window. The youngest child, a boy, crosses his eyes, their whites round and large in his face. Jack turns away.

Climbing the hill towards the freeway, a little of the morning's mist remains. Tiny beads of water form against his windshield, sent shivering upwards as he speeds towards his exit. He flicks on the wipers, listens to them scream. His face is fully awake now. He pokes at the newly crowned tooth with his tongue. Its edge is rougher than he expected, at its centre a ridge. He bites down on it, testing, as he pulls into the parking lot. His usual space is free and he swings into it, facing the water, and kills the engine. He listens to it tick, wonders why his heart is racing. Two lone fishermen sit on the pier below him, their backs to one another. A single seabird parades back and forth between them, head cocked. He leans his head against the headrest, closing his eyes.

'Call me when you get there,' Elsa said to him once, and he looked at her strangely.

'To work? Why?'

'I don't know.' She was looking out of the window, sky silver behind her. 'Sometimes I just worry.'

'There's nothing to worry about,' he said then, but now he isn't so sure.

He straightens up, removes the keys from the ignition and gets out of the car. Taking his work belt from the back seat, he locks the door and leans briefly on the roof, looking out at the bridge. *Sometimes I just worry*. The moon is already visible, a ghostly outline low in the blue sky. The sun is just beginning its descent to the sea.

He heads for the office, his shadow stretching out ahead of him. His jaw is beginning to ache and he runs his tongue over the tooth again, wincing. There is nobody around, which is unusual. He goes to his locker and takes out his jacket and hard hat. Normally Miller can be found here at this time of day, but the room is empty, and – perhaps it is his imagination – it seems only recently so, a weight in the air like a sentence left hanging. The door to the safe box where the trucks' keys are kept is hanging open, three sets inside, but he sets off on foot instead. He glances back at the empty room as he leaves, unnerved, and closes the door carefully behind him.

Back out in the sunlight, he trudges towards the bridge, the belt clinking against his thigh. He runs a hand over his jaw, the beginnings of a beard prickling against his rough palm, and presses a tentative finger against the tooth. The ache intensifies under pressure, but the swelling is all but gone. At the entrance to the walkway, he shields his eyes against the sun. He sees the section of scaffolding, about a quarter of the way down, and starts walking towards it. But as he gets closer, he sees the others gathered at a point much nearer to him, their fluorescents flashing in the sunlight. They are grouped together by the railing and a crowd is forming behind them. His stomach lurches. As he watches, one of the yellow figures lights a flare and drops it into the water below.

A minute later, they begin to disperse. His colleagues head back to the scaffolding, the crowd moved on by Andy and a policeman. The little pickup trucks spring to life one by one, and by the time Jack has reached the spot, Miller and Alex are the only ones left, talking quietly to a lone Highway Patrol officer who has just arrived at the scene. She writes on a small notepad, nodding as they speak.

'Hey, dude,' Alex says in a low voice, stepping away from the conversation and clapping Jack gently on the shoulder. 'How's the tooth?'

'Fixed. Jumper?'

'Uh huh. Two. A couple, I guess. We were just getting ready to move on when Andy saw them.'

'Went straight over?'

'Yup. Holding hands. Fucking sad, they looked young.'

He doesn't want to do it but he can't stop himself looking over the railing. The flare still smoulders, bobbing animatedly on the waves like a bird. In the distance, the coastguard's boat approaches. He glances back at the walkway. Miller, clearly satisfied that his role is complete, stomps away in the direction of the office, leaving the officer to stand alone, scratching her ear.

'You got plans tonight?' Alex asks Jack, stooping to tie one of his bootlaces. 'Some of the boys are heading out for beers.'

The boat is closer now, close enough for Jack to make out the two figures on board, both dressed in white hazmat suits. One holds a long pole, its end hooked. Several layers of thick plastic are folded on the deck, a corner lifting repeatedly in the breeze.

'No,' Jack says. 'I've got no plans.'

2007

Late in July, he flies to New York for a week. He tells Beth that he is taking the job — a simple bit of rebar with a friend of Franklin's he met years ago — because it is a good chance to see Aimee, but in fact he does it because it is a good chance to be elsewhere. He hates himself for thinking that, but the walls of the house, its once unthinkably airy rooms, are drawing closer and closer. Beth's cleaning, her constant, high-speed chatter, the false brightness of her smile: they gnaw at him. He often finds himself thinking *The baby* and he hates himself for that too. When he leaves, he holds her longer than she means to let him, and he calls her from the car, from the plane.

He hasn't told Aimee he is coming and perhaps this is because he cannot be sure he is. Plans change so often now; Beth is too sick, Beth is too afraid, Beth has decided she would rather do this, or this. He goes instead to the bar she works in, hoping to surprise her. It is plain and unassuming; a black leather awning, double black doors. He goes inside, out of the oppressive evening heat, and squints into the liquid blue light.

Plain, unassuming, and a strip club. Girls writhe in the pools of pink and purple like eels caught in tanks. He thinks of Cara, all those years ago, and this, as many things do, makes him think of Ginny. He thinks of her often. He regrets that, back then, he thought of her never.

'Can I help you?' A hostess approaches him, dressed in black satin, the small bulge of flesh between the strap of the dress and her arm vulvic and mesmerising.

He flounders guiltily, though it's not – by any means – his first trip to a strip club. 'Does Aim—' He stops. He does not want to know. He turns and leaves, ignores her calling after him.

In a bar down the street – normal lights, sports channel, fully clothed female behind the bar – he leaves a message on Aimee's machine, telling her that he is in town. She could be a hostess, he assures himself. She could be the manager. This brings with it images of brothel madams and hip-hop pimps, and he drinks a little faster. Best not to know.

He watches the game and he drinks his drinks and he waits for Aimee to call. A woman sits down beside him, dumping her small handbag on the bar between them. Its chain link strap slithers into a puddle and the bag lolls sadly towards him. The woman crosses her legs and then uncrosses them. She leans on one arm and then the other, and when the bartender approaches, she waves commiseratively, as if they are meeting after a mutually bad day.

'I don't know what I want,' she says, a cheerful warning.

'Okay,' the barmaid says. They both wait.

'What's that green stuff?' Her hand, extended close to his face, smells of meat.

'Midori.'

'Okay. That.'

'With lemonade? Soda?'

The woman shrugs, bored. 'I don't know. Champagne. Why not.'

'We don't sell champagne by the glass.'

'So bring me a bottle.' She turns to Jack. 'You'll drink with me, right?'

He looks at her and then at the barmaid. Assistance is not offered. His silence is taken as affirmation.

'Thanks,' he says, a wine glass of champagne in front of him.

'Green stuff?'

'No. I'm good.' He turns back to the screen.

She crosses and uncrosses her legs again. The spiky heels of her shoes clack against the metal stool. 'I'm feeling very sad,' she says, and he looks down into his glass. He thinks of Beth, scrubbing imaginary stains; singing softly to herself as she moves, on and on, endlessly through the rooms of the house. 'Will you ever be happy?' he has asked her before, but he doesn't want to ask this woman the same.

'I'm going to be a father,' he says instead.

2013

It takes a week, but eventually, Elsa works up the courage to knock on Pearl's door. The house has been quiet, no TV sounds or children crying. She thinks of taking her sketches but at the last minute decides against it. She has bought flowers and she fiddles with them as she waits on the step. After several minutes pass without a sound, she is forced to accept that nobody is in. Back at home, she walks through the house, thinking about her neighbour, thinking about Carrie — *What have you done to my baby* — and of Sam — *Why do you do it?* Somehow, without her realising, her phone finds its way into her hand. She listens to it ring, her head resting against the wall.

'Hello?'

'Hi.' She straightens up. 'It's me.'

Her mother's voice instantly brightens. 'Hello, sweetheart. We were just talking about you.'

'Were you? How come?'

Her mother hesitates. 'It's kind of a long story, actually.'

'Is something wrong?'

'No, no, not at all. We've just had some news, that's all.'

'About what?'

'I don't want to spoil it. Anna's probably trying to call you right now.'

Her heart speeds up. 'She's getting married!'

'Well, no, not exactly …'

'Is she okay?'

'She's fine, she's fine. Anyway, anyway, how are you?'

A heat is travelling through Elsa's body. Sweat beads against the phone. 'I'm fine. Everything's fine.' She swallows. 'Actually, Mum, can I call you back in a second? Jack's just walked in.'

'Okay, love. Send our love to him.'

Elsa hangs up. Jack has not just walked in. Jack never just walks in. He is always expected, she is always expecting. And now, it seems safe to assume, Anna is also expecting. She turns the idea around in her mind, trying to find a new direction from which to approach it. She goes to the fridge and takes out a half-empty bottle of wine, unstoppers it with her teeth. Pouring a glass, she steadies herself against the counter. She drinks the wine down in three, four sips, and pours another. Taking the bottle back to the living room, she finds her phone and dials Jack's number. She listens to it ring, again and again until the line disconnects. She pours another glass and calls him again.

Take some time, a voice says to her from long ago. *Take some time to yourself. Think it over.*

'"For wide is the gate and broad is the path",' she says aloud, though she can't remember the rest of the quote. She gets the message. Destruction. No way back.

TELL HER. That part she remembers perfectly. She tries to unpick the letter, tries to understand it. He is a man with a secret, that much is clear. She cannot remember if she is talking about the jumper or Jack.

She quickly becomes drunk. She opens another bottle and turns on the television. Every so often, she remembers and picks up her phone, dials his number again. It becomes a tic, a habit. To stop would be disastrous. When she isn't listening to it ring, the phone beside her is silent. Her sister does not call.

Come on, don't overreact, Jack tells her. *She's not a baby any more.* She turns the television up. She looks down at her phone. She drains her glass and picks it up, dials his number again. She hits Play on an old episode of *X Factor*, watches Simon Cowell cast a proprietary arm across the back of Britney Spears's chair. Her breathing begins to slow. She settles lower in her chair.

As the evening draws on, she forgets to call. Sheltered in her small sitting room, with her back to the road and the concrete wall of the yard outside gathered protectively across the window, she is safe. The velvet air of the room creeps slowly in from the corners, the darkness soft and inky. It seeps like a tide, surprising her each time she glances up from the screen or her glass and finds it closer, deeper.

When Jack's key finally turns in the lock, the darkness is complete and the television is on mute. The door huffs cold air into her sanctuary and the light in the hallway stutters into life. She hears him remove his jacket, then his boots, and then:

'You here?' he calls. She stands up, her legs stiff.

'In here,' she replies, staggering towards the light switch.

'Hey,' he says, appearing round the door. His breath is warm and malted. 'You okay?'

She nods, and he passes her. In the kitchen he stares into the fridge and she watches him from the doorway, hair falling unnoticed over her face as she leans against the frame. He takes out a beer and opens it. 'Sorry I missed your calls,' he says, flicking the cap towards the bin. 'I left my phone in my car. What was it?'

She takes a step towards the table. 'You're late home,' she says. 'Where have you been?'

'Just grabbed a quick beer with Alex.' He flicks through the stack of post on the counter. *Banish serpents disguised as lovers.* She reaches for the back of a chair to steady herself, forgetting the wine glass in her hand. It somersaults in slow motion towards the ground, shattering on impact.

Jack looks up at the sound, and then his face hardens.

'You're drunk,' he says. 'For fuck's sake, Elsa.'

She reddens. 'So are you!'

'I've been out with friends, not sitting in the house getting trashed all day!'

'Well, good for you for having friends,' she exclaims. 'My only friend here is an eighty-year-old woman, I'm sorry about that.' He stares at her. 'An old lady and Simon Cowell!' she yells, and she laughs. 'Living the dream. Living the American dream.'

He grabs his beer from the side. 'I'm not talking to you when you're like this.'

'Like what?' When he doesn't reply, she raises her voice even further. 'Come on. What am I being like?'

'You're acting crazy.'

'You're making me crazy!'

He stares at her as she stands among the shards. There is horror on his face and something is swelling up around them, something which chokes her, rising up and towering over them, ready to fall. *Say it*, they think, pleading with each other. But the moment passes; the wave runs weakly flat upon the shore, and he hands her the brush from behind the door and leaves.

The pieces of glass glitter up at her as she sweeps them into the pan. They watch her and she watches them and all the while something is building inside her, a fury which spirals rapidly up, hot and harsh in her throat. She rises, kicking the dustpan aside. In the living room, an American football game is on the television, and Jack stares fixedly at it, drinking his beer in long, swift swigs. She turns her back on him as she plugs in the stereo, turns the radio up as loud as it will go. *THE BAY CAR COMPANY* it crows, the faint hiss of static turned monstrous by the speaker. The sudden rush of anger is dissipating, taking with it the fug of wine,

(Taking you the places you want to go)

both settling, solid and resentful, immovable, in her chest. She presses her forehead to the window, stares out at the yard.

The advert travels through her, words vibrating in her chest.

What am I doing here? Her breath has fogged up the glass; she slowly draws a cross through it with the tip of her finger.

Why did he let me come? She turns sharply from the window, but the words catch in her throat.

Jack is still sitting in his chair, but his face is in his hands

(From Oakland to Golden Gate)

and

his body is wracked with silent sobs. They travel through him as she watches, horrified, his shoulders heaving

(A service you can trust)

and then she is

across the room. She curls silently into the corner of his chair and presses her face to his back,

(Let us take you where you need to be)

her arms around him. The muscles of his back tremble beneath her, and the part of his shirt which is underneath her face becomes slowly wet. After some time – though neither could say how much – has passed, he lifts his head. She moves away, lets him lean back. She rests her head on his and they sit in silence, watching the stars which appear in the dark sky beyond the window. The radio plays on and the TV fills the room with flickering light. Somehow, without knowing when, she falls asleep.

2007

They are late for Denny's wedding and these days they are always late. He paces back and forth, from room to room, looking and trying not to look at his watch. He hears the tap run, again and again, and he wonders how it can be that there is any skin left on her hands at all. Eventually he goes upstairs and stands by the door. He does not knock; he listens to her moving through the thin wall, and he thinks of the baby turning circles inside her. He puts a hand to the door and he looks at his watch and suddenly he does not care what time it is. He puts a hand on the door handle and he decides to open what is closed; what he or she or both of them have closed.

She is sitting on the bathtub and her dress is red and reminds him of the day they first met.

She is sitting on the bathtub and her skin shimmers softly, her hair streaming down her shoulders.

She is sitting on the bathtub, looking down at the floor.

She is sitting on the bathtub, and there is a test on the floor.

There is a test on the floor and she sees it as he does, she moves for it as he does, but even though she is quick, he is surer. He picks it up and he looks at its small, digital window and he looks at the key printed on the plastic beside it, and he looks again.

'You lost it,' he says, but already he knows that this isn't true.

'I'm sorry,' she says. She worries at a piece of hair, her eyes big and wide. 'I didn't mean—'

'You lied.'

She is not afraid, not ashamed. She looks at him with her head on one side; confused, beseeching. 'I thought it *could* be true, I wanted—' She is coming towards him and this he can't bear.

'I slept with someone,' he says, and even though he didn't mean for the words to escape, he enjoys each of them viciously. There is a thundering from somewhere; somewhere far off or somewhere inside, he can't be sure.

She stops, her face blank. 'I didn't mean to lie,' she says. 'But it can still be true. We'll have a baby. Won't we? We'll have a baby.'

'Are you listening to me? I slept with someone. I cheated on you.'

'I love you,' she says, but his words have made a hole. He

watches its smouldering edges take hold, its flame catching. Her eyes narrow. 'Who?'

'A woman I met in New York.' He thinks of the sticky melon taste of her mouth, the meaty smell of her hands.

She closes her eyes and it is some time before she speaks. 'We'll be okay.'

'We are not okay!' The words and their volume frighten him, and it is this fear which propels him forwards, it is this fear which erases the anger, lets him see her standing there, small and gold and in her red dress. He gathers her to him, and he speaks into her hair. 'I'm sorry, Beth, so sorry, but I think this is over. I think you need help.'

She puts her small hands on his, she puts her small hands on his face. 'Shhhh,' she says, and she strokes him and he sobs. 'It'll be okay,' she tells him. 'It will all be okay.'

2008

The test is on the floor, the phone in her hand. Kieran's voice in her ear is clear though sound is distorted.

'Get rid of it, please.'

Hours later, there is a conversation, there is an argument. There are tears. He seems small then, inconceivably so. His eyes are hard, hers swollen and sore. Things are swollen and sore and aching. She stands while he sits, staring up at her.

'Think of me. Think of my career.'

There is no career. There are degrees, two, and rejections, many. There is her.

'I can't do this, Elsa.'

Her heart hardens, her body stone. 'But I can't do this for you.'

His face softens, her hands in his. 'Please.'

*

A week later, in a doctor's office, there is blue paper on a bed and a screen turned away from her. An image is printed, placed face down on the desk. Her finger is taken by gloved hands, a pin pressed into its pad. A single streak of blood on the piece of paper, its type recorded. She answers the questions carefully, a pause for thought before she speaks aloud, because she cannot trust the words which might come out. Her responses are written down, added to a brown cardboard file. The face-down image slides in beside them, out of her sight.

Another week later, it is over. She lies in bed and she doesn't cry. She lies in bed beside him, her back to him while he sleeps. She flicks through pictures on her phone in the faint orange light of the street outside. They are all of him; his face from every angle, in every light. She turns over and watches him sleep. She is ashamed but her heart beats faster. He still makes her heart beat faster.

2013

There is an accident. Jack passes it on his way
to work. It is a Wednesday morning and the
fog is particularly persistent, the air sodden. The
windows of his car are beaded with it; the flashing
lights of the emergency vehicles repeat in each, the
glass alive and blue. He turns his face away as he
drives on.

They have not spoken of the night he cried.
Realising she was asleep, he lifted her carefully
and carried her to bed. Climbing in beside her, he
buried his face in her hair and closed his eyes. He
did not sleep; not at first. But he was calmer. He
let the sound of her breathing, regular and feather-
light, coax him down. As the sky began to grey, he
let himself dream.

The next morning, she watched him and he
saw that she was remembering. He made himself

meet her gaze, and when she asked, in a small voice, 'Are you okay?' he nodded.

'I'm fine,' he said. 'Just tired.'

He says it again to himself now. *Just tired. I'm fine. I'm okay.*

Arriving at work, he realises he has left his phone behind. The mystery calls continue; they continue to be unanswered. And yet not to have it beside him, not to see it ring, fills him with terror. Like the age-old question of the tree in the woods, he wonders: if nobody is there to watch the phone ring, is the call really happening?

Inside, he straps on his harness. Andy is at the locker beside him, talking quietly on his phone.

'Oh, she did?' he says, and then, 'Yeah, send me a picture.'

Behind them, Alex lurks, texting. He hums as he does it, smirking, and Jack eyes the phone in his hand. He slams his locker shut.

'All set?' Andy asks him, and Alex whoops.

'Go, team!'

Jack follows them out, fists clenched in his pockets.

'I'm thinking the Spanish place for the bachelor party,' Alex is saying. 'I talked to Rosie and she said there's no problem with you guys ordering a stripper. Of course, I didn't tell you that. You came up with it all by yourself.'

But Jack isn't listening. He keeps his head down as cars slide past them, the grey creeping on.

'Alex!' Chase waves from across the road. 'Could use you over here.'

'I'll catch you in a while,' Alex says, and Jack nods. His jaw feels tight and he puts a hand to it, trying to loosen it.

'You okay?' Andy asks.

'Yeah. Just tired.'

'Take it easy up there, yeah?'

'Yup.'

Clipping himself to the safety wire, he makes his way up the cable behind Andy. The steel is slippery and his boots squeak as he walks. He glances down at the water. The foghorn has begun to sound, a hoarse bleating which shivers across the bay. His hair is damp and his skin feels sheer like ice. He fumbles through the checks on each fitting with numb hands, discarding his gloves.

As he works, he remembers the first time she took his hand. It was New Year's Day, the morning after the night before, and the first threads of panic were beginning to worm their way out through his heart. *I can't do this*, he was thinking, but each time she came closer, each time her body brushed against his, each time she looked up at him, there was a surge instead. Walking out with her – *I'll walk with you*, she'd said. *I'm going to see my friends* – he tried not to look at her. It would be easier that way, better. *Better to let her go now*, he'd thought, and as he did, her hand slipped into his. She did it with such ease, so naturally, not even pausing in her sentence, and he stared down at it, at the place where they were joined; her small, white hand pressed against his, the fingers entwined.

Take my hand. The image will not leave him alone. The fog

forms soft fingers, the wind sings a Beatles song. If he had his phone, he could text her the lyrics. The rain begins in earnest, fat drops falling down his collar and splashing his boots.

Within an hour, their radios crackle into life.

'Come down.' Miller's voice is sludgy in the storm of static, the words difficult to distinguish. 'Head in.'

'I thought he'd never ask,' Andy says.

'Shop?'

'Guess so.'

Coming down the cable, Jack's boot slips, momentarily leaving the steel surface. He swings dizzily off-balance, the clip of his harness clicking against the wire, before finding his footing again. He takes a shuddering breath, staring down at the road below, at the chord which runs beneath it.

'You okay?' Andy asks from above him, and he finds he cannot answer.

Back on the pavement, Chase and Alex huddle into their hoods. 'Bitch of a day,' Chase says, and Jack laughs. They look at him, confused, as the single gull-like sound fades into the fog. He shrugs.

'Let's get inside.'

They walk towards the workshop. The fog has become so thick above the water that through the railings there is only white. He runs a hand through his hair, tries to focus on what Alex is saying

'– I keep telling her, why does it matter? It's just one day –'

but there is a thumping in his ears; just distant, a pulsing drawing slowly closer.

'Yeah,' he says. *Tell her.*

'Uh oh,' Chase says in a low voice. Up ahead, looming out of the fog, a man stands at the railing, bracing himself against it with both hands. He looks down over its edge into the nothing and the white. Three hands go automatically to their radios. Jack's is not one of them. His heart stutters in his chest, the thumping getting louder. His mouth is dry and he struggles to swallow.

But the man thinks better of it; or hasn't thought of it at all. He pushes himself away and turns sharply, walking towards them. They watch him pass, grey overcoat swinging.

'Be a good day to go though, huh?' Alex says, glancing over the railing. 'Like stepping into a cloud.'

'Yep,' Jack says. *A good day to go.*

The workshop is sheltered from the rain but not warm, its small windows clouded and icy. A single radiator rattles against one wall, clanking at intervals. Jack doesn't know many of the crew who work here; has been fortunate enough with the weather that this is the first shift to be rained off. One of the shop crew, a tall, thin man called David, parks in the space beside his. They have often exchanged a few words at the beginning or end of a shift: a how's-it-going here, a let's-have-a-beer-some-time there. He can put names to most of the other faces, but not much more. For their part, he is simply Jack, the New Guy.

It's David who comes over now, offering tasks to people at random. He gives Jack a single clap on the back as he passes. 'Think they could use some help over there,' he says, gesturing towards a corner at the far end of the room, where stacks of safety equipment are lined up in rows. Arriving there, Jack and Alex are given the task of sorting through an old supply of safety clips, discarding any which are worn or rusty.

'Great,' Alex says, sitting down on the floor. 'This'll make the day go fast.'

'Better than being out in the rain.' Jack picks up a clip with a peeling red rubber coating and examines it.

'I guess.'

They sit in silence for a few minutes, occasionally tossing one of the clips onto the pile with a musical clink.

'How's Elsa?' Alex asks.

'She's good.' Jack pushes the lever of a clip open and closed, open and closed. 'A bit homesick, I think.' He thinks of her in the kitchen, the wine glass shattering at her feet. *Living the American dream.*

'Her visa must be up soon.'

'Yeah, end of the month.'

'She applying for a new one?'

Jack squeezes the sides of a clip, studying it. 'I guess. I assumed she would.'

'She wanted to work, right?'

'Yeah. I don't know.' He tosses the clip aside. 'It's not a

problem. I can look after us.' There is a sharp, sheering sound coming from a machine in an opposite corner of the workshop. It shrieks as metal is passed through it, the sound cutting through the air like a blade.

'She must get bored though.'

'I don't know. Maybe.'

'I should get Claudia to give her a call. They can go for lunch or whatever.'

'That'd be good.' *You're making me crazy.*

'Hey,' Alex says, reaching for another tub of clips. 'You ever figure out what the deal was with that old lady and the little kids?'

'No. I haven't seen them around in a while.' *Only us.* The pulsing is growing louder; his head throbs with it. He clicks his jaw, rubs a hand over his eyes.

'You sure you're all right?'

'I'm fine.' *Things will be okay in the end.*

'Here.' Alex holds out a hand, and Jack stares blankly down at it. *Take my hand.* 'The clips?' Alex says, gesturing to the tub beside Jack. 'Those ones okay?'

Jack nods. Alex stands and picks up the tub. He looks down at Jack. 'You don't look too hot.'

The pulsing is so loud he can feel it behind his eyes. Rain batters against the windows. His mouth fills with water. He tosses another clip onto the faulty pile. 'I'm fine,' he says, and the words unfurl weakly out of his mouth, struggling for air. 'I'm going for a piss.'

'Take it easy, man,' Alex says, but Jack is already heading for the door. He is dimly aware of Andy looking up

Jack, you okay?

and of Eddie delivering the punchline of a joke

Because she thought she had wings!

as he passes them, his heart pounding. He throws the door open, sucks in air. The corridor is draughty and smells of urine and bleach. He pushes open the door marked WC. There is a dented steel urinal, a brown-streaked sink and two cubicles. He locks himself in one, taking in rapid, shallow breaths.

An extractor fan in the top-left corner of the wall opens directly to the outside, and the air is thin and cold. For a moment, looking up at it, the world rights itself. There is a sense of clarity, of balance, and then Jack bends at the knees and vomits into the stained toilet.

When he is done, he straightens up and leans back against the door. He takes a few deep breaths, the pressure on his chest easing, and looks out through the slots in the fan. The sky has lightened, the sound of the rain lessened. Soon it will be time to go back to work.

2007

They come almost every hour at first. Over the weeks, the flow fades, until it is one person a day, sometimes two. Then it is phone calls, emails. They invite him to dinner, or to stay for the weekend, and each time he declines. When some time has passed, they leave him alone completely.

At first, though, they come every hour.

'I'm so sorry,' they tell him.

'I can't understand,' he says.

'We're praying for you,' some tell him, and at this he stares, blankly, at the wall.

They bring flowers, though never actually give them to him, never place them in his hands. Instead they busy themselves with the bouquets; they find vases, glasses, splay out the stems. They find them a place among the others, a wall of quickly fading life.

'It's my fault,' he says, and all of the people and all of the flowers shake their heads. *No*, they breathe, but in the no he hears only yes.

'Is there anything we can do?' they ask.

Later, when the steady rush begins to slow, they say, 'Have you thought about what you'll do now?' and he pauses.

I'm going to leave, he thinks, but to them he says nothing.

'Let me help you pack up her things,' her mother asks him, and he tells her no.

'Let me help you pack up her things,' his sister instructs him, and he nods.

'She was a wonderful person,' they all say.

'She was,' he replies.

'It's a dreadful tragedy,' they say.

'It is,' he replies.

'She lost control of the car,' they say.

'She didn't,' he replies.

2013

City Hall, a grand and imposing building, sits in the middle of the run-down and broken-beyond-repair Civic Center. As a building, Elsa has often thought, it feels at times apologetic, at others as if it is resolutely looking the other way and hoping it can soon makes its escape. Today, to her, it feels resigned. She takes a seat a third of the way up its pale grey steps and pushes her hair away from her face. Around her, people without homes sit in small groups or alone. The air is sharp and cold, the sun defiant. She turns her face up to it.

At her feet, in one of her shopping bags, is a yard of soft white cotton. She's not sure yet what it will be: a baby blanket, a set of burping cloths, a trio of bibs. She has spoken to Anna this morning, for the third time this week. Her sister is feeling well, everyone is excited. There is a due date and there will be a flight just before or soon after, and those are the only concrete details of the roles that either sister will play in this new stage of their relationship.

People pass by, and in doing so, expose their faintest flaws to Elsa. A young mother, her toddler daughter in a fluffy coat and pink buckled shoes, looks anxiously at her phone as she tugs the little girl past. Her eyes are shaded and lined, and just a little red. Elsa looks at her own phone, knows how she feels.

She closes her eyes briefly, leans back against the step. The military jacket is soft with wear now, its funnel neck smudged with make-up and fragrant with perfume and the smell of frying food. In her pocket are gloves, white-and-rust striped soft wool, which Jack gave her on Christmas morning, but there is something appealing in the way the wind numbs her fingers as the sun warms her face.

A couple in their early thirties pass, hand in hand and carrying several large shopping bags. As she talks, she lays her head occasionally against his shoulder; each time his fingers squeeze hers a little tighter. To the untrained eye, they are content, but Elsa, looking closer, can see the tightness in his jaw, the uneasiness in her eyes. They have argued, or they will argue – nothing serious, nothing long-lasting; probably only a fraught and irritable kind of bickering. She is certain of it.

She is a little jealous of them, actually.

Two teenage boys fly past on skateboards, both laughing. One hits an uneven patch of pavement and is sent hurtling from the board in an ungainly series of hops while the other sails on down the street. Collecting his skateboard, the fallen boy glances up at Elsa. As their eyes meet, he pauses, his brow furrowing. He considers her like this for just a second or two, and then, with a brief sort of nod, he is gone again.

There has been no mention of further letters, and a part of her is sorry. With more of them, she is sure, she would find out their cause; understand what serpent this man took as a lover, why it drove him to the bridge. Now, with only one, she can't reason him away, can't dispel him from where he hovers, a cloud over them, threatening a storm. She is frightened that as time goes on, he will be joined by more and more, the traces of the people who jump filling up their little house, pulling up the picket fence.

Claudia and Alex will soon be married, and that brings with it hope. Does Alex talk to Claudia about what it is like? She is too afraid to push Jack any more, too frightened of the rejection. Her walks to the bridge, though, have become a little bolder; have taken her to the beginning of the walkway. There, she looks down at the steel beam which runs below it and imagines how it would feel to lower your weight carefully onto it, to look down at the iron-grey water below. At the entrance to the bridge is the first of many emergency phones. It has a sign beside it: 'Crisis Counselling', and then: 'There is hope. Make the call.' Often, on the long bus ride back to Potrero, this is what she remembers.

A group of four twenty-somethings pass by her steps, each trying to comfort a tall, younger-looking man who swears intermittently and kicks at the ground. 'I'm such a fucking twat,' he says, in an English accent, and then, 'Eighty fucking dollars.'

'Come on,' one of the girls, who has a faint accent – Swedish, perhaps, Elsa thinks – says. 'Let's just go back to the hostel.'

'She's right,' another says, a small girl who also has an English accent. 'Let's go back and work out what to do.' As she speaks, she glances at one of the other boys; dark-haired and unshaven, so far silent; and in that glance Elsa sees a flash of flesh, of secret sex.

'Oh, fuck it,' the tall English boy says. 'Let's just carry on. I'm not getting it back, am I? Let's at least get pissed so I can forget about it.'

And then they are gone. She listens as their voices fade away. She wonders what it would have been like to be in a strange city with Jenn, or with Lily, to share bedrooms with strangers and take buses with strangers, to have secret sex with strangers. They went the summer after graduation, Jenn and Lily, with Max too; trains through Europe and sleeping bags in stations. They sent her postcards. Sitting here, she wishes she had kept them. Sitting here, she wishes she had been there too.

'It's a bad idea to sit here,' a man says, and he sits down beside her.

'Why's that?' she asks.

He shrugs. 'Not safe. That's what they say, anyway.'

She turns to look at him; at his shock of reddish hair, his straggly beard. His skin is yellowish and dirty. He wears a long-sleeved T-shirt and filthy combat trousers. In his hand is a large can of beer. 'I don't really listen to what people say,' she says. 'I feel safe enough. What about you?'

'I feel drunk.'

'I think that's kind of the same.'

'Maybe,' he says. He takes a drink from his can and is silent for a while. 'You're sad,' he says eventually.

'Aren't you?'

He considers this, looking out over the road. Across the street, two homeless men have begun to argue, their voices rising steadily. 'No,' he says. 'Not exactly.'

'There is hope,' she murmurs.

'You should go home,' he says, and she smiles.

'Where's your home?' she asks.

He finishes his drink and puts it carefully beside him. 'I don't know any more,' he says, locking his fingers together between his knees.

'Me neither,' she says.

'You do.'

'How do you know?'

'I can tell.' He waves a hand at her. 'You have a look about you. Like you belong somewhere.'

'Oh.' She sinks back against the step and looks out. The fight has subsided; the two opponents now on opposite sides of the road.

'You'll be okay,' he says.

'Will you?'

He sighs. 'I think you should go home.'

'Can I fix things?' she asks.

'Will he let you?'

She frowns. 'I'm not sure.'

' "There is hope",' he says. 'Right?'

She stands up, unzipping her jacket. 'I'd better go,' she says, and she puts it around his shoulders.

2008

Months are lost, the days a long, terrible
chain of nothing, of bleak grey mornings
and throbbing head; curtains drawn, bottles
lined up along the wall. Money is running out, an
eviction notice fluttering against the door. He sleeps
rarely but hardly moves and they often hammer
on the door until his heart beats in time with their
fists. When he lets them in, their faces loom large
in the room: Franklin, Nicole, Aimee. They sit
him up, they clean him. They wash the blood from
his hands as best they can, tear strips from T-shirts
to stem the flow. Franklin repairs the dents in the
walls, Nicole paints over them. They take away
his car keys and so he learns again to walk, pushes
handfuls of coins across counters, stumbles back
with his bottles. Franklin writes him cheques which
he never cashes, paper pile soft in the house of glass.

The year draws to a close and the walls can no longer be repaired. His fists go through them and glass smashes against doors. He rages and he yells. He tears his things from the closet because the empty space beside them is too much to bear. Catching a glimpse of his face in the mirrored door, he puts a fist through it. The old instincts surface and the fist flies again, and then a foot, and then it is the kicker, it is his head. After that, there is black. After that there is Aimee, and with her, his father. His father lifting him. His father standing over him, handing him coffee. He sits on the edge of an unfamiliar bath while his father shaves his face and tears roll steadily down his cheeks. He lets his father lead him onto a plane as he has so often before. He presses his face to the window and looks back as the city shrinks away.

Rehab is weeks of white; tapping heels and squeaking doors, clipboards notes ticking clock. When it is over, his father is there again, rusted car idling at the end of the drive. 'You look better,' he says, and Jack shakes his head. 'You'll get better,' his father says, and he puts the car into drive.

He takes him back home – Jeff's home, not Jack's – and it is just the two of them, just the two of them in their places in the silent Seattle house. There are no beers and there is food. 'You learnt to cook,' Jack says, one evening, his voice hoarse.

'I went to prison,' his father says. 'I had to learn something.'

Aimee is back in New York but she calls each evening; talks to him about nothing, saying everything. They are long days of remembering, cold and exposed. Beth; Beth is everywhere. His father doesn't ask questions and they continue on in the small circles of the house; wake, move, eat, sleep. There is no work, little conversation, but gradually things become less fragile; begin to harden over, to take his weight. The chance of slipping through to what is beneath lessens a little each day.

Often, though, the cracks appear; a misplaced foot somewhere, a thought straying too far from safety, and somehow he can't move. He stares at the wall and the terror travels through him. When this happens, his father sits beside him and waits, hunched forward over his knees.

'I can't do this. I can't carry on,' he says, one afternoon, and his father looks back at him.

'You can,' he says, and then there is a figure at the door. 'It's going to be okay,' his father says, and then his mother is kneeling in front of him.

'Come home with me,' she says.

2009

Their arguments stretch into days and then into weeks. Doors are slammed, plates thrown. Words are said in anger and left marooned between them, crowding up the small space. It is always her apology, even when it has been his argument. Kieran works long shifts at the bar, a career in design finally abandoned – temporarily or for ever, it is not yet clear. He comes home late and crawls under the sheets beside her, smelling of cigarette smoke though it is now illegal to smoke in bars.

She turns to him one night, pale grey light between them. 'You're cheating on me, aren't you?'

He gives a simple nod. 'Sorry.'

She doesn't leave, though she hates herself for it. There has been too much invested, too much discarded. She stays and she cries. She stays and she tries to make things right. Sitting in a hairdresser's one Tuesday after work – the cheapest she can find, where the magazines are dog-eared and soggy, and the smell of peroxide hangs in the air – she stares at her face and is suddenly, horribly frightened. She looks at the floor as the long pieces of her hair fall limply down.

'What do you think?' the stylist asks, and Elsa runs a hand across the back of her neck where the skin is soft and newly exposed.

'I don't know,' she says.

Back in the tiny flat, she waits patiently for him to come home, tucking it behind her ears, letting it swing forward again. Lipstick dries chalky on her lips. When he arrives home he is surprised and then he smiles.

'You cut your hair.'

'Yes.'

He walks towards her with his prowling, languid walk. 'It looks nice.'

His hands are in it then, the perfumed scent of the salon shampoo hazy in her throat. He lowers his face to hers and kisses her. His lips feel strange, a stranger's. She tries to mould them with hers, tries to find their shape. He pulls away.

'Sorry. I can't. I – I just don't feel that way any more.'

It is too difficult to process; she steps away, blinking, and begins to undress. As she falls asleep, she thinks brightly that this is the first time in a long time that he has apologised. She watches him leave for work the next morning. She sits in silence and waits for him to come home.

A month later, he leaves for ever. From their studio straight to someone else's bed; whose, she never discovers. She spends her work days trying not to cry and the hours at home staring at the wall, dry-eyed.

And then it is January, another new year. After weeks of being asked, she finally accepts an invitation to lunch with two girls from the office. Thai, a new place just down the road from their building. Set lunch six pounds starter main and small glass of wine. She orders spring rolls and green curry (vegetable). Wine white.

The two girls are younger than her but they earn more money, have worked their way up whilst she was still studying. Their sentences are always questions: did you hear about did you see can you believe. Is it me or. She treads water in the flow, stops attempting to answer them.

'What do you think, Elsa?' they say occasionally, and she can only shrug.

'You're so quiet,' they tell her. 'You're a right dark horse.'

I never used to be, she thinks. *Is it me or.*

The bill arrives and is split between three cards. 'You had green tea,' the girls tell her. 'Don't forget to add that on.'

'Better get back to the hellhole,' they say. 'Did you hear about –'

She zones out. *Four hours left*, she thinks, standing. Four hours until she can go home and be silent on her own. Taking her coat from the back of the chair, she catches it, tipping it over. It clatters loudly against the floor.

'Whoops,' one of the girls says.

'Easy,' says the other.

She bends to right it, her face flushed. Straightening up, she pushes her hair out of her face, and someone places a hand on her back. She whirls around and he is standing there. Max.

'All right, Miss Unwin.'

'Max.' She hugs him tightly, afraid to let go. He pushes her gently back, grins at her.

'You look good, Els. You changed your hair.'

She feels suddenly, embarrassingly tearful. 'It's so nice to see you.'

'What are you up to now?'

She waves a hand at her colleagues, now lurking in the doorway. 'Just some boring sales shit. What about you?'

'PhD. Final year. I live with Jenn.'

'That's amazing. How is she?'

'She's great. Look, give me your number. No, wait. Let me give you our address. Pop over tonight, we only live down the road. Surprise her.'

'Really?'

'Yeah, of course.'

She scribbles it into her diary, hands shaking. 'Thanks, Max. I — I really needed this today.'

He grins. 'Whatever. See you later, yeah?' He heads back to his table. 'Bring a bottle,' he calls over his shoulder.

2013

She moves her hand through the water, watching the ripples. The bathtub is short and her knees rise out, two peaks amongst the steam. Her toes tap against the bottom; an agitated, irritable beat. In the house next door, Pearl looks up from her book, peering through her glasses at the window. The street outside is silent and grey. She watches it for a few seconds, then shrugs and returns to her page. In the bath, Elsa flicks at the surface of the water, watches the ripples spread.

They fixed her. Jenn and Max. Lily. Barney. Slotted her back into their circle; nights of wine and food and laughing, mornings waking up on Jenn and Max's sofa. Lily found her a flat-share, helped her pack up the studio and leave it behind. Barney, finally looking his age in smart shirts and suits, recommended her for a new job; another desk job, but the days behind it less dull, the money twice as generous. *They fixed you*, she thinks. *And now where are you?* She stands up suddenly, the water running off her in sheets. Wrapping herself in a towel, she thinks of Max. A sunny Sunday in Clapham and the two of them stand at the bar, waiting for their drinks. It is the fourth round and she is feeling drunk and suddenly, looking up at him, with his scruffy hair and his glasses – worn more often now, a sure sign they are getting old – in his jeans and flip-flops, she is overwhelmingly grateful. 'Thank you,' she says, and he looks at her quizzically. 'For being there,' she explains, and the drinks begin to arrive. He rolls his eyes and hugs her, says, 'We've always been there, mate – you only had to ask,' but when they are at the door to the garden, he turns back, his face serious.

'You're fucking better than that, Elsa. Don't forget it, okay?'

She wraps the towel tighter around her and storms out to the bedroom, leaving damp footprints in her wake. In front of the wardrobe, she gazes at her clothes, at the suitcase beneath them. She runs a hand across them, grabs a fistful of fabric. But before she can pull, the anger subsides. She lets her fingers walk over to his side, takes a handful of his shirt instead. She puts it to her face and breathes.

When his key turns in the lock, she is sitting in the kitchen. He is cautious coming through; his steps slow. When he appears in the doorway, they look at each other, their eyes sad. They smile small smiles.

'Where have you been?' she asks.

'Just for a drink.'

'I can't do this any more,' she says, still sitting.

'I'm sorry. I should've texted.'

'It's not that. It's this. I can't keep pretending.'

He leans against the frame. 'What do you mean?'

'You know what I mean. This – *us* – it isn't right, it isn't normal.'

'We aren't normal, Elsa.'

She looks down at the table, her voice growing smaller. 'But I don't want that any more.'

'And what do you want?'

It is a genuine question but she looks up, her features hardening. 'You aren't even going to say sorry? I've been *trying*, Jack. I've been trying to make this a home for us, I've been trying to help you.' Her hand begins to slap the table as she speaks. 'I wanted this to work. I came here for *you*.'

Cornered, the words escape him in a panic. 'I never asked you to!'

She stares at him. 'Yes, you did.'

'No, I didn't. I said you could come. If you wanted. I didn't ask you to. I never promised you anything, Elsa. I thought you understood.' He trails off, helpless. 'I said you could come,' he says again, softly.

She lets out a shocked laugh. 'You're going to throw me under the bus over *semantics*? You fucking shit, Jack. You fucking shit.'

With a sudden horror, he sees what is happening. He takes a shaky step forward. 'Elsa, please. I didn't realise. I'll try.'

'It's too late,' she says, her eyes fixed on a worn patch on the floor. 'It's just too late. Can't you tell?'

'It's not,' he says, firmly, crossing the room in three swift steps and taking hold of both her hands. 'It's *not*.' He finds that he is shaking his head, over and over, childish and defiant. 'It's not too late,' he says again.

Finally her eyes meet his, the two of them perched on the precipice. He grips her hands tighter. *Take my hand*. 'Please don't leave me,' he whispers, and she hesitates. Her hands squeeze his. She presses her lips together and he crouches down in front of her. 'Please.'

She puts a hand to his face, strokes his cheek. 'If we could start again,' she says, thinking suddenly, wildly, of Kylie Minogue and a car journey, and he nods.

His phone begins to ring. The sound rolls through the small kitchen in sharp swells. 'I'm on call,' he says, and he lets it ring.

'You're on call,' she says, and she pushes the phone towards him. He answers and the sound of his voice still runs through her in waves.

She stares down at her hands on the table. *You're fucking better than that*, she thinks, but then she remembers them spinning on a beach. She remembers him carrying her up the stairs on their first night here, remembers his face, close to hers. *I love you*. He hangs up the phone and she pushes her chair back and stands.

He takes a couple of uncertain steps towards her and she looks up at him, a strand of hair falling back down from its untidy knot. Slowly, she steps; one small bare foot onto each of his. She wraps her arms around his neck and lays her head on his shoulder. His body goes slack and he pulls her closer. He pushes his face into the crook of her neck.

'I'd better go,' he says, the words muffled against her skin.

Arriving back at the bridge, he is faced with the strange half-light of almost darkness. The shadows shift as he moves, the sound of his footsteps skittering ahead of him. As he jogs towards the entrance, he is sure that people passing in cars turn their heads to watch him. Their pale faces glide by, the moon drifting slowly upwards. The wind is picking up; it lifts the hairs on his arms and whistles gently over the water.

Alex is waiting for him at the walkway's gate, already in his harness. He holds out another to Jack.

'Who is it?' Jack asks, taking it.

'Some chick,' Alex says. 'Crazy bitch. Someone's called the psych ward and they're on their way.'

'Great.' The procedure is simple here, Miller's favourite. *One distracts, the other grabs.*

'You wanna grab?' Alex asks. 'Or me?'

'Let's just see how it goes,' Jack says. As he tightens his harness, he notices that his hands are shaking.

'Cool. You okay?'

'Yeah. I just want to get home.'

'Me too,' Alex says. 'Let's do this shit and get out of here.'

They are jogging now, almost halfway to the first tower. A final pair of gulls fly overhead, wings clapping softly in the darkness. Somewhere in the city, Matthew sits beside his youngest son's bed, watching him sleep. He looks up at the ceiling and smiles.

Out on the bridge, Jack and Alex draw closer to the scene. A police car reverses hastily whilst an officer diverts traffic across into other lanes. The car bumps onto the pavement, its headlights directed at the chord. Jack can just make out a figure there.

'Here we go,' Alex says. One of the Highway Patrol officers approaches them; Jack recognises him from Eve's jump. His straw-coloured hair looks silver in the twilight, and Jack's stomach turns. 'She's not making a whole lotta sense,' he says, 'but she's responding. If we can just keep her talking—'

'Yeah, we got it from here,' Alex says, and he gives Jack a nudge. 'Be safe,' he says, and then he pushes through the small, huddled crowd, and chooses a place about ten feet down to climb over the railing.

Jack hitches himself over, secures his harness. Only then does he allow himself to look properly at the woman. Her dark hair is shorn off at the shoulders, frizzing at the edges. She is perhaps in her mid-thirties, though it is hard to tell in the unfolding darkness, and through the streams of black make-up which run down her cheeks. Her jaw moves continuously, her mouth opening occasionally to accommodate it. *She's not crazy*, Jack thinks. *She's a crackhead*. But when she speaks, he's immediately sure that the initial diagnosis was right.

'Stay back,' she says, hunching into herself. She is clinging to the railings with one hand; the other, finger pointed, stabs back and forth between Jack and Alex. 'I know who you are. I know who sent you. You're with *them*.'

'We're not with anyone,' Jack says firmly. 'What's your name?'

'Bells ring in churches,' she says. 'Marriages, dresses. Death. Dying. Jumping.'

Alex groans and her head snaps towards him.

'Dog fucker,' she says. 'Fucking dog fucker.'

'Nice. You kiss your mother with that mouth?' Alex asks, unwrapping a stick of gum with one hand and folding it lazily into his mouth.

'I do a lot of things with this mouth.' Her eyes dart to Jack. He looks away from her, out at the bay.

'Oh yeah? You wanna tell me about that?' Alex has, in Jack's silence, assumed the role of distractor.

'Sure.' She leans towards him, swinging wildly from the hand which grips the railings. Jack knows that this is his moment to move, but his body is suddenly heavy. He looks down at the water below him, and then out at the city. The moon hovers above it all with a strange, luminous stillness.

'Jack!' Alex's voice brings him back with a lurch and he twists, dizzy, his arm extending, his fingers brushing the woman's. She jerks away but he is quicker now, he darts forwards. His hand closes around her wrist, and then he sees. He fights the urge to push this woman away, forces himself to keep hold of her. He pins her arms to her sides and wraps her in a headlock. *Got her,* he thinks, and then: *Elsa*. He feels the woman's breath, hot on his neck. The hot breath becomes wet as her teeth pierce his skin. 'Stop fighting,' he tells her, and suddenly, finally, he hears the words himself.

He only loosens his hold for a second, but it's enough. Her arm flies outwards, pale and liquid in the moonlight, and only as it gets close does he see the silver. As the blade pierces his throat, he feels only relief.

When they are dying, these are the things they will remember. They will see it all; see the things which came before, the things which came between them. They will remember words whispered in ears, lips leaving soft scars on skin. They will remember the fall but this time they will see it coming, they will see where they came undone.

31 December 2011

After a year installed in Essex with his mother and Robin, her new husband, he is on more solid ground. The first months are delicate; his mother tender, Robin respectfully distant. Gradually, they find him work on building sites. He commutes there and back, has breakfast made for him, dinner waiting, sleeps on clean sheets in a tightly made bed.

But finally, the time for the cord to be cut arrives, along with a job opening too good to be refused: a shopping centre in central London which guarantees at least a year's work. Another huge expanse to be filled with things to be desired, things to be coveted, another block of concrete to be peopled with teenagers and mothers and persons passing through. The thought sickens him, but also comforts; the world continues on and there will always be things to be built, things to be secured and maintained.

He rents a room in a house-share in Clapham. His housemates are friendly, young and Australian; three boys, three voices, loud and uncompromising, laughing and teasing, £435 pcm. A year passes and London is all that there has ever been. America is a place where the disasters belong to others; where oil rigs explode and orcas kill theme-park employees. His father calls and he speaks to him because he is indebted. But each time he holds the phone he is afraid; the line live like a snake, the connection it opens unstable and vicious. Soon they communicate only by email. Both are more secure in this medium.

And now the year is over, its last day dwindling into its twilight hours, and he is walking downhill to a bar that Charlie, the youngest of his housemates, thinks will be 'awesome'. His hair is just cut, his shirt ironed for the first time in months. Trailing behind the others, he watches the sky darken. Another year behind him. He tucks it safely there, a further layer between him and another life. Reaching the bottom of the hill, he keeps his eyes always forward.

'You know what you need?' Charlie says, glancing back at him.

'What's that?'

His friend throws an arm around his neck. 'You need to get laid.'

Jack shrugs. 'I'm not really like that.'

'Course you are. Come on, Shark Finn! It's New Year, the perfect hunting ground!'

'Yeah,' one of the others says. 'Shark Finn!' They begin a series of short, throaty barks, ruffling his hair.

'Fuck off,' he says, shrugging them away, but he can't help smiling. Sometimes they are infectious.

Reaching the bar, pints are bought and he takes his own warily. He glances around – *Anyone watching?* Of course they aren't, rehab is miles and years behind him. People are already flooding into the small venue and the sky outside is a clear and vivid dark blue, the rare sight of stars strange and celebratory. Charlie points out the girls he will try his luck with; each blonder, thinner, more po-faced than the next.

'What's your type?' he asks, and Jack doesn't know. 'Dude,' Charlie says, his eyes already a little wild. 'You need to get a life. You're in London. Start living.'

As the hours pass, the music grows louder and the punters surge around him, he allows himself to be tugged away from the group. He looks around at the girls in their tight dresses, their cut-away T-shirts. He tries to imagine what it would be like to be with one of them; tries to remember the way someone else's skin feels against his.

By the bar now, his elbow finding a sticky spot to rest, he glances at his watch. The music is loud and the ceiling low, a slow-moving sea of sound around him. Someone's body bumps his, an elbow digging into his side. But he is not someone who would throw a punch now; instead he extends a firm hand to assist the stranger away, easy now, no trouble here.

'Sorry, mate,' the stranger says, round-faced and starry-eyed, a bottle of Prosecco in hand.

'No worries.' End of conversation, move on, no trouble here.

But the stranger stays, a lopsided grin spreading. 'You having a good one?'

He sighs, he sips. 'Yeah, it's all right. You know.'

'Yeah. I'm Barney, by the way.'

He shakes hands, still wary. 'Jack.'

'Bit of a shithole, here, isn't it?'

'Yeah. A bit.'

'Want some of this?'

He glances down, panic spreading through him. But only the bottle of Prosecco is waved. 'Nah, you're all right, mate,' he says, relieved, and he looks away.

Barney is looking behind them; his unfocused eyes narrow and then light up. 'One sec.' He darts through the crowd like a fish. Returning a second later, he drags someone else behind him; the crowd parts momentarily and Jack catches a flash of grey dress, a low swoop of dark hair across a pale cheek.

'My new friend,' the stranger is saying to her. 'Meet my new friend.'

2013

It is warm, and everything is still. The house on Potrero is filled with a beautiful spring light; winter has finally departed. He is lying on the bed, Elsa beside him. She sits with her back against the wall while he lies, looking up at her. He runs his fingers along her bare leg, the skin soft and firm.

'It all went wrong,' she says, and he nods.

'Everything will be okay,' he says. 'Things will be okay.'

'Everyone has secrets,' she says, and he presses his lips to her thigh.

'When you wake up, we'll be home,' she says, and she runs a hand through his hair.

'I love you,' he says.

'I love you too,' a voice says, laughing, and he tries to open his eyes. The lids are heavy, sticky, and when he moves his head there is a bolt of pain which travels through him like fire.

'Take it easy,' the voice says, and this time his eyes open. The room is white and too bright and he squints, afraid to move.

'Jack?' A figure looms into view, and he winces, nauseated. 'Am I that ugly?' the voice says, and the face swims into focus. Alex grins down at him. 'Good morning,' he says.

His memory returning, Jack tries to sit up. An IV drip runs into his left hand, and as he lifts his head, another white-hot bolt of pain runs through it. 'How long was I out?' he asks, wincing as he attempts, this time successfully, to lift himself to a sitting position. He puts a hand to the thick bandage on his neck.

'An hour. You went into shock and they sedated you. Pussy.'

'That's not a very friendly way to talk to someone who just got stabbed in the throat.' His voice cracks, his mouth dry and sore.

'It's just a scratch. You're gonna be fine.'

Jack rolls his eyes. 'Thanks for the sympathy.'

'Okay, seriously?' Alex sits down beside him. 'You scared me out there. Twelve stitches. And a fuck-load of blood.'

'Did she jump?'

'She's fine. We hauled her ass over just before you hit the ground. You don't remember?'

Jack shakes his head. 'I just remember it coming towards me.'

'Crazy bitch.' Alex lowers his voice suddenly, turning towards the door. 'Shit, I forgot. Her sister's out there. She wants to see you.'

'Why?'

Alex shrugs. 'To thank you. They already talked to me. The brother-in-law tried to give me a hundred bucks!' He considers this. 'I don't know why the hell I said no.'

Jack smiles weakly.

'So shall I tell her to go away?'

'No. Send her in. I'm fine.'

'Take the cash,' Alex advises, and disappears into the hallway. Jack runs a tentative hand over his neck again. Beneath the bandages, the area is tight and tender, but he thinks that maybe Alex is right; the damage is superficial. The thought sends a sudden shock of fear through him. *Elsa*.

'Hi.'

He glances up at the woman standing timidly in the doorway. Her face is blotched and puffy, and she has a ragged tissue clutched in one hand. 'Hi,' he says. 'Come in.'

She tries to smile and comes towards the bed. 'I'm Tess,' she says, reaching out a hand.

'Nice to meet you, Tess.' As he shakes her hand, he notices the dried blood on his own, and withdraws it quickly.

'I just wanted to say thank you, for what you did for Bella.'

Jack nods. 'It's all part of the job. She gonna be okay?'

'I hope so. She's in the right place, at least. If I'd known she'd gotten this bad, I would've done something sooner. If I'd known ...'

Her eyes fill with tears.

'Hey,' he says softly. 'It's okay. It'll be okay.' There is someone else he has to say these things to. Someone else to catch.

Tess presses the heels of her hands to her eyes, nodding. 'Yes,' she says, straightening up. 'I hope so. I should go. I'm so sorry ...' She trails off.

'Take care of yourself,' he says, and she smiles and turns away.

'Thank you,' she says, and when she reaches the door, she turns back. 'Good luck,' she says, and then she is gone.

When the sound of her footsteps has disappeared down the hallway, Alex reappears. 'Looks like all the crazy in that family went one way, huh?'

Jack tuts. 'Have you called Elsa?'

'No, dude, sorry. I had to give a statement to the cops. And I wanted to be with you when you woke up.'

'Where's my phone?'

Alex fumbles through his pockets. 'Here.'

With shaking hands, Jack scrolls through to the number of the Potrero house. As he hears the first ring, he glances down at himself. 'Get me my clothes,' he says to Alex.

The phone rings, each ring seeming longer, seeming to stretch further away from him. They echo hollowly in his head and his heart begins to thud.

'Hello?'

He slumps in relief. 'Elsa.'

'Hi.'

'I'm on my way home, okay? I'll be home soon.'

Her voice is tearful but he is sure he hears a smile. 'Okay,' she says.

'I'm coming home,' he says again. 'I love you.'

'I love you too,' she says, and he has to rest his head against the wall because the relief is too great.

'I'll explain everything,' he says in a whisper, but he is already hanging up. He draws in a deep breath, closes his eyes. He turns to Alex. 'Give me my clothes,' he says again.

'Jack, they want you to stay overnight. You lost a lot of blood—'

Jack holds out his hand. 'Clothes.'

Alex shrugs and points to a small pile on the chair. 'At least let me get a doctor …'

'Just go get your car.' Jack tugs the IV line out of his hand. 'It's time for me to go home.'

As they drive, Jack presses his forehead to the glass and lets the orange of the street lights roll slowly over his face. They fight for space, together in his head; Beth and Elsa, Eve and Bella. His father watches over him and they are the same, they are liars, they are lovers. Against his better judgement, he loves. He thinks of her, her feet on his, her arms around his neck. He thinks of her, watching him leave. He remembers her, on New Year's Eve, looking up at him. He remembers her on New Year's Day, her hand slipping into his. His fists clench in his lap, his nails digging into the palms.

'You okay?' Alex asks.

'I hope so,' he says, and then they are outside the house.

'You gonna be okay?' Alex asks again, and Jack nods. 'Call me tomorrow,' Alex says. 'Stay home. Stay with Elsa.'

'Believe me,' Jack says, opening the door. 'I intend to.'

He climbs out of the car, his head swimming. 'Thanks, Alex,' he says, leaning down.

'No worries. Take it easy.'

Jack claps the roof of the car. 'Drive safely.'

There is a light in the bedroom and he looks up at it as Alex drives away, its small warmth in the dark. *I should let her go*, he thinks, but he knows he can't. *We're tied together now*, he thinks, and he thinks again of the first time she took his hand. He sees clearly, for the first time, the simple beauty of falling.

His hand shakes as he turns his key in the lock, and he has to put the other out to steady himself on the frame. The warm air of the house creeps slowly out, and he takes a shaky step inside. Taking off his boots, he looks down and sees the dark flowers of blood on them. He staggers against the wall and pauses, breathing slowly. The downstairs is dark and when he has regained his balance, he makes his way carefully up the stairs. He holds onto the banister and when he reaches the top, he calls out to her.

'I'm home,' he says softly, but she is gone. He stands in the doorway, looking at the empty room, the neatly made bed. He stands in front of the wardrobe, looking at the space where her clothes were, the place where her suitcase stood. He sits down on the bed and picks up the set of keys she has left, holding them carefully in his hand. Everything is stopped. He is not sure if he is breathing.

He lets out a single, solitary choking sound; a sob, perhaps, or just a gasp, a reflexive need for air. He manages to stand, and staggers down the stairs, his whole body heavy, his whole body steel. In the living room, he stumbles against the wall, his fingers finding the light switch.

And she is there.

She is there, her suitcase beside her. She is there, looking sadly, hopelessly back at him.

'I couldn't go,' she says, her hand still on the suitcase. 'I couldn't go,' she says again, and this time there is a plea there.

'There are things I need to tell you,' he says, and she smiles.

31 December 2011

Dressing that night, a heaviness settles over her. It is her least favourite night of the year; everything overpriced and oversubscribed, everyone underwhelmed always. Beside the bath, where the last suds are still stranded on the enamel, are a glass and an empty wine bottle. Drinking alone has, as it usually does, made her lazy and morose. She looks at herself in the mirror, at the new dress, at the make-up she has carefully applied. She fights the urge to rub it off. The new lightness of living is beginning to fade, the future seeming difficult and far off again. She turns away from the mirror, resolute, and picks up her bag. She clicks off the light and leaves the house, heading into the dark in heels which are not easy to walk in.

She meets Max and Jenn on the high street, and together they walk down the frosty hill. Lily and her boyfriend and Barney are already in the pub, their texts becoming increasingly impatient. Lily's levels of drunkenness can usually be measured by her use of exclamation marks; in the most recent text, Elsa counts five. Approaching the pub, she almost slips on an icy patch; Jenn's hand locking around her arm and keeping her upright. A girl is sitting on the pavement outside, shouting into her phone.

'It's New Year's Eve!' she yells into the mouthpiece, clutching the phone in front of her face. 'Sort your life out!'

'Festive,' Jenn says, holding the door open for Elsa.

Inside, the air is muggy and thick. Max, as usual, spots an opening at the bar. 'What do you want?' he asks, and they press in behind him.

'The dress looks great,' Jenn tells Elsa.

'So does yours.'

'Here.' Max puts plastic shot glasses in their hands. 'And again,' he says, when they bang the empty glasses down on the bar, handing them another.

'Max!' Jenn swats at him.

He shrugs. 'Start as we mean to go on.'

They make their way through the crowd to their friends. Barney is drunk already, his cheeks red and his voice loud. He hugs Elsa too tightly, lifts her off her feet, and she laughs. Barney always makes her laugh. There is a part of her, growing each day, which wonders if Barney – silly, sweet Barney, with his bad jokes and his sweaty top lip – could be the right person for her.

Lily seems distant, distracted; her new boyfriend nowhere

to be seen. 'Have they had a row?' Elsa asks Barney, and he nods. She tries to keep Lily close, hugs her often. Barney buys bottle after bottle of Prosecco, splashing it over her fingers as he pours it into her glass.

She looks around the room, at the bodies pressed together, the mouths forming words. Her fingers are sticky with Prosecco, tacky against the stem of her glass. Barney is dancing now, dark patches forming on his shirt, sweat shining on his cheeks. She drinks more, her cheeks warm. Lily begins to cry and Jenn ushers her away.

'Be back in a sec,' she tells Elsa. 'You stay here.'

After an hour, she makes her way out to smoke a cigarette filched from Max. She stands alone, a little way apart from the group of smokers huddled under the heater fixed to the window's canopy. It is beginning to rain, fat drops of it pattering around her, the thin plume of smoke rising obstinately from her fingers. She thinks about leaving. She thinks about a bath, or her bed. She puts down her half-empty glass and drops the cigarette half-finished, crushing it under her heel.

Her steps echo down the street, the sounds of the bars behind her fading. She is drunker than she realised, the cigarette making her head swim. She is halfway up the road when she thinks suddenly of the night at the union, escaping home to Kieran. She shakes her head, chiding herself. She does an about-face and walks quickly back the way she came, heels clacking against the pavement.

She collects her glass from its spot on the pavement, but,

back inside, has sudden visions of blackouts and date-rape drugs. She peers into the glass, swaying slightly in her shoes. She holds it up to the light and studies the liquid inside.

'Hey.' Barney's hand closes around her wrist. He is really drunk now, his eyes bleary and red-rimmed, his mouth moving slowly, spit forming at the corners.

'My new friend.' His hand is on her waist, moving her forwards. 'Meet my new friend.'

Author's Note

Whilst this is a work of fiction, the role Jack and his fellow bridge workers play in preventing suicides is very much a real one. I originally read about it – and became instantly obsessed with the idea of writing a novel on the subject – in an article by Scott Ostler, 'Saving Lives Just Part of the Job', published in the *San Francisco Chronicle* in January 2001. It's still available online, and is essential reading for anyone wanting to find out more about the ironworkers of Golden Gate.

Perhaps understandably, the Golden Gate Bridge Authority are not eager to publicise the rate at which people travel to the bridge to end their lives (not all are recorded, but on average, it's at least one a fortnight). They therefore politely declined to allow me to interview any of the men who currently work on the bridge. However, I was very fortunate to be assisted by members of the Ironworkers Local Union 377, one of whom had previously worked on Golden Gate for twenty-five years. All of the men at Local 377 were extremely kind, if a little baffled at what the strange British girl was doing at their HQ with her notebook.

The building blocks of Jack's career are entirely factual – from the apprenticeships he begins with, to the tactics he and the other Golden Gate employees use to try and talk someone off the chord. Some artistic licence has, by necessity, been taken – I have never, for instance, been inside the workshop at the bridge, though it does exist – but every effort has been made to keep Jack's life as a Golden Gate ironworker as close to reality as possible.

This book is dedicated to my wonderful dad, who put me on the plane to San Francisco in the first place, but there are a number of people who made my time there so memorable, and I'm extremely grateful to them: Kat Luper, Avi Nocella, Mirjam Tideman, Hannah Tries, Lorenz Fuelle, Theo Negri, Aurore Zelaziak Czerwony, Katherine Coogan, Renee Gratis, Matthew Beytebiere, Anke Olschina, Alex Peel and all the other lovely guests and staff who made Pacific Tradewinds such a great place to be in December 2011.

Back in the UK, I was lucky to have support and advice during the writing of this novel from some truly fantastic readers, and as always I am totally indebted to them: Hayley Richardson, Jo Unwin, Carrie Plitt, Ian Ellard, James Smythe, Shelley Harris, Archana Rao and Lisa Baker.

Cathryn Summerhayes has been a magnificent agent and Beth Coates a dream editor – it's been an absolute pleasure to work with you both on this, so thank you. Thanks too to Alice Broderick, Victoria Murray-Browne, and all at Vintage.

And to Richard, Margaret and Daniel Cloke, who put me on planes, welcome me back again, make me laugh, listen to me cry, and put up with each and every ridiculous decision and scheme I continue to cook up: THANK YOU. No matter where we all are, you are always home to me.

www.vintage-books.co.uk